Praise for Mary Herbert . . .

"The Clandestine Circle . . . has an excellent, imaginative plot. It is suspenseful, exciting and often impossible to put down. It . . . has a little bit of everything: action, adventure, fantasy, romance and comic relief. An exciting page-turner."
—*Florida Today*

The Linsha Trilogy

City of the Lost

Linsha Majere has been assigned to a post on the edge of the known world, charged to coordinate the Solamic Circle's mission with the Legion of Steel and the local dragon overlord. But when barbarians from across the sea invade, it is all Linsha can do just to stay alive.

Flight of the Fallen

The invading Tarmak armies have crushed all opposition, scattering the last of the resistance. They are now strengthening their forces in preparation to bring all the Plains of Dust beneath their heel. A desperate band of freedom fighters is gathering to strike before it is too late, but a traitor in their midst may bring all to ruin.

Return of the Exile

Linsha survived the great battle of the Plains, but she is now prisoner, fearing all her friends dead. Her only chance to keep her vow to protect the dragon eggs is to marry the feared Akkad, the leader of the Tarmak invaders. On the far-away island home of the Tarmak, she finds hope in the most unexpected place of all—among her enemies.

THE LINSHA TRILOGY

City of the Lost

Flight of the Fallen

Return of the Exile

THE LINSHA TRILOGY

RETURN OF THE EXILE

Mary H. Herbert

RETURN OF THE EXILE

Cover art by Matt Stawicki
Map by Dennis Kauth
First Printing: February 2005
Library of Congress Catalog Card Number: 2004113600

9 8 7 6 5 4 3 2 1

US ISBN: 0-7869-3628-2
ISBN-13: 978-0-7869-3628-1
620-17722-001-EN

U.S., CANADA,   EUROPEAN HEADQUARTERS
ASIA, PACIFIC, & LATIN AMERICA   Wizards of the Coast, Belgium
Wizards of the Coast, Inc.   T Hofveld 6d
P.O. Box 707   1702 Groot-Bijgaarden
Renton, WA 98057-0707   Belgium
+1-800-324-6496   +322 467 3360

Visit our web site at **www.wizards.com**

FOR KEITH

After two kids, three dogs, twelve books, and twenty-two years, you are still my Chosen.

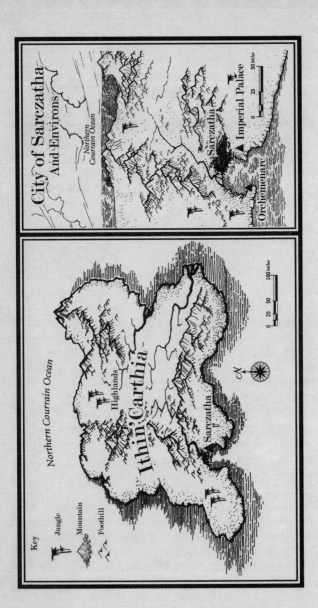

Across the warm waters of the northern Courrain Ocean the storm rolled with fire in its teeth and a wind that howled like the damned. A vanguard of the changing seasons, the storm churned over the waters, rolling south and east along the prevailing currents toward the continent of Ansalon. It was monstrous and powerful, armored in dense, gray clouds and clothed in driving curtains of rain that obscured the sky. Its gale-force winds drove huge waves before it that clawed at the horizon and seemed to drown the world in water.

It was, Linsha thought, an appropriate backdrop to her moodturbulent, angry, and frightened. She yanked her cloak off—for what little good it had done—and tossed it behind her. Taking a tighter grip on the safety line, she leaned forward over the prow of the ship into the teeth of the storm. The wind tore at her hair. The flying spray stung her face. Behind her, the ship groaned in the strain of fighting wind and water. The one sail left rigged for some control snapped in the gale like breaking bones. Voices shouted in Tarmakian, but Linsha ignored them.

The ship crested a large wave and plunged down the far

side into the furrow. A green wall of water crashed over the bow. The weight and momentum of the water swept around Linsha's legs and struggled to break her hold on the rope.

It would be so easy, a perverse little thought whispered in the darkness behind her eyes. All she had to do was let go. *Take one more step.* Release ten fingers and she could put an end to the pain. The rope burned into her hand. It would be so easy—one small movement, then into the water and peace.

The wave swept by her as the ship began its difficult climb up the next comber. Linsha shook the stinging salt water out of her eyes and spread her feet. She took a step forward closer to the high prow and looked at the oncoming wave. It was a particularly large one crowned with spume and streaked with silver foam.

Her clear green eyes swooped down to see the slope of the water that fell away at her feet. The ship's prow sliced through the crest of the wave. She stared down, mesmerized by the massive power of the sea around her, unaware that her hands tightened around the ropes. Why not? she thought. What was left for her? Why couldn't she just let go now?

The ship dropped away beneath her, and water crashed over her. Her feet slipped on the wet deck and were washed out from under her by torrents of rushing seawater. Linsha was aware that her body was being buffeted by the cold, rushing wave, but the one thing that stood out with painful clarity was the feeling of the thick wet rope digging into her hands. Her muscles ached, her shoulders hurt, and the rough hemp tore the skin from her fingers and palms, yet she could not force her hands to let go.

The water subsided, draining away over the timbers of the ship. Aching and drenched, Linsha climbed to her feet on the tilting deck and waited while the ship climbed laboriously up the next wave. She sensed movement behind her and tensed, wishing for the thousandth time that she had a weapon. A sword, a dagger—even an eating knife would be welcome.

Arms came around her and hands clutched the rope beside hers so she was penned in the circle of his arms. His body pressed against her back as if he felt she needed his steadying influence.

"Haven't you had enough of this?" A strong masculine voice yelled in her ear. He had to shout over the roar of groaning timbers, howling wind, and thunder.

Animosity crushed any other thought or emotion in her mind. She would have given almost anything to slam an elbow beneath his ribs and kick his traitorous carcass into the storm-tossed waters. But she had not become a Solamnic Knight and worked for years to attain the highest rank of Knight of the Rose to lose her temper and kill the only chance she had left to regain her honor. Her honor and a small clutch of brass dragon eggs were all she had left, and because of a vow she made to the dragon overlord Iyesta, the two were inextricably tied together.

With every scrap of self-control she had left, Linsha twisted her lips into something resembling a smile and yelled back, "I like storms."

"You are the only one," Lanther replied. "All the other women are seasick below decks." He seemed as unshaken by the storm as she. "Why are you standing out here on the bow? Are you trying to drown yourself?"

"Why not?" she replied with icy sarcasm. She had lost many good friends, seen an entire Solamnic circle and most of a Legion cell die. Lanther had taken away her companion, Varia, and driven away the one best friend she had ever found. Her life had become nothing but defeat, dishonor, and misery, and she saw nothing but defeat and slavery in her future. She smiled a brittle sneer. "Why shouldn't I let go and die here before things get worse?"

Lanther laughed, a genuine guffaw of caustic amusement.

"Because you are too stubborn. And I still have your precious eggs locked away in a safe room in Missing City. If you want them to survive, so must you."

At that moment the ship dropped under their feet and began its rush down the backside of another huge green comber. Linsha took a deep breath and held it. Water slammed over her head. It poured around her, over her, a gray-green monster that roared in her head and filled her ears and nose with salty water. She kept her feet this time, hugging the high prow with both arms. It would be too much to ask, she thought, that Lanther get washed overboard.

The ship wallowed in the heavy water, then slowly righted itself in time to meet the next wave.

Linsha exhaled and shook the water out of her eyes. She had to admit this vessel was well-built. It was a version of a trireme, a sleek, oceangoing warship built by the Tarmaks from a design that borrowed heavily from the minotaurs' shipcraft. It was tough, fast, and maneuverable. Even so, she decided she'd had enough of her negative thoughts, enough drenching, and enough of the man standing behind her.

She angled her body against the solid wood of the prow and was about to push away from the man when she heard a wild voice cry from the crow's nest on the mast. She could not see anything in the driving rain, but apparently the lookout did, and the crew accepted it. The shouting and activity below deck grew louder. More Tarmaks came up on the main deck while others took their places at the oars.

Lanther's arms tightened around her and his dripping face split into a grin. "Don't leave now. We're almost there. The seas will grow calmer as we sail around the point. Stay and see the Orchemenarc."

Linsha's heart sank. *Almost there.* The words banged in her head like a sentence of doom. For over fourteen days she had survived on this crowded ship with one hundred fifty Tarmak warriors, twenty female prisoners, trunks and chests full of stolen treasure, one coffin, and barely enough food and water to last the journey. As uncomfortable and miserable as it was, as long as they were still at sea, she could ignore the passage of miles and the increasing distance between herself and her home. Now she could no longer avoid the truth that she had been taken from her homeland and borne into the distant reaches of a far sea, away from home and family and the aid of anyone who might have stirred to help her. She felt the painful sensation tighten her throat still further, and heat rushed into her face. Tears would be next, she knew, and she swore she would never cry in Lanther's presence.

Another wave came. It surged around her and cooled her skin. She fought back the grief and self-pity, fought back the tears. She was a knight, a Majere, the child of Heroes, and the sole protector of a clutch of dragon eggs. She could not, nay would not, give in now.

Soaked and seething, she stayed where she was and thought no more of letting go. She still could not see any indication of land, but it seemed, as she watched the roll and pitch of the waves, that the storm was lessening. The wind had dropped somewhat, and the waves were not as rough. The change must have been noticeable enough for the captain, for he suddenly bellowed orders to his crew. Tarmak seamen, as tall and muscular as the warriors, swarmed up the two masts and released more sail.

Linsha watched with mingled respect and frustration as the tough fabric unfurled, snapping and dancing in the wind. Swiftly the sailors tied down the sails and dropped back to the deck. A drum boomed once on the rowers' deck below, Linsha heard a shout, and in one smooth movement the ship's oars dropped into the water and bit into the waves. The drumbeat set the rhythm, and the oars began their steady lift and pull. The ship leaped forward.

"We are moving into the lee of a large peninsula," Lanther told her. "When Lord Ariakan came here, his ship landed to the north on the western edge of the continent. He did not come to Sarczatha until later."

Linsha shuddered at the mention of *that* man, the Dark Knight who first found the land of Ithin'carthia many years ago before the Chaos War. He should have drowned on the voyage there, or back, or just left well enough alone and allowed the Tarmaks to continue killing each other in peace. But no. He had seen potential armies in the Tarmak warriors and brought thousands of them back to Ansalon to fight in his legions. The Brutes, as they were known, were responsible for thousands of deaths all over Ansalon. They fought not just in the service of the Dark Knights but for their own motives as well, and now they had their eyes set on the Plains of Dust as a new extension of their conquests.

Another wave crashed over Linsha and her companion, leaving them breathless and drenched, and that was the last of the large storm waves. Pushed on by the oars and the wind in the square sails, the ship sped out of the teeth of the storm into the shelter of the large land mass.

Linsha blinked in the rain and saw it at last—a dark, indistinct line on the horizon. All too soon the blurred shadows became high hills, rain-soaked grasslands, and tall bluffs of gray stone.

"There!" Lanther said. His finger indicated a promontory that jutted out of the peninsula. At its tip sat a great, hulking mass of walls and forbidding towers. A single light burned in the highest tower, a light so bright it sheered through the stormy gloom as a brilliant beacon. "There is Orchemenarc," he told her proudly. "My father helped build it. It marks the entrance to the harbor."

Linsha remembered his father had been a Knight of Takhisis stationed with the Tarmaks as a liaison. She bit back the rude comment that came to mind and merely watched as the ship sailed closer. She wasn't surprised to hear a Dark

Knight helped construct a thing like that. It exuded a grim power and vigilance that made her skin crawl.

The waves had settled from large combers to mere rollers that smacked the sides of the ship and splashed its occupants with flying spray. The pitch and roll of the vessel eased to a more comfortable rise and fall. Overhead, rain still poured down, but the lightning had faded away and the wind had dropped to a stiff breeze. The gray afternoon light dimmed toward a stormy evening.

Linsha heard the captain bellow another command and the drumbeat below deck boomed faster. The oarsmen leaned into their oars. Driven by sail and oar, the Tarmak ship charged by the dark walls of the fortress and aimed its bow into a large natural harbor carved like a half-moon into the limestone hills.

For the first time Linsha saw the mouth of a river and the high hills that lifted on either side. To the east of the river she saw stone buildings and edifices rising level after level from the sand beaches of the harbor to the grass-crowned foothills that vanished into the mist and rain. This was the Tarmak capitol city of Sarczatha. Five hills it covered with busy streets, large buildings, temples, and teeming markets. On a high bluff farther to the east, she noticed another sprawling complex of stone buildings. They were barely visible in the failing light.

It wasn't the size of the city or the beauty of its colorful architecture that took her breath away. It was the sight of the vast fleet tied at anchor in the harbor that made her blood run cold. Row after row of the sleek, deadly war vessels rocked at their moorings, crowding the smaller pleasure craft, fishing boats, and cargo ships. She shot a look at Lanther and saw with growing alarm an expression of grim satisfaction on his rugged features. After he had revealed his real identity and assumed the leadership of the Tarmak as the Akkad-Dar, he had allowed his facial hair to grow into a trim beard in the manner of many of the Tarmaks. In the gray light of the fading day, his bearded expression looked forbidding, hardened by the purposeful intensity of a zealot.

He saw her look and the arrogant grin returned. "There lie the instruments of our final subjugation of the Plains. From those ships we will launch an invasion that will carry the Tarmaks as far west as the Kharolis Mountains and as far north as the New Sea. We will go deep into the Silvanesti Forest." His hand swept out to encompass the entire fleet. "We will sweep the Plains clean of the tribes and clans, rid the forest of those pitiful refugee elves, and destroy the last vestiges of resistance. Even Sable in her lair will think twice before invading our empire."

Linsha, who had met the monstrous black dragon face to face, said, "Oh, she may think twice. But she won't let second thoughts stop her."

His grin spread even wider. "Then perhaps we'll have to add her blood to the Abyssal Lance."

Linsha stopped listening. She did not want to hear any more of his boasting and certainly no more of the dreadful Abyssal Lance. That cruel weapon had killed Iyesta and badly wounded Crucible. She still didn't know if the bronze was dead or alive. She wondered briefly if the lance was on this ship or if Lanther had left it in the Missing City. Given the opportunity, she'd toss it into the ocean.

She turned her attention back to the harbor and the fleet of warships ahead. From the highest tower of the Orchemenarc a horn sounded a welcome that rang through the harbor. It was taken up by signal horns on almost every ship until the wet afternoon rang with music. Figures appeared on the decks and on the distant docks of the city's waterfront. Shouts of welcome and loud cheers could be heard even over the rhythmic boom and splash of the oars.

With the eye of a spy, Linsha counted the ships as they sailed through an open passage toward the central wharf.

There were fifty-two at least, some with double rows of oars, some with triple, and all with the small swiveling catapults on the ships' bridges, the reinforced prows, and the capacity to carry one hundred fifty to two hundred highly trained Tarmaks. Worst of all, they were poised and ready to swoop down on the Plains of Dust, whose defenders were already depleted and demoralized.

Behind her, Lanther put his hands on her shoulders and forced her around to face him. He kissed her hard, his lips and tongue salty against hers. Then he laughed with pleasure and left her alone while he returned to the ship's bridge. Linsha spat on the deck where he had stood and shook her head as if to rid her nose of a foul smell. She had agreed to marry the traitor, to be his wife. But being with him now, unmarried and unescorted, took all of her resolve. How was she going to bear their time alone as husband and wife? Thank Kiri-Jolith that was in the future, because at the moment she could not conceive of it. At one time she had considered him a friend, and if he had pursued more than a friendship with her, perhaps she would have considered it. But that friendship was dead, drowned in the blood of too many friends and forever replaced in her heart by terrible memories and unending grief. The only feelings she had for him now were murderous.

Drawing a deep breath, she pushed her salt-drenched hair out of her eyes and trudged back to the hatch below decks.

The only ally she had now was time.

While Linsha dripped her way below deck, the Tarmaks furled the sails, drew in the oars, and guided the ship alongside a long pier where a crowd waited in the rain for their arrival. Drums beat a welcome from nearby ships and signal horns sounded across the harbor.

In her small cabin beneath the bridge, Linsha listened to the noise above and wondered how long it would be before the Tarmaks dragged the women out to be paraded with the crates of steel, gold, jewels, and other precious items stolen from Iyesta's hoard. Anticipating sooner rather than later, she packed their few belongings then wrapped Callista in a blanket and urged the young woman to drink a little water.

The courtesan lifted drooping eyelids. Although she was accompanying Linsha as her serving maid, she had been seasick most of the voyage, and Linsha spent most of the time caring for her. Not that it mattered to Linsha. She had never had a maid, lady-in-waiting, serving wench, or even a cleaning woman in her life. Nor had she wanted one. But this seemed the only way to protect Callista from being included in the tribute of female slaves Lanther had brought for the

Tarmak emperor. Lanther, who once favored Callista, had agreed to the arrangement.

Callista's wan face turned even paler when she saw what Linsha was doing. "We're there, aren't we?" she said softly.

"Yes," Linsha said. "Tied at the pier if I am not mistaken. Solid ground."

While Linsha finished the meager packing, the courtesan pulled her blanket closer and sat up, swinging her feet over the side of the bunk. Perhaps the mention of land gave her strength, or perhaps the cessation of the wild roll and pitch of the ship helped, for she drank some water, ate a few crackers, and staggered to her feet. She stood swaying gently for a few minutes, but she was upright and a little color returned to her flawless cheeks. She even managed enough strength to run a brush through her long hair. She eyed Linsha's soggy clothes and storm-blown hair critically.

"You look like something the dog dragged off the beach. Aren't you going to change?" she asked, but she knew the answer. The two of them were opposites in so many ways.

"No." Linsha shook her damp curls. They were stiff with salt and as bedraggled as her wet clothes. "It's still raining. No point in drying off if I'm just going to get wet again."

They heard loud voices and screams from the two cabins beside them and knew the Tarmaks were coming for them. A fist pounded on their door before it was yanked open and the large, bearded face of one of Lanther's guards glared through the opening. He said something in the harsh, guttural tongue of the Tarmaks and stamped on.

Linsha hid a sneer. She'd always had a talent for languages and from the Tarmaks' first appearance in the Missing City, she had been trying to learn their difficult tongue. During these past two weeks on the ship, she had listened to the warriors and sailors at every opportunity and believed now she was beginning to understand the Tarmaks' rhythm, syntax, and many of their swear words.

She hoped the time would come when this would prove to be a valuable asset.

Trying to dredge up some resignation, she shouldered her sack of belongings and led the way out of the cabin. Callista followed silently, her blanket pulled over her fair head like a shawl. The bevy of slave girls was passing by, escorted by several burly Tarmak guards, and Linsha and Callista simply mingled in. Lanther had not told them to do otherwise, and Callista was anxious to get off the dank, dark ship. Linsha was too despondent to care what they did.

At the tail of the line of anxious, weeping women, Linsha and Callista walked out of the hold into the rain. Callista, still weak from seasickness, had to lean on Linsha's arm as they walked across the deck. They followed the young women and guards across the plank onto the pier and up to a busy wharf where they came to a halt before a large group of Tarmaks, both male and female, who had gathered to meet the ship.

It was the first time Linsha had seen Tarmaks of both sexes, and she was impressed in spite of herself. The females were nearly as tall as the males, equally as graceful, and they handled themselves with dignity and some measure of self assurance. Their skin had the deep tan of people who spend much time outdoors, and most wore their long hair in a single braid, unlike the men whose hair was often twisted into intricate knots.

Both men and women were clothed in loose, comfortable clothing designed for a warm climate. The females wore wrap dresses or loose skirts, and the men wore knee-length pleated kilts or tunics and baggy wrap pants. Although the men adorned themselves with gold jewelry and the feathers of exotic birds, only the warriors wore the white feathers in their hair, and the women seemed to avoid any obvious decoration.

Some of the Tarmaks Linsha saw seemed to be very important, for she noticed there was much talking and bowing between a group of males in headdresses of gold set with red gems and Lanther, the ship's captain, and several of the officers. She could also see another large group approaching the edge of crowd, a group accompanied by a canopy and a sizable display of banners and pennants that sagged in the gusty rain.

She was staring at the oncoming entourage when she felt someone move behind her. A rough hand shoved her out of the way and a Tarmak moved into her place beside Callista. She staggered, landed on the balls of her feet, and like a cat she regained her balance and twisted around to see a large male pull the blanket out of Callista's hands.

The courtesan made a sound of protest and tried to pull back, but the blanket was yanked away, revealing her fair hair and uncovering her beauty. The other nineteen girls from the Missing City had darker hair, black or brown or reddish auburn; none had Callista's hair that fell like a shimmering veil of gold or a face as fair an elf maiden's. Even pale and weary from the voyage, Callista was the most exquisite of the human women and, to the Tarmak eye, probably one of the most exotic.

The Tarmak's heavy features lifted in a leer and he pinioned the courtesan's arms in a tight grip. To Callista's credit, she did not scream. Her blue eyes darkened with anger and turned to Linsha in a silent appeal for help.

Linsha studied the situation for one quick instant. The Tarmak before her was not one of Lanther's. If he had been on the ship, he would have known this woman was untouchable. She noted the scars on his legs from the Tarmaks' notorious war games, the heavy calluses on his hands, and the muscles that bulged on his arms and chest. He had a full beard and long hair braided with the white feathers of a warrior, and he wore the traditional short sword that was heavy enough to decapitate a horse. She acted fast while she still had the advantage of surprise.

With the speed of a backstreet cutthroat, she shifted her weight to one foot and lashed out at the Tarmak with the other. Her soggy boot landed firmly just above the hem of his pleated kilt. The impact made him gasp and loosen his hold on Callista. As the Tarmak tilted forward in pain, Linsha swung the palm of her hand up to smash into his nose. It was like smacking a bullock, but the stunned Tarmak groaned and toppled. Using his weight and the right leverage, Linsha caught his arm and flipped him over the edge of the wharf. The splash he made going into the water was most satisfying.

Linsha stared down at him floating in the choppy water, and for one brief second she considered jumping in after him. She had done something similar once to save Ian Durne, but he had been just a Dark Knight assassin. This Tarmak, she decided, could sink or swim without her.

She turned back to the dock and came face to face with half a dozen angry warriors, their swords drawn and pointed at her. All around her wary faces stared at her in surprise and unpleasant consideration. Linsha sneered at them and spat a single word in the Tarmak language. Her effrontery gave them pause just long enough for Lanther to reach her.

"That is not a polite word, my dearest," he said. "Do you have a death wish?"

The warriors drew back before the Akkad-Dar while one explained in a spat of heated words what had happened. At Lanther's command, they sheathed their swords and stood glowering at the woman they believed to be a slave.

Lanther peered over the edge of wharf then turned his back on the fallen warrior. "Why did you do that?" he demanded.

She drew herself up to her full height. "The oaf tried to touch Callista. I have a reputation to establish."

A single eyebrow rose on Lanther's face before his vivid blue eyes began to twinkle and he burst into appreciative laughter. "An excellent beginning, my lady." He bowed to her.

He switched to the Tarmak tongue and, speaking to those around him, grated through a long string of sentences.

Although Linsha only caught a few words, she could see the effect of his intent on the faces around her. The Tarmaks relaxed; a few smiled. The warriors appraised her from head to toe and shrugged. No one, Linsha noted, made any effort to go after the warrior in the water or even throw him a line.

"Are you going to leave him there?" she asked.

Lanther made a dismissive gesture. "He was stupid enough to let himself be tossed in. He can find his own way out."

The press of Tarmaks parted behind him. The guards, the canopy, and several dignified-looking old Tarmaks in robes of blue approached escorting one of the most massive males Linsha had ever seen on two feet. His girth made most minotaurs look skinny. He stood a good seven and a half feet tall, and his grizzled bushy hair and beard added even more height and bulk. A magnificent headdress made of beaten gold and the tail feathers of a large bird crowned his huge head. On his shoulders was draped the pelt of a black panther. A golden torque hung about his neck, and his arms were bound with gold arm rings. He stood under his canopy in the falling rain and looked over his people with the immovable assurance of a mountain.

Every Tarmak fell to one knee and clasped their upraised hands together. Callista and the slave girls stared with frightened eyes until the guards forced them to kneel as well. Only Lanther, the slaves hanging grimly onto the poles of the canopy, and Linsha, who crossed her arms and looked unimpressed, remained on their feet.

Ignoring Linsha for the time, Lanther threw open his arms, and his face split into a huge smile of welcome and pleasure.

To Linsha's astonishment, a young, rather damp Tarmak woman cried out in delight. She sprang back to her feet, broke away from the stately entourage, threw herself into Lanther's arms and kissed him in such an embrace of ardent passion that Linsha's mouth dropped open. She turned her head and looked at Callista kneeling behind her, missing the startled, wary look that passed over Lanther's features.

Curious, Linsha eyed the young Tarmak. The woman stood a healthy six inches taller than Linsha and was certainly in better physical shape. While Linsha had suffered through almost five months of deprivation, struggle, poor food, wounds, and illness, this woman must have been running up mountain slopes and butchering cattle in her spare time. She had the same athletic grace to her build and motion as the males and a formidable upper body strength that spoke of years of weapons practice. Her fair skin was darkened from a lifetime spent outdoors, and her black hair was braided into the single, utilitarian braid laced with polished stone beads.

Lanther gently but firmly pushed the Tarmak woman back a step and explained something to her in her own language.

Whatever it was he said to her, Linsha could see the woman was not taking it well. Her face darkened with anger and a scowl turned her excitement to ugly scorn.

The huge male under the canopy rumbled a question or two to Lanther in a voice that reminded Linsha of boulders rolling down a hillside. The Akkad-Dar bowed low. Taking Linsha by the arm, he pulled her over to face the huge Tarmak and launched into a much longer explanation. Linsha understood only bits and pieces, but she caught the gist of it. Lanther was apparently extolling her virtues as a warrior. At one break in his narrative, he pointed over the dock and into the water, which elicited a chuckle from the big Tarmak and looks of curiosity from the others close by.

If the men of the group were interested by Lanther's tale, the woman was not. She put her hands on her hips while Lanther talked and focused her unfriendly glare on Linsha. Her dark brown eyes bore into Linsha's with unadulterated animosity.

"What's going on?" asked Linsha. She pushed her hair out of her eyes and tried to ignore the insidious little chill that slid up her back.

Lanther switched to Common and said, "My lady, I would like you to meet Khanwhelak, Emperor of Ithin'carthia, Lord Subjugator, Chosen of Kadulawa'ah. I have told him of your prowess as a warrior."

With a grim smile, she swallowed her obstinate pride. Clasping her hands, she bowed to the Emperor. She might toss the odd Tarmak warrior into the water, but she knew enough to back away from dangerous shoals. This giant of a Tarmak could crush her with one hand or order a dozen warriors to hack her to bits.

Lanther bowed as well and added something else, but a sharp word interrupted his speech. The young woman stalked up to him and launched into a long diatribe laced with furious gestures and loud words directed equally to Lanther and the Emperor. Linsha did not need a translator to catch the derision and disdain directed at her or the heated argument the woman was heaping on both males' heads. Linsha wondered if she was a relative to be allowed to address the emperor in such tones.

The Emperor let her rant for a short while before he cut her off with a single word. He said something to Lanther that seemed to calm the woman a little, but Linsha saw the Akkad-Dar's jaw muscles tighten and the scar on his right cheek turn a darker red. She wiped the rain from her eyes and wondered what had just transpired.

The Emperor shouted something to his people, who cheered with great appreciation, then he and his guards, accompanied by Lanther and the ship's officers, proceeded up the broad road away from the wharves and disappeared into the busy city streets.

Linsha watched them go while her apprehension grew. She and Callista had been left behind with the slave girls and no clear idea of what they should do next. The Tarmak woman glared down her aristocratic nose at them, turned her back, and left with a toss of her long braid.

"Isn't she a charmer?" Linsha muttered, helping Callista to her feet.

"If she were in my business, she would use chains and whips," the courtesan replied with a note of professional disdain. She pulled her blanket back over her damp hair, looked anxiously at the little huddle of young women, and asked in a soft voice, "What do we do now?"

Her answer came swiftly in the guise of a squad of warriors. The ten Tarmaks quickly herded the slaves, the courtesan, and Linsha into a wet, miserable group and escorted them through the busy waterfront to a paved road that wound up the slope of a high, broad hill. Linsha took the lead of the group and walked after the guards with her head held up and her eyes scanning the city around her. The other women fell in behind her.

They walked through wide streets busy with pedestrians, carts, wagons, and numerous four-legged animals. Linsha saw mules, goats, dogs, and some odd creatures that she had never seen before. She saw chickens and ducks that might have been brought from Ansalon, furry animals that looked like hornless goats with long necks, tiny golden monkeys that scampered through the trees, and spotted cats the size of foxes.

The buildings of the city were constructed of stone and wood and were painted in bright colors. None were over three stories tall and most had flat roofs and wide, colorful awnings that sheltered doors and shop windows. Tarmaks of all ages and both sexes went about their business in the rain beneath the colorful awnings or under parasols that moved and twirled in a rainbow dance that made an unexpected contrast to the drab, wet day.

In the Missing City autumn was setting in with its gales and frosts and impending cold, but the climate on Ithin'carthia's southern foothills was semitropical and—to Linsha's thinking—downright warm. Everywhere she looked she saw flowers trailing, vining, and clambering over rock walls and buildings. Flowering shrubs grew in pots or in yards. Flowering trees, native to the continent, bloomed in parks and gardens. Linsha saw large butterflies, something that looked like a dragonfly with iridescent wings, and small birds of brilliant hue flying among the blossoms. She had thought the Brutes were a rough, uncultured people, yet looking around this large, populous city she began to realize there was far more to them than the first impression of bloodthirsty savage. Their buildings were well made and maintained, their green spaces brimmed with gardens and walkways, prosperous markets sat at many intersections offering buyers tables of merchandise and food laid out in neat displays under canopied roofs that kept shoppers dry. Everyone, from the warriors who strutted together along the streets to the mix of laborers and human slaves who moved busily about their tasks, looked healthy and clean.

There were many large buildings whose purpose Linsha could not identify, while there were others she recognized as storehouses, shops, workshops, public houses, kitchens, livestock markets, and clothiers. Near the edge of the city she saw a large tannery and a metalworking shop. Close by was an armory and another huge complex with training fields and what looked like step pyramids and temples.

The road swept on past the barracks on its large hill then curved to the southeast and began to climb up a taller hill. Linsha tried to look ahead, but clouds and rain obscured the heights and hid the foothills in fog. Around her, the city's buildings gave way to terraced fields and vineyards.

The girls behind her slowed and looked around with huge apprehensive eyes, but the guards would not let them dally. The group trudged on through the rain up the road to the top of the hill. Beyond the crown of the hill the farmland gave way to level grass fields cleared of all trees and undergrowth. At the higher elevation the wind blew harder, driving the rain before it.

"Look," Callista said softly. One hand tightened around Linsha's forearm while the other pointed toward the fields.

Linsha followed her gesture out toward the far edges of the fields, out into the wind and the pouring rain, and felt a chill grip her heart. If the ships were poised and ready to sail toward Ansalon, certainly there would be warriors to man them. Unit after unit, the *ekwullik* and the larger *dekullik*, of Tarmaks trained and marched on the grassy fields, oblivious to the weather that stormed around them.

"There must be thousands out there," Callista whispered.

"At least," Linsha grated. "See there? They have cavalry, too. They weren't very good on horseback the first time they came to the Plains, but they're learning. Gods, look at that maneuver. They're almost as good as the Plains tribes."

Linsha would have stood in the rain and watched the distant army in its training, but the guards moved her along with the others, and Linsha did not argue. They rounded another curve in the road and saw for the first time the large complex of buildings sprawled on the top of the high promontory that Linsha had seen from the ship. Girdled by high walls, it looked very imposing and very secure.

"The Emperor's palace," a guard said to her in rough Common. "You will stay here. In the Akeelawasee."

"The A . . . keela . . ." She tried to repeat the unfamiliar word. "Place of—?"

"The Chosen Ones," the guard answered.

The Chosen Ones? Linsha did not like the sound of that. Chosen for what?

The road leveled out and led straight and true to a towering gateway that opened through the first high wall and into a courtyard lined with guards. From the court, walkways led through arches in numerous directions to stables, barracks, storehouses, armories, and the outer service buildings of the palace. The main road continued across the courtyard between a row of menacing statues that resembled lions in various poses of attack. They had been carved from polished sandstone, and they glowered down on passersby. Beyond the lions the roadway passed through a second wall and timbered passage and into a second court where more guards stood in silent vigilance and more pathways guided one to other parts of the palace. Finally a third wall rose before the women, and they were led into the largest and most impressive square of any palace Linsha had ever seen.

The square spread out one hundred feet on both sides of the entrance to high walls painted a dazzling white and to impressive buildings whose purpose Linsha could only guess. A broad flight of stairs led down to the cobbled square that stretched about two hundred yards ahead, past a large statue, to the foot of a second stone staircase that climbed with dignified grace to a magnificent five-storied hall. The hall had been painted a brilliant blue and its numerous columns were red. Its two-tiered roof and soaring peaks gleamed gold even in the stormy light of the fading day.

There was no sign of anyone in the square until a Tarmak guard called a question. It was answered by another voice somewhere close by. A Tarmak warrior stepped out of the shadows of the wall and gestured to another who stepped out of his place and opened a large door in the wall. Linsha realized with a start there were probably dozens of warriors stationed silently in the corners, doorways, and arches that led out of the square. The hushed group of wet women began to move reluctantly toward the door, driven on by their guards. Linsha and Callista moved after them.

The guard who had spoken to her earlier extended his spear and blocked her way. "Drathkin'kela. You do not go there. You—" he pointed to Callista and herself— "You go to Akeelawasee."

"Yes," Linsha said crossly. "You said that earlier. Isn't that where they're going?"

He laughed a deep rumble of enjoyment. "Those? They are slaves. Tribute from the Akkad-Dar to the Emperor. Our glorious emperor will take them himself. If any survive, he may keep them or give them to his guards."

Linsha's brows lowered. "What do you mean 'if any survive?' "

The Tarmak made a sharp sound of derision. "Human womans are too small. Fragile. The Emperor is a powerful warrior. He is not . . . gentle."

Linsha looked disgusted. "He is not a lightweight either."

"Poor things," Callista said softly, her large eyes filled with sympathy for the women disappearing through the door. Her hand tightened even more on Linsha's arm.

"This way." The guard pointed his spear toward the hall on the far side of the square. Taking the lead, he walked across the smooth cobbles, fully expecting the two women to follow.

Linsha took one last look at the women from the Missing City then followed him, her arm steady under Callista's apprehensive grip.

Halfway across the square they came to a series of narrow bridges that spanned a stone-laid waterway where a river had been diverted to flow through the square in a gentle arc. The effect was serene and added a balancing element to the large open stone space. It also provided an excellent way to slow down an enemy trying to attack across the square. Linsha wondered what other tricks the Tarmaks had disguised in this place.

As they walked across the remaining distance to the stairs at the great hall, Linsha took a closer look at the statue posed at the foot of the stairs, then she took a second look. Although the artist's execution and interpretation of his subject had been fanciful and a little too exotic, the basic shape was all too familiar. The statue was of a dragon that stood crouched protectively, one taloned foot upraised and its toothy mouth open in a snarl. Its wings were half furled; its cold eyes stared malevolently at passersby.

Linsha stopped at its feet and looked at the head ten feet above her. "I didn't know this land had dragons."

To her surprise, the guard bowed low before the statue. "No dragons here. They are sacred to Amarrel. This was Methanfire, dragon of the Akkad-Dar's father."

The Dark Knight's dragon. A blue, if the painted scales were accurate. Linsha's thoughts roved back over everything she could remember about the Tarmaks and dragons. Except for the previous warlord, the Akkad-Ur, she had never seen one on dragonback. The general had also worn a necklace of dragon's teeth and a mailed shirt of dragon scales. Where had those come from, and why had he worn them? Were they trophies from a kill or a way to honor dragons? On the Plains, the Tarmaks had aided Thunder in killing Iyesta, then they abetted in the death of the blue. They tried to coerce Crucible into joining them, then nearly killed him. What did the Tarmaks think about dragons? She really didn't know. She would have thought they hated the great beasts, but here was one practically venerated in the front porch of the emperor's palace. The guard had said they were sacred to Amarrel. Amarrel, she remembered, was the demigod Lord Ariakan had supposedly impersonated in order to convince the Tarmaks to join him. Maybe it was his influence that sparked this respect for something the Tarmaks seemed to both love and hate.

Shaking her head, she moved past the dragon statue and

followed the guard and Callista up the stairs to a set of large double doors bound in brass and set in a frame of some kind of polished red wood. The guard pushed open a door and led them inside out of the rain. Linsha and Callista paused on the threshold for a moment, their mouths open in astonishment at the size and ornamentation of the vestibule. Mosaics in bright geometric patterns spread over the floors, and murals of Tarmak battles covered the walls. A row of gilded columns gleamed in the dim light. The guard turned left and hurried the two women on. Their eyes wide, they moved through broad corridors past more chambers and council rooms, and all the rooms that they could see were adorned with polished woods, magnificent wall hangings, and painted frescos of fantastic animals and bloody battle scenes. This was certainly more than either had expected.

The Tarmak had always struck Linsha as a race bent solely on destruction. It had not occurred to her that their civilization was quite ancient and somewhere in the midst of their warfare they had found time to build magnificent palaces and learn the deeper aesthetics of art and expert craftsmanship.

After some minutes of walking, they approached a set of large double doors flanked by two enormous guards fully armed with swords, knives, and small round shields. The doors were set in a round opening and carved into a screen of ornately twisting vines and flowers. A word spoken by their escort elicited a slight bow by both Tarmaks, and the door was opened wide.

A smaller male Tarmak in a simple white tunic and leather kilt hurried forward to meet them as if he had been waiting by the door for just such an opportunity. The warrior explained his mission. Linsha listened to his voice and caught the Akkad-Dar's name. She also heard the odd title the guard had used earlier. The Drathkin'kela. What was that supposed to mean? Betrothed? Intended? Idiot? Whatever it was, it was enough to prompt the elderly Tarmak to jerk his head. For a second his eyes sought her face and an expression of astonishment flickered across his features. Immediately the look was hidden, and he clasped his hands and bowed low, revealing a bald head.

The guard bowed to Linsha. "The Akeelawasee," he said and propelled the two women through the door.

Linsha turned around to ask him a question, but before the words were out of her mouth the doors slammed in her face.

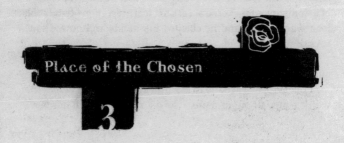

Place of the Chosen

3

Greetings, Lady," said the servant by her elbow. He was an elderly fellow only an inch or two above her height. His wrinkled skin seemed more reddish than most Tarmaks and his ears were not as pointed. A simple sleeveless tunic of bleached linen hung on his thin frame, and a knotted blue rope was tied around his waist.

He bowed again and indicated the way down a long hall. "If the Drathkin'kela will follow me," he said. Any hint of surprise was gone, and his expression assumed a bland servile mask under an awning of thick eyebrows. His voice, when he spoke, was soft and modulated as if trained to avoid giving offense.

Linsha took it any way. She was still feeling disgruntled. She crossed her arms and refused to move. "You speak Common well. Do you know more than just a greeting?"

"Assuredly, Lady. I speak several languages well, including Tarmakian, Damjatt, Nerakan, and your Common."

She studied the man's wrinkled face. He had light gray eyes, which he kept respectfully lowered. "Then tell me what this 'drathkin-kela' means. I am a Knight of the Rose, a trained warrior, not some silly female you can throw names at like a dog."

He clasped his hands, a movement Linsha began to realize was a sign of respect. "Lady, the words are a title the warriors of the Akkad-Dar have given you. It means roughly 'dragon friend' or 'chosen of the dragon.' "

"Oh." Linsha's arms dropped and her hand moved to the dragon scales that hung on the chain around her neck. Her fingers clasped the scales under the wet wool of her tunic. "Is that a good thing?"

He gave her faint smile. "To them it is. Even though you are a human, you have been granted a place in the Akeela-wasee where you will be treated with honor and respect."

"Even though I am a human," she repeated dryly. He made no mention of her status as Lanther's betrothed. She wondered if Lanther had told anyone yet. "You must have learned Nerakan and Common from the Dark Knights."

The man nodded. "Sir Bendic tutored me. A very skilled linguist. He learned Tarmakian in a few months."

"Tarmakian I recognize. What is Damjatt? I thought that was the breed of horse the Tarmaks use."

A wry glint lit his pale gray eyes. His thin mouth lost its smile. "The horses were once ours. Our pride and joy." He paused then went on. "My people are the Damjatt, the people of the high grasslands. We were the last free tribe to fall before the Tarmak military might. Now we are merely beasts of burden, like our horses."

"If you were the last," Callista put in, "who was the first?"

"The Keena. They relied too heavily on their jungle to protect them."

Linsha tilted her head in thought. The name sounded familiar to her. She had heard that before. Then she had it. Lanther had called in a Keena to seal their betrothal before they sailed, and a pair of Keena had guarded the dragon eggs when Lanther showed them to her. "Are they priests?" she asked.

"Those that survive. They are a deeply religious people, and those that still remain have found a place among the Tarmak as priests, seers, scholars, and . . . other things."

Linsha snorted an unladylike sound. The Tarmaks obviously hadn't treated their neighbors any better than they treated the people of the Plains. Feeling disgruntled, she strode forward without waiting for the servant or Callista. "What is this place?" she demanded as they hurried to catch up.

"It is the Akeelawasee," the Damjatt replied.

"Which means what?"

"The Place of the Chosen Ones, Lady."

Linsha glanced around. They were walking down a long corridor already dark with evening shadows. A few oil lamps spilled pools of light on the stone floors and illuminated delicate murals and decorations painted on the walls. It was so quiet she could hear the rain pounding on the roof. "Chosen for what?" she finally asked.

"For the emperor and the royal family. These females— or women as you call them—are the wives, daughters, concubines, and family of the emperor." He stopped before a large door, threw it open, and waved the two women in. They stepped onto a gallery that overlooked a large room. Bright light filled their eyes, and a swarm of sounds buzzed around them.

Linsha blinked in surprise and looked down. She'd had no real previous conceptions about the Tarmak women. In the war for the Plains she had only dealt with the warriors and their ferocious, bloodthirsty lust for war. She'd never given the females much thought. A "Place of the Chosen Ones" brought to mind images of pampered women lolling about indolently on soft pillows waiting for their master's pleasure. She hardly expected something that reminded her of a Solamnic training facility. The white-painted room was brightly lit with lamps that hung from the high timbered ceiling and cast a yellowish glow over the space below. Spread across the room were several dozen tall, muscular women engaged in various forms of exercise and physical training. All had tanned skin, dark hair, pointed ears, and all looked as fit as warriors.

Linsha stared.

The servant saw her face and tried to explain. "Lady, among the Tarmaks, all are instilled with an ideal of military virtue and discipline. The males are taught to fight and the females are expected to bear children to continue the glory of the Tarmak Empire. In order to bear healthy children, the women must also be healthy, so they are given vigorous exercise, a simple diet, taught faultless discipline, and—"

Linsha cut him off. "Oh, really? Faultless discipline? What about that one?" She pointed to a far corner of the room where an altercation seemed to be in progress. The young woman she had seen on the docks with Lanther had come in through another door and interrupted an older Tarmak woman working with stone weights. Her loud, insistent voice drew everyone's attention.

"Well," the servant said quietly, "possibly except for that one."

"What is your name?" Linsha demanded. She didn't mean to be so brusque, but nervousness and her bad mood were making her short tempered.

He hesitated, watching the conflict below with some nervousness, then said, "In this place I am called Afec. I am the apothecary and one of the elder slaves of the Akeelawasee. I have been told to bring you to the Empress."

Linsha glared at the two Tarmaks arguing in the corner. "There is one?"

"Assuredly. Tzithcana is the Emperor's first wife. She is the . . . matriarch. Is that the word?"

"Yes, if I understand what you mean."

Afec hunched his shoulders and looked worriedly at her.

"Lady, if I may say. It would be best if you would obey the Empress's commands. You are under the Akkad-Dar's protection, but in here the Empress is the supreme ruler. If she does not accept you, you will not live long enough to lodge a complaint."

A sudden shout from below brought the room to a standstill. Every person watched as the young Tarmak woman stalked across the room to the foot of the gallery stairs and pointed up at Linsha. She burst into another furious stream of Tarmakian. She must have said something shocking because the women around her gasped and stared up at Linsha.

Linsha felt her temper straining at the bit. She'd had about enough of this female and her vitriolic verbal attacks, and she still didn't know what galled this woman so. She started to move forward when a hand brushed her arm.

"Drathkin'kela—" Afec said in a low-pitched warning.

"My name is Linsha Majere," she snapped.

"Lady Linsha, the Empress demands respect, obedience, and self-control. Do not react to Malawaitha. The Empress will deal with her."

Linsha's green eyes flashed with anger, but the sense of his words reached her. If she had to live in this place for now, it would be better to abide by their rules and strive for a good impression. Perhaps the Emperor did not mind if she tossed a warrior in the harbor, but the Empress might not appreciate a brawl before she'd even met Linsha.

Linsha squared her shoulders under her wet clothes, lifted her chin, and indicated for Afec to take the lead. With Callista behind her, she marched down the steps and walked onto the padded floor of the exercise hall.

The tall Tarmak woman charged up to her, her mouth already forming the words of a loud accusation. Her face flushed with anger, agitation, and hurt.

Linsha stopped and waited. She made no reply or effort

to back away; her expression remained unmoved. Unflinching, she glared at the Tarmak's face as the woman vented her anger in no uncertain terms. Linsha just wished she could make some form of reply.

"Malawaitha!" The name snapped like a whip across the woman's loud tirade.

Linsha was impressed to see the fiery, volatile woman abruptly snap her mouth closed and stand straight, almost in perfect Solamnic attention. Silence filled the room to the rafters where the sound of rain drummed on the roof.

From the far side of the room, the large woman strode across the floor. Watching her approach, Linsha knew without a doubt this was the Empress of the Tarmak Empire. No other female in this room compared in height, breadth, or air of arrogant self-assurance as this first wife of Khanwhelak. She moved toward the small group like a warship at ramming speed with full sails and oars. Her broad face was suffused with irritation and anger; her gray eyes darkened like an approaching storm.

Linsha did not even wait for Afec's cue. Clasping her hands, she bowed low to the Empress. Callista and Afec quickly followed suit and remained that way as the Empress swept up.

Only Malawaitha waited a moment too long to bow. A powerful backhanded blow knocked her to her back. She lay on the floor without a word or a tear, staring up at the matriarch like a child who finally realized it was time to be silent.

The Tarmak Empress snapped a question. Afec bowed even lower and his calm, soothing voice gave an answer.

Linsha, her nerves tight as a bowstring, could only wait. She had experienced this same feeling of wary, tense obedience the first time she met Commander Ian Durne, the captain of Lord Bight's personal guard. He had exuded the same unquestionable authority and iron control as this formidable woman.

31

The Empress drew a deep breath into her ample chest. There was none of the soft-cheeked, white-haired, gentle-voiced grandmother about her. She was taller than Linsha by a head, probably twenty years older, and as weathered as oak. Her dark hair had become mostly gray and was pulled back in a tight bun for exercising, accentuating the austere lines of her face and the force of her gaze. Born into a militaristic society and raised in the Akeelawasee she was a handsome female, muscular, and seemed well satisfied with her position as first wife. She said something to Afec that included the title "Drathkin'kela."

Afec said to Linsha, "The Empress demands to know what you have around your neck. Jewelry is not normally permitted here."

Linsha's hand flew to her throat and touched the gold chain that gleamed at the neckline of her tunic. Reluctantly she pulled out the two dragon scales. One brass scale from Iyesta and one bronze scale from Crucible hung from the chain that had been a gift from Lord Bight. She didn't know why Lanther allowed her to keep them since he despised Crucible and was partly responsible for Iyesta's death, yet he had never tried to take the chain from her or even suggest that she put it away. She hoped the Empress would be equally as understanding. She stood warily as the matriarch reached for the scales and fingered them thoughtfully.

"Did you earn these?" the Empress asked in a very rough Common. Her accent was so thick that Linsha barely understood her. But she filed the information in the back of her mind. The Empress could speak Common, albeit not well, so it was likely she could understand more than she could speak. Linsha realized she would have to be very careful when she spoke to Afec or Callista in the Empress's presence. She pondered the scales between Tzithcana's fingers. The Empress asked her if she had "earned" them. Did the Tarmaks consider dragon scales to be badges of honor or signs of disgrace? She decided to be honest.

"They were gifts of friendship, Empress," she said as distinctly as possible. "From two dragons I greatly admired."

A sudden pang of loss flared unexpectedly in her heart. She had admired, respected, and befriended Iyesta and still missed her very much, but she had grown to love Crucible. Although she had known of him since her time in Sanction, she had become very close to him during their months together on the Plains of Dust. Their companionship had turned into a deep friendship of trust, respect, and a genuine mutual liking that made his deceit and lies to her that much more painful when he finally revealed his human identity to her. She bit her lip hard and used the pain to fight back the unexpected grief. Crucible was gone. Probably forever. There was no point in harboring any feelings for him.

She blinked and lifted her eyes to meet the Empress's. The woman's intense eyes bored into hers as if she could strip every mask and pretense and peer into the exposed soul. Linsha did not look away. She had endured too much in her life to be intimidated by a mere stare.

At last the old woman nodded once. She walked around Linsha, studying her arms and shoulders and legs. She felt the bones in Linsha's hips and the calluses on her hands.

"Take tunic off," said the Empress.

With a grimace Linsha pulled off her wet outer shirt and stood in front of the Empress in her damp undertunic. The matriarch continued her inspection of Linsha's muscles and scars. She poked Linsha so much she made her feel like a mare at a horse fair.

"This wound?" she asked, stabbing a finger at a new red scar on Linsha's upper arm.

"Crossbow," Linsha replied.

"Your hands?"

"Burns."

33

"These?"

"Swords."

The Empress stared like a basilisk for another moment or two, then she clapped her hands, her appraisal finished. The other female Tarmaks gathered around, each studiously ignoring Malawaitha on the floor. Pointing at Linsha, the Empress spoke to the women in fast emphatic words that offered no chance for argument. When she finished with them, she growled to Linsha, "You are thin. You are weak. You must work. Afec will be your servant."

"I have a servant," she dared to say.

The Empress cast a contemptuous eye at Callista. "This one is too small. She will work. Afec will guide you on path of a proper Tarmak. Will teach you our ways. He will speak for you to others until you have learned our tongue."

Linsha bowed.

Satisfied, the Empress turned her back on Linsha and reached for Malawaitha with a large hand. She yanked the woman to her feet and thrust her forward toward a door in the far wall.

The young Tarmak shot a venomous look over her shoulder at Linsha before she fled the room, the Empress close on her heels. The door slammed behind them. Abruptly the crowd of women broke up as they all hurried back to their chosen tasks. Sounds and voices filled the silence again.

Linsha heard a faint sigh of relief beside her. "You did well," Afec said quietly, giving Linsha a brief bow. "The Empress has accepted you. For now."

"Afec," Linsha said in tones that made Callista take a step out of the way. "Who is Malawaitha and why is she so angry at me?"

The old Damjatt sighed again. "She is a minor daughter of the Emperor. She has always been full of challenge and desire."

"And why does she dislike me? The other Tarmaks don't seem to be upset."

Afec glanced at the door where the young woman and the Empress had disappeared. "She is betrothed to Lanther Darthassian. She thinks you have come to take him from her."

A heavy knock on the frame of her narrow door brought Linsha awake before dawn. She yawned and stretched to a sitting position, and for the thirtieth time in as many days, she thought sadly of Varia. The owl had been her constant companion for over five years and habitually woke her in the morning by bouncing on her and hooting softly in her face. It was a far better awakening than this unfriendly, impersonal slam on the door. By Kiri-Jolith, she missed her friend. She didn't even have the solace of knowing what had happened to Varia. Lanther had refused to let her see the owl before they left the city and would not tell her what he had done with the bird. Nor had she been able to ask since they landed in Ithin'carthia. The one advantage that she could see about being sequestered from the male population was she hadn't seen Lanther for almost two weeks.

She groaned and rose as Callista slipped into the tiny room with a basin of cold water and a cup of juice. The courtesan looked tired. She had a soft gray look about her eyes and a sag in her shoulders. It was little wonder. Linsha estimated by the time she finished with all the work the palace servants were required to do that she had only four or five hours before she had to start again. The small blonde smiled at Linsha and handed her the juice.

Linsha grimaced. "This dodgagd juice is foul. Where do you suppose they get it?"

Callista laid the basin on a stand. "You don't want to know. But I am told it is very good for the blood flow. And good blood flow means—"

"Strong muscles, and strong muscles mean healthy babies, and healthy babies mean a greater Tarmak nation," Linsha said by rote. "I swear if I hear any more about Tarmak babies, I will hurt someone." She spoke in a loud voice knowing full well she could be heard through the thin screens that separated her from the other sleeping chambers of the barracks-like dormitory.

But Callista was not so bold and replied in a much lower tone. "I know. They are single-minded. The servants say there are seven women with child in the Akeelawasee—and five of them are the Emperor's get."

Linsha grimaced at the mere mention of the Emperor and pregnant women spoken together in the same breath. It reminded her of the slave women brought from the Missing City. She hadn't seen one of them yet, and she could only hope they were still alive. Her thoughts hurried on while she pulled a clean sleeveless shirt over her head. The rumors of babies brought something else to mind she had noticed earlier.

"If all these females are breeding little Tarmaks like rabbits, where are the children?" she asked.

Callista straightened out the blankets and rolled up the sleeping pallet to look busy in case someone passed by the door. "The royal children are in another part of the palace. Their mothers feed them and visit them until they are about seven, then the boys are sent to a military camp and the girls are sent somewhere else for schooling and physical conditioning."

"Seven?" Linsha repeated, horrified at the thought. At

seven she had been happily ensconced in the center of her family, surrounded by loving parents, grandparents, and a brother who still called her by her family nickname. "I can hardly imagine that. A child should be with its family."

Callista agreed. "My mother may have been a courtesan, but she kept me with her until her death." She paused and a pale twinkle lit her blue eyes. "Have you had children, Lady Linsha?"

Linsha gave a snort. "I had a horse once."

Then there was no more time for talk. A bell rang in the corridor calling the women to their first exercise period of the day. Linsha groaned. She had been in this place for about fourteen days and she had come to loathe that bell. It ruled her life like a slave driver, holding her fast to the rigid routine of the Akeelawasee. What, she wondered as she stretched a little, did the common females do? If they were bound to this sort of royal routine, nothing would ever be done.

She was about to leave the cubicle when she suddenly turned and looked at Callista. "How do you know what the servants are saying? Do you speak Tarmakian already?"

The courtesan waved a casual hand. "Servants talk. A few speak Common. They're all slaves from different areas. There's even an old woman from Solamnia who was left here by the Dark Knights. She talks to me often. Oh! Another thing I heard. The apothecary, Afec? Some of the older slaves say he is a prophet. They say he has visions sometimes." She giggled. "It's probably from all the fumes from his herbs and medicines. Maybe he'll have another vision of how we can escape from here."

Linsha grinned. "I'll ask. Keep your ears open. Let me know what else 'they' say."

Callista's humor abruptly faded and she held out a hand. "One last thing. Malawaitha has been away being 'properly chastised.' Whatever that means. But someone said she was coming back soon."

"I'll watch for her. Thanks."

Malawaitha, Linsha thought as she jogged outside to join the noblewomen. Afec had told her the emperor's daughter had been sent out of the palace for a while as punishment for her temperamental outburst to the Empress, but no one had said where she had gone or what was happening to her. It had been rather nice not to have to worry about the fiery Tarmak stabbing her in the back or ambushing her during one of their long runs.

The gods knew this place had taken some getting used to. Even her first few years in the Solamnic knighthood had not been as regimented as this. She and all the other royal women rose before dawn for a cup of foul dodgagd juice and a three mile run over the palace grounds followed by calisthenics and swimming. Then there was breakfast, more exercise, a massage, a light midday meal, more exercise, and any work the Empress saw fit to hand out. Then there was music lessons or weapons practice, gymnastics, a small evening meal, discussions on what Linsha could only describe as beauty lessons, and then it was bedtime when all the females had to retire to their personal cells for sleep. The routine was so set and so predictable that she was already perishing from boredom. She was too accustomed to setting her own times, making up her own mind, doing things in her own manner. She liked reading books, visiting with friends, riding her horses, eating different foods, facing challenges, using her mind! Here there was nothing to do but exercise, eat dull food, and sleep. It was enough to drive her mad.

On the good side though, she noted while she jogged along the same dull dirt path, the food, the rest, and the exercise had done her a world of good. After so many months of war and hunger and strife, she desperately needed the food to rebuild her strength, the rest to rebuild her stamina, and the mindless exercise to regain her old skills. She truly felt better than she had in months.

She was so deep in thought that she did not pay much attention to the grounds around her. She had already seen this path fourteen times in a row and examined it carefully for some means of escape. Unfortunately, the grounds were walled in by high stone barriers and frequently patrolled by Tarmak guards. There was no way out that she had been able to see, yet. This morning the sun was barely up and a heavy dew drenched the grass. The shadows were still thick under the trees, but the sky was clear and promised another warm sunlit day.

There were so many other women out running that Linsha paid scant attention to the footsteps pounding behind her. Suddenly a hand struck her between her shoulder blades and shoved her off balance. She staggered sideways, slipped on the damp grass, and fell to her knees. One knee scraped something hard, and pain streaked up her leg. Linsha looked up in time to see Malawaitha run by, a nasty little smile on her face.

"Malawaitha, wait! I'd like to talk to . . ." Linsha yelled, but the Tarmak woman kept running and soon disappeared among the trees.

Wincing with pain, Linsha climbed to her feet and continued jogging. She didn't look at her knee. It was obviously scraped, and if it was bleeding, the blood would help clean out the wound until she could find some water and a bandage. This time she ran with her full attention pinned on the track ahead. If Malawaitha could do something like this, she wouldn't put it past the Tarmak woman to try to ambush her in any one of the groves of trees along the trail. When she heard more runners come up behind her, she slowed a little to allow them to catch up with her. Better to run in a group than by herself. The other Tarmak women in the Akeelawasee tended to ignore her, but at least they didn't shove her into the dirt.

By the time she reached the end of the morning run, she

had blood dried in streaks down her shin. The Empress, waiting at the end of the path, spotted the bloody injury and snapped a word to Afec standing patiently nearby. There was no sign of Malawaitha. Linsha bowed to the Empress as was customary and said nothing about the petty incident with the Emperor's daughter. She would bide her time and wait to see if this animosity would continue.

The old slave shuffled forward to meet Linsha. "Lady, you must clean that before you can enter the eating hall. It is unsanitary."

"Undoubtedly," Linsha replied. She looked down at her knee and frowned. The knee was scraped as she suspected, but there was a short deep cut just below the kneecap as if she had fallen on a sharp stick or a pointed rock. Annoyed, she followed Afec past the dining hall and through an archway into a large garden basking in the morning sun.

Linsha slowed to look around. A few small trees grew in the well-tended beds, but most of the plants she could see looked like herbs. She recognized a few from her own land—feverfew, thyme, marigold, and sage. The rest were new to her, probably culled from the highlands and jungles of the Tarmak island. Their scents filled her nose as she walked along the side of a building after Afec.

At the far end of the building, the Damjatt entered a small room and invited her to enter.

The room must have been Afec's workroom, for the only pieces of furniture in it were a large table, a smaller work table, and row after row of shelves neatly stacked with bottles, boxes, jars, stacks of linens, and bowls. Dried herbs hung from the ceiling. Another rack held small bottles of powders, unguents, and liquids of various colors. A brazier burned on the worktable, heating something that slowly bubbled in a cooking pot and smelled similar to horehound.

"I wanted to warn you before you ran," Afec said, indicating that she should take a seat on the large table. He bustled around the tables and shelves as if he was very familiar with the room. "Malawaitha has returned."

Linsha studied the dirty, oozing scrape and the cut on her knee. "Yes, I saw her."

She watched while Afec collected a basin of water and a clean cloth. His short stubby fingers played over the jars and boxes for a moment then plucked a stoppered bottle and a jar out of the rack.

"I know you've told me Malawaitha is betrothed to Lanther, but what if one of them changes their mind?" she asked. "Do the Tarmaks break their betrothal vows?"

The Damjatt poured a small amount of a clear liquid into the bowl of water and brought it to the table where Linsha sat. "This will sting a little." Gently he swabbed her knee with a cloth dampened in the water.

Linsha sucked in her breath. It did sting! Yet the pain was not enough to distract her from her chain of thought. She was about to repeat her question when Afec finally answered her with innate discretion.

"It can be done if the Emperor wishes it. However, Malawaitha is a beautiful, headstrong, willful, ambitious woman with the desires of her father's family. Unfortunately she has her mother's blood and intelligence." When Linsha looked blank, the old servant gave a slight shrug and went on. "As you might have noticed, the Tarmaks set great store by rank and position, but their ideas of rank are not always based on birth or even bloodlines. Often it is earned. The warlord Lanther is a good example. He is not a Tarmak, but his skills impressed them so much that he was adopted by the Emperor's brother and became a high ranking leader in the military."

"So what does this have to do with Malawaitha?" Linsha asked. "Isn't she the daughter of the Emperor?"

"Yes, and that grants her some rights and privileges of rank. But her mother was a slave. Unless Malawaitha marries a high-ranking leader or official in the court, she will forever remain a second-rank female in the Akeelawasee."

Linsha couldn't think of many things that would be worse. The second-ranked females, she'd noticed, rarely left the grounds of the women's compound and were often given the most mundane work such as spinning, simple weaving, cleaning equipment, and taking turns caring for the numerous offspring that lived in another part of the palace. She could little blame the energetic, ambitious Malawaitha for wanting something better.

"So she has set her aim on Lanther."

Afec nodded while he cleaned the cut on her knee. "Some years ago. She saw him at court functions and at the games, and she tried to convince her father to let her marry the human. Even though he was not of the People, he was of higher rank and could bring her status up. She convinced the Emperor to arrange a betrothal. Then Lanther and the Akkad-Ur planned the attack on your land. Lanther left our city and was gone for almost three years. Now that he is back, Malawaitha plans to continue where she left off."

"But I am in the way."

Afec glanced at her keenly from under his thick brows. "Malawaitha certainly thinks so. If I may ask, Lady, why are you here? I do not believe it is to enjoy our customs. Are you wishing to marry the warlord?"

Linsha laughed at the irony of the whole thing. She couldn't help it.

Afec, startled by the bitter fierceness in her eyes, set down the bloody cloth and studied her. His wrinkled face grew thoughtful. "You do not wish this?" he said curiously.

"No," she replied, shaking her head. "I do not wish it. But it is a matter of honor and a clutch of dragon eggs."

To her surprise, the Damjatt brightened with interest. "Dragon eggs. Did you bring them with you? They have great medicinal power. I would be pleased to see an egg in its entirety."

A suspicion sounded in Linsha's mind. Where had he seen dragon eggs, and what did he mean by "its entirety"?

"How do you know about dragon eggs?" she asked, careful to keep her voice mild and unemotional. "Was the Dark Knight's dragon a female?"

"No, no. Methanfire was a male. There were eggs from other dragons."

"What other dragons?" This time Linsha could not contain her interest or her rising intensity. "Are there dragons on this island? What did you do to the eggs?"

The quickening of interest died in Afec's demeanor as quickly as it came. Something must have come into his mind, for he hastily retreated behind his mask of reticence and bowed low, his hands clasped in front of him. "It was a long time ago, Lady. When the previous healer was teaching me the craft. She had boxes of dragon scales and pieces of shells that she used in her potions and medicines. They have not been renewed in a long while."

"So you have had no other dragon on this island than Methanfire?"

"None that I have seen," he muttered and bent to his task to avoid any more questions.

Linsha stifled her irritation. She had a feeling he was not telling her the whole truth, but she wasn't sure what the whole truth could be. He seemed to know something he did not want to share, but if there *was* something the old Damjatt was hiding, it would have to be wheedled out of him later when he had forgotten this conversation.

"Lady, the cut is deep and will be sore for a few days. But it will heal." He dabbed a creamy unguent on the scrape and wiped his hands on a clean cloth. "If you have a problem with it, please let me know."

Linsha nodded and slipped off the table. She had come to know this Damjatt better the past two weeks. In spite of her intense loathing of this place, she had grown to like the old servant. He had a quiet dignity that appealed to her and an indefinable inner strength that gleamed behind the bowing head and clasped hands of his slave's status. He was efficient, solicitous without being fawning, and a well of useful information—at least information he felt she should know. Apparently dragons were a subject he didn't want to discuss. Callista's words came to mind, and Linsha wondered briefly if there was any truth to the rumors from the servants quarters that Afec was a prophet.

She followed him back across the cloister and entered the dining hall. At a table on the far side of room, she saw Malawaitha lounging amidst a group of the younger females. Probably they were her friends and siblings, Linsha thought. They seemed pleased to see her.

Ignoring Malawaitha's presence, Linsha found an empty table and sat down. The Tarmaks usually sat on the floor and ate together at a low table spread with bowls of food and cups of beverages. The women did not drink as much wine or ale as the men, but they partook of fruit juices, water, and a powerful concoction of leaves, bark, and the gods knew what else called tazeer. According to Afec, it was a recipe handed down for generations that was supposed to help the body, strengthen the mind, and increase fertility. Linsha thought it tasted like swill and yearned for a cool cup of mead, a mug of her grandfather's spring ale, or even a scorching cup of kefre.

As soon as she was seated, Callista brought a bowl of hot cereal that contained some sort of grain Linsha didn't recognize. Steam rose from the gelatinous mass in the bowl, and a smell similar to slightly moldy wheat wafted over the table.

Linsha stifled a groan. Didn't these people break their fast with anything else? She didn't mind hot cereal once in a while when she could have it with cream and honey. But not like this, freshly boiled and unflavored. And not every day!

"Don't they serve meat around here?" she grumbled.

"Where are the sausages? The steaks? The venison and mutton? The hams and pickled pigs feet?"

Afec blanched. "Pigs feet? You truly eat such things?"

"All right, I am jesting about the trotters. I never liked them either. But meat! Why don't they serve meat here? Even our evening meal is nothing but soup, soup, flat bread, and soup. This is worse than being under siege. They overcook the vegetables, the fruit is soft and overly ripe, and this stuff should be fed to horses." She shoved the bowl away. She knew she was being childish, but she didn't want to stop. She was hungry, Chaos blast it, and not for this slop. "Soups, stews, tubers, boiled grain, and not a scrap of meat in sight."

"Don't forget the fish," Callista added.

"You are fed well," Afec protested at the same time.

Linsha threw up her hands. "Fish! I am sick of fish. That's all we see are bits of fish." Her voice was growing louder, and she made no effort to lower it. "And what about chickens? Or eggs? Don't you ever eat chickens?"

Afec stood motionless by her side, hoping she would not attract the attention of the Empress. "We do not have enough chickens. They were brought from your country and are considered a great delicacy."

Callista nodded, ever helpful. "They don't seem to have much meat. I've been in the kitchens. What meat there is goes to the Emperor and his warriors. It helps strengthen their . . . *attributes.*" She winked at Afec, whisked off a few dirty bowls, and hurried away to fetch a pitcher of tazeer.

Linsha watched her go with a faint smile. The courtesan had a touch of deviltry in her petite frame that often came out in the presence of the gloomy Damjatt. Although neither she nor Linsha had ever asked, they both assumed from the pudgy look of his body and the higher-pitched timbre of his voice that Afec was a eunuch. It was the only way he would be tolerated in the Akeelawasee with all the royal women.

The reminder of Afec's position in this place sobered her a little. He was as much a prisoner as she, yet he complained little. He had not even said a word of protest about being assigned to a foreigner who whined about the food and couldn't control her bad moods. She settled back to her seat, drew the bowl back, and stuck a spoon in the thick porridge. To avoid eating for another few minutes, she asked, "Why do the warriors get the meat? Is there some sort of religious or moral rule?"

"Lady, most of the meat is served to the males because it is they who fight for the glory of the people. Women who are with child are also given meat in hopes that their baby will be a male. The rest of the population must eat the fish, grains, and vegetables." A sadness came over his face, much like the look of regret he had revealed when he talked about his own people and their horses. "It was not always that way," he added so softly that Linsha barely heard him.

She lowered her voice. "What changed?"

"This land is too populated. The Tarmaks have spread like locusts. They cut back the jungles for fields and for wood. They overgraze the grasslands with their cattle and sheep. There is not enough arable land left to support all the people."

His words clicked in Linsha's mind and a few pieces of understanding fell into place. "No wonder they want Iyesta's realm," she said. Images of green fields, the rolling Toranth River, the woods, and the herds of fat cattle took form in her memory and for a moment a homesickness pierced her heart with the force of an arrow.

Someone moved behind her. Suddenly she felt something hot and sticky splat on her neck. The heat stung her skin.

"Malawaitha!" Afec cried. Red-faced he gave her a carefully worded reprimand.

A smooth, silky voice answered in an apology so patently false Linsha wanted to laugh. "Oh, Small One, I am so sorry.

I didn't—" Linsha could understand that much. The rest was a string of Tarmakian beyond her current understanding, but she understood what Malawaitha was doing. The Tarmak was hoping to needle her into attacking her in the presence of the Empress, which would put Malawaitha in a more favorable light and land Linsha in trouble. Linsha curled her lip. This female obviously didn't know some of the initiation traditions for young Solamnic Knights. She was an amateur in comparison.

With iron control Linsha remained sitting and casually reached up to her neck. It was the cooked cereal as she suspected. Coolly she scraped off some and flipped her hand in the direction of Malawaitha's voice. Her aim must have been good for she heard the woman give a hoot of anger.

The Empress's voice cracked across the noise of the hall. "Malawaitha! You will stay away from the Drathkin'kela."

Malawaitha bowed once in the direction of the Empress and stalked away.

Linsha hid a snarl. She was understanding more and more of the Tarmakian language and catching more of the nuances of their speech. Her self-control had paid off again. Unfortunately she had a feeling that the unmarried Tarmak woman had a vindictive streak as long as the King's Road. Linsha wiped the rest of the cereal off her neck and vowed she would not break. She would not allow this jealous, spiteful female to goad her into a fight over something she didn't want.

"Lady," Afec said apologetically. "I'm sorry. I did not see her."

Linsha accepted his apology with a wave and plunged her spoon back into her bowl of porridge. Disgusting though it was, the cereal sustained her and gave her strength through the long mornings. She knew she was going to need all the strength she could muster for a while if she was going to ward off the attentions of Lanther's betrothed long enough to find a way to get home.

Linsha's resolve was sorely tried over the following days. As she suspected, Malawaitha tried time and again to irritate, anger, or cause injury. The weather remained mild after the big storm, which allowed the women to spend much of their time outdoors running, wrestling, swimming in the garden pool, or practicing with the long sticks or the bell clubs. All of these activities gave Malawaitha ample opportunities to harass Linsha without attracting the Empress's attention. She found ways to trip Linsha on the trails or pitch rocks at her from behind trees. She grabbed Linsha's ankle one afternoon and pulled her under the water until Linsha was half dead from lack of air. Whenever she could get away with it, she chose Linsha as a partner during practice skirmishes with the bell clubs, sticks, or wooden swords and fought with such a vicious intensity that Linsha found herself covered with lumps and bruises.

Fortunately none of the other women joined Malawaitha in her petty spitefulness. They were too cowed by the Empress. But they looked askance at Linsha as if they expected her to do something, and they did not help her. Most of the time they turned away from the human woman in their midst and pretended she did not exist.

This frustrating state of affairs went on for another six days until one evening Malawaitha slipped up beside her in a dim corridor on the way to the evening meal. One moment Linsha saw someone slide out of a darkened room as she passed and the next a hand grabbed the chain around her neck and yanked. The strong chain did not break but tore into her skin and pulled her off balance. Pain burned into her neck.

Yet the pain did not burn nearly as hot as her fury. Without a sound she spun and swung a vicious punch into Malawaitha's midriff just below her breastbone. As she hoped, the Tarmak was completely unprepared for such a move. Her fist sank into Malawaitha's unprotected belly and drove the air out of her lungs. The tall woman grunted and doubled over, her hands clutching her stomach.

Linsha's fingers closed over Malawaitha's long braid and yanked her head up to Linsha's eye level. "Touch these scales again and I *will* kill you."

Malawaitha did not understand the words, but she caught the intent of Linsha's threat quite clearly. "One day Lanther will give *me* scales," she hissed in her language. "And you will be food for the Emperor's dogs."

Linsha translated most of it and almost made a slip by snapping a reply in Tarmakian. Instead she bit her lip hard and thrust Malawaitha away from her.

At that moment the Empress sailed into the hall, followed by her slaves and several of the lesser ranked females. She raked her dark eyes over both women and her expression darkened.

"There is blood on the neck of the Drathkin'kela. What have you done now?" she demanded of Malawaitha. Without waiting for an answer, she strode up to Linsha and examined her neck and the chain with the dragon scales. Angrily she turned on the younger woman. "I am ashamed for you. You know the rules of the Akeelawasee, yet you flaunt your desires in our faces. There are times to challenge and times to let patience rule your actions. Do you understand?"

Linsha did not entirely understand. There seemed to be layers of meaning in the Empress's choice of words that were beyond her limited comprehension of Tarmakian. But Malawaitha understood quite well. She bowed low and stood meekly when the Empress said to her slave, "Take her to the Room of Chastising and give her seven lashes for the attempted theft," then she swept on to the dining hall with her servants in her wake.

Linsha watched them all go until she was alone in the

hallway once again. Slowly she turned on her heel and walked back to the dormitory where her sleeping cell gathered the first shadows of evening. Her appetite forgotten, she lay down on her pallet and her fingers closed around the dragon scales. A deep, wrenching longing welled up inside to see her friends again. Any friendly face would do: Sir Hugh with his blunt easy grin, Leonidas (preferably without his crossbow), Falaius Taneek, or even the healer, Danian, with his hawk and his red-haired apprentice.

But more than anyone else, she desperately wanted to see Varia and Crucible. Especially Crucible. She would not have believed it was possible back there on the fields of the Red Rose, but the big bronze had become a vital part of her life. When she rejected him without giving him a chance to explain or giving herself time to think, she had torn her life apart. She had sent him away to live or die without her, and now all she had was an aching vastness in her heart and a regret that grew larger in her mind like a cancer. She wanted so much to see him again, to sit in the comfortable, reassuring circle of his neck and tail and talk to him as they used to do. Perhaps in time she could understand why he hadn't told her about his human shape, the shape she had known so well as Lord Hogan Bight. Perhaps. But now it was probably too late. She was trapped in this distant land where he could not find her, held hostage in a palace with a hateful rival and a promised husband she despised. Crucible, for all she knew, was dead.

Linsha lay on her pallet in the gathering darkness and silently cried for lost friends. It was a long time before she found the solace of sleep.

Malawaitha's Choice

5

'm invited to a what?" Linsha said, hanging upside down from a bar. She was using the bar to strengthen her stomach muscles by doing upside down sit-ups. It was an exercise she hated, but the results were worth the effort.

"The Akkad's initiation," Afec said patiently for the second time. "There will be a ceremony and a feast."

"What is this ceremony?" Linsha asked while she bobbed up and down.

"During the afternoon the Emperor, his guards, the high-ranking warriors, the priests, and certain officials of the court perform rites to prepare the dead Akkad-Ur for his journey in the afterlife. They then complete the ceremony to name Lanther Darthassian as the Akkad-Dar, the new warleader of the Tarmak hosts."

"And I have to go to the ceremony?" Linsha inquired.

"No. Women do not attend military ceremonies."

"Why not?" she demanded. Sweat ran down her face, or rather up her face, and dripped on the mats below. She puffed for air every time she swung her upper body upward. "I've been to plenty. Several initiations of rank, several knighting ceremonies, a vigil for a Legionnaire. I went to a military wedding, too, and I've seen my share of military tribunals."

Afec sighed, knowing she wasn't paying strict attention. "Women do not attend military ceremonies. That is simply Tarmak tradition."

"Fine. Fine. I don't want to go anyway." She swung up again, grabbed the bar with her hands, and dropped her legs to the ground. "So what is the feast? Will Lanther be there?"

"The feast is held for the entire court. The Akkad-Dar has specifically requested that you attend."

"Oh?" She wiped her face thoughtfully with a small towel. "And he will be officially instated as the warleader. I wonder what he plans to do about Malawaitha."

"I'm sure I don't know," Afec replied. "But for your sake I hope he treads carefully. He will not want to insult the Emperor."

"I don't suppose I could just slip out, go down to the docks, and catch the next ship back to Ansalon?" Linsha said, half in jest, as she stretched to ease her aching abdominal muscles.

Afec looked appalled. "Lady, I beg you. Do not do that. There are no ships that go to Ansalon except the military fleet. You would be caught and put to death, and the warleader himself could not prevent it."

Linsha had been talking partly in a wishful way, but the adamant tone of the old slave gave her pause. While she had examined several ways of slipping out of the palace, she hadn't had a way to check out the city and look for any avenues of escape from the island. The news that there were no ships that sailed to Ansalon—anywhere on Ansalon—was bitter indeed. She had given her word that she would marry Lanther, but if an opportunity to escape made itself plain, she had already decided she would take it. The mere thought of slipping away from her fate, no matter how unlikely, had stayed in the back of her mind like an escape door. As long as it was there, the impending marriage did not seem so fearsome. Now Afec had nearly closed that door. She forced the emotion from her face to hide her disappointment and picked up a ladle of water.

"So," she said before she took a long drink. "What do the proper ladies of the Tarmak wear to a feast?"

———————————

The feast was held two nights later in the huge square before the palace audience hall. While the men were occupied with their rites, the slaves and the women of the Akeelawasee set up tables, brought in lanterns, and hauled in armloads of garlands, flowers, and greenery for decoration. A space was left open for dancing, and slaves set up a platform for the musicians.

At sunset when the setting sun streaked the sky with orange and the peacocks screamed in the gardens, the men returned to the palace square that was aglow with golden light, to tables laden with food and wine, to music, and to the women of the palace arrayed in their finery. Benches had been brought out of the audience chambers, and one of the Emperor's gold plated thrones had been placed at the top of the stairs where he could view the feast from his exalted height. A huge awning shaded the throne, and banners bearing his crest of springing lions hung on poles on both sides.

While every person bowed low, the huge Tarmak walked ponderously up the steps and took his seat in the golden throne. Gongs sounded, drums beat, and from a side door, a dozen kitchen slaves staggered in carrying a huge platter with the entire carcass of a roast bull on a bed of green boughs. They placed the platter on a table at the foot of the stairs for the Emperor's inspection and stood back to wait.

The Empress, resplendent in a long linen robe of red and a cape decorated with the feathers of jungle birds, strode to the table in the shadow of the stone dragon and, wielding a knife, sliced a portion off the tenderloin. After placing the steaming meat on a dish, she carried it to the Emperor and offered a taste of the most succulent morsel.

The Emperor voiced his approval with a single grunt, then he pointed to Lanther standing near the foot of the stairs. The Empress took the dish to the new Akkad and offered him the second taste. Lanther, too, nodded his acceptance. Taking the knife from the Empress, he began to carve the roast bull into large pieces that were placed on smaller platters and carried to the tables scattered around the square. The crowd watched him hungrily. At the Emperor's signal, the musicians began their first piece, a typical Tarmak composition filled with drums, gongs, and the squall of Tarmak pipes. A shout rose from the waiting crowd and everyone made a rush for the food and wine.

Linsha stood back in the shadow of a wall and watched glumly as the Tarmaks crowded around the tables like hungry wolves. Slaves circulated through the gathering with trays of fruit, goblets of wine, cheese, and rounds of bread. Other tables held platters of roast birds, stuffed peacocks, roast mutton, pickled fish, steamed vegetables, and sweets of many varieties. But all of that food was being ignored for now while the Tarmaks stuffed themselves on the roast beef.

"It is a rarity for them," Lanther said quietly beside her.

Linsha felt her heart quicken. She hadn't seen Lanther since the ship arrived and she was taken to the Akeelawasee. She had wondered how she would react to him when she finally saw him again. Would she be pleased to see a familiar face? Angry that he had not sought her out before this? Furious that he was betraying another woman for her? She faced him and looked him over carefully before she made any reply.

The days of rest and steady food had worked well for him too. He looked fit and healthy and immensely pleased with himself. His hair was longer and braided in Tarmak style with white feathers and beads of bloodstone. His beard had been neatly trimmed and its dark, grizzled color helped to frame his brilliant blue eyes. A loose-fitting robe of deep blue draped his broad shoulders and opened in the front to reveal a fine-woven pair of loose pants held at the waist with a jeweled belt. He looked very much the part of a high-ranking nobleman and warlord.

Taking her hand, Lanther made a slight bow. "It is a pleasure to see you, Linsha. You look beautiful. Almost as lovely as the first time I saw you."

"And why not?" Linsha tried hard not to snap. "I have been kept as well as any prize brood mare."

He chuckled. "The Tarmak ways are rather different from what you're used to, but you will come to appreciate the advantages."

"When pigs fly," Linsha muttered under her breath.

The Akkad-Dar didn't hear her. Still holding her hand, he pulled her into the light of a hanging lamp and turned her around so he could admire every line of her costume.

In spite of her desire to wear her old tunic and stained skirt, Linsha had been given a silk wraparound dress that was the customary garb of the Tarmak noblewomen. She quickly learned the large piece of silky fabric could be worn several ways. Some wore the sleeveless dress over one shoulder or with loose robes, fringed shawls, beaded collars, or light sashes. A few, especially the younger, unmarried women, wore them tied around their hips, completely bare above the waist. Linsha had refused that variation and wrapped the golden fabric as high under her arms as she could manage and borrowed a large, feathered wrap from the pile of accessories made available to her. Although Callista had dressed her hair for her, Linsha, like the other women going to the court feast, was allowed neither cosmetics nor jewelry. Instead the women decorated their faces and arms with the Tarmak blue paint that was applied to their bodies in thin lines and geometric designs. The only other thing Linsha was permitted to wear were her dragon scales on their golden chain. Dressed in this fashion she felt neither comfortable nor beautiful, yet Lanther stared at her in a most disconcerting way.

"You look lovely. Why don't you remove the wrap so your true assets can be most appreciated?" he suggested.

"What? My scarred arms?" she said between her teeth. "Who wants to see those? Besides, look how many birds gave up their lives for this wrap. I feel obliged to honor their sacrifice."

He pulled her close and wrapped an arm around her waist. "There will be one more ceremony tonight. As the Drathkin'kela you may come to witness it, if I choose to take you." There was a keenness and luminosity in his eyes she didn't like.

She shrugged and would not look at his face. "Why would I want to come?"

He breathed softly in her ear, "I have brought a dragon egg."

Linsha stiffened. Her eyes flew to his like a striking hawk. "What do you mean? We left those in the Missing City. Why do you have one here?"

But Lanther only smiled. "You must come to see it."

Linsha was smart enough to catch the implied threat. If she wanted to see the dragon egg, she would have to humor him. Reluctantly, she pulled off the heavy feathered wrap and tossed it to a passing slave woman. Feeling very self conscious, she allowed Lanther to lead her to a table where he fixed her a plate of the hot meat, roast birds, and fish. He carried her plate to a special seat arranged for him across from the dragon at the foot of the stairs and left her there while he loaded a plate for himself and collected a flagon of wine and two goblets.

Linsha simply stood and held her plate while the noise and laughter swirled around her. She did not like the Tarmak music nor the slave dancers who had come out to the square to entertain the diners, and the sight of all these Tarmaks eating, dancing, laughing, and enjoying themselves was more than her stomach could stand. She had complained about the lack of meat several days before, but now that she had a plateful before her, she could not touch it.

Lanther laughed at her when he returned. "Sit," he said, urging her toward a high backed chair. "Tonight you dine in the presence of the Emperor and his Akkad."

Linsha bit back an unladylike retort and forced her legs to bend so she could sit down. The laden gold plate sat heavily in her hands. Lanther gave her a goblet of wine then plunged into his meal.

Since there was nothing else she could do, Linsha picked at the meat with her fingers, wondering if she could get any of it down without vomiting. She would rather have some of the bread and cheese to help settle her stomach, but Lanther hadn't offered any of that. Apparently the meat was good enough for the Akkad-Dar and his woman.

"You're not eating," Lanther pointed out. He shoved a piece of fish in his mouth and jabbed a finger at Linsha's plate. "It would be an insult not to eat the gift of the Emperor."

Linsha glanced up the stairs to the Emperor who sat in his throne and shoveled massive amounts of meat in his mouth from a platter the size of a trough. Two of his lesser wives held the platter while a third kept it full from the tables below. The Emperor, as far as she could tell, was paying no attention to anyone else. She hunched down in her difficult dress and tried to pick at her meal. This was going to be a long evening.

By the time the night descended and the single pale moon rose above the mountains to the east of the city, the feast was well underway. The young bull had been stripped, and a few people sat around the tables cracking bones and sucking noisily at the marrow. The hungry celebrants had moved on to the other offerings and gorged themselves on the fish, fowl, roast mutton, and side dishes. Wine was brought out in huge ewers and poured by the pitcherful. While the court ate and drank, dancers, musicians, singers, and jugglers performed for the crowd and the Emperor. The noise level in the square rose appreciatively and it wasn't long before the music grew faster and louder and the feasters had replaced the dancing girls in the dance space. Other people talked and laughed in small groups scattered all around the square and drank copious amounts of wine. Some, already feeling the effects of the wine and rich food, cavorted in the stone waterway.

From her seat by the stairs, Linsha watched the jugglers for a while because she enjoyed juggling and hoped to learn a few tricks. Soon she grew bored with that and watched the revelry around her, wondering if she could slip back to the women's quarters without anyone noticing. She was tired and out of sorts and very lonely in this mass of Tarmaks. Lanther was talking to some of the Tarmak officers, and no one else felt inclined to speak to her. Callista had not been allowed to attend, and there was no sign of Afec. Linsha found herself wishing for a friendly voice and a little peace and quiet.

Across the walkway the stone dragon glowered down at her, reminding her too vividly of another ugly, horn-headed blue dragon. She glanced up to watch the bats swoop and flutter at the edge of the light where a feast of large moths gathered, drawn by the torchlight. Beyond them stars glittered on the velvety night sky. A few clouds scudded across the stars driven by a stiff westerly wind. Behind the black mass of hills to the northwest, Linsha saw the faint flicker of distant lightning in the heart of a thunderstorm. There would probably be rain later that night.

"Akkad-Dar," said a sweet voice in Tarmakian, "I wish you many congratulations on your new rank."

Linsha nearly choked. She whipped her head around and saw Malawaitha bowing low to Lanther.

"Thank you, " Lanther said curtly, making little effort to be pleasant.

The Tarmak officers he had been talking to grinned to one another and stepped back to watch.

Malawaitha rose to her full height and gave the Akkad-Dar a brilliant smile. As a young, unmarried female, she had chosen the alternative style of the wrap dress and wore hers around her hips, well below her ample bare breasts. A magnificent garment of woven gold threads and shimmering beads hung about her neck and draped over her breasts like golden raindrops. Her long hair hung unbound and fell down her back in a dark cascade. She did not seem discouraged by Lanther's lack of interest.

"My lord," she pressed on, "I have wanted to talk to you since your return home. Why have you not visited the Akeelawasee?"

"I have had many duties, Malawaitha," he said.

She moved closer to him, completely ignoring Linsha. "Of course you have. But tonight the court feasts together. There is plenty of time for eating, dancing, and talking. Do you remember how we used to talk? We have shared much pleasure in our quiet walks in the garden. Please come talk with me. I have much to tell you."

Although the two were speaking in Tarmakian, Linsha was able to follow the gist of the conversation fairly well. Afec's lessons were beginning to pay off. She wasn't certain of the several translations for the word "talk," but Malawaitha's body language made her meaning perfectly clear. Linsha wondered how Malawaitha's request would settle with Lanther. Had he lost all feeling for this girl or did he still hold some regard or desire for her? Now that she was pushing her suit in front of others, how did he plan to deal with this without angering the Emperor? Keeping her expression deliberately blank, Linsha watched the two with interest and wished fervently she could take her dragon eggs and go home. Lanther and this woman deserved each other.

The Akkad-Dar chose to ignore Malawaitha and her obvious invitation. He turned back to the officers and resumed his conversation.

Malawaitha's face reddened. She flashed a look of utter hatred at Linsha. Slowly she bent her leg and knelt on one knee behind Lanther. "My lord," she said looking up him with proud eyes. "Have you forgotten your promise to me so quickly? You have given your word to my father."

Lanther's mouth tightened in irritation and he finally looked at her. "Get up, Malawaitha. You look ridiculous down there. I have a land to conquer. I free you from our binding. Go back to the Akeelawasee, find a husband appropriate to your rank, and give birth to babies suitable for our glorious armies."

Linsha could not help but feel the tiniest twinge of pity for the woman. Malawaitha was a warrior, a headstrong, tenacious fighter with the heart of a lioness. She should have been born to the Plains tribes or to the centaur clans where her fierce wants and her passionate ambition would have been appreciated. Instead she was forced to live among the royal Tarmak women where she was as caged and repressed as the Damjatt and the Keena. Linsha sensed it had taken all of Malawaitha's determination to kneel before the Akkad-Dar and plead for her forsaken cause, and Lanther had just coldly kicked her aside. This, Linsha knew, would not end well.

But Malawaitha tried one more time. "Lanther, as Akkad-Dar, you may take several concubines. I do not mind being second wife to this human if it means I may have you as husband."

Linsha nearly choked. She hid her reaction by swiftly stuffing a bite of meat in her mouth and chewing furiously. Any thought of pity for Malawaitha vanished like a candle flame in a high wind. Marriage to Lanther would be bad enough, but she would plunge a knife in his gut and suffer the consequences if she had to include this vicious Tarmak slut.

Lanther cast a quick glance at her then laughed. "No, Malawaitha. This human will be enough for a wife. She has fought beside me, saved my life, earned my respect. She is a friend of dragons, a rider of horses, and the daughter of a great sorcerer. Through her, my sons will rise to rule an empire that will bring glory and riches to the Tarmak people. I need no other wives. Or concubines."

If the comment had come from someone else—practically anyone else—Linsha would have felt complimented and pleased by such an accolade. Coming from Lanther the words only stung and irritated.

To Malawaitha, the words did more than sting. The color rose in her face in a hot flush of anger and humiliation. She rose slowly to her feet and stood haughtily glaring down at Linsha. She said nothing, but Linsha could see the fury raging in her eyes.

The hairs rose on the back of Linsha's neck, for she realized the Tarmak woman had suddenly become very dangerous. She forced a mask of uncomprehending curiosity and looked from Malawaitha to Lanther and back. "What did she say?" she asked Lanther in Common. "Why is she so angry?"

"She wants more than she deserves," he said, dislike ripe in his voice.

Malawaitha did not know his words, but she caught his tone and something deadly flickered in the brown depths of her eyes. Wordlessly she spun on her heel and hurried up the stairs toward the Emperor, her back rigid in unreleased animosity.

"Was it something you said?" Linsha said innocently.

Lanther gave a snort of laughter. "I know better than that.

You understand much more than you let on, and I'll wager my best horse that you know exactly what she wanted." He stopped laughing as he watched Malawaitha bow before her father, and the humor vanished from his visage. Tension tightened the muscles around his nose and mouth. With an abrupt gesture, he dismissed the officers. His hand closed around Linsha's wrist and hauled her to her feet.

Her body stiffened. She could feel the heat from his bare skin and could hear his rapid breathing.

"The time has come," he hissed. "You will have to challenge Malawaitha to a *ket-rhild*."

Suspicion burned like acid through her thoughts. "A what?"

"A duel," he said. "She has become a problem. We need to dispose of her before she causes more difficulties."

Linsha heard the words and did not believe what her ears were telling her. Challenge her to a duel? Dispose of her? "What are you talking about?"

He took her hand and raised it to his lips. "Power is the only thing these people respect. I am now their Akkad, the warleader of thousands. I deserve a woman more befitting than a second daughter. By the laws of the Akeelawasee, only a woman may challenge another woman. You are my first choice, so you must initiate the challenge."

She snatched her hand away. A feeling of cold certainty chilled her to the bone. She shot a glance at the woman talking vehemently to her father. "You manipulating bastard," she snarled. "You've known this all along. She's not just some slave girl you can drop at your whim. She's the daughter of the emperor. The only way you can get rid of her without offending him is to make me do it."

He leaned forward, his lips pulled back in a tight smile. "Beautiful and clever. You will be the mother of a dynasty."

She backed away from him, an eerie burning in her heart as if a hot darkness was gathering around her. Her hand itched to rip his eyes out, but she knew it would be a useless gesture. "I am a Knight of Solamnia. I cannot and I will not do your dirty work. You have already humiliated her. Let her go. I will not murder her. Not for you or anyone else."

She turned her back on him and would have walked away, but he grabbed her wrist again and yanked hard. She lost her balance and fell to her knees by his feet, His fingers dug into her wrist, grinding the bones together.

"Lady Knight, you will not only challenge Malawaitha to a *ket-rhild*, you *will* kill her, or your eggs will be given to my priests and used any way they see fit."

Linsha glared up at him, trying to ignore the pain in her wrist. "You promised those eggs to me if I married you."

"I cannot marry you if Malawaitha is betrothed to me."

"Why don't you just take her as a second wife?"

He hauled her to her feet and said, "You know Malawaitha. She would try to kill you at her first opportunity. No, she must be put aside in the Tarmak tradition, a Trial by Opposition, and you are the only one who can do it."

Linsha twisted her wrist out of his grasp and stood staring at him as if pinned by the gaze of a basilisk. How could she do this? If she bowed to his demand and challenged Malawaitha for no better reason than Lanther's desire to be rid of an encumbrance, then she would violate her oath of honor as a Knight of the Rose. This was murder. Plain and simple. Rose Knights were expected to be the defenders of justice, not assassins.

But if she did not agree, she was endangering the eight small lives she had sworn on her honor to protect. Both oaths bound her, and she would have to break one to keep the other.

Her thoughts twisted around like snakes. Her lungs felt tight and heavy. Gods, she swore, where lay the path of honor? Where was the justice in this trap? She struggled for a moment over the problem of what Lanther would do if she refused. She knew his manipulative and cunning character well. There was no doubt in her mind that he would turn over the eggs to the priests for their foul rites and probably drag her back to the Missing City just to watch. Then what? Would he kill Malawaitha anyway? Dispose of her quietly later? Would her gesture to save the woman be for nothing?

A clear image came to mind of Iyesta—magnificent, proud, gleaming in the sun. Her words came to Linsha's mind as clearly as if the dragon spoke them aloud.

Not as a Solamnic. I want your word of honor. It is stronger and more binding than your vows of Knighthood.

Her personal word of honor had proven stronger in the past. It had saved Lord Bight and Sanction. It had prompted her to swear an oath to a dragonlord, and it had led her half-way across the world. She had vowed to protect those eggs. They were all she had left.

Lanther saw the acceptance gather reluctantly in her turbulent green eyes. He strode to a guard, said something to him, and took the Tarmak's tall spear. He shoved it in her hands. "Take this to her. Just say *ket-rhild*. She'll understand."

Linsha took a deep breath and wrapped a hand around the spear shaft. In spite of the noisy revels around her, she was trapped in silence. She felt old, heavy, and damned with a sense of honor that tore her to pieces. With a slow step she walked up the stairs toward the Emperor and his daughter. They looked at her; their expressions registered surprise.

She reached Malawaitha and looked up into her face. There was a cloud of envy, hurt, and anger in the taller woman's features, and a dawning of understanding.

Linsha bowed to the Emperor then she raised the spear overhead and shouted over the music and laughter, *"Ket-rhild!"*

Startled Tarmaks close by fell quiet.

Then Malawaitha snatched the spear out of her hands

and raised it over her head. A piercing ululation, somewhere between a scream and a warcry, reverberated between the stone walls, cutting through the rest of the noise and music like a blade through soft butter.

Linsha felt her blood run cold from the memories of that awful cry. She had heard too many variations of it in the Missing City and on the Plains of Dust. She looked out over the square, half expecting the entire male company to reply in kind and come charging up the stairs to hack her down where she stood.

Malawaitha shouted something to her people that Linsha did not understand. But the crowd did. The Tarmaks roared their approval.

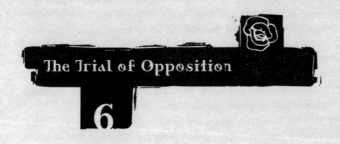

The Trial of Opposition

6

fec materialized beside her. Where he had come from Linsha had no idea, for she had not noticed him earlier. But now he stood beside her, his aged face clouded with worry.

"A *ket-rhild*," he said sadly. "Oh, Lady Linsha, why? What good will it do?"

"I have to," she said, her words edged with steel.

The old Damjatt licked his lips. It was hard to read his expression for his features were blurred in shadow. "The Akkad-Dar has forced this," he guessed, his voice held low. "He wants to be rid of her.

Before she could answer, Lanther bounded up the stairs and bowed low to the Emperor. He spoke quickly—too fast for Linsha to follow—and gestured toward the Tarmak woman with obvious concern.

"What is he saying?" Linsha said under her breath to Afec.

"Lanther is opposed to a Trial," the old slave whispered, fidgeting with his knotted belt. "He does not want to risk the Emperor's displeasure."

A huge gust of emotion blew through Linsha, leaving her

gasping somewhere between shrieking and tears. *I'm not going to fight that cow over him. She can have him.* The words rang in her head and beat to get out, but she bit her tongue hard. If she wanted the eggs, if she wanted to save the lives of those baby dragons, she had to follow through with this farce. But if Lanther didn't keep his part of the bargain, she vowed she would skin him alive with a dull knife.

Malawaitha replied in Tarmak in a long, furious harangue that involved many gestures toward Linsha.

The Tarmaks below watched in fascination.

The Empress approached from the crowd at that moment, and Malawaitha voiced her acceptance to the challenge again to the matriarch of the Akeelawasee. The Empress listened impassively.

"She has the final word in this," Lanther said quietly to Linsha. "She knows the two of you and will judge if you are fit."

"What if she says no?" she asked, watching the two women talk.

"She won't. She believes Malawaitha can kill you."

The Empress held up a hand to cut off Malawaitha's impassioned flow of words then moved close to the throne to confer with the Emperor.

"And you don't?" Linsha said. "You're not worried about me?"

"My dearest Linsha, of course, I am concerned. Malawaitha is in superb condition while you are still suffering from the effects of the war." He twisted suddenly and clasped her elbow in a tight grip, all the while keeping his eyes fixed on the Empress and the Emperor. "But you are a child of destiny, Drathkin'kela. You must do this for our dynasty."

Linsha did not bother to reply. Dynasty be damned, she thought. The man was lost in his delusions of glory. She watched the imperial couple talk together and knew there was no need for suspense, for she was sure she knew the Empress's response. The Tarmaks could not resist a good fight, especially one between an outsider and one of their own.

Her face showed none of these thoughts when the Empress walked to her and stopped. "You have challenged," the Empress said in her rough Common. "Malawaitha has accepted. What is the reason for this challenge?"

Linsha stifled a powerful surge of irritation. By the gods, she didn't want to do this. What was the point? Why couldn't they just talk about this? She loathed Malawaitha, but not enough to want to kill her. Or be killed by her. Resentment, tinged with a red tint of apprehension, filled the look she flashed at Afec, the only one who seemed to be slightly sympathetic.

"Est Sularas oth Mithas," she whispered. My honor is my life—or death, she thought. Then she squared her shoulders. "I challenge for the right to be the Chosen of the Akkad-Dar." She said it loudly for all to hear and listened in cold silence while Afec translated for her.

The blood rose to Malawaitha's face. Something hot and dark flashed in her eyes. Her strong body, her demanding personality, faced Linsha with thunderous malevolence. She smiled. She stepped back and with a powerful thrust, she jammed the point of the spear between two stones so the spear stood upright between the two women.

"Drathkin'kela, you shall have time to prepare. Afec, take her and ready her for the Trial," ordered the Empress.

Readying her for the Trial, Linsha discovered, involved removing all her clothes in spite of her protests and painting her skin blue with the Tarmak warpaint. Although slave women applied the paint, Linsha found the whole operation

69

to be embarrassing and nerve-racking. Surely they didn't expect her to go out in front of that crowd and fight in nothing but blue paint? Of course not, they replied, only the men did that, and they gave her a tiny loincloth and a fighting harness that held her breasts in place and left everything else exposed.

While the blue paint tingled on her skin and slowly dried, she longed for her Solamnic armor with the kingfisher and the rose embossed on the breastplate that had been made especially for her. The breastplate, the greaves, the gauntlets, the helmet . . . everything had been lost when Thunder destroyed the Citadel. Now she was reduced to blue paint and a loincloth. Blue wasn't even one of her favorite colors.

"I don't want to fight like this," she told them, feeling peevish and nervous at the same time.

The women did not understand her words and continued to rub the paint into her skin.

The paint did have one advantage though, one she remembered from the wound she received in the ambush at Iyesta's palace. A crossbow bolt had pierced her arm and caused a nasty wound, but Tarmak warriors had pulled the bolt out and slathered the blue paint on her wound. The injury had healed in less than half the time something of that sort usually needed. She suspected the blue paint had healing properties in it that bordered on magic.

As soon as the paint was dry, Afec ordered the slave girls to leave. He looked her over critically for a minute or two, then he shook his head. Gently he touched the dragon scales hanging on her chain. "Malawaitha has a long reach. Do not let her get you in a strong grip. She knows how to break necks. If she has a weakness, it is her arrogance and a tendency to lean too far forward in her swings." His lips thinned to a line, and he hesitated as if unsure if he should take the next step, then he said, "Wait here."

He was gone only a few moments. When he returned he

was carrying a cup and a small stoneware jug. He unstopped the jug and poured out about two full swallows of a thick greenish-gold liquid. "This is a special drink the Damjatt devised for their warriors. It gives strength and clarity of mind and improves endurance."

Linsha eyed it dubiously. "Do the Tarmaks drink this?"

He laughed. "The Tarmaks believe their own strength is sufficient and anything else is false. I fix this as a tonic for the slaves and the women during childbirth. But it does help, and tonight you will need all your skills and resources to fight Malawaitha."

"And kill her?"

"It would be best now," Afec told her. "If you do not, she will destroy you."

Linsha picked up the cup and stared at the contents. "What will the Emperor do if I kill his daughter?"

Afec's worry grew deeper. "I don't know. He should abide by the law of the *ket-rhild*. But he is the Emperor, and his mood is often unpredictable."

How ironic would that be? Linsha thought. Lanther tricks her into killing Malawaitha so he can marry her, but the Emperor has her executed in a fit of rage and grief and Lanther is left alone with the eggs.

"Thanks," Linsha said dryly. Feeling queasy, she drained the cup to the dregs. The liquid slid down her throat in a warm slide that seemed to ignite a fire the moment it hit her stomach. Energy rushed into her bloodstream and sizzled into her muscles. Her eyes widened in surprise.

"Let's go," Afec said. "Before that wears off."

He hurried her out of the palace and into the torchlit square where the crowd of Tarmaks and Malawaitha, now dressed in very similar garb, waited for her.

Linsha stood on the steps beside the Emperor and bowed low to him and to the crowd. She looked out over the square and saw the Tarmaks had been busy while the slaves painted her blue. A large area in front of the palace steps had been cleared away and was now ringed with excited onlookers. Malawaitha stood in the center of the space gently swinging a long-handled axe in one hand.

By the gods! Linsha took in a deep breath. Afec wasn't joking when he said his tonic gave clarity of mind. The scene before her burned into her mind in sharp detail and magnificent color. Sounds were louder, clearer; the light from the torches and lamps shone brightly and dispelled the darkest shadows. She looked up over the palace walls and saw the brilliant streams of lightning dance across the northwestern sky. The storm had moved closer while she was inside, and she could feel the wind rising over the palace and could sense the approaching rain. The gathering energies of the storm tickled her skin like the souls of the dead, but this time she relished the touch and felt the power energize her rather than drain her. She lifted her arms to the coming thunderstorm and drew in a deep breath of cool air.

This was a good night. If she was to die tonight, then so be it. But there was one thing she wanted to do. With the Damjatt tonic firing her body and mind, she took her thoughts and hopes and extended them far out into the night. She knew she was too far away to reach Varia or Crucible by way of the shared link in her mind, but she had to tell them whether they ever heard her or not.

Varia, you are my friend, this night and forever. Crucible, forgive me.

The owl's dark eyes popped open, and her head swiveled around to look at her surroundings. Her location did not amaze her, for she was where she expected to be—in a cage hanging in the headquarters of the Tarmak commander in Missing City. But something had startled her out of a moment of sleep. She pivoted on her perch and glared around the room at the Tarmak guards that stood at the doors and at the officers that sat at a table laughing and drinking. It was late afternoon by the slant of the shadows on the floor, and the owl usually napped this time of day. Yet deep in the quiet of her sleeping mind she had heard a voice, a beloved voice of someone she believed to be long gone. She had only heard a single word, *Varia*, and it was enough.

Linsha was out there far beyond the normal reach of their ability to communicate, and still she had found a way to send a word. Agitated, Varia fluffed her feathers and paced back and forth on the stick the Tarmaks called a perch. She would have to get out of this cage.

"You, Dog!" one of the officers snapped. "That bird is awake. Feed her."

A Tarmak warrior stepped away from his position by the wall and slouched over to the cage. He pulled a dead mouse out of a basket sitting close by, opened the cage door, and tossed it in. Looking morose, he closed the door and resumed his place by the wall to wait for his next order.

Varia made a chuckling sound that made the Tarmak whip his head around to stare at her. From what she could understand of Tarmakian, that particular warrior was serving a sentence for failure to perform a certain task. His punishment was to serve in the Dog Units as a servant, errand runner, cleaner of privies, or doer of any other distasteful task his superior officers could think of until he was properly chastised and remorseful. He had been put in charge of catching mice for the Akkad-Dar's owl and feeding her whenever she was hungry. What he didn't know, what most of the officers didn't know, was that Varia could talk and think.

She settled down her perch, hunched her head into her shoulders, and turned her round, wide eyes on the Tarmak warrior by the wall. She would give it some thought. There had to be a way out of this cage and out of this building, and once away she would seek help. Linsha was out there, still alive and still thinking of her. She had to get away.

***

"Linsha," Lanther said beside her. "It is time."

Linsha started violently out of her reverie, and the deep animosity she felt for him came snarling back. "If I die, wash this god-awful paint off before you bury me."

"The Tarmak burn their dead," he said and handed her an axe similar to Malawaitha's. He stepped back when she snatched it out of his hands.

She stared at it for a moment, long enough to see it had a handle about two feet long and a blade with a long curve, then she glared down at the woman waiting for her. In a startlingly fast change of mood, her contemplation of the night ended and her fear vanished in a sudden onslaught of rage. Every pent-up frustration, every concealed irritation, every anger she had kept under control joined together and burst into a firestorm that roared through her mind and burned away every civilized restraint she had. She thought to give a Solamnic warcry, but the sound that came out of her throat was a primal scream of fury that was more animal than human.

Lifting the axe, she charged down the steps and attacked Malawaitha like a demon spawned of Chaos. The young Tarmak woman fell back. Malawaitha had thought she was weak and unwilling to fight, but now everyone knew otherwise, and after a moment or two of desperate parries, Malawaitha settled down and fought back.

The battle was not pretty, nor was it fought with any rules. The axes both women wielded were sharpened to a razor edge, and the long handles could be used like a staff weapon or a club. Malawaitha had the strength and training of years in a Tarmak school. Her skills with the axe were better and her endurance was greater, but she was too accustomed to her practice drills and the limited scope of her experience with other styles of fighting to defeat the Rose Knight easily. Linsha, trained by Solamnic Knights and thugs alike, had a fighting style that spanned many skills and weapons. She fought with fist and foot and fingers and teeth, and she fought with such an inflamed fury that it surprised even herself.

Deep in the center of the clouds of red rage that roiled in her head, Linsha kept a desperate grip on a small struggling core of self-control. She'd heard the term "beserker" before, but she had never experienced such a transformation until now. Her common sense whispered that yes, her rage was fueled from days of pent-up animosity, disappointment, loneliness, and guilt, but there was something more, something artificial that boiled in her brain and set her blood on fire. She wanted to damage Malawaitha, to spill her blood, and tear her to pieces by any means possible. It was both frightening and exhilarating.

In the cooler, detached center of her self-control, a little thought said, Be smart. Use your rage to your advantage. Don't give in completely to the fury.

Easier said than done.

Linsha swung her axe up with both hands and just barely blocked a powerful swing by Malawaitha that would have removed her arm if it had connected. The shock jarred down her bones. Malawaitha grinned with malice and switched the handle to her left hand and swung again. Linsha ducked out of the way and landed a kick on the Tarmak's ribs. Breathing heavily, she danced out of Malawaitha's reach while her foe gasped for air. Linsha did not give her a moment to regain her strength. Malawaitha was too well trained with the battle axe. She knew how to hold the intricately carved brass handle that could slip so easily in a sweaty grip. From years of practice she understood the weight of the blade and how to use it to its greatest advantages. She knew the best way to use the butt end of the handle to smash it into Linsha's nose or eye or mouth. With her longer reach and greater strength, she swung the weapon with bloody efficiency and skill. Linsha's only hope was to stay out of the way of the blade and try to wear Malawaitha down before her own strength waned or this beserker flame in her body died.

With a wild shout, Linsha leaped again at Malawaitha. Her foot lashed out and deflected the axe far enough for her to knock the young Tarmak's feet out from under her and send her crashing to the ground. She swung her blade toward her enemy's head.

Malawaitha twisted out of the way and made a swipe at her ankles that forced Linsha to leap away. In that moment Malawaitha catapulted to her feet and faced Linsha again.

The crowd cheered wildly.

Linsha saw the pleasure in Malawaitha's eyes, saw the sneer of confidence that she would soon be the victor. Her anger rose to new heights that seared away almost every sense but her sight. She felt no pain from aching muscles, or the bangs and bruises on her arms and legs, or the shallow slash on her abdomen, or the tingling of the blue paint on her skin. She did not taste the blood that trickled over her lip or hear the crude shouts from the spectators. All she saw, all she wanted to see, was her opponent. She noticed how the sweat glistened on Malawaitha's face, and blood from a deep graze on her shoulder gleamed red against the blue paint. Her eyes followed the Tarmak's every movement, every shift of her dark eyes, every twitch of her face.

They traded blows again, their blue bodies struggling back and forth across the stone paving. Their axes clashed viciously, blade against blade or blade against handle. Soon they both bled freely from lacerations on their arms and upper bodies. Linsha's cheek and eye swelled from a hard blow from Malawaitha's elbow, and the young Tarmak limped from a battered knee cap.

This can't last much longer, Linsha's inner thought told her. Although she couldn't feel the fatigue yet, she could see her muscles trembling with the effort of movement. Malawaitha, too, was struggling for breath and for balance, and she was less accurate in her attack.

Linsha bared her teeth. Gods, she loathed this woman. Malawaitha was the figurehead of everything she hated about the Tarmak—the arrogance and tyranny, the bloody-minded stubbornness that kept her trapped here, and the malice that meant only harm to herself and her friends.

Why—

Linsha swung her axe.

—doesn't—

She swung again, bringing the blade down hard on Malawaitha's in time to the words that pounded in her head.

—she—

The axes crashed, sending a shock down Linsha's arms.

—just—

She gritted her teeth and struck again.

—fall!

The blades clashed together a fifth time and Linsha felt the blades lock. The handle slipped in her weakening grasp. The blade deflected off her foe's axe and slid sideways in her sweating palm. The unexpected twist threw her off balance, and she staggered and fell against Malawaitha's arm. Her axe slid from her aching hand and crashed to the stones.

The Tarmak woman staggered sideways under Linsha's weight and lost her hold on her own weapon. Seeking an advantage, she managed to snatch Linsha's hair and drag her down with her. The two women landed side by side on the ground.

All at once Linsha felt an arm snake around her neck and she found herself pinned in a death grip with Malawaitha's arm locked across her throat. She felt the Tarmak's embrace tighten around her like iron bands. She tried to breath and realized she could not draw in a breath. Her throat was being crushed beneath Malawaitha's powerful forearm and her head was immobilized.

Malawaitha's breath blew hot on her ear. "I will kill you slowly with my hands," she hissed in Tarmakian.

Linsha could not reply. Pain registered in her mind, screaming in her neck and back and lungs. Blood pounded in her head and behind her eyes. Panic clawed at the rage that still fired her mind. Her hands tore at Malawaitha's arm, but she might as well try to tear out stone. Her vision blackened as her eyes strained again the mounting pain and pressure in her head. Her feet kicked, trying to connect against Malawaitha's shins or knees or feet. It was all of little use. The implacable pressure on her throat continued to crush the life out of her.

Then her fingers touched a familiar hard disk hanging at her neck. The chain was caught under the Tarmak's arm, but the two dragon scales lay free on her chest. Linsha snatched them. She knew from touch which was which. Lord Bight had edged the bronze scale with a thin rim of gold. However, Iyesta's scale had been given on the spur of the moment and there had been no time since to match the rim. The brass scale was hard as metal, thin as a disk, and sharp enough to do damage. Linsha's fingers angled it and slashed the curved edge down Malawaitha's forearm. The Tarmak made a gasping noise, but she did not scream or loosen her grip. Her strength ebbing, Linsha tried again. Desperately she slashed Malawaitha's arm a second, a third, a fourth time. She could tell the scale was cutting deeply into the woman's arm, because she shuddered each time and her blood ran down warm and slippery onto Linsha's chest. Yet still she clung tenaciously to Linsha's throat.

There was no air left in Linsha's lungs. Her mind was shutting down; her head throbbed. Frantic now, she summoned the last tatters of her waning strength and hacked the dragon scale against the back of Malawaitha's wrist. Something gave beneath the edge of the scale.

A sound somewhere between a gasp and a choked-off scream burst in her ear, and the Tarmak's arm slid off just enough for Linsha to gasp for air. Her throat hurt abominably and her air passage felt pressed flat, but a thin stream of air slid out of her aching lungs and blessed fresh breath flowed in. She gasped again and coughed. Malawaitha shifted under her, and the woman's uninjured arm moved as she sought to get another grip around Linsha's neck. The terror of being pinned again shot a burst of energy through Linsha's flagging muscles. She lifted her head as high as she could manage and brought it down hard on Malawaitha's face. Pain shot through her head, but she guessed from Malawaitha's cry that it was not as bad as the damage done to her enemy.

Taken by surprise, Malawaitha had taken the full brunt of Linsha's head blow on her nose. Groaning, she clapped a hand to her injured face. Linsha rolled off and scrambling to her hands and knees, she sought for an axe. The Tarmak scrabbled away from her, blood streaming down her broken nose and pouring from her arm. They both saw the closest axe at the same time.

Both women lunged for the weapon. Malawaitha's longer arm reached the axe a fraction of a second sooner, but Linsha's hand swerved in mid reach, bunched into a fist, and smashed a powerful upper cut into Malawaitha's broken nose. Blood splattered them both. The Tarmak sagged over the axe, stunned by the blow.

Trembling with the effort, Linsha lunged after the second axe, crawled to her feet and stood over Malawaitha, the axe dangling in her hand. The tonic Afec had given her still sizzled in her brain, but the red killing lust had gone, leaving only regret and a deep sadness at the waste of all of this. She stared down at Malawaitha through a sparkle of tears and listened to the crowd around her scream for blood. They wanted a death; it didn't seem to matter whose.

"Live or die?" she offered in Tarmakian so softly only Malawaitha could hear her.

For a long moment there was no answer. The young Tarmak lay face down on the stones, wheezing for air and bleeding profusely. Overhead, lightning flared in the clouds that now covered the sky. Linsha could hear the thunder rumble over the voices of the spectators.

Malawaitha moved. Slowly she pushed herself to her knees to face Linsha and hefted the axe. "I will never share Lanther with a human," she spat through the blood in her mouth.

"Lanther betrayed you," Linsha replied sadly. "If you had helped me instead of fought me, you wouldn't have had to share him with anyone." Then, knowing there was no other way to end this duel, she slammed Malawaitha's axe out of the way and brought her own weapon around in a swift arc that sliced into the woman's neck and sent her head dropping to the ground.

The body stayed upright, swaying gently a moment, before it toppled forward and lay still on the stone paving. Linsha threw her axe to the ground. She stood still in the center of the watching Tarmaks and lifted her eyes to Lanther. The first few drops of rain splattered on the stones around her.

Urudwek's funeral

7

ightning cracked in the sky over the palace, and thunder rumbled into the hills, but the Tarmaks paid little attention to the approaching storm. They watched as Malawaitha's body collapsed to the stones. Without a moment's hesitation to regret her death or mourn her passing, they burst into a wild chorus of warcries, vociferous shouts, and a spate of appreciative applause. The dead woman had failed and was gone. The victor had fought well, with surprising ferocity, and had won her position as the Chosen of the Akkad-Dar.

The Emperor rose from his golden throne. He nodded once to Linsha, shouted a command to his people, then moved ponderously into the palace followed by his slaves and the Empress. The Tarmaks shouted with pleasure, and every man and woman carried their goblets, plates, clothing items, musical instruments, and in some cases each other up the stairs and into the large audience hall. Slaves brought the tables, the benches, the lamps, and the wine. The feast, it appeared, was moving indoors.

Linsha did not move. She stood by Malawaitha's body and stared down at the corpse, her face expressionless. It was all she could do to stay upright.

Afec was the first to reach her through the streams of people moving up the stairs. He touched her arm and looked worriedly into the stormy green eyes that turned to look at him.

"What did you put in that drink?" she demanded.

He looked slightly embarrassed. "I may have given you a larger dose than you needed. In the rush of the moment, I did not take into account your smaller stature."

Lanther joined them. His blue eyes sparkled with pleasure and pride as he slipped his blue robe over her shoulders and hustled her toward the stairs.

She was too tired to argue. The only thing keeping her on her feet was Afec's tonic. She had a feeling that when it wore off, she would collapse like a sail in a dead calm. Just once she glanced back and saw Afec kneeling by Malawaitha's body, his head bowed, while slaves collected her head and gathered her body to be carried off. At that moment, the rain dropped out of the sky in a deluge of pouring water, and Lanther pushed her inside the large double doors of the audience hall.

She hoped he would take her back to the Akeelawasee where she could lie down, have a long drink of water, and have her injuries attended to. The swelling on her left eye was getting so bad she could barely see through the puffy flesh, her throat hurt, and the laceration on her stomach stung like fury under the blue paint.

"We're going this way," he said, pushing her in a different direction, away from the festivities.

"Lanther, please," she contested. "I've had enough."

"We're going to see the dragon egg."

He would tell her nothing more in spite of her protests and questions until they had walked through several long corridors and stopped in front of a door.

Linsha fell silent and studied the entrance. While many of the other doors in the palace were lightweight barriers of red-colored woods carved with geometric patterns, this door was massive, dark, stained with age, and decorated only with two iron straps added to the door for strength. Two of the emperor's guards stood on either side of the door like ponderous statues and looked neither left nor right.

She glanced at Lanther through her one good eye, but he held his finger to his lips and shook his head. She became aware then that they were not alone with the guards. Other Tarmak warriors were coming silently down the hall carrying torches. They formed a line behind the Akkad-Dar and waited patiently, although for what Linsha had no idea. She hoped they were not here for the dragon egg, for that thought made her very uncomfortable. No good could come of Tarmaks and dragon eggs together. But surely Lanther wouldn't let any harm come to the egg. He had promised them to her. She had fought for them.

A drumbeat, slow and measured, echoed down the corridor, and the warriors moved quickly to either wall. Clasping their hands in front of them, they bowed low as a procession moved majestically along the hallway toward the gathered warriors. Linsha expected to see the Emperor in front, but as the long line of Keena priests, warriors, and attendants came into her view, the first thing she saw was the casket from the ship's hold carried on the shoulders of six burly warriors. Beside her, Lanther bowed low.

Linsha's battered face darkened into a frown of anger. She knew who was in that coffin—Urudwek, the Akkad-Ur, the previous general of the Tarmak armies and the man who had led the invasion of the Missing City, ordered the massacre of the Wadi camp, and murdered her friend, Mariana. The Tarmak should be consigned to the darkest depths of the Abyss, not brought home in honor for some ridiculous burial ceremony.

Lanther grabbed her wrist and pulled her over into a bow. "Do it or they will kill you," he said in no uncertain terms.

Although her hands clenched into fists and her stomach was tied in knots of anger, Linsha bowed low as the two guards pulled open the massive door and the casket was carried ceremoniously past her into the lighted passage beyond. The priests and attendants followed, and behind them walked the Emperor and his guards. The huge Tarmak inclined his head to Lanther. The Akkad-Dar, keeping a tight grip on Linsha's arm, fell in behind the Emperor and behind him came the remaining warriors.

The procession moved in time to the beat of a drum—slowly, reverently—along the corridor and down a long flight of stairs to a lower level beneath the palace. From there, they continued downward on another flight of steps that spiraled deeper and deeper below the lowest levels of the building into the native stone of the promontory itself.

Linsha tried to pay attention to where they were going. She was a trained spy and a Solamnic Knight of the highest order who should have been making mental notes and absorbing everything she could see of this new experience. But she was feeling lucky just to stay on her feet as she trudged down the neverending stairs after Lanther. Her body ached from an unbroken chain of knocks, scrapes, cuts, bruises, and sore muscles from head to foot. That horrible tonic still rumbled in her stomach and fizzed in her head, and the smell of the blue paint and Malawaitha's blood on her chest made her nauseous. Worse, the smoke and dancing light from the torches left her dizzy and lightheaded. She prayed they would reach the end of the stairs before she fainted or vomited. She wasn't sure which might happen first.

Thankfully the procession came to the last of the stairs before she lost control of her head or her stomach. They proceeded along a gently sloping course through a broad corridor. The darkness was intense, broken only by the torches carried by the priests and warriors.

Linsha lifted her head and sniffed the air. There was

something very reminiscent about this place—a smell, a feeling, a touch of cold, dank air that reminded her of the maze under the Missing City or the caverns under Sanction. She guessed they were in an underground complex in the heart of the promontory. Was this where the Tarmaks buried their honored dead? Were there tombs down here? She groaned and rubbed her throbbing temples.

She plodded onward behind Lanther, concentrating on keeping her feet moving and her body upright. She could hear the Tarmaks talking softly around her, but she paid little heed to what they said. It was too much effort to translate the guttural Tarmakian. They could be talking about the latest crop harvests for all she cared.

"Linsha," Lanther said quietly. "Look ahead."

Through her open eye she saw a flickering light curving around a large arched entrance at the end of the passageway. The light was yellowish and danced like firelight. In fact, Linsha realized, there was an odor of smoke on the breeze that wafted up from the archway. Her curiosity stirred. She looked around as the procession walked down the last length of corridor and passed through the archway into the lighted cavern. Linsha's interest took a sudden leap. They had entered a large, natural cave with a high ceiling and smooth walls. To Linsha, it looked like a sea cave carved out by water, and she wondered how close this place was to the harbor. A stone walkway extended around the walls of the cavern for perhaps twenty feet in either direction before dropping down a long curved ramp to the cavern floor. Torches sat in brackets every few feet along the cave wall, and a row of imperial guards stood stiffly at attention along the gallery wall that overlooked the cavern.

Linsha eyed them curiously and was about to ask Lanther a question about tombs when she caught a familiar sound. Over the sonorous beat of the drum, the shuffling of feet on stone, and the hushed voices of the warriors, she thought she heard the faint sound of something massive breathing. It was an unmistakable sound once she knew what to listen for—the slight brush of scales rubbing together, the bellows-like rush of air through a long neck, the rustle of leathery wings. A dragon! Linsha had spent enough time in the company of Crucible to be able identify his breathing in total darkness. This was not Crucible's inhalation. Whose was it? She broke away from Lanther, pushed herself between two massive guards and peered over the edge of the wall into the cavern below.

Her breath escaped in an audible gasp. Perhaps fifty feet below lay a dragon curled on a bed of sand. It was too dark to see what kind of dragon it was, but enough torchlight reflected off its scales to see it was a metallic. Her fingers tightened on the stone rim of the wall.

"But I didn't—" she started to say.

A large hand fell heavily on her shoulder. She wheeled, expecting Lanther, and was startled into silence by the stern face of the Emperor looking down at her.

"Drathkin'kela, it is time," he rumbled in Tarmakian. "Come. There is much to do."

Feeling stunned, she walked down the ramp to the cavern floor beside the Emperor and came to a halt perhaps twenty feet away from the dragon. In the added light of the new torches, Linsha was able to see the dragon was a brass—a young one from its size. It slept heavily, curled in a tight, protective ball, its head tucked under a wing. She started to walk toward it, but the Emperor took her arm again and called for Lanther. For the sake of self-preservation she did not yank away from the huge Tarmak, but she could not take her eyes off the dragon. A hundred questions swarmed in her mind, and all she could do was stand and look.

The Akkad-Dar came forward proudly to stand beside Linsha. The warriors gathered in a semicircle around them. Priests bustled back and forth, setting up for a ceremony of sorts Linsha didn't understand. Urudwek's coffin was laid on a large, flat stone that bore unmistakable scorch marks. In a moment the activity stopped and the gathering fell quiet. The dragon, Linsha noticed, did not stir.

To her right a Keena priest in a sleeveless black robe began to chant what sounded like a long prayer to some god whose name she didn't recognize. She listened for a moment or two, then her tired mind lost interest and she studied the dragon instead. What she saw worried her. The brass was obviously not in good health. Linsha had seen Iyesta in the peak of good condition and knew what a healthy brass dragon should look like. It should not look so thin. The dragon's bones pushed up beneath the scaly skin, and its brass coloration looked more like green patina than polished metal. Scales were missing in large patches around its muzzle and back. Worst of all, Linsha knew, it should not be so deep in sleep that it did not respond to a crowd invading its nest. It was possible the dragon had gone into a dormant sleep for self-defense, but Linsha wondered if there was something else wrong. Young brasses were too gregarious, too curious, too interested in life to shut themselves away deliberately from things going on around them. Were the Tarmak doing something to it?

A sharp pain in her hand stunned her out of her wandering thoughts, and she came back to the ceremony to find the Emperor had cut the palm of her hand with a sharp knife. Blood oozed from the shallow wound and trickled down her wrist.

"Enough!" she cried. "If you want blood, I have plenty leaking out from other places."

But the Tarmaks and Lanther ignored her. The Emperor cut Lanther's palm as well, and to Linsha's disgust he pressed their two hands together to mingle their blood. The warriors cheered their approval. The Emperor appeared stiff and formal, less than pleased, but he made a speech about the skill, prowess, and courage of the Akkad-Dar, how he had made an excellent choice for a mate, and how the Akkad-Dar would further the cause of the Tarmak empire. Linsha swayed on her feet and decided that if she was going to vomit, now would be a good time. The Emperor proclaimed the betrothal between the Akkad-Dar and the Drathkin'kela to be official and threatened a heinous death to anyone who tried to put them asunder. Linsha stifled a yawn.

To her relief, that part of the ceremonies seemed to be over, for Lanther pulled his hand away and the priests turned from them to the coffin on the slab of stone. A young priest carried out an ancient text bound in leather and tied with silk cords. It lay cushioned on a silk pillow and was presented with due reverence to the chief priest. The older Keena carefully opened the vellum pages and began another long series of chanted prayers.

Linsha caught the name of Amarrel and little else. The priest spoke too fast for her to follow. "Oh, please hurry," Linsha muttered, rubbing her aching temples.

Lanther heard her as he wiped the blood off on a cloth provided by an attendant. He nodded sympathetically. "It will be over soon," he whispered.

A second attendant approached with something in his hands covered with a red cloth. Lanther uncovered the item and lifted it for Linsha to see. It was the golden mask of the Akkad.

Linsha bit back a cry of dismay at the sight of that metal face. Too many times she had looked into the dark eyeholes and suffered at the hand of its wearer. Too many evil memories were attached to its ornate surface.

Lanther simply smiled and slid the mask over his face. The torchlight gleamed on the polished surface of the mask and flickered on his bare skin as he raised his arms to the coffin of his friend and general and joined in the prayers for the dead.

Feeling sick, Linsha pulled the blue robe tighter around

her and eased back out of the way. She did not want any part in any more Tarmak ceremonies. Fortunately, the warriors did not seem to be paying attention to her now that the betrothal ceremony was completed. They were concentrating on the death rites for the old Akkad and on the priests who were chanting prayers and scattering his coffin with some kind of oil and herbs. Linsha slid a few steps back and glanced around again. No one paid her any heed. Dropping the robe to the sandy floor, she moved away from the torches and the gathered warriors and eased slowly around the wall toward the dragon. She stayed in what shadows there were and made no sudden movements to attract attention.

It took her several minutes, but when she finally reached the dragon's side the priests were still droning and no one had called her away from the beast. In the uncertain light of the torches she took a closer look at the dragon and was stunned by what she saw. Kiri-Jolith, she thought in horror, what had the Tarmaks done to this poor creature? The dragon was not bound by chain or rope, but the scars of some sort of bond clearly marred the dragon's legs. Its sides were mere slabs of ribs and its neck looked thin and hollow. Even its smell was wrong. Linsha knew from experience that brasses had a distinctive odor similar to hot sand or hot metal. But this one smelled of rotted seaweed and diseased flesh. High on its back, Linsha spotted another wound that looked hideously familiar—a patch of blackened scales about the size of a platter. She had seen a wound like that only on one other dragon—Crucible, and he had nearly died from it. Her anger rose again. How could they? How could anyone treat a dragon like this?

She spotted several scales lying on the sand where they had fallen from the dragon's body. Keeping her movements slow, she bent down and palmed one before anyone noticed. She wasn't sure if she would need a scale from this dragon, but taking the scale wouldn't hurt the animal and she thought maybe she had a use for it. She shot a quick glance over her shoulder and when she saw no one was looking, she placed her hand on the dragon's foreleg.

Magic was what she needed now. Not much, just enough to boost her flagging energy and draw on her ability to read auras. She had tried not to use magic since she had learned the spirits of the dead, trapped in the world and under the thrall of the Dark Queen Takhisis, drew the powers of magic out of anyone attempting to use it. But it occurred to her now that this was a different land, a land separated from Ansalon by many miles and peopled by tribes that believed in Takhisis. Maybe magic would still work here. With that hope, she closed her mind to everything around her and concentrated on the power that existed naturally inside her. Goldmoon had taught her many years ago how to use the power that she called the Magic of the Heart. Linsha was not good at it, but she had practiced the spells enough to be able to help heal herself, to read the invisible auras of any sentient being, and to communicate with a few receptive minds. Perhaps, with a little luck, she could scan this dragon's aura and learn a little more about it.

"Drathkin'kela!" The title snapped across the silence in the cavern and startled Linsha out of her thoughts. It was the Emperor's voice.

Linsha cursed under her breath and drew her hand away from the dragon.

"Linsha!" Lanther called. "Stand back from her. It is time for the cremation."

Her? So the dragon was female. Frustrated, Linsha held on to that bit of information while she tucked the scale close to her palm and walked back to where she had dropped the robe. There was no easy place to hide the scale in her battle harness or loincloth, so she picked up the robe and in the motions of putting it back on, she slid the scale carefully under the leather supporting her right breast. If no one looked carefully at her in the gloom of the cavern, the scale would be safe enough. She pulled the blue robe tightly around her and shuffled over to the join Lanther. If they were going to cremate the body, maybe that meant the ceremonies were almost over and she could go back to the peace and quiet of the Akeelawasee.

But if the chief priest was planning to set fire to the Akkad-Ur's coffin, he was not going about it in the usual manner. Instead of using a torch or a flame of some sort and setting alight the oil, he and two attendants walked over to the brass dragon, pulled her head out from under her wing, and stretched out her neck so that her head pointed toward the coffin and the stone slab.

Linsha watched in growing dismay. What were they doing to her?

The priest raised a hand toward the dragon and began a chant that Linsha knew was no prayer. It sounded more like a spell. His attendants picked up a bucket containing a liquid and poured the contents into the dragon's mouth. They had to lift her head up and clamp her mouth closed to get her to swallow it. In less than a minute she gagged and coughed and sneezed. One large eye slowly cracked open.

Linsha's eyebrows rose. What was this potion?

"Sirenfal, rise and bow before me!" the head priest shouted to the dragon.

The warriors made sounds of excitement and awe as the dragon slowly lifted her head from the sands.

Linsha wanted to cry. There was no energy, no interest in the dragon's listless gaze. The flesh of her head was shrunken around the large fluted faceplate that was the distinctive characteristic of brass dragons, and scales were missing from her neck in large patches.

"What is the matter with her?" Linsha asked Lanther.

He shrugged. "It's not your concern."

Linsha bit back a retort. The dragon was fully awake now

and watching the priest as a cat watches a deadly viper. Her lips were curled back in a silent snarl and her head swayed dizzily from side to side.

The priest snapped a command. The dragon hissed at him and tried to stand on all four feet, but the priest raised his other hand in a gesture the dragon obviously recognized and feared, for she dropped back to the sand and obeyed his command. She took in a deep breath and blew a blast of super-heated air directly at the wooden coffin. The fiery air rolled over the oil-soaked coffin and set it burning in an intense conflagration.

"The Tarmak believe they are honoring their warleader by sending him to the afterlife on the flame of a dragon," Lanther explained, watching the smoke rise to the ceiling.

"While killing her in the process?" Linsha said. "What is the logic of that?"

He gave a patronizing chuckle and did not answer her. Linsha fumed while she watched the Akkad-Ur burn to ash. The priests were making their prayers when she glanced up and saw the young dragon had regained some of her awareness. Her eyes were more alert, and she was looking around as if searching the cavern for something. Perhaps, Linsha thought, she had caught the scent of someone different. Linsha's hand slid under the robe and grasped her two scales. Swiftly, before anyone could hinder her, she gathered what energy she had left, drew on the latent power of the scales, and sent a brief thought into the mind of the dragon. It was much harder to do this across a distance, but she had to try.

Eat. Rest. You have a friend here. I will try to help.

The words must have reached the dragon, for Sirenfal's head swiveled around and she stared directly at Linsha with eyes the color of light amber.

Who are you? The question rang in Linsha's head.

A friend of Iyesta's.

As Linsha hoped, Sirenfal recognized the name of the

greatest of all brasses, for she made a small involuntary sound of hope. Unfortunately, the sound drew the attention of the chief priest, who glanced suspiciously at the dragon then followed her gaze to Linsha.

Linsha guessed she had only a moment to do what she could. Gathering every memory she could recall of Iyesta and Crucible and the fall of the Missing City, she opened her mind to the dragon and was about to pour it all out when the chief priest shouted a command and tightened his hands into a fist. His attendants drew out a leather bag and dumped a handful of yellowish dust into the dragon's face.

The brass moaned piteously. She tried to keep her eyes on Linsha, but the priest's sedative was too much for her. She sneezed once and subsided to the sand. Curling back into her tight ball, she closed her eyes and tucked her head under her wing.

Linsha felt her own strength drain away like water. The last vestiges of Afec's tonic fizzled away, and the attempt to reach the mind of Sirenfal had taken her last reserves. Her skin broke out in a clammy sweat and the pain in her head began to pound. She wrapped her arms around herself and sagged against Lanther. He caught her and held her tight, his eyes deeply worried.

"Where is it?" she mumbled. "Where is the dragon egg?" Her eyes rolled up in her head, and she passed out in his arms.

Dragon Dreams

8

'm sorry, my lady. I should have realized this would be too much. You have fought a *ket-rhild,* and by rights you should be back in the Akeelawasee."

The voice droned in her ear as Linsha felt herself carried to the wall and carefully set down, her back to the cold stone. Her eye opened a crack, and a face swam into her vision. Lanther. Blast it all, she thought, she must have only been out for a minute or two. She slouched down, her legs in front of her, her shoulders sagging, and closed her eye again. Lanther left her alone to return to the warriors congregating around the smoking slab and the ashes of the Akkad-Ur. Linsha tried to sleep. Every muscle in her body screamed that she needed rest. But she couldn't find a comfortable position, and in her mind danced her own words. *Where was the egg?*

She hovered on the edge of consciousness, her body half asleep and her mind half awake. Where was the egg that Lanther promised? And who was this Sirenfal? What was she doing here in this condition? When would all of this be over? She shifted against the wall and felt the chill seep into her bones. She shivered and did not stop.

A sudden cheer pulled her attention to the crowd in the

cavern. Her eye opened again to see two Keena priests bring in a large metal box suspended between two poles. The box was big enough to carry . . . a dragon egg? Linsha's eye opened further and she pushed herself up the wall to a better sitting position.

Reverently the two priests laid the box on the smoldering ashes atop the hot slab and stood back. One handed the Akkad-Dar a pair of heavy leather gloves. The box must have been hot, for even with the gloves Lanther moved quickly to remove the lid and lift the contents onto the slab. The warriors crowded around, blocking Linsha's view.

Linsha struggled to her hands and knees. She still couldn't see past the bulky bodies of the Tarmaks. A strong suspicion gave her the strength to pull herself up the wall to a standing position, and at that moment Lanther held the object overhead for all to see. The Tarmaks cheered.

Linsha stifled a cry. An oblong shape, little more than two feet long, lay in his gloved hands. It gleamed in the torchlight with a polished pale gold sheen. It was a brass dragon egg. Her egg. Linsha struggled forward on legs that had the strength of gelatin, but before she had made it three steps, Lanther lowered the egg and she heard a sickening crack.

Her heart fell to her feet. "Lanther, you bastard!" she screamed.

Surprised and startled Tarmaks turned and gave way before her furious advance. She shoved and staggered her way through the ring of warriors to the slab and Lanther in time to see him thrust a dagger into the top of the egg, where a small hole had already been started.

"Hold her," Lanther ordered.

Two warriors snatched Linsha's arms and pinned them behind her back, giving her no chance to get closer. She didn't have the strength left to fight a butterfly, let alone two burly Tarmaks. Her face twisted into a mask of grief and disgust.

"How could you?" she cried. "You gave those eggs to me."

He grinned his mischievous grin of old. "I gave you dragon eggs that are safely lying where we left them. This was one I kept out for myself for this occasion. Now, be quiet and watch. This is a rare opportunity. Females are not usually allowed to attend these ceremonies."

Before her stricken gaze, he continued to stab the dagger into the egg until he had cut a circular hole in the top. He pried off the cut piece of shell and poured the contents of the egg into a large stone bowl.

Appalled, Linsha stared as the small, slick dragon embryo squirmed once or twice in the puddle of albumen in the bowl before it lay still. It was perfectly formed and more developed than she expected it to be. Tears ran unnoticed through the blue paint on her face.

Lanther turned to face the warriors and raised his dripping dagger high. "The feast of dragon blood will be prepared tonight! Who will drink the *Awlgu'arud Drathkin?*"

A shouted roar from the warriors answered him and echoed through the cavern. While the Emperor, the Akkad-Dar, and the warriors watched, the two Keena priests chopped the dead embryo to small pieces, mixed its body with the bloody ruined contents of its egg, and added hot water. They also mixed in powders and other liquids, something dark that looked like blood, and some herbs and wine until they had made a revolting-looking soup. The drummer beat on his drum once more and the attendants sang a harsh, discordant chant that grated on Linsha's shaky self-control. She watched, sickened, as the priests stirred the contents of the stone bowl and let it steam gently on the hot slab. When the potion was ready, the high priest fished through the hot contents and pulled out the dragonlet's tiny skull. He filled it with the liquid and bowing, handed it to the Akkad-Dar.

Lanther raised the skull in a salute. "Hail to the godson, Amarrel, Keeper of Dragons, Champion of the White Flame and beloved of the goddess, and hail to the Dark Queen, mistress of the world and ruler of the dead!" With a bow he passed the skull to the Emperor who drank the contents in a single swallow.

Lanther and the Tarmaks roared their approval. As the warriors pushed forward for their taste of the potion, Linsha felt the grip on her arms loosen. Her two guards, eager for their own share, released her and pushed her back and out of the way. Linsha staggered several steps, bent over, and vomited on the sand. Her legs trembled beneath her; her head throbbed with pain. She wanted no part of this savage ceremony, but she did not have the strength left to climb the stairs back to the upper levels of the palace. She had to lie down and she had to do it now. Wiping her mouth, she looked up and saw the dragon curled up in its induced state of sleep. The dragon was a stranger. But Linsha was a prisoner, too, and in the brief moment of mental joining, Linsha had sensed a desperate loneliness and fear in Sirenfal that matched her own. She felt drawn to the dragon and empathetic to her plight and hoped that Sirenfal wouldn't mind a little company.

Growing weaker by the moment, Linsha forced her legs to walk to Sirenfal's sandy nest. She felt the heat of the brass dragon radiate outward like a warm oven, and gratefully she fell to her hands and knees and crawled until she could sit up against the dragon's bent leg. In spite of the shouts of the Tarmaks and the beating of the drum, she was asleep before her head settled against the brass scales.

<hr />

She came to a state of awareness in a chamber of pale shadows. Looking around, she thought perhaps she was still in the dragon's cave. The air was damp and smelled of stone and saltwater; the spaces echoed around her. But if that was where she was, some time had passed, for the Tarmaks were gone and the cave was silent and empty. There was no sign of Sirenfal. Light filtered in from somewhere overhead and reflected on a pale mist that swirled in from an opening she sensed but could not see.

Who are you? The voice, light and feminine, spoke directly into her mind.

Linsha peered into the dim fog around her and saw only more shadows. "I told you. I am a friend."

So you say. But you wear the paint of a Tarmak warrior and you attend their ceremonies.

Linsha studied her skin, which was indeed still blue. Only the pain, the tingling, the cuts, and the bruises were gone. "I am a Knight of the Rose of the Solamnic Order and a friend of Iyesta. I was captured and brought here because of a debt of honor."

It must be an important debt.

"Iyesta asked me to protect a clutch of eggs."

A sharp intake of breath somewhere close by cut across her words. She paused, staring harder into the mist.

"I have not been very successful so far," she added.

Sirenfal's thought came back heavy with sadness. *If there is even one left, you have been more fortunate than I. The Tarmaks destroyed my entire clutch.*

Linsha climbed slowly to her feet. Her pain and nausea were gone. In fact she felt nothing, not even the chill of the mist gently wafting around her. "How long have you been here?"

A lifetime. The answer came sighing back. *About eight years, I think. Their priests and that dreadful man captured me with spells and stole my eggs. I think they killed my mate.*

Linsha was horrified. "How could they keep you imprisoned?"

Because I am a dragon? There was a soft earthy chuckle, and a petite, delicate woman stepped out of the mist and stood in front of Linsha. Her light brown eyes bored into Linsha's jewel green ones. *Even dragons can be vulnerable.*

"Sirenfal."

The woman nodded. She was as beautiful as an elf maiden with honey-gold hair that swept around her shoulders and fine-boned features that looked like porcelain.

Linsha was not surprised. Some dragons could easily shapeshift and often did so for a variety of reasons. Bronzes in particular liked to shift their forms and many spent years disguised as humans—a fact Linsha knew all too well. She met Sirenfal's sad gaze without judgment or fear, only curiosity. The dragon woman did not look well. Her gold hair hung limp around her thin face, and her skin was pale and drawn. She had none of the vivid life and vivacious quality of Iyesta in her human form. She seemed more of a wraith, a thin shadow of her younger self.

The man called Lanther has taught these Keena priests how to use spells created by the Dark Mystics. They in turn have taught him some of the secret potions of the Keena. They keep me sedated and under thrall while they experiment on me, harvest my scales, and leech my magic. They killed my eggs in those horrible ceremonies.

Linsha listened, appalled by the dragon's misery. A terrible suspicion crept into her mind, prompted by the memory of the discolored wound on the dragon's back. "Do you know of the Abyssal Lance?"

Sirenfal's slender frame shuddered. "They experimented on me," she whispered, using her own voice as though too afraid to share her thoughts.

"Linsha!" A voice harsh and loud boomed in the cavern. Sirenfal started in fear, took a step back from Linsha. Her form began to fade.

I must go. Must not let him know. The mist swirled around her.

Instinctively Linsha held out a hand in comfort and

farewell, but she did not speak for fear of drawing the hated voice to the dragon.

"Linsha! Wake up! It's time to go." Lanther's words cut through the gloom and shadows, and suddenly Linsha snapped awake.

She was back in the cavern at night with the Tarmak warriors, the torches, the smell of smoke and the stink of the potion. She was back with Lanther. Blinking in the torchlight, she looked up at his face hidden behind the golden mask and stifled a surge of loathing. The presence of the dragon was gone, but the intensity of her sadness and the injustice of her plight filled Linsha's mind and heart, kindling a new hatred for Lanther. How could he have done something like that to a dragon? Any dragon? Is that what he had had in mind for Crucible? Experimentation. Study. Harvesting. Leeching. The words sat like curses in her thoughts. When he held out a hand to help her to her feet, all she could do was stare at it. She hadn't really noticed before how scarred and blunted his hands had become from years of fighting, hostile weather, and incidents with thorns, knives, dragon scales, and the gods knew what else. These were the hands that tortured and killed dragons, murdered her friends, and wielded a magic she could not understand. It was all she could do to force her fingers to touch his and accept his aid to climb to her feet.

As soon as she was upright, she snatched her hand away and stepped back from him as if avoiding a plague carrier. She was still weak and unsteady on her feet, and the pain was back. But she felt a little stronger after her short nap, and the nausea was gone. With luck and determination, she should be able to make it back to the Akeelawasee without Lanther's assistance.

She glanced back at the sleeping dragon and felt something stir in the back of her mind that she hadn't felt in a while—compassion. For the first time in days the black depression that had oppressed her lifted slightly, like a pall of smoke stirred by a fresh wind. Although she realized she had been dreaming, she did not doubt for an instant the validity of her conversation with Sirenfal. She had dreamed with dragons before and found the results to be quite interesting. Like Crucible before her, Sirenfal had chosen this private way to communicate with her in the hope that she would understand.

Fortunately Linsha had. She had an affinity with dragons that she did not fully comprehend, an affinity that was stronger and more powerful than most humans possessed. Where it came from, she didn't know, but for as long as she could remember she always felt comfortable in the presence of most dragons, and they responded to her in kind. Even Sara Dunstan's aloof blue companion, Cobalt, had allowed her privileges he would have seared other children for if they had dared try. Sirenfal, Linsha knew, had taken a huge risk to communicate with someone who was still an unknown stranger, but perhaps she, too, sensed the sincerity of Linsha's attempt to reach out to her. Linsha vowed to herself that Sirenfal's trust would not go to waste. The dragon was wounded, ill, and in desperate need of help. Surely as the Drathkin'kela, Linsha could find some way to help a dragon.

She followed in Lanther's footsteps up the long stairs ahead of the long line of Tarmak warriors. Several times while she trudged up the steps she wanted to stop and rest, to catch her breath and let her aching muscles relax. But the warriors pushed up behind her and she would not show any more weakness before them this night. She forced herself on until her legs burned and her lungs panted and the ache in her head felt like a blacksmith was forging implements on her skull.

By the time she finally reached the door leading back into the first level of the palace, Linsha was trembling with exhaustion again. The therapeutic effects of her nap and her dream with the dragon had vanished. All she wanted was a bath and a bed. As soon as she entered the hall, she veered away to escape down the hall to her quarters.

Lanther caught her arm. "Come with me. We must talk."

Talking to Lanther was the second-to-the-last thing she wanted to do with him. "Now?" she snapped. She made no effort to hide her antagonism and irritation. "I am tired beyond measure. I had to fight a useless duel, then you dragged me to a cave to watch you torture a dragon, cremate my enemy, and kill a dragonlet you had promised to me. I have nothing to say to you."

Ignoring her, he removed his golden mask, handed it to an attendant, then took her elbow and propelled her down the hall and out a small door that opened into a beautifully manicured garden. The storm had passed, leaving the air cool and damp, and the moon spilled milky light over the trees and flowerbeds. All around them, tree frogs croaked an endless chorus in the darkness.

"I have some things to say to you," he said and pushed her down onto a stone bench.

Linsha winced. The cold wet stone made an uncomfortable seat when all one wore was a scrap of loincloth. She pulled her elbow out of his grasp, laid her head in her hands, and groaned. Would this night ever end?

"You fought well tonight," he said, pacing slowly in front of her. "It is a shame Malawaitha had to press her suit."

Linsha did not bother to reply. She hadn't had the time or the peace to think about Malawaitha and her needless death.

He went on. "Fortunately the Emperor is impressed with you. He has finally given me his blessing to marry you, and he made arrangements with the High Priest to hold the ceremony in five days."

Linsha sat upright, aghast. Five days. *Oh, gods, come back now and blast me where I sit*, she thought.

Lanther stopped pacing and glanced up at the full moon. He took a deep breath. "The ships will be provisioned within the next week," he said rather hurriedly. "I intend to sail for the Missing City before the next new moon."

Linsha froze in a deluge of fear, anger, and disbelief. Had he meant what she thought he had just said? Surely he wouldn't do that to her. "You said, 'I.' You do mean 'we.' We're going back to Ansalon together." She spoke more in desperate hope than conviction.

Lanther crossed his arms and continued to stare at the moon. "Take you back to war and deprivation? I think not. No, no. You will stay here where I know you are safe and respected, and where you cannot find a way to slip through my grasp. You will stay here and await my return."

It was only with the greatest self-control that Linsha was able to stop herself from leaping off the bench and ripping his eyes out with her dirty fingernails. "I would prefer to go with you," she forced herself to say rather than give voice to the shriek that banged at the back of her throat.

"I'm sure you would," he said.

"You wanted me to stay by your side, fight with you. You asked me to be the Empress of the Plains. Now you want to leave me here like some second rate concubine?"

"It would be better," he agreed.

"What about the dragon eggs? They are my bridal gift. I want to see them." There was a note of rising hysteria in her voice that she couldn't stop. She couldn't believe what he was saying, couldn't accept it. To be left here on this island, in this prison of women. Married and possibly pregnant. With no one but Callista to keep her company. She would never see her home again, never see her family. She would never have a chance to find Crucible and Varia.

"The eggs will be well cared for," he assured her.

Linsha's fragile self-control broke and she sprang to her feet. "Like you cared for the last one?" she yelled through her dry and aching throat. "No! I don't believe you. I have to go back to the Missing City. You can't leave me here!"

"I can and I will. You are my betrothed, and in five days you will be my wife. You will remain on Ithin'carthia to bear my son." His final words boomed like a death knell in her ears.

Preparations

9

Linsha had to admit the Tarmaks knew how to treat a battered body. No sooner had she returned to the Akeelawasee than she was met by the Empress. Callista hovered in the background, her eyes huge with worry and consternation. Behind her waited Afec, looking cool and inscrutable, and several attendants.

Uncertain of the Empress's reaction to Malawaitha's death, Linsha clasped her hands and bowed low. "I apologize for killing a daughter of the royal family," she said in a low voice.

The matriarch snorted indelicately. She looked Linsha over carefully from head to blue toes, nodded a few times, and replied in her difficult Common, "She accepted a challenge and lost. Do not apologize." With a snap of her fingers, she held out her hand for a glass of dodgagd juice, which a servant swiftly handed to her. She passed it to Linsha. "I am told you marry in five days. You will stay here when Akkad-Dar leave."

Linsha heard Callista's gasp of dismay over the subdued noises in the room. She barely nodded an affirmative and drank the juice. For once its strange taste did not repel her,

105

and the cool liquid was a welcome relief to her sore throat and overworked body.

The Empress clapped her hands and Linsha found herself surrounded by Callista, Afec, and the two female slaves. The women bustled her to the bathhouse where they scrubbed the blue paint from her body, massaged her aching limbs, and treated her bruises with cool water. Fortunately she remembered the brass dragon scale in time and slipped it out of her leather battle harness before anyone noticed. As soon as they were finished, Afec gave her a cold compress for her swollen eye, washed her superficial wounds with the stinging liquid and rubbed the thick unguent into the cut on her palm and the long laceration on her stomach. Callista brought her more juice and a bowl of soup. Linsha thanked them all, gave Callista an encouraging smile, and returned to the comparative peace of her tiny room. Although she wanted to talk to Callista and Afec, she gave in to the demands of her body and lay down on her pallet. Sleep found her before the blanket settled over her.

"Would you be able to get your hands on some dark green clothes or fabric in the next day or two? Dark gray would also work." Linsha lay flat on her pallet, trying to stretch her muscles back into some semblance of working order. She cocked her good eye at the courtesan to see if she caught the significance.

Callista didn't. The only subterfuge she knew involved the arts of her profession. Her fair face looked down at Linsha in confusion. "I suppose so. Why do you need such a thing?"

"An assassin I once knew told me dark green is a better color to wear when you are sneaking around in the dark. It is much harder to see than black, which tends to stand out in shadows."

The two women were alone in the sleeping quarters that morning, for the Empress had excused Linsha from the dawn run. It was a good thing she had, Linsha decided, because she wasn't entirely sure she could stay on her feet. Running was out of the question.

"Are you planning to sneak somewhere?" Callista asked with a slight smile.

Although they probably were alone in the sleeping rooms, Linsha lowered her voice to a murmur and told Callista about the dragon in the cavern beneath the palace. "I want to talk to her without a pack of Tarmaks gathering around—and without the High Priest. He and Lanther have a power over her that will be hard to break."

"Do you know what it is?"

"No. But Afec may be able to help me."

Callista drew in a breath. "Could this Sirenfal fly us home?"

Linsha did not reply immediately. The same notion had occurred to her already and sparked a tiny seed of hope in the gloom of her mind. But she remembered the dragon's obvious weakness and the pallor of her scales. She didn't know if Sirenfal was in any condition to fly across the bay, let alone all the way to Ansalon. She did not know either how to get the dragon out of the cave, how to slip past the Tarmak guards, how to get out of the Akeelawasee with Callista, or the answers to a host of other questions. She needed first to talk to the brass dragon. "Maybe," she said at last. "If many things go right."

"What about your marriage?" said Callista. "Will you go through with that?"

A chill shivered down Linsha's shoulders. "I will do what I must," she said.

Unbidden and unexpected came an image of a tall man with broad shoulders, hair the color of dark gold, and eyes that burned with the wisdom of a dragon over a hundred years old. She had seen him fiery with the intensity of passion to save his city, strong with command in an emergency, and silly with the joy of life while playing in a fishpond. He had saved her life several times, and when the need arose, he left his city behind to help her. If only he could help her now. *Please*, she silently begged the empty firmament. *Please let him still be alive.*

With Callista's help, Linsha eased some of the kinks out of her sore limbs and made her slow way to breakfast. To Callista's surprise, Linsha ate her gruel, the juice, and everything in sight without grumbling, and after breakfast she went to the small lake to swim in the warm water.

Although the swim helped, Linsha knew from past experience it would be several days before her body returned to a semblance of normal after the abuse it had taken the night before. Ten years ago a night's sleep, a good meal, and a swim would have had her back to her practice exercises and feeling fit as a young colt. But her body was experiencing its age and the years of fighting that had taken their toll. She didn't recover as quickly as she used to, which meant she was going to have to work hard the next few days and be extremely careful if she was going to do any good.

When her swim was over, Afec came to fetch her and took her to his infirmary for an examination of her injuries. Linsha allowed him to walk in first, then she closed the door firmly behind her. He glanced up curiously just as she tossed the brass dragon scale on the table. It flew in a gleaming arch that caught his eye and landed with a metallic *ting* on the wood table. Afec's eyes widened; his gnarled fingers reached for the shining disk.

Linsha took two rapid steps to the table and slammed her hand over the scale. "What do you know about this dragon?" she demanded.

Shutters fell over the old Damjatt's face, and he withdrew to a respectful distance from Linsha and made a slight bow. "Only what I've heard, Lady," he said.

Linsha did not move. "And what did you hear?"

He peered behind her and out the window where the shutters were partially open to the morning breeze. "I heard once or twice," he replied softly, "that there was a dragon in the old sea caves beneath the palace."

"You've never seen it."

He shook his head, his eyes on the floor at her feet. "It is forbidden. Only the priests and warriors and those chosen by the Emperor or the Akkad may go down there."

Linsha thought for a moment then picked up the dragon scale and laid it in the old slave's hand. His seamed face crinkled into a large smile. He held the scale to the light, admiring the sheen and color.

Linsha had deliberately polished the scale until it gleamed, and she was gratified to see her small ploy had worked. Assuming a casual air, she sat on the worktable in front of him and held out her cut palm. Never had she been able to figure out why some people thought it necessary to cut the hand for a blood oath. Why not the forearm? Or the buttock? Or the little toe? Something that would not interfere with one's grip on a sword. Fortunately the Tarmak paint once again had performed its magic. The cut on her hand and the slash on her stomach were already healing well, and her eye did not seem as swollen.

"Her name is Sirenfal," she said as if adding an after-thought. "She's a young brass dragon."

Still holding the scale, Afec bustled around his worktable and shelves, collecting his medicines, cloths, and water. "A female you say? And she's young?"

"She has only laid her first clutch of eggs."

The old Damjatt dumped his things on the table beside her and took her hand distractedly. "She has eggs?"

As Linsha hoped, he sounded fascinated. She caught his arm and asked, "Why would the warriors and the Emperor smash an egg to make a soup of some sort?" She described the breaking of the egg and the mix of ingredients that went into the drink.

His hand fell to the knotted belt at his waist and clutched the knots in his fingers. "They did that? I have only heard rumors. Are there any more eggs left?"

"Not of hers. Those are gone. This egg was from the Missing City. It was part of a clutch I swore to protect."

"What a waste," he murmured.

"Yes. So what are these rumors you've heard?"

Afec shrugged. "You know how talk passes among servants. I have heard that the drink you described is an old potion handed down among the Keena priests."

"All right. But what does it do?" she insisted. "It couldn't have had dragon eggs as the main ingredient in the beginning."

"No. I've told you. We have no native dragons on Ithin'carthia. The addition of a dragon's egg was the Akkad-Dar's suggestion. I believe the potion was made by the Keena originally as a way to increase virility."

Linsha's eyebrows rose. "And what does the egg do?"

He gave a dry, raspy chuckle. "Adds its innate magic to the brew. It changes the nature of the drink to a kind of general tonic. It is supposed to improve one's natural abilities—strength, stamina, virility."

"No wonder the warriors crave it," she said and wondered if a talent to use magic was one of those abilities that could be enhanced by this potion. That could explain much about Lanther. "The dragon eggs are hard to come by, so the Tarmaks have made a religious ceremony out of the preparation."

Afec stared. "Did they give you any?"

She made a face that answered his question clearly. "I doubt they share that with women. I think Lanther just wanted me there to show what he can do to the eggs if I don't obey."

"What was the dragon doing during the ceremony?"

Linsha hid a secret smile. She had captured his full attention. Now she wanted his sympathy and cooperation. Afec was an old man and a slave, yet he knew the palace well, and while he was not a priest, he seemed to know much about healing and medicines. He did not have a great regard for the Keena or the Tarmaks either. He could be her best ally. With that in mind, she told him everything she could remember about Sirenfal, the dragon's condition, and what the priest used against her.

When she finished, he stayed quiet for a long while and concentrated on cleaning her hand and the slash on her stomach. He checked her bruises and her black eye. He rubbed a cream on her wounds that tingled with the same heat as the blue paint.

"What do you plan to do?" he said at last.

"Why do you think I'm going to do anything?" she asked.

For the first time the old servant lifted his eyes to look directly into hers and gave her a knowing smile. Linsha was charmed. There was a sparkling vigor to his gaze and a depth of intelligence she realized he had kept camouflaged behind his subservient bows and lowered lids.

"I have watched you, Lady," he said. "You would not be here, alive and preparing for a union to the great Akkad if you were not strong, resourceful, and tenacious. You are named the Drathkin'kela for good reason. I don't believe you will let this young one languish in misery if there is something you can do."

Linsha knew without a doubt that he meant what he said. She could only hope that he had the courage to help her and remain silent. "I need to talk to the dragon without the Tarmaks listening to every word," she told him. "You said the dragon was in a sea cave. There must be an entrance somewhere out on the cliff face."

She paused, tilted her head. Through the window she could hear insects buzzing in the bright sunlight and the faint rustle of the wind through the slender trees in the garden. Then she heard the sound again that had caught her attention—the slap of sandaled feet on the stone paving.

Afec patted her arm and switched subjects without a moment's hesitation. "Rest today. Let your muscles recover. Tomorrow we will discuss the marriage rites and your duties as a Tarmak wife."

The sandaled feet paused at his door and a knock shook the door just as it was shoved open. Two of the Akeelawasee guards and a stricken-looking slave woman hurried into the room. The slave woman's linen shift was dirty with sweat stains and blood, and she carried a wrapped bundle in her arms.

"Afec," the woman said in Tarmakian. Tears trembled on the edge of her lashes. "Loruth's babe was delivered a short while ago."

Neither Linsha nor Afec had to ask if the birth had gone well. The grim faces of the guards and the woman's distress were clear enough. Linsha hopped off the table and watched with interest while the slave laid the bundle down and unwrapped it. Inside the woven blanket, a large Tarmak infant startled at the sudden exposure to light and cool air and began to cry lustily.

Linsha studied the baby, a little boy, and could see nothing wrong. It had been hastily cleaned and its umbilical cord was still attached.

Afec pointed to the small foot. "What did the midwife say?" he asked the slave woman.

"He is *marthtok*," she sniffled.

The old healer sighed. Linsha looked puzzled. *Marthtok?* What did that mean?

"I am forced to agree." Afec picked up the squalling baby. "A pity. And the mother?"

"She is resting. Once the midwife pronounced the infant *marthtok*, she refused to look at it. It is her second loss. There will be no more."

Linsha grew even more puzzled. Why were they talking as if the baby was dead when he was right in front of them crying noisily? She watched astonished as Afec cut the umbilical cord, dropped it in a jar of alcohol, and pulled out another smaller jar. He slathered a liberal amount of a greenish cream on the baby's umbilical wound and handed him to the guards. The woman began to cry softly. While the guards carried the naked baby away, the slave snatched up the blanket and hurried out in the opposite direction.

"What was that about?" Linsha asked, watching Afec wipe his hands thoroughly on a cloth. "What does *marthtok* mean?"

"It means the babe is deformed. He will not be allowed to live."

"What?" she gasped. "He looked fine."

"He had a clubbed foot. To the Tarmaks any deformity or defect in a baby is a death sentence. A child with a clubbed foot does not become a warrior, therefore he has no value. He is a blight on society and must be disposed of."

"And the mother went along with that?" she exclaimed, shocked by such a thought.

"She is Tarmak. She has no choice. Nor would she want it." Then his voice chilled with a cold Linsha had not heard before. "And I do not try to stop them because the fewer Tarmaks there are the better."

Linsha strode to the window and looked out, but the guards had already disappeared. "What will they do to him?"

"He will be left on a high hill to die. The goddess will take his spirit and perhaps send him back in a better body."

Linsha shuddered. "That's barbaric. What are these Tarmaks?" she cried. "They eat dragon embryos and murder their own young."

The old healer nodded. "Among other things. But at least that little fellow will not feel anything." He moved around the room putting things away.

She turned around and pursed her lips thoughtfully. "The cream. You put something in that green cream."

"It has a heavy numbing sedative. I usually use it on adults before I have to cut into the body or make stitches."

Linsha shot a look at the red umbilical cord floating in the liquid and decided not to ask what other potions and medicines he knew that might require something like that. Her shock and anger slowly subsided, leaving a mental aftertaste in the back of her mind that left her slightly queasy. There had to be way off this island and away from these people. There had to be!

"Now, Lady, if you will return to the sleeping quarters and rest. We will meet to discuss your marriage this afternoon."

A pang went through Linsha's heart—whether of fear or anger she couldn't decide. She clamped down on it and banished it to the back of her mind. She still had four days—much could happen in four days—and there were other things to think about. Sirenfal lay ill and mistreated. If that wasn't enough to occupy her mind, she could kill any thoughts of self-pity with the memory of the small dragon embryo lying in the pool of it own blood or the infant boy being carried out by Tarmak warriors to die alone on an empty, heartless landscape.

Shaken, she thanked Afec and walked outside where the hot sun baked the stone walls and a cloudless sky arched overhead. She considered Afec's advice then rejected it. The heat of the day felt good on her aching shoulders and her thoughts were too restive to give her peace. She wanted solitude and space to think.

Knowing the gardens would be busy on a fine day like this, she skirted the lawns of the exercise fields and took the running path around the perimeter. The walled enclosure that formed the grounds of the Akeelawasee covered a rectangular area of about ten acres. It was by far the largest open area in the confines of the Imperial palace. Linsha had explored much of it in the hope of finding a way out, but the walls were heavily guarded, and so far she had not found so much as a mouse hole. She reviewed her memories of what she had seen. She had only searched out of habit, knowing an escape attempt toward the city or the interior was doomed. She hadn't thought about an escape toward the sea, and she'd never bothered to see how close the walls came to the cliff edge.

Her muscles felt warm in the morning sun and her joints were a little more limber, so she broke into a gentle jog that carried her slowly around the small lake, through the copses of trees and flowering vines and out into the open lawns of the farthest reaches of the Akeelawasee. It seemed odd to be out here without Malawaitha to harass her. She hadn't realized how much the Tarmak woman had preyed on her mind until the vindictive bully was gone. Callista had told her that Malawaitha was buried without fanfare in an unmarked grave somewhere in the palace gardens. Although the regret lingered, and more than a little guilt still gnawed at her, Linsha felt as if a great weight had been removed from her thoughts.

Trotting on, she drew closer to the enclosing wall of the garden, and for a while she followed the path in the shadow of the high stone barrier. She felt the eyes of the guards on her back and ignored them. Let them watch. All she wanted to do was look.

She came to a particular rock formation that jutted out of the ground like the prow of a ship. It was blanketed with lichen and tenacious wildflowers, and it served as the turning point on the trail. From the rock, the trail curved to the right and wound its way toward the opposite wall. The shorter connecting wall, the wall that paralleled the cliffs, was out of sight beyond a low rise and a tall hedge of evergreen shrubs.

Linsha slowed to a gentle walk and veered off the path as

if she were simply out for a stroll. Meandering through the grass, she found a narrow path, probably made by sentries, that followed the wall and made its way up the rise and through a thin break in the hedge. The shrubs grew tall and thick and crowded her in their dark green, fragrant foliage. Then she was through, and she stepped out into a different world.

Behind her, past the hedge, the palace gardens were lush and well tended, but here on the edges of the promontory, the greenery had been stripped away and there was nothing here but stone walls and wind-swept rock. She walked forward. Perhaps twenty feet away was the fortifying wall, a massive structure about ten feet thick and thirty feet tall. A narrow stair climbed up to the parapet at the top of the wall and a small guard tower that overlooked the wall and what lay beyond. She could see two guards on the walkway standing with their backs to her, but she knew there were probably more around. Both Tarmaks were well armed and carried bows already strung. It would be better to let them know she was there, she decided, than surprise them and end up with an arrow in her chest. She shouted a greeting in her roughest Tarmakian.

The two Tarmaks whirled in surprise, and as she suspected, two more came running from the tower. They glowered down at her, jabbering at her in Tarmakian too fast for her to follow and gesturing for her to turn back. She calmly ignored their gestures and walked up the stone steps to the walk. Clasping her hands, she bowed to them politely.

"Can any of you speak Common?" she asked.

"Drathkin'kela," one warrior replied in a rough voice. It was the *ketkegul*, the warrior in charge of a unit of ten. "You should not be here. This is not for women."

She bowed again and said a silent thank you. Courtesy was her weapon here, and she was not yet fluent enough in Tarmakian to feign such politeness.

"I am not here to get in your way, *Ketkegul*," she said. "I just want to sit on the wall and watch the sea. I want to feel the wind and the sun." She angled herself slightly so he could clearly see the bruises on her throat and on her eye. "I am not like the other women. You know what it is like to ride horses on the open plains and sail the vast seas. I have done that. I have fought in battle like you, and I have ridden the great dragons. This place—" she waved back at the palace behind her— "is beautiful, but my spirit chafes in there. I just want to see something beyond the walls. I will stay out of your way. I promise."

The *ketkegul* looked perplexed, and Linsha offered him her most persuasive smile. He'd probably never had a woman from the Akeelawasee come out and ask to sit on his walls. He talked for a few minutes with his guards while Linsha waited, and eventually he nodded to her.

"You may stay for a short while, but you will go when I tell you. And Ruthig will stay with you."

She glanced up the towering Tarmak he indicated and shrugged. All four of them could stand around her, as long they let her see beyond the wall. With deliberate care she chose a place in full view of the Tarmaks, climbed carefully to the top, and sat down cross-legged on the sun-warmed stone. The wind from the sea teased her hair and filled her nose with the smell of saltwater. She closed her eyes and inhaled deeply. The wind was out of the west, and although she could smell nothing but warm rock and cool sea, she fancied that this same wind had swept over Ansalon a few days before and still carried some essence of her homeland on its capricious breezes.

She had come a long way to look over this wall, but she did not look down immediately. Instead she cast her eyes to the sea beyond the harbor, to the northern Courrain Ocean that gleamed a blue-gray in the late morning light and rolled endlessly south toward home and freedom. She looked far beyond the distant shores of the bay, past the dark towers of the Orchemenarc, and concentrated on the hazy horizon between water and sky, and when she had that vision indelibly etched into her memory, she closed her eyes and turned her focus inward to the secret recesses of her heart and the power she knew beat there.

She had not tried this in a long while simply because she had failed so often it was hardly worth the effort. But she had learned why from Danian at the gathering at the Grandfather Tree—the spirits of the dead drained the power for their own purposes. She had never learned why the spirits had been trapped in the living world or why they needed the energy; all she knew were the effects of their desperate hunger. But this place was far from Ansalon and the wars that plagued that troubled land. Maybe, just maybe, the souls were not here.

She drew deeper into herself, putting away the discomforts of her sore eye and aching throat, her wounded hand and stiff muscles, until the world receded from her and she found at last the tranquility she had so desperately missed. Her heartbeat slowed; her muscles relaxed. Slowly she gathered the mystic power of her heart and spread it out through her body to soothe her pain, strengthen her limbs, and invigorate her mind. It flowed through her body, a warm, tingling intoxication that fired her body and her spirit. The spell was almost complete when she felt the familiar faint tickle on her face and neck. The power suddenly drained from her like water from a broken cup and there was nothing she could do to stop it. The spell broke and vanished. She sighed. Apparently there were hungry souls here, too, and the magic was gone for now. At least the spell had worked long enough to serve its purpose. She felt stronger and more vigorous than she had in days.

A hand prodded her back and she heard a voice say, "Drathkin'kela, the guards will be changing soon. You must go."

She pulled herself back to the world, to the external sounds of the sea below her, to the smells, and the heat, and the wind. Opening her eyes, she looked at the sea's horizon then let her eyes slide slowly downward until she was staring at the edge of the cliff. Her face lightened into a broad smile.

fec was waiting for her when she came back from the midday meal. He looked her over carefully and said, "I know my skills are as good as any Keena's, but I don't believe I have seen anyone heal as fast as you. The swelling is almost gone from your eye, the bruises are gone from your throat, and look at your hand! The cut has closed over already."

Linsha made a noncommittal shrug. "That blue paint works wonders," she said.

Of course he didn't entirely believe her, but when she wasn't more forthcoming, he led her to a quiet room away from the noise and bustle of the early afternoon activities and spent an hour telling her the schedule of events of a royal Tarmak wedding and her expected role.

She listened for a while and picked up the gist of the ceremony. There would be many prayers, a blessing of the couple, and a procession where she had to walk while Lanther rode a horse. The bride was supposed to be accompanied by family and attendants, but since Linsha had none, she would walk alone as befitted the Drathkin'kela. There seemed to be much talking and feasting involved. That was good. She didn't even want to think about—let alone discuss—the wedding night. She understood from Lanther's pronouncement the night before that the wedding night would begin immediately and wouldn't end until he set sail for the Missing City. Her mind balked at that and began to wander elsewhere while she thought of ways to hide a small dirk in her dress. Or did the Tarmaks wed naked like they fought? Now there was an image that made her stomach churn. No, Afec had mentioned a dress at one point. Her thoughts trailed away on another tangent.

A yawn sneaked up on her and slipped out before she could stop it. If Afec noticed he did not stop. He continued in his modulated voice telling her about her greetings to the Empress and the Emperor. Obviously the marriage of an Akkad was an important event and the Tarmaks made the most of it with much drinking and feasting. She yawned again, and this time Afec broke off his talking and sent her to her pallet with strict instructions to rest.

Before he left her, he gripped her wrist. "Do not plan anything for tonight," he whispered. "I am looking for something that might help. If you wait, I feel the weather will change tomorrow."

Linsha squeezed his hand in reply and without argument went to her room. She was smiling. It seemed she had a new weapon in her arsenal: an ally.

Linsha did not think she had slept at all, but when Callista entered the tiny sleeping chamber, she started awake and saw the room was nearly dark. The buxom courtesan laid a small lamp on the table and posed in place.

"What do you think?" she asked, pride and a little mischief clear in her voice. Linsha squinted in the dim light and saw the courtesan looked rather more buxom and plump than usual under her plain linen shift.

Callista flashed a grin, reached under her shift, and pulled out a wad of dark fabric. "Tarmaks do not pay attention to slaves. I found these in the laundry and borrowed them." She laid the clothing on Linsha's recumbent form and dropped down beside her to see her reaction.

Sitting up, Linsha held the clothes up to the light. The busy courtesan had found a dark green silk tunic—probably from one of the minor nobles who lived in the second circle of offices, treasuries, and craft rooms. The pants were a pair of heavy silk formal pants that on a tall Tarmak would reach only to the knees. On Linsha they were baggy and came neatly to her ankles.

Linsha hugged the courtesan in gratitude. "These will work quite well. Thank you!"

"If they help us get off this forsaken island, I would steal the wardrobe of the Empress herself," Callista replied fiercely.

"Are you sure you want to risk an escape?" Linsha asked. She wanted to be sure of the young woman before she committed either one of them to such a risky endeavor. "We do have a choice. We can stay here and hope Lanther will eventually come back for us. We can wait here and hope Crucible is still alive and tries to find us. Or," she paused, her intent in deadly earnest, "we can try to convince Sirenfal to fly us out. *If* we can find a way to release her, and *if* she is strong enough to fly."

The courtesan studied Linsha's expression, her cornflower blue eyes half-lidded in thought. "I don't think either one of us believes Lanther will ever free us from this island." Rubbing the silk between her fingers, she asked, "Do you think Crucible is still alive?"

Linsha did not answer at once. She saw again in her memory the field of battle wreathed in smoke, stinking with blood and littered with the dead. She remembered the pain in her hands and the unutterable exhaustion and grief that overwhelmed her. Before her stood a man, badly wounded and bleeding heavily, a man half-dead from the evil dart she had pulled from his back. He had lied to her and betrayed her trust for as long as he had known her, yet the need to see him again burst on her like an arrow piercing her chest. She covered her face with her hands.

To her surprise, Callista put an arm around her shoulders. "You miss him, don't you?" she whispered.

More than I ever imagined, Linsha said to herself. But to the courtesan she replied, "I don't know if he's still alive. And if he managed to survive the battle, I don't know if his wings healed enough for him to fly."

"So Crucible is out." Callista said firmly. "Then I say here we are and here we will stay unless we do something for ourselves. I do not want to stay."

The courtesan's gentle gesture and firm words were enough to help Linsha regain her self control. She rubbed her face hard and forced her memories back into the cellars of her mind. She needed her wits with her if she was going to penetrate the palace's defenses and make her way undiscovered to the dragon's cave.

All she had to do now was wait for Afec.

The fourth day before Linsha's union to Lanther passed as any other day in the Akeelawasee. The day came hot and clear. Linsha ate and exercised by herself, since the other women avoided her and she completely disregarded them. She felt stronger and less sore, and her eye was almost back to normal. Late that afternoon when the Tarmaks dozed in the afternoon heat and the insects droned in the acacia trees, Linsha had to endure another long discussion about Tarmak traditions and the responsibilities of a royal wife. After one tedious lecture, Linsha made an indelicate noise, rolled over on her back in the grass, and said, "Why don't you just say the husband has all the rights, all the fun, all the privileges, and the wife does nothing more than jog in circles, lay on her back, and have babies?"

Afec tilted his bald head. "Do you want children, Lady Linsha?"

She sighed at the very idea. "My dear Afec, I am thirty-four years old. I have been a Knight of Solamnia for almost twenty years. My days to want children can be numbered on one hand, and they vanished years ago."

"But what about the Akkad-Dar? He is expecting you to bear his sons."

"He can expect all he wants. I will never—"

She stopped in astonishment when the Damjatt leaned over and laid his hand on her mouth. "Don't make rash vows, my lady. Do what you must to survive. A Damjatt philosopher once said, 'Seeing into the darkness is clearness. Knowing how to yield is strength.' "

Her eyes opened wide then narrowed in speculation. Gently she took his hand and lifted it from her lips. Still holding his callused fingers, she said, "Is that what you've done, Afec? Do you see into the darkness? Is that how you survived so long?"

His face looked weary to her and his skin seemed thin and dry. He closed his eyes, and for a moment, Linsha thought he had fallen asleep. But eventually he sighed and made an answer. "When I was a little boy, my clan was over-whelmed by the Tarmaks. They took the young people for slaves and slaughtered the rest. They made me a eunuch and put me to work here. It was only after that I started having visions. I have been in the palace nearly fifty years, serving the Tarmaks, biding my time. I thought it was too late for me, but now you are here. You have spirit and compassion. And you *fight*." His voice dropped until she could barely hear him. "You are the Drathkin'kela."

Linsha pushed up on her elbows and stared at him, her mouth slightly open. The intensity of his voice surprised her; the meaning of his declaration took her breath away. His tone was unmistakable. It was pure *awe*.

She was about to make some sort of reply when he climbed stiffly to his feet and looked toward the palace brightly gleaming in the afternoon light. "If you will excuse me, Lady. I will leave you to your contemplation. The Empress wishes to see you tonight so that you might choose a dress. I will come for you when she is ready."

Linsha, whose idea of formal dress involved armor and polished chain mail, looked over the array of colored robes and long dresses and immediately lost interest. The Empress's rooms were much more intriguing. No tiny barracks-style sleeping chamber for her. The Empress had a large suite of rooms for herself and her slaves that included a meeting room, dressing rooms, a private bedchamber, and a bathing room. The entire suite was decorated with exquisite fabrics, leopard pelts, potted trees, and various weapons.

Afec cleared his throat, drawing her attention back to the clothing. Linsha shrugged. She couldn't have cared less what she wore.

The Empress surprised her though. After fitting her with a green wrap dress that barely gave her room to take a stride, she presented Linsha with a long-sleeved black robe embroidered with a blue dragon that curled sinuously around the sweeping hem.

"Your *quartal*," the Tarmak woman said proudly.

Linsha looked so quizzical that Afec hastened to explain. "You have no family to represent you, so you have no family *quartal*. Umm, that is what you might call a family crest or a clan emblem. All the old Tarmak families have one. The

125

Empress thought a dragon would be appropriate for you."

Linsha thought about that and ran her hand lightly over the exquisite blue silk embroidery. It was a blue dragon, a dragon of evil, a minion of Takhisis. But it was a *dragon,* and something about it reminded her of Cobalt, Sara Dunstan's remarkable blue. It seemed better to Linsha to have her own symbol than to be faceless in the presence of the Akkad-Dar. Bowing, she expressed her thanks to the Empress.

After the meeting, Afec escorted her back to her quarters. At the wide door into the building, he handed her the robe and the green dress. As he passed it to her hands, he made a respectful bow and murmured so only she could hear, "When you go to the dragon, use the powder for the guards only in an emergency. Wear the belt. It will protect you from the priests' magic. The liquid is for the dragon. Make her drink it. It will help her regain her strength."

Linsha saw two woman approaching and quickly laid a hand on his wrist. Without a change in his expression, he nodded goodnight and shuffled away. Holding the dress and the robe and the items he had hidden in their folds, she watched him go until he disappeared in the direction of his small workroom.

She hurried into her sleeping chamber where she hung up the wedding finery and hid the small items with the dark green tunic and pants under her pallet.

With the patience born of a hundred past clandestine missions, she lay down on her pallet to wait.

Sometime close to midnight Linsha woke to the cry of the wind under the eaves. Lying still for a time, she listened to the sounds of the sleeping room, and when she heard nothing more than the moan of the wind, the creak of the timbers in the roof, and the common noises of the sleeping women, she rose silently to her feet. She gathered the bundle of clothes and the items she had collected and held them close to her body, then she wrapped a blanket around her shoulders. If anyone found her and asked, she would say she couldn't sleep and was going to the privy. However, there was no need for subterfuge. The sleeping quarters remained quiet, and the halls were empty. Linsha hurried down a corridor and slipped outside.

The wind greeted her with a roar and a bite. The clouds she had seen in the western sky had bulled in after sunset and now covered the entire sky in a black velvet wrap. The clouds' consort, the wind, roared and rolled over the palace grounds with a strong smell of rain on its skirts.

Linsha took a deep appreciative breath of air and hurried to the cover of a thick planting of shrubs and trees. She changed into the dark clothing, wrapped a gray scarf around her head, and tied Afec's knotted belt around her waist. She hadn't had a chance to ask him why he felt the belt was important to ward off the priests' magic, but it made a good place to hang the small bag of powder and the container of liquid he had given her, a pair of archer's gloves, and several lengths of a strong lightweight rope she had borrowed from the exercise room. She shoved her light tunic and the blanket out of sight and rubbed dirt over her hands, face and ankles. In this gloomy night, she knew she would be very difficult to see.

A shadow among the tossing shadows, she flitted through the windy night across the grounds to the hedge and stood at last at the foot of the circling wall. If she was right, the guards would be changing soon, which would give her the distraction she wanted to slip over the wall.

Low voices spoke on the parapet above her, and Linsha abruptly realized the change of the guard was already occurring. On silent feet she eased up the stairs by the tower and pressed into the darkness where the tower bulged out from the wall. An archway bisected the tower to allow the guards to pass through and to give them access to a ladder that led up into the higher levels of the watch turret. Linsha peered cautiously through the tower entry and saw six guards quietly conversing along the wall on the other side. Three were leaving and three would be staying. Or four. Hadn't she counted four the other day?

Footsteps clattered overhead and a trap door suddenly opened in the tower ceiling. A guard climbed down the ladder and hurried to join the others. Another conversation ensued between the two watch leaders.

Linsha eased into the darkness of the tower archway, straining her ears to hear their voices. It was difficult to catch what they said over the roar of the wind and the crash of the surf below, but she thought she heard the Tarmak words for sick and three.

The Tarmaks saluted one another then four marched for the stairs, leaving only three on the walls. Linsha grinned. Apparently one of this guard unit was ill and they didn't feel it was important enough to replace him on a night like this. So much the better.

Before the Tarmaks decided to move in her direction, she whisked out of the entry and snatched out a length of rope that already had a loop tied at one end. Tossing the loop over a crenellation, she settled the rope as far down as it would go and pulled the loop tight. In the deep gloom of the cloudy night, it was barely visible against the stone, and only if you knew where to look for it. She slipped on the archer's gloves—the only type of gloves she had been able to find—cast a quick look at the tower, and let herself down thirty feet. As soon as her feet touched the ground, she followed the base of the wall away from the tower toward the narrowest width of ground.

From the base of the wall to the edge of the rocky escarpment was a mere six paces, a very difficult width to utilize if you were crazy enough to attack the palace from that direction. The land had been cleared of brush, rocks, and any kind of cover, but Linsha had the distinct impression that the wall in this section was not so much to keep enemies out as to keep people in. The other day when she sat on the battlements she had seen that this wall was the only one. Unlike other, more vulnerable sections of the palace that had two large defensive walls, this part had one, and one steep, rocky promontory that jutted out into the sea.

She found the place she wanted and eased out away from the wall. On a moonlit night she would have been hard pressed to creep away from the wall without being seen, but she was lucky on this black, gusty night. As long as she did not attract attention with sudden movement, she should be able to creep over to the eroded crevice she had noticed earlier and drop out of sight.

The palace wall remained quiet. No horns blared. No harsh Tarmak voice yelled at her from the wall. No arrow slammed into her back. Only the wind roared over the stone walls and tugged at her body as she scrambled down the worn crevice and picked her way carefully to the steep edge. Fortunately the face of the promontory was not a sheer cliff like the high bluffs near the Missing City. The land dropped abruptly to the sea, but there was enough slope to make the descent possible. She debated with herself about using one of her two precious remaining lengths of rope as a safety line then decided to do it. She didn't know what lay at the foot of the promontory. She might need a rope. It was better to be cautious than end up a broken wreck at the bottom, so she tied off a long length and climbed down the rocky face as carefully as she dared in the dark and tempestuous winds.

Rock by rock she crept along the steep slope, testing with her feet, feeling her way down. She watched as best she could for a crack or a shaft that might lead into the dragon's cave, for she remembered in her dream seeing light filter through an opening in the wall of the cave. But if an opening was there, she did not find it in the dark.

Halfway down, she paused to give her aching arms a rest and saw the pale wash of waves breaking below her. They seemed to be washing up on a beach or a gravel bar or a shelf several paces away from the foot of the stone wall, which gave Linsha hope that she would have an area to walk upon as she searched for the cave entrance.

Her rope held through the long descent down the rugged slope until the last ten feet. As soon as the end reached her fingers, she tied a knot and anchored the rope on a slight outcropping where she hoped she could find it again on the way back up. She climbed cautiously down a few more feet, then her aching fingers slipped on a lichen covered rock, and she fell backwards off the rocks. She landed jarringly hard on her seat and was immediately soaked from her buttocks to her feet. For a painful moment she sat breathing hard, unsure whether to laugh at her absurd position or cry from the pain in her tailbone. She was on a small gravelly beach, a shelf of sorts, which extended from the foot of the promontory only about seven or eight feet into the water. Driven by the wind and tides, waves washed up the tiny beach.

Dripping and sore, Linsha climbed to her feet and looked both ways along the escarpment. There had to be an entrance to the sea cave. There had to be! She was staking a great deal on that fact. But she didn't know exactly where it was, and she didn't want to stumble onto a Tarmak guard in the dark. Which way should she go?

Just then the rain came. There were only a few warning drops before the clouds opened wide and dumped a deluge of rain on the land below. Linsha's upper body was soaked in seconds. By sheer good fortune, she was looking to the right when she saw a brief flash of red light. It lasted only a heartbeat or two before it vanished in the torrents of rain, but it was enough for her to see a brief glimpse of a guard and a blackness behind him that could be the entrance to a cave. She shielded her eyes from the driving rain and made her way slowly along the rough foot of the promontory to the place where she had seen the light.

She was cold and thoroughly drenched by the time she reached the place where she had seen the guard, but the rain, the pain in her back, and the cold of the wind were nothing to the elation she felt when she saw the cave entrance. It was not very high, perhaps fifteen to twenty feet at its highest point, yet it was low to the ground, smooth, and wide enough for a sinuous brass dragon to slip through.

She proceeded with caution to the mouth of the cave and peered inside to find the guard. If there was one guard, there could be more.

There were two. She saw them sitting by a miserly fire hardly big enough to heat a cup of water. A lantern encased with a reddish glass sat on the floor beside one of them. They had chosen a rocky shelf to sit on that was higher than the main floor of the cave and protected from the wind and flying spray by a bulge in the cave wall.

Linsha found some shelter just inside the cave's mouth and studied the situation. She quickly realized that she would not be able to slip by. The cave was not big enough to hide her movement from the sharp-eyed Tarmaks, and the guards didn't look like they were planning to go to sleep any time soon. She could try to lure them outside, but if their suspicions were aroused they would be doubly dangerous.

She felt for the leather pouch Afec had given her and pulled it out. What was it? He didn't tell her how to use it, only to save it for an emergency. She opened the small bag and took a sniff. The escaping fumes hit her brain and almost knocked her senseless. Her head whirled. She sagged against the rock wall, fumbling to close the bag. Ye gods, she thought, that was a fast acting powder. If a single smell would do

this, what would a face-full do? She had to take several deep
breaths to clear her lungs and head.

Slowly her thoughts slogged out of the drug-induced fog.
Perhaps a frontal approach would work. She unwrapped her
scarf, tore off the driest section she could find, and formed a
small bag. Using extreme caution, she poured a small amount
of the power into the fabric and tied the scarf piece with a
loose knot. She swung the knot a time or two to check its
swing, then she rose to her feet, covered her face with her
hands and staggered into the cave.

"Help me!" she cried.

Sirenfal's Promise

11

The Tarmaks leaped to their feet. The nearest one was reaching for his sword when Linsha's makeshift bag hit him in the face. Dusty powder flew into his eyes, nose, and mouth, and he collapsed like a dead man. The second guard managed to unsheathe his sword before the powdery bag struck him. Linsha leaped by his falling body and ran about ten paces to escape any floating powder before she whirled and crouched to face her opponents.

There was no need. Both Tarmaks lay on the floor, their bodies limp, their eyes rolled up in their heads. Cautiously she approached them. When she saw they were still breathing, she dragged them to their fire and arranged them in realistic sleeping positions in case other Tarmaks came to check. She hoped they were on the same schedule as the other guards in the palace, which might give her a few hours before anyone came along. She considered borrowing one of their weapons, then thought better of it. She wanted the guards to be as groggy and confused as possible when they regained consciousness. A missing weapon would be sure sign someone had been there. She brushed away every mark of footprints and left everything untouched. With luck she would be in and out before the guards woke up.

One thing she did borrow was a small brand from the fire. Its glowing end was better than nothing in the ebony dark of the cave. Leaving the guard post behind, she walked carefully into the depths. The cavern smelled strongly of seaweed and saltwater, and echoed with the sounds of the rain and surf outside. Its floor was covered with gravel and sand. Almost immediately she found a narrow trail that led from the entrance to the interior, and she gratefully followed its lead.

She had gone no more than a hundred feet or so when she saw a faint glow ahead. She stamped out her brand and tread softly toward the light. Moving warily, she kept on the lookout for a barrier, a ward, or anything that kept the dragon trapped in the cave. Surely there was something that held the brass in the cave besides intimidation and some combination of poisons and sedatives.

If there was a barrier in the cave, it wasn't readily apparent to her. She was able to walk the entire length of the passage without difficulty. The light grew brighter the closer she drew to the larger cavern. She pressed against the wall and crept small step by small step toward the opening. Her eyes scanned the interior. The bulk of Sirenfal lay in the same place where she had been two nights before, in much the same position. Her head was tucked under her wing and her breathing was shallow and regular. Torches flickered on the upper level where the stair tunnel entered the cave, but Linsha could see no sign of guards or priests. Was it possible the priests had so much faith in their concoctions and spells that they left the dragon unguarded?

She eased her head out of the shadows of the cave opening and peered into the cavern. No one shouted or yelled a challenge, so she eased a little further inside the big chamber. The walkway above was empty, and except for the scorched stone platform there was nothing and no one on the cavern floor. Rainwater poured though an opening in the high ceiling and fell in a thin stream into a shallow gathering pool. Muted sounds of the storm echoed dimly through the cavernous spaces.

The dragon's tail twitched on the sand.

Surprised and hopeful, Linsha's breath hissed through her teeth. "Sirenfal."

The brass's wing rustled slightly then her bright eyes peered over her folded wing. "I knew you'd come," she whispered. "Be quiet. There are guards at the entrance up the stairs, and a priest sleeps in a small room over there." She lifted her head a fraction higher. "How did you get past the sentinel?"

Linsha trod silently over the sandy floor, keeping the dragon's body between her and the stairs. As soon as she reached the dragon, she ducked down behind her.

"The guards? I knocked them out."

"No. The sentinel in the wall. There is a magic alarm of some kind that is supposed to stun intruders. My own magic has failed, but I was told the ward is still working."

Considering the state of magic on Krynn, Linsha rather doubted it. Nevertheless, some old artifacts and ancient spells remained viable. Linsha lifted the ends of the wet knotted belt tied at her waist and ran them through her fingers. "Afec gave this to me to ward off spells. Could that have helped?"

Sirenfal cocked an interested eye to study the belt. "Ah, knot magic. I have heard some Damjatts believe in its power to protect. You should keep that belt with you."

Linsha made a mental note to thank Afec and secured the belt with another knot, just to be sure it did not fall off. She touched Sirenfal's shoulder.

"You look better," she said quietly. "Your scales are brighter."

I have not eaten, replied Sirenfal in Linsha's mind. *I knew they were keeping me drugged with something, but I ate anyway because I had no hope. Tonight I buried my food when they did not watch."*

"Why? Why was tonight different?"

I wanted to see what would happen. I need to know if the drug will wear off quickly or if I need to avoid food until we can escape.

Linsha felt a bud of elation blossom. "Escape? Are you sure that's what you want to do?"

The dragon's response shot back in alarm, *You do not? I thought that's why you came. To work out a plan.*

"Yes, yes!" Linsha hastened to assure her. She leaned against the dragon's warm bulk and grinned at the shadows around them. "I just want to be sure you are aware of the danger."

I know more of our danger than you do, Sirenfal told her. *I am not well and I never will be again. When the Tarmaks experimented on me with the Abyssal Lance, they left splinters in my back. The splinters are small, insignificant, but they are there, and like the lance, they have the power to kill. One day, the splinters will reach my heart and I will die. If that happens while we are flying —*

Linsha interrupted her. "Then we will deal with it then. Do you want to risk it?"

Sirenfal did not move, but her body trembled with her emotion. *To be free of this place? To fly with the wind? To see my home and find my mate? I would risk anything. Just help me out of this horrid cave and I will take you anywhere.*

"Can you take two? I have a friend who has helped me survive these long days. I cannot leave her behind."

One or two, it will not make any difference to the splinters. I believe my wings will carry us—at least to the nearest island.

Linsha nodded. "Then before we lose the chance, take this. A healer gave it to me and said it was for you."

Sirenfal's light brown eye rolled around to glare suspiciously at the flask Linsha removed from her belt. *I will take nothing made by those Tarmaks. I have had enough misery from them.*

"This was made by my friend, Afec, a Damjatt, a slave in the Akeelawasee. He is fascinated with dragons and only wants to help you." Linsha popped off the cork and sniffed the contents very carefully. "It smells good," she said, surprised.

The one who gave you the belt? Very well, then, agreed the dragon. She opened her mouth just enough to allow Linsha to pour the contents over her tongue. *Oh! It does taste good.* She licked her lips and sighed. *That is the best thing I've had to drink in a very long time. Please give him my compliments. Is it meant to do anything?*

Linsha tilted her head, perplexed. "I don't know."

So what do we do now? Sirenfal asked. *How do you plan to get me out?*

"What is keeping you here? Why do you not blast them and fly out?"

When the priests and that Akkad-Dar man first brought me here, they broke my wings and kept me asleep. I think my wings have healed now, but I am chained to this wall and my food is always full of their poisons.

Linsha listened to the brass's words in her head and felt a deep sadness. The Tarmaks had not only broken her wings and chained her leg, they had almost broken her spirit. Most healthy, self-respecting adult dragons would have tried to fight their way out of this cave years ago. But the Tarmaks had kept this young one in such a state of bondage and fear that she believed in her own captivity. Maybe now she and Sirenfal could change that.

"I must be married in three days," Linsha said.

Yes, I heard. To the Akkad-Dar. Will you go through with it?

"Not if I can change it. He has already told me he will not return me to my home. How much time do you need to regain enough strength to fly?"

Sirenfal thought for a moment or two. *A few days would help me.*

"Then in two days I will try to come to you. We will get out of here together."

Voices echoed in the tunnel above, sending shivers down Linsha's back.

Sirenfal's mental voice took on an overtone of panic. *Get out. Go while you can. I will wait, two days, two hundred days.*

Linsha leaned over the dragon's back, hauled her long nose to eye level and said fiercely, "No. If something happens to me, find a way to get out! You can do it! Go to the Plains of Dust and find a dragon named Crucible. Tell him about me. You have to promise!"

Sirenfal's eyes gleamed with a sickly light of fear, but she seemed to take strength from the intensity in the woman's voice. She bowed her head and closed her eyes. "I promise," she told Linsha softly.

Like a deer before wolves, Linsha broke for the passage opening, sprinting with all her strength as the voices in the stair tunnel grew louder. As soon as she was in the shelter of the darkness beyond the torchlight, she slowed and turned for one last look at the brass dragon. Sirenfal had returned to her former sleeping position, head under wing and tail curled around her body. Voices echoed in the cave around her, and to her dismay, one voice sounded like Lanther.

Linsha did not wait to see if she was right. Fear put speed in her feet and led her back on the path to the small entry cave where the two guards still slept by the embers of their fire. Outside the rain fell in the sheets and the wind howled around the island.

Linsha woke to the sound of the bell calling women to morning exercise. With a groan she rolled over to her back on her damp pallet and stared at the ceiling. She hoped never to go through another night like that again. Climbing down the cliff and entering the dragon's cave had not been extremely difficult, nor had escaping the cave. The guards had still been unconscious when she slipped by them and hurried out of the cave. Going back up the cliff in the heavy rain had been almost impossible.

The trouble had started when she realized the waves, driven by the powerful winds and incoming tide, washed up against the stony face of the promontory. She'd had to fight her way back through water that sometimes surged up around her hips and threatened to drag her out into the bay. Finding the rope she had left anchored ten feet up the slope had not been easy either. She struggled back and forth along the rocky slope where she thought she had left the rope and finally found it when she saw it flapping loose in the wind.

But if it hadn't been for that rope, she would never have made it back up the cliff face. Instead of a dry descent in the dark, she had a miserable ascent on steep rocks turned slippery and treacherous from the rain. By the time she reached the top of the promontory, her entire body hurt. Bruised and breathless, she'd had to rest before she could even consider climbing the rope up the palace wall. The driving wind and rain helped shield her from Tarmak eyes and kept the guards huddled down behind crenellations or in the tower, but they also buffeted her against the stone wall and made the rope as hard to hold as a wet snake. Her arms and legs, already tired and sore from the treacherous climb up the rocks, trembled and burned by the time she lifted her head over the wall and flopped on the walkway like a gasping fish. Guards or no guards, she'd huddled in the shelter of the tower to regain enough strength to haul up her rope, stumble down the stairs, and return to the women's quarters before she was missed at dawn. She'd hid the dark clothes, retrieved her own wet tunic, and hurried cold and wet to her pallet to snatch an hour's sleep.

Now, like it or not, it was time to get up.

Callista stopped in the doorway. "Thank goodness you're back," she whispered. She came in bearing a cup of hot spiced tea and the usual dodgagd juice. Linsha gratefully drank them both.

She groaned and lay back for a moment, her eyes closed. "We will go tomorrow night," she told Callista in a hushed voice. "Before the ceremony. We will need warm clothes, water, and food if you can get it."

Callista grinned in delight. "I will."

Although she was sore and bone-weary, Linsha went out for her morning run with the other women. She wanted to appear as normal as possible and give the Tarmaks no reason to be suspicious. But she received a nasty shock when she came in from her run. Two large Akeelawasee guards waited for her at the dining hall. They were from the *ketkullik* that usually guarded the entrances and walls of the women's enclosure, not the eunuchs who were permitted inside, so their presence created a stir among the women. The females looked askance, talked behind their hands, and gave the big guards a wide berth. The Empress did not look pleased either, but she made no attempt to have them removed. The guards stood behind Linsha while she wolfed down her meal, and they followed her every step through the morning.

Her thoughts and emotions went through a crazy whirl of fear that the Tarmaks had learned of her clandestine visit to Sirenfal. Had the guards in the cave outpost recognized her? Had she left footprints? Had the dragon been forced to reveal their plans? Her guards said nothing to her. They only watched with cold eyes and dogged her every move. They wouldn't talk to her even when she demanded answers. Yet they did not search her belongings for ropes or stolen clothes or the carefully hoarded pouch of powder from Afec, and they did not try to drag her before Lanther.

She wished she could talk to Afec, who might know what was going on. But with the guards on her heels, she did not dare approach him for fear of drawing undue attention to him. She waited hopefully for him to come to her in the afternoon for another lecture on Tarmak customs, but the Damjatt was nowhere to be seen, pushing Linsha into more dreadful speculation that perhaps the Tarmak had imprisoned him and were torturing him for his knowledge of her plots. When he did not appear by evening, Linsha grew truly worried. She could not think of a day when she had not seen him somewhere around the Akeelawasee busy at his tasks.

As exhausted as she was, Linsha could only sleep in fits and starts that night while her brain ran over every worry and fear she had concocted. She hoped fervently the guards would be gone the next morning, but one look at Callista's face at dawn told her they were still there just outside the sleeping quarters.

"What are we going to do?" the courtesan murmured while she served the juice. "If the guards stay with you, we won't be able to get out of here."

"I know, I know," Linsha replied, her mood made sharp by lack of sleep and her own deep apprehension. "Do you know where Afec is? Have you seen him at all?"

"Not since yesterday. He received orders to attend the priests."

"That does not sound good," Linsha muttered.

"No." Callista put a dainty hand on Linsha's arm and tried to smile. "I have the water and the food we need. I am trying to find some warm tunics or cloaks. What do you want me to do tonight?"

Linsha felt a cold feeling of dread and worry squirm in her stomach. Gods above, tonight was the last night she would be free to stay away from Lanther. They had to escape. Somehow, they had to get away from the guards, climb down to Sirenfal's cave, and get the dragon out of there. By Kiri-Jolith, she missed Varia. She hadn't realized until this separation how much she had come to depend on the owl for her courage, her intelligence, and her willingness to spy. She could really use the owl this night.

Instead of an owl, she had a feisty courtesan and stubborn old eunuch. They were doing their best; it just took a little getting used to. "I will feign illness and try to convince them to allow you to stay with me, so you won't have to sneak out of the servants' quarters," she said. "Maybe they'll find Afec, too."

Callista nodded and went to fetch the basin of water for Linsha's washing while she went outside for her run. As Linsha feared, two Tarmak guards fell in behind her, and this time they followed her around the path of the garden for her entire run. They stayed with her through the day, from the morning meal through the exercise schedules and her swim in the lake, to her evening meal and the quiet time before the women retired to bed. Linsha refused to eat her dinner and dragged herself to her quarters where she planned to have Callista inform the Empress that she was ill and would someone please summon Afec.

Instead she was met at her cubicle door by a Keena priest in a sleeveless black robe. Callista stood behind him looking pale and sick with fear.

"Drathkin'kela," the priest addressed her with a bow. "If you will accompany me, the priestesses are waiting for you."

"Why?" Linsha cried. Her most basic instincts wanted to back up and make a break for the wall, but the two armed guards stood directly behind, blocking her path.

"If you will come with me," the Keena said, and he took her arm and pulled her toward the hall.

Linsha cast one agonized look back at Callista and was forced to follow.

There would be no escape that night.

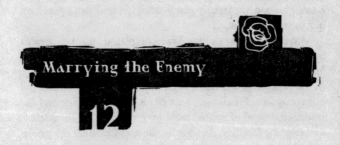

 insha couldn't decide whether to be intensely irritated or very relieved when the Keena took her to another room in the palace and left her in the care of four priestesses. The women, dressed in black robes, wore their hair cut very short and hid their fair skin with a dark red cosmetic powder. Talking among themselves, they led Linsha to another room on a subterranean level where a deep pool of water formed a small underground grotto. To the music of drums and cymbals, the priestesses stripped Linsha, tossed her clothes away, and made her soak in the pool. They scrubbed her several times with a granular soap until her skin burned and then washed her hair with scented cleansers. When she was thoroughly clean, she was asked to step out, and in front of a roaring fire the priestesses rubbed her skin with oils and flailed her with branches from a tree that grew on the island.

It was the branches that finally triggered a vague memory in Linsha's mind of something Afec had said during one of her momentary lapses of attention. Ritual purification. The chosen of a high-ranking Tarmak warrior had to be purified and prepared the night before the marriage ceremony. She had not listened to most of his description of the rites, for she had hoped to be gone by that night, but the Tarmaks—or Lanther—had apparently not trusted her and put a guard on her to insure she stay.

As soon as the flailing was completed, the priestesses braided her shaggy curls as best they could, then they draped her in a clean blue cloth and the head priestess blessed her in Tarmakian in the name of Berkrath, a goddess Linsha did not recognize. Finally she was given a glass of wine and the traditional meal of cooked meat for energy, bread for fidelity, and eggs for fertility. As soon as she was finished, the priestesses led her to a small room and told her to sleep. She would need her strength the next day.

Linsha vowed she would not sleep—she had to find some way to get out. But the priestesses must have put something in her food, for the next thing she realized hours had passed and the women were waking her for the next step of her preparation for marriage. A sick certainty chilled her to the bone. She would have to go through with this. There would be no escape from the island in time. She would have to marry Lanther and possibly submit to him if she wanted to live through the next night and keep the eggs safe.

The dressing and the morning preparations took a mind-numbing eternity. Linsha, who was not used to primping or taking more than five minutes to put on a dress, was cleaned again and rubbed with more scented lotions. Priestesses painted a geometric design of blue dots on her face—probably in lieu of cosmetics she guessed. Her hair was decorated with beads and white feathers. Her nails were cleaned and stained with a golden brown powder that made them gleam like polished wood. Even her dragon scales were polished and set reverently against her scrubbed skin. Then the Empress brought the green dress and the dragon robe, and Linsha was carefully dressed.

The entire operation reminded Linsha of the one doll her parents had given her before they accepted the fact that she was determined to join the Knighthood. She had played with the doll for one day, dressing it and playing with the wool hair until she had it just to her liking, then she propped it in the corner and never played with it again. She wouldn't have been surprised if the Tarmak women propped her in the corner and left her there.

Unfortunately they didn't. To the beating of drums and clanging of cymbals, they escorted her upstairs and took her outside into the hot sun where they processed out of the palace and into the large field where the warriors usually exercised and trained. Once again, the court was assembled in their finery. The black-garbed Keena priests and priestesses led her through the crowd to a large awning in front of the Emperor and his empress. The two royal Tarmaks inspected her and gave their approval.

Lanther arrived on horseback in much the same manner, escorted by shouting warriors, throbbing drums, and slaves carrying pots of burning incense. He looked particularly imposing in the Akkad's gold mask and the dragonscale cuirass that reflected the sunlight like a polished brass mirror. His blue eyes brilliant behind his mask, he bowed to the imperial couple and then to Linsha. She was taken to Lanther's side, and before the entire assemblage, the high priest took a silk cord and bound Linsha's wrist to the Akkad-Dar's. In a droning, high pitched voice, he intoned several long-winded prayers in Tarmakian.

Linsha listened and watched but said nothing. She was sweating profusely in the heavy robes, and her head ached. Beyond that she felt numb. The anger and fear that bubbled below the surface had disappeared into dark cracks, and everything else in her head erected a massive wall and hid behind it. She had nothing to do or say for a while, nothing that required a response, so she simply stared at a place far beyond Lanther's left shoulder and wished in a silent prayer that Crucible would come winging over the wall.

A loud cheer startled her, and suddenly Lanther took her roughly in his free arm and kissed her fiercely. "Soon, my dear wife," he hissed in her ear.

Linsha twisted out of his grasp and pulled her wrist out of the loose cord. Her face darkened with anger. "I fulfilled my part of the bargain," she snapped in Common. "You *will* fulfill yours."

To her annoyance, he laughed and held up a gold chain for her to see. On the chain hung a key about the length of her first finger. "This is my gift to you."

"A key." Her words were heavy with disbelief.

"A key. To the special chamber in the Missing City where nine brass dragon eggs are gently incubating. It is for you."

She refused to touch it. "And what good will that do," she cried, "when I am left behind in this prison of a breeding farm?"

He twirled the chain around his finger and said, "You do not know without a doubt that I will leave you here for the rest of your life. There may come a day when I will take you to our new realm to rule by my side."

"You mean when Crucible is dead and the Plains of Dust lie under your heel?"

"Yes." He nodded with a chuckle. "Around then. You and our son may come to the Missing City and you will see your eggs."

For a painful moment Linsha almost yanked the chain off his finger and threw the key away. It was worthless as far as she was concerned. He would never bring her back to the Plains, and since the eggs were in the Missing City, they might as well be on the far side of the Ice Wall for all the good they did her. Her fingers reached out, grasped the chain, and very slowly, as if lifting a great weight, pulled the chain into her hand. *Throw it away! Throw it away!* Her mind demanded. But her heart could not give up the hope, no matter how slight, that some day she might stand on the threshold of the chamber and see the brass dragon eggs once more. She pulled the key to her chest and clenched it so tightly the metal bit into her skin.

With a triumphant grin, Lanther took her arm, whirled her around and marched her to a shaded pavilion where seats had been arranged for the newly joined couple, the Emperor, and his retinue to watch the Tarmak games played in Lanther's honor. Apparently the games were not open to the public, for the only people in the audience were the inhabitants of the imperial palace. Those of high rank lucky enough to have a seat in the shade quickly took their places, while everyone else sat on the ground and found what shade they could under a collection of brightly colored parasols.

There was very little fanfare. The first combatants took the field, swords were drawn, and the duel commenced. Linsha had heard the fights in Tarmak games were often to the death, but this time the fight stopped when one of the duelists was knocked unconscious. Too bad, she thought morosely. If they killed each other in large enough numbers, there wouldn't be so many to reinforce the garrison in the Missing City.

The rest of the afternoon passed in a blur of bloody contests, competitions of skill and daring, and a wicked game that involved several vicious wild boars, an inflated pig's bladder, and two teams of Tarmaks armed with knives. Linsha didn't watch most of it. Her mind wandered alone on dark and distant paths.

When evening came and the wounded were hauled off the field, the Emperor's court retired excitedly to the palace courtyard for another feast of roast bull, various dishes, and vats of wine. Linsha scanned the crowd of servants for

Afec or Callista, but she saw neither of them. Her anxiety, ignored through most of the afternoon, came back in ever-increasing shock waves like the warnings of a volcanic eruption. She sat beside Lanther, ignored her food, and felt her anger and resentment feed on her fear and build to an explosive force. If something didn't happen soon, she feared she would explode.

The waning moon rose over the hills to the east, the night grew late, and still the dancing and feasting continued. It could not last forever though, and much sooner than Linsha would have liked, Lanther rose from his chair and signaled to the Emperor. Khanwhelak nodded and suddenly a great cheer and outburst of raucous shouts filled the courtyard. Warriors came and lifted Linsha and her chair high on their shoulders. Everyone still able to move clapped and followed the warriors as they circled the courtyard carrying Linsha who clung to her pitching chair with all her strength. Following Lanther, the loud, boisterous group trooped through several hallways of the palace and came out into a garden Linsha hadn't seen before. The garden was heavily planted with shrubs and groves of trees so each clearing had a feeling of solitude and seclusion. Moonlight painted the trees, and somewhere nearby came the sound of a fountain. The entire group came to another clearing surrounded by a lush grove of tall, stately bamboo and there in the center sat a small, airy building with the same style of arched roof as the palace. A door stood wide open, pouring warm lamplight on the dark pathway.

Linsha eyed it suspiciously. Afec hadn't mentioned this. As she feared, the warriors put her down and handed her over to Lanther with many ribald comments and jests. They pushed her toward the door, then the entire group turned on its collective heel and disappeared into the night back the way it had come. A thunderous silence settled over the grove and its delicate house. Linsha felt her body begin to tremble. An almost overwhelming urge to flee shivered in her muscles, but before she could move Lanther pulled her into the house.

In a daze she stood on the threshold and looked at the interior. It had only a single room, a bridal chamber with large windows open to the breezes that played in the garden and a huge bed piled with soft pallets and pillows. It took Linsha a minute to notice Callista and another male servant standing by the bed. They bowed low to the newly joined couple.

"The pavilion is ready, my lord Akkad," said the male servant to Lanther. He indicated a tray of cooled wine, goblets, and sweetmeats, then he helped the warlord remove his mask and cuirass.

Callista hurried to Linsha and gently removed the dragon robe. "I have brought your things, my lady, if you wish to refresh yourself. There is a basin of water and some cloths." Then she said as softly as she dared, "Afec sends his congratulations."

Linsha's eyes met Callista's in a dagger-sharp glance. "He is well?"

"Yes. He was sent here to prepare this house for you. It is the pavilion used by all the imperial family on the five nights following their marriages. You will stay here with Lanther until he leaves for the Missing City. Afec told me to tell you that if your head pain returns, he has left a bottle for you in the small cabinet by the wash table."

"You are dismissed," Lanther snapped at both servants.

Callista dared not dally. She gave Linsha a sympathetic squeeze on her arm. "Good night, Linsha," she said quietly, then her voice dropped even lower. "Afec says don't kill him. If you do and the Tarmak catch you, they will torture you for days. If you get away, we will try to wait for you."

"Out!" Lanther bellowed.

The courtesan bowed low, and with her most impish grin, she winked at Lanther and hurried out after the male servant. The door closed behind her, leaving Linsha alone with her husband.

Linsha stood still for a moment and eyed him coldly, then she walked toward the wash basin Callista had left for her.

Lanther sat down on the bed to remove his sandals. "Callista had a lot to say," he said idly.

"Yes," Linsha replied, busy with the cloth and the cool water. Her face was dusty and hot and the blue paint design itched. "She was giving me advice."

He chuckled. "You are no virgin to need advice from a prostitute."

Linsha made no reply. She had found a folded fabric bag that contained her few clothes, a pair of sandals, her hair brush, and buried in the center lay a certain leather pouch, some dark green silk clothes, and two coils of rope. Linsha's eyes began to glitter with a dangerous spark. Under the guise of applying a hint of perfume and brushing the braids out of her hair, she palmed the leather pouch.

"Does this house contain a privy?" she inquired in a cool detached manner. "I fear I drank too much wine during the feast."

He nodded and indicated a door leading out of the room. "It is there. But do not think to slip out a window or make a break for the Akeelawasee. This garden is surrounded by guards."

"I wouldn't dream of it," she growled.

She picked up a candle and stalked out, slamming the door between them. The privy turned out to be a tiny, one-person room attached to the pavilion by a very short walkway. She made use of it for her own comfort as well as his suspicious nature, and while she sat she carefully poured hot wax onto her palm. The wax burned for a moment before it cooled, but while it was still pliable, she smoothed it over her hand to form a thin protective layer. As soon as she finished and smoothed down her dress, she poured a small handful of the sedating powder into her hand. Her heart began to race; her stomach twisted into a large knot.

She managed to screw a smile of sorts onto her face before she went back into the room. Lanther had poured more wine and doused most of the lamps. Only a few candles remained to light the room with a soft romantic light. Linsha knew she would not have to approach him. He would come to her.

She stepped into the room, her hands clenched into fists beside her, her entire demeanor stiff and apprehensive. He did not hesitate. He strode to her, pulled the candle from her hand, and wrapped his arms around her, pinning her arms to her sides.

Linsha could scarcely breath in his embrace. She could feel his intense need for her, and the reality of it sickened her. She didn't want this man, and she knew at that moment that she could never bear to give herself to him even in pretense. She squirmed to pull her arm loose, but his hold was too tight. His lips trailed down her neck and his hands moved over her back. Her wrap dress fell loose and remained between them only by the pressure of his body against hers.

She forced herself to relax. Pushing every feeling of revulsion aside, she made the lightest hint of a moan and leaned closer to him.

"Thank Takhisis you are mine now," he said huskily in her ear. "I have waited too long."

She felt his arms release their tight grip around her enough to move further down her body. She squirmed just enough so she could take a deep breath. He grinned at her, misinterpreting her action, and she smiled in return. Taking her breath, she held it and pulled her arm loose. She raised her palm and blew the powder into his face.

Lanther coughed and choked once then toppled to the floor with a heavy thud.

Linsha looked down at him. "You'll have to wait a damned

sight longer," she snarled at his unconscious form. Suddenly her own head swam and her eyes unfocused. She realized belatedly that talking while that powder was in the air was not such a good idea. She quickly staggered away and sat down on the bed where she could breathe without falling over. For a short time she breathed slowly and deeply to clear her head, and while she rested she stared at Lanther.

The temptation to wrap her fingers around his neck and apply pressure to the artery just under the skin was almost more than she could bear. Her fingers itched to throttle him or smash the wine ewer into his skull. He was a menace, a constant danger to her world and her life. He had not hesitated to betray the encampment at the Scorpion Wadi, murder Sir Remmik, or order the slaughter of hundreds of defenders in Duntollik. If given the opportunity he would return to the Plains of Dust and kill anyone in his path to an empire.

She forced her teeth to unclench and took several more relaxing breaths. She wanted to kill him, wanted it so badly she could feel it like a fever. But she couldn't. She would let him live for now. If he came at her with a weapon, she would not give a second thought to killing him, but even without Afec's warning, she knew she was not like Lanther. She was a Knight of Solamnia, Order of the Rose, trained by the Oath and the Measure and sworn to accept honor as one's guide. She could not in good conscience kill Lanther while he was helpless and unarmed. She just hoped she didn't live to regret her decision.

Of course, that didn't mean she couldn't gag him, tie him, and make him completely uncomfortable while she made her escape. Quickly she doused the candles and worked silently in the ambient moonlight to truss the Akkad-Dar very tightly and gag him so he could not make a sound. Just in case a passing sentry decided to peer in an open window, she heaved Lanther up on the bed and covered him with a blanket, and just to be sure he did not wake anytime soon, she dusted him with more powder.

When she was satisfied, she went to the small cabinet under the wash basin and found a clear glass bottle filled with a dark liquid that gleamed with the faintest hint of red when she held it up to the candlelight. She was unwilling to leave it behind, so she wrapped it in the cloth bag and tied it to her stomach. After that it took only a moment to change into the dark clothes, tie Afec's knotted belt around her waist, and tuck the pouch of powder into her waistband. She still had the wax on her palm, but she decided to leave it for now. If any of it remained, it might come in handy later. She slipped through a window as stealthily as a cat and slid into the shadowed groves of the garden.

Her mind worked fast as she moved carefully from one patch of shadow to the next. She wasn't sure where she was in relationship to the Akeelawasee, but if she could find that she could find Callista and slip down the promontory one more time. The thought of the courtesan climbing down the long rock face gave her pause, yet they really had no choice. She did not want to assault the guards on the stairs leading down to the cavern if she didn't have to.

So all she had to do was avoid the guards, find the Akeela-wasee, get Callista, go over the wall, and climb down the steep stone cliff to awaken the dragon. She just hoped the night and the sleeping powder lasted that long.

13

Linsha found the main palace building and the door leading within. She watched the shadows by the walls and the dark corners, and when she saw no one move, she slipped inside.

Something shifted behind her. She heard the brush of sandals on the wooden floor and suddenly a clammy hand clamped over her mouth.

"Quiet," hissed a voice in her ear. The smell of herbs and incense filled her nostrils. Afec.

Linsha relaxed and nodded once.

He backed away, gestured for her to follow, and led her to an empty room just a few paces away. "I hoped you would be able to flee him," he whispered.

Linsha gave him a hug. "Are you all right?" she demanded. "Where have you been?"

He hugged her back but quickly backed away, looking nonplussed and embarrassed. "Busy. Preparing for your marriage ceremony. Among other things, I was sent to prepare the royal pavilion. Was it to your liking?"

"It was to Lanther's." She held up a quick hand to forestall any worries. "I did not kill him—hard as that was. He sleeps in bed, where he should be this late at night."

Afec bowed in agreement. "As it should be. Did you bring the bottle?" When she nodded, he pantomimed pulling a cork. "Good. Now you take that to her. If she is asleep, pour it in her mouth. Make her drink it. It is a tonic to counteract the spells of the High Priest and renew her strength."

Linsha patted the bottle under her shirt. "Is this what we gave her the other day?"

"It is very close. This has . . . more. To help her fight the poisons of the Keena."

"Do the Damjatt have the same potions?"

"No. We have learned to make our own." He took her elbow in the dark and led her silently to the door. "There are only a few hours of darkness left. You must go fetch the dragon. As soon as she is strong enough, fly with her away from here."

Linsha stopped in her tracks. "But I have to take Callista. I cannot leave her behind. And what about you? We cannot just leave you. Come with us."

Afec shook his head vehemently. "I have been down to the caves to see the dragon. She is not strong enough to carry three. You go release her. I will fetch Callista. We will wait for you by the lake in the garden of the Akeelawasee."

The plan sounded reasonable to Linsha—much more reasonable than trying to help Callista climb down the rocky promontory. But the thought of leaving Afec behind did not sit quietly. There had to be some way to help him.

"What if—"

He cut her off. "Come," he beckoned. "I know other ways to the lower levels of the palace."

Light of foot, they passed out of the room and trod silently into the maze of back corridors and small stairs that only the slaves and servants knew well. They saw a few guards and one patrol along their way, but Afec stayed in the shadows and avoided their attention. They went down about three floors before they stepped off a flight of stairs into a dark hall that disappeared into darkness in both directions.

"I must go this way to the Akeelawasee," Afec told her. "If you go to the right, you will come to a small door that opens to the main stairs leading down to the cavern. It is forbidden for slaves to go that way, so I can only tell you what I've heard."

Linsha reached for the knotted belt to return it, but the old Damjatt touched her hand. "Take it. I can always make another."

They parted quickly and went opposite ways down the long corridor. Linsha followed the way Afec had indicated and soon found the hall ended in a stone wall with a guard standing stiffly at attention. A small oil lamp hung from a sconce on the wall beside him and lit the area with insufficient light. Behind him she could see a narrow door.

She pulled loose the powder bag and hefted it experimentally. There wasn't much left, but if all went well, she wouldn't need much more. Too bad really. The powder was very useful. Since the wax was nearly gone from her palm, she made another impromptu bag from a strip of her tunic and added a little powder. She swallowed hard to moisten her dry throat, then she strutted forward in her baggy dark clothes as if she had every right to be there and knew exactly what she was doing.

"You!" she snapped in clear Tarmakian. "Where does that door lead?"

The guard was a young Tarmak, probably placed on guard at that quiet door late in the night to practice patience and self-discipline. He looked very startled to see her.

"Drathkin'kela, what are you—" he began. He got no further.

Linsha walked swiftly to him, so close she could smell the old sweat on his body and the fat he had rubbed into his leather gear. He took a step back in alarm, and she swatted his face with her powder bag. The pale powder flew out in a cloud, forcing her to leap back out of the way. The Tarmak crashed to the floor with a clatter of weapons. This time Linsha did not hesitate to take weapons. She removed his dagger, belt axe, and the short, powerful sword strapped at his waist, then she rolled him out of the narrow patch of light and into the dense shadows. The weapons felt good in her hands. She shoved the dagger and the axe in her belt, held the powder bag in one hand, and gripped the sword in the other. It felt like an old friend.

Cautiously she opened the door and peered in. As she hoped, it opened onto a small alcove to the side of the dimly lit staircase that led down to the dragon's cave. In her bare feet she padded quickly down the stairs, keeping a careful watch for any guards on the way. The steps remained empty, and when she reached the last step she saw the tunnel was clear to the cave opening. At the entrance to the cave, however, there were two warriors standing to either side of the door. Both looked alert and very imposing. These Tarmaks guarded the main entry into the sacred cave and were far different opponents than the untried youth at the side door. She would not be able to slip up on them either, for the tunnel cut straight and clear from the stairs to the cave with no cover other than the dark shadows from one torch to the next.

Linsha frowned. There was no time for finesse and no room for error. She had to dispatch these two quickly or she would never be able to revive Sirenfal in time to meet Callista before daylight. It seemed very important to get away before the sun rose, before Lanther revived. She did not want to face his wrath, nor did she want Sirenfal to have to fight the Tarmaks. The brass would need all her strength to fly across the Courrain Ocean.

She pressed into a shadow and tried to think. She had no throwing knives and no bow. Just sleeping powder, a sword, and her reputation as "Friend of Dragons." The frontal approach had worked before. The Tarmaks did not seem to be able to conceive of a woman approaching them unarmed as anything but a curiosity and a nuisance.

She pushed the dagger and axe around behind her back and wrapped her hand around the bag of powder where it could not be seen. Reluctantly she left the sword behind. It had only been hers for a short time, but it was too obvious to carry. Lifting a torch from its sconce on the wall, she stepped out into the corridor and walked boldly toward the guards.

"Good morning," she called. "The Akkad-Dar is sleeping well." She chuckled meaningfully. "But I cannot. He gave me permission to visit the dragon."

The guards exchanged glances. Although her Tarmakian was more than a little rough, they seemed to understand all of it. The question was, Linsha thought, would they accept it?

"The dragon's cave is forbidden to women," one guard told her.

Linsha continued to walk toward them. "I've already been here, remember? I remember you. You helped the priests prepare the funeral pyre and stood guard at the foot of the steps in the cavern."

The guards looked uncertainly at each other again, and Linsha pressed her point in her most arrogant tone of voice.

"I'm not like the other women. I have fought to the death and won. I am the Chosen of the Akkad-Dar. Do I have to go back to him and tell him you did not allow me access to the dragon's cave when he has already given his permission?"

By this time she had almost reached the two Tarmaks. They glowered down at her, their expressions tense.

"I shall ask the priest Imshallik if you may enter," one guard told her.

He was turning to go into the cave when Linsha threw the bag of powder and hit the other guard in the face. The first guard whipped around, drawing his sword as he turned, and he met Linsha's dagger coming around to strike his stomach.

The Tarmak blade sank in deep just below his ribs. He gave a grunt of surprise, clutched his wound with one hand and with the other brought his sword around to chop her head off.

Linsha ducked the blow and lunged toward the second guard who lay sprawled on the stone floor. Her hand reached for the dusty powder bag, snatched it up, and threw it at the wounded guard. It grazed his head and flew by to hit the wall behind him. Linsha thought she had missed him with the bag, but the light graze had been enough to shake powder loose over his face. He staggered, fell to his knees, then toppled forward onto the dagger still embedded in his stomach.

Satisfied, Linsha retrieved another sword and dagger and hurried into the cave. The guards had warned her that a priest was somewhere within. As late as it was, she hoped he slept in the room Sirenfal had mentioned. Perhaps she should ensure he remained asleep.

Quietly she ran into the cave and hurried down the stairs to the main cavern floor. She saw Sirenfal asleep by the wall, but she turned away from the dragon and slipped over to the doorway that led into the priest's sleeping room. The room was dark and silent. The bed was empty. Where was the Keena?

Linsha muttered several frustrated words under her breath and dashed to the dragon. This time the brass did not rouse at her arrival. She lay curled tightly in a ball. Her eyes were firmly shut. She was barely breathing.

"Oh no." Linsha hissed. The dragon seemed to be in a state of dormancy. She knew dragons could put themselves in a deep hibernation, but she could not believe Sirenfal had done this to herself intentionally, not after their talk only three days ago. The brass had been truly sincere in her desire to escape her captivity. Which meant, Linsha decided in growing anger, the priests had probably drugged her again.

Desperate, she heaved at Sirenfal's head and pulled it out from under the dragon's wing. Staggering under the dead weight of the dragon's big head, she tugged and pulled and finally stretched the neck out onto the stone floor. She untied the bottle under her tunic and brought it out. Afec had said to pour it into the dragon's mouth, so Linsha hauled open Sirenfal's mouth and, holding the dragon's upper jaw with one hand, she poured the thick, dark liquid over the dragon's tongue.

Obviously the dragon could not swallow while she was asleep, so how did the liquid get into her stomach? Linsha wondered. Maybe it didn't have to. Maybe it absorbed into Sirenfal's blood through her mouth. She didn't know, and Afec hadn't told her. She just had to trust the Damjatt and hope this tonic worked quickly.

She dropped the bottle and spread her hands over Sirenfal's forehead. Her eyes closed as she concentrated on the power of the dragon scales hanging around her neck. She focused the power and send it inward to the dragon's mind. At this close proximity, she should have no trouble reaching Sirenfal's conscious thoughts—if there were any. Yet she found nothing. The dragon was completely unconscious and her thoughts buried under a shroud of dense obscurity. Linsha wished she had the talent to reach deeper. All she could do was try to talk to her and perhaps lead her closer to consciousness.

Sirenfal. I am here. It is time to go. You have to fight this! I have given you a tonic. Find it in your body and put it to use. It will help you, if you want to leave this place. She went on, sending her message to the unconscious dragon with growing urgency.

All at once a massive pain exploded in her back. Linsha cried out and fell sprawling on the floor beside the dragon. The high priest in his black robes leaned over her, a staff in his hands and a look of utter fury on his rugged face. Several Tarmak guards stood behind him, and one held a bloody dagger in his hand.

"Where is the text, woman?" snarled the priest. "What have you done with it?"

Linsha had no idea what he was talking about and had no time to give it further thought. The priest reached into his robes and pulled out an amulet of dragon's teeth hanging on a cord around his neck.

Linsha struggled in the hands of the guards. "Sirenfal!" she screamed. "Wake up!"

The priest laughed, a nasty sound that reverberated through the cave. "The dragon cannot hear you, and the Akkad-Dar will not save you." Holding the amulet in his hand, he reached out to Linsha.

She saw his hand coming and threw herself backward in the Tarmaks' hold. She looked frantically for her powder bag, but she had left it in the tunnel beside the wall where it had fallen after she threw it at the guard. The warriors tightened their grip and held her still.

The priest's hand touched her face. Pain bright and agonizing exploded in her head, and yet, even as the priest's magic ripped away her strength and tortured her mind, she realized this was not as bad as the time the Akkad-Ur or Lanther had used this spell on her. Either the priest was not as strong or something was interfering with his magic.

Then she had no more time. The Tarmaks dragged her up the stairs away from Sirenfal and into the tunnel. She sagged in their hands in despair. Her chance to waken the dragon was gone. She would be taken to Lanther, and if he was lenient he would punish her and imprison her somewhere where she would never see the light of day again. If he was not, she would die.

***

Silence crept back into the cave.

Solitude returned.

The Tarmaks were gone; the human was gone. There was no sound except for the distant crash of waves that washed quietly through the sea tunnel. On the cold stone floor of the cave, the empty bottle lay unseen in a shadow by the wall.

Then another sound intruded into the quiet—the sound of scales scraping on stone.

The dragon stirred.

Linsha felt herself hauled up the long flight of stairs, and she could do nothing about it. Every time she moved or tried to object, the priest touched her and sent his magic ripping through her head until she thought her skull would shatter at the merest touch of his fingers. Eventually she stopped struggling and simply let them drag her through the halls and out a large door.

It wasn't until she heard voices of other guards that she opened her eyes and recognized the large, flattened cobbles of the huge courtyard of the imperial palace. Torches still burned in the sconces, and a few slaves moved around the tables making a desultory effort to clean up. Then she remembered with start that this was her wedding night and the feast that had been going on in the court when she and Lanther were escorted out was probably over. The Tarmaks, those that could still move, had retired.

"We found her in the dragon's cave," the priest explained to a *ketkegul*. "And the Text of the Amarrel is missing. I would like to see the Emperor."

"Send someone to check on the Akkad-Dar," the officer said to another guard. "If she has injured or killed him, the Emperor must know."

"Where did those two come from?" the priest asked.

Linsha lifted bleary eyes to see what he was talking about and gave a start of horror. Afec and Callista stood terrified between three Akeelawasee guards. One of the guards held several old leather bags.

"We caught them trying to leave the women's quarters. They had stolen goods with them. This one is a slave, so I was going to report them to the Empress."

Linsha caught the priest looking at her thoughtfully then studying the Damjatt and the courtesan. For Afec's sake, she prayed he did not make a connection between them, but it would be hard not to.

"We must take all three before the Emperor," the high priest said. "I believe they are working together."

The officer was about to say something when a shadow swept over the court. Darker than night and faster than a storm, it blew over the palace with a powerful gust of wind and was gone in a blink. The Tarmaks looked up in alarm.

Linsha threw back her head and screamed, "Sirenfal!"

The meeting in the courtyard disintegrated into chaos. Shouts of warning sounded across the palace grounds, and bells rang a warning on the high walls and towers.

But the cries were too late. The stars blacked out as a large shape winged over the courtyard, wheeled and came back, crashing down like a burning star. Linsha heard the unmistakable flap of large sail-like wings and wrenched free from her stunned guards. She screamed a warning to Afec and Callista and dropped to the ground. She was just in time. The wind from the dragon's powerful wings knocked the Tarmaks off their feet and sent the smaller Keena tumbling. The stones trembled under her landing. Linsha heard a snarl of anger and recognition. The high priest screamed. She lifted her head to see the priest scramble to his feet and try to raise his hands, but Sirenfal was not the sedated, fearful creature he was used to. She flung a mouthful of heavy chain at him that caught him across the thighs and sent him sprawling. With a flip of her wings, the dragon leaped up and came down on his body with all four feet. Turning her head, Sirenfal opened her mouth and sent a jet of superheated air blasting through the open door of the palace. Fire exploded in the wooden roof of the great hall, lighting the court with a lurid glow.

An arrow slammed into the stones by Linsha's head. She struggled to stand upright. "Sirenfal, let's go! Now, before more warriors arrive!"

The dragon, still standing in the red mess that had once been her tormentor, squealed with glee. "Hurry then. I have things to do."

Linsha did not pay strict attention to the dragon's words or her meaning. Her head still ached from the magic and she was frantic to get Callista and go. The Tarmak guards were climbing to their feet, drawing their swords. If they attacked the dragon and damaged her wings, there would be no journey home. One guard close to Linsha was still on his knees. He saw Linsha at the same moment she looked at him. He threw himself after her to bring her down. Years of training overcame her pain and weakness. She spun on her heel, bringing her right foot around in a vicious kick to his head that knocked him sideways and sent him crashing back to the cobbles. Before he could recover, she kicked him again and snatched the sword that fell from his nerveless fingers.

Another stream of hot air from the brass dragon blasted the high wall of the courtyard where guards stood loosing arrows at her. Stones exploded in the intense heat, and more fires erupted in the buildings around her. The dragon roared with delight.

Linsha felt the heat of the fires even in the center of the court. It was like standing in the middle of an oven. Frantically she looked for Callista in the growing smoke and running figures. She finally saw her standing over Afec, menacing an Akeelawasee guard with a dagger.

"Gods," she breathed, amazed at the courtesan's audacity. Gripping her sword, she sprinted for the small group. The big Tarmak guard saw her coming and turned his attention to her, away from the small blonde with the little weapon.

Behind him, Callista moved, her beautiful face set in a mask of grief and rage. Linsha saw her and screamed the Solamnic warcry to keep the guard's attention focused on her. Swift and deadly, Callista's dagger flashed in the light of the fires as she took a flying leap onto the Tarmak's back and brought the edge of the dagger across his throat. Blood sprayed over his neck and chest. The guard fell forward onto the stones, and Callista fell on top of him. He struggled to roll over as his blood pooled over the cobblestones.

Callista clambered off his body and spat a name at him Linsha had only heard in the streets of the Missing City. She looked up at Linsha with tears in her eyes. "Afec—!" was all she could say.

Linsha's eyes fastened on the fallen slave. She thought he had just dropped to the ground when the dragon came, but she could see now there was blood on his white robe. Too much blood. Crying, she knelt beside him and took his hand. He was not dead yet, but she could see he was almost gone. "Thank you," she said.

A flicker of a smile settled on his aged face. "Take this," he murmured, trying to push a large sack into her hands. "For you. Read it. Ariakan was . . . not Amarrel. He was . . . *not.*"

She took the bag just to please him, for his words did not sink in right away. She was too concerned for him. She leaned over and whispered in his ear, "You are free."

The smile remained. The life behind it escaped at last.

"Linsha!"

Her head snapped up. Her blood ran cold. It could not be. She had given him enough powder to keep a draft horse asleep for a day. How could he be awake? How could his voice ring over the uproar in the courtyard? And yet, there he stood on the steps of the palace, the fire behind him, his face stained with rage.

"Lanther." The name came out like a curse.

Linsha did not wait to see what he would do. She dropped

Afec's hand, snatched up the bag, and bolted for the dragon. "Callista! Sirenfal!" she screamed. "Time to go!"

The young brass heard her and extended a foreleg. Linsha and the courtesan scrambled up her leg and barely made it to her back before the dragon crouched and sprang up into the night sky. The dragon's wings stretched up then beat in a powerful downstroke that helped fan the fires she had set in the palace. The force of her take-off flattened the two women to her neck.

"Hold on!" Linsha yelled to Callista as the dragon veered away from the palace.

The warning was needless, for the courtesan had her arms wrapped around Linsha's waist like bands of iron and her head buried in Linsha's shoulder.

She glanced down once and saw Lanther still standing on the steps. His face was turned toward them. In his hand was a sword. A cold shiver jolted up her spine.

She turned to look ahead. The palace fell away behind them, and she saw the field where the marriage games had taken place. They were headed the wrong way.

"South, Sirenfal!" she shouted over the creak of the dragon's wings. "We have to go to the sea!"

"Not yet," the brass answered in a tone as hard as steel.

Linsha looked down again and saw the Tarmaks' city spread away beneath them, dotted with torchlight and filled with sleeping people.

The dragon's breath seared across the large barracks-like building Linsha had seen on her arrival. The building burst into a conflagration, and in its fires Linsha saw hope.

"Sirenfal! Leave the city! You don't have the strength!"

"No!" howled the dragon. "They took my eggs! They took my mate! They ruined me! I will kill them all!"

"Listen to me! Take your revenge, but use your head! The ships down there in the harbor will sail for Ansalon in five days! You can save our land. Burn those ships!"

The dragon's body dropped in a dive that took Linsha's breath away. She clung on, hoping desperately that Callista could hold. She heard the courtesan's voice rise in a shout, then all sound was lost in a tremendous roar from the furious dragon. A jet of boiling air streamed from her mouth.

Linsha saw the harbor below. There were the ships tied side by side, many of them filled with food, weapons, armor, and the supplies of a conquering army. The dragon's breath struck the wooden vessels and ignited them in an instant. She soared over the harbor burning every ship she could see, then she swooped around and came back to incinerate the ones she'd missed. The harbor below turned into a maelstrom of raging fires. She angled around again and incinerated the wharves, the docks, the warehouses, and the piles of stores that sat on the docks waiting to be loaded. Her eyes burned with reflected fires, and the light set her scales glowing like molten brass.

She was breathing heavily when she circled around for a fourth time, and her flying seemed labored.

"Sirenfal, we'd better go," Linsha advised, staring down at the burning harbor.

The brass didn't argue. She fired one more blast of heated air into the city itself, then she turned south and winged into the fading night.

Over the Ocean

14

The sun tinted the eastern horizon before Linsha finally stirred and glanced over her shoulder at Callista. In spite of the tension, the smoke smudges, the dirt, and the blood the courtesan still looked lovely. She met Linsha's eye and gave a nervous giggle. Linsha started to chuckle, and a moment later both women howled with laughter in a great, freshening release of tension, fear, and pain. They laughed so hard tears came to their eyes, and their faces turned red with emotion. Sirenfal cocked her head to listen.

"Sirenfal, that was magnificent!" Linsha gasped. "I have never seen a sight so beautiful as you sweeping over that palace. How did you get out of the cave so quickly?"

The dragon slowed her flight and angled her wings to catch a rising sea breeze so she could glide for a while. Her face had an expression of glowing joy. "The liquid you gave me . . . I don't know what it was. I have never had a feeling like that. I heard you come into the cave and talk to me, but I couldn't move or speak." She snorted a hot spurt of air. "That priest put something in my water yesterday morning and forced me to drink it. I felt paralyzed. It was awful. I wanted to answer you, but I couldn't. Then you gave me that liquid.

My head started to buzz! My heart beat faster, and suddenly I was awake—gloriously and mightily awake. I broke the chain holding me and came to look for you."

"Thank Kiri-Jolith you did," Linsha said gratefully. "Thank Afec for that liquid." She twisted around to Callista and asked, "What happened to him? How was he killed?"

The merriment died from Callista's blue eyes and she sighed at the memories. "When Sirenfal flew overhead, one of the Akeelawasee guards tried to pull us inside the palace. Afec fought him. He told me to run to you and get away. He fought the big guard to keep him away from me." She wiped her eyes with the palm of her hand. "Why would he do that? Why would he sacrifice himself for us?"

Linsha did not reply at first. Afec had been an unexpected gift in a foreign world, a friend and an ally. She thought back over the time she had spent with the old Damjatt, his hidden intelligence, his quiet manner, and his determination to help them get free. Thinking of him reminded her of the sack Afec had pushed into her hands. What could be so important? She pulled open the drawstrings and lifted out an ancient book bound in leather and tied with silken cords.

"By the gods!" she breathed. "It's the text the priests were reading that mentioned Amarrel, the Warrior Cleric. He stole it! Why would he give this to me?"

Callista tried to shrug while keeping a tight grip on the dragon. "What did he say to you? Didn't he speak Amarrel's name?"

Linsha dredged her memory for the words she had scarcely heard. "He said Ariakan is not Amarrel."

"Didn't Lord Ariakan convince the Brutes he was?"

"Yes," Linsha replied. She had to shout to be heard over the roar of the wind. "But if he wasn't . . . who is?"

It was all too big a puzzle to worry about now. They still had to find their way home. Linsha tucked the book carefully away in its bag and said a silent prayer of farewell. She pulled out the ends of the knotted blue rope belt around her waist and admired its handiwork. Afec would never be forgotten in her lifetime. "At least he won't have to suffer Lanther's wrath," she added at last.

The courtesan shifted carefully behind her. "Lanther." She chuckled. "I assume he did not have the wedding night he was hoping for."

"I'd say not."

"Good. So, do you think your Tarmak marriage is legally binding in Ansalon?"

"I don't think so, or I am going to have some explaining to do." A pang of hunger in her stomach diverted her attention to a subject more pressing. "What supplies do we have? Were you able to bring anything?"

Callista showed her a single waterskin and a small bag of food she had kept concealed under her clothes during their escape. It wasn't much, and it would have to be carefully rationed, but with some self-discipline and a stop or two along the islands that bordered the Blood Sea of Istar, they might be able to make it.

The women talked a little more before they settled down on the warm, broad shoulders of the dragon and took turns trying to sleep. Sirenfal flew on, the open sea before her and a rosy dawn on her left.

Linsha was the first to awaken hours later. She opened her eyes and stared blearily at the world around her, wondering why the sky was moving at such an odd angle. Something was changing—rapidly downward. She sat up, suddenly alert and worried for Sirenfal. Below her the sea rushed up to meet them, and as far as she could see there was nothing but water in gently rolling waves.

"Sirenfal?" she called worriedly.

"I'm sorry, Linsha. I have to rest. My wings aren't accustomed to flying anymore," the dragon told her. She had to struggle to maintain her controlled flight while she dropped toward the water, and there was a wheeze in her breath Linsha had not noticed before.

"Rest? Rest where?" Linsha said incredulously.

"Well, down there. I can't swim like a bronze, but I can float. I just need to rest my wings."

There was no time to answer. Linsha had just a moment to steady the sleeping courtesan as the dragon braced her legs in front of her. Her wings tilted to brake her speed, and she touched down on the surface like a huge swan. Warm water sprayed out in her wake; a wave washed over Linsha's legs. Callista came awake with a scream and grabbed Linsha's waist. Then they were down, settling in the sea, while Sirenfal's wings spread out on the water like outriggers to help hold her bulk on the surface. A sigh of relief whistled out her long nose.

Linsha peeled Callista's fingers off her waist. "We're safe on the dragon," she said as much to reassure Callista as herself. She felt the waves gently rock the exhausted dragon. "You can take off this way, can't you?" she asked after a while.

"If not, you can get off and push," came the brass's drowsy retort. She curved her neck and pulled her head down just like a swan and let herself float. "We're in the southern current," she told Linsha. "We're still moving toward home."

The dragon fell quiet, and Linsha decided to let her rest. Remarkably, Callista had survived the entire landing and still sat upright on the dragon's broad back. Linsha debated about trying to sleep again, but she was wide awake now. She looked at the sun still shining hot in the west. She looked at the dragon and the waves, and without a second thought she gave in to impulse. Her clothes flew off, and she dove into the warm water.

With lazy strokes she swam beside the dragon, diving

around her and splashing like a child to wash the stink of the Tarmaks off her body. Eventually she stopped to rest against Sirenfal's wing.

"Where did you learn to swim like that?"

She glanced up to see Callista staring down at the waves in suspicion and fear. Her blond hair had been tied back in a pony tail, and her face and arms were still smudged with soot and dirt and smeared with blood.

"My brother taught me the strokes, but Crucible taught me to enjoy the water," Linsha said. "Why don't you join me?"

A grimace marred the courtesan's lovely features. "I can't swim," she admitted. She blinked and stared down at Linsha. "Where did you get that key? I don't remember seeing that before."

Linsha's fingers touched the scales and the key hanging on the gold chain. "It was a gift from Lanther."

"A key?" Callista said dryly.

"It's supposed to be the key to the chamber where the eggs are being kept."

"Do you believe him?"

"I'm willing to take the key back to the Missing City and try it."

"Who is Crucible?" Sirenfal's tired voice asked.

"He was my friend," Linsha replied.

"Tell me about him."

Linsha climbed up to the dragon's back, pulled her grubby clothes on, and sat in the warm breeze to drip-dry. "It's a long story," she sighed.

"We have the time," Callista pointed out. "I haven't heard the whole story either."

So while the dragon rested, rocking gently on the waves, Linsha told them both about Crucible and Lord Bight, Iyesta, Lanther, Sir Remmik, and the fall of the Missing City. She hadn't meant for her tale to be anything more than a quick, cool assessment of the bronze dragon, but once started the story came out in full passionate detail. Neither Callista nor Sirenfal interrupted her once. They listened avidly to the end, when Linsha told Sirenfal of her meeting with Lanther and his promise of the eggs.

When she finally stopped and stared silently at the darkening sky, Callista said, "Gods of all, Linsha, I had no idea."

A faint glint of tears shone in the corners of Linsha's eyes, and she whisked it away before anyone noticed. "Yes, I hadn't realized what a tale it becomes when you put it all together." She retrieved the water bag and took a small swallow to ease her dry throat.

"Do you know if Crucible is alive?"

She shook her head. "He was badly wounded by the Abyssal Lance. I don't know if he survived it."

Through her knees Linsha felt a faint shudder run through the brass dragon at the reminder of the Lance. The old black wound made by the splinters of the Lance lay close to Sirenfal's neck ridge almost under Linsha's seat. The scales around the scar looked warped and discolored, and the flesh that she could see beneath them felt hard and hot to the touch.

"Are you all right?" she asked the dragon.

Sirenfal's wings rose and flapped slowly in the wind to dry. "I am just weary. I will fly for a while and rest again. One thing I should know: Where do you want to go? What about Kern or Nordmaar? We must try to avoid Malys at all costs."

No one disagreed. The huge red dragon, Malys, was the largest and the most dangerous dragon in the world. She could and gladly would eat a young brass like Sirenfal for a snack. Her realm lay to the south and west in the region now called the Desolation that formed the southern border of the Blood Sea of Istar. To avoid her, Linsha knew Sirenfal would have to fly due south, skirting the Blood Sea, then swing southwest around Silvanesti. That way was longer and

spent much time over open water, but it would stay clear of
Malystryx. Or she could fly far to the west and come south
between the realms of Khellendros, Malys, and Sable. Neither
way looked inviting.

"I know it's a long way to go, but I need to go to Iyesta's
realm, the Plains of Dust. Where do you want to go?"

"As far as I can." The dragon fell quiet and did not speak
again for a long while. She paddled around into the wind,
lifted her wings to finish drying them, then said, "Hold
on!"

They did, and the dragon stretched out her neck and
flapped her wings with all her might. As she pumped her
wings, her body moved slowly forward and rose laboriously,
streaming water behind her.

Linsha and Callista clung to her back and willed her into
the air.

Her belly cleared the water, then her back feet, and finally
her tail. At last she was airborne. Sirenfal rose to a comfortable altitude and settled into a strong, steady beat that carried
them south over the undulating leagues of the Courrain
Ocean. The sun settled in the west, burning a golden path
across the sea before it sank and left the sky to the brilliant
swaths of stars in their strange constellations.

With little else to do but hold on, Linsha let her thoughts
wander. She was delighted to be free of Lanther and the
island of the Tarmaks, but so much still preyed on her
mind, and she'd barely time to assimilate everything that
had happened. As far as she could tell, she and Callista had
been on the island about three weeks, which meant they
had been gone from the Plains for well over a month and a
half. Who knew what had happened on the Plains in that
length of time? Or what had happened to Varia, Crucible,
Falaius, Leonidas, and the defenders of the Plains? Her time
in the Akeelawasee had been almost worse than fetters, yet
it had given her a badly needed chance to rest and recover

from the war. She had learned much about the Tarmak and had improved her skill with the language. She had met Afec, a Damjatt of inestimable qualities, and she had found Sirenfal.

Of course she had also been forced to fight the Emperor's daughter, marry the Akkad-Dar, and kill at least one Tarmak guard. She'd probably made an implacable enemy of Lanther, but on the other side of the coin Sirenfal had burned the Tarmak fleet. With winter settling in to the southern Plains, it could be half a year or more before the Tarmaks rebuilt their ships and sailed again for the Missing City. A great deal could happen in the span of six months; many things could be accomplished. Would she be alive to see it? What should she do next?

Callista must have been thinking along the same vein, for she said, "What are we going to do when we get back?"

Linsha turned her head to the courtesan, surprised by the similarities of their thoughts. "You're optimistic. We haven't even seen dry land yet."

"I know." Callista sighed. Her teeth were chattering, and she was shivering in the cool night air. "But planning ahead takes my mind off the more immediate possibilities, like freezing, drowning, dying of thirst, being eaten by Malys . . ." Her voice fell to a slight murmur that only Linsha could hear. "I can see well enough that Sirenfal is not well. I saw many dragons come and go in Iyesta's realm, and I have never known one to look as ill as this one. Will she survive the journey?"

Linsha listened to Sirenfal's wheezing exhalations and felt the struggle in the wing muscles near her legs. "I don't know," she answered.

"Then we'll hope for the best," Callista said. "That's why we left Ithin'carthia in the first place. So what do we do when get to the Missing City? Obviously I can't go back to work there as long as the Tarmaks are in control."

A picture of Callista with a dagger in her hand facing

the warrior surfaced in Linsha's mind, and she smiled at the memory. "You could join the militia—what's left of it. Where did you learn to cut throats like that?"

"In the militia. Well, from my father really. He was a captain in Iyesta's militia. He never married my mother, but he cared for me and taught me a few things about fighting and self-defense, and he left some coins for me when he died. I thought about joining the militia because of him." She shrugged. "But I decided staying in bed late was much better than getting out early, so I followed my mother's profession."

"Are you sure you want to go back to the city? There are other places you could go."

"I know. Perhaps I will. Meanwhile, maybe I could help you?"

Linsha rubbed her temples where a dull ache still lurked in her skull from the priest's magic and the lack of food. "You would be welcome," she said. She knew what she was up against. She would take help from anyone willing to offer, especially someone with Callista's courage. "First though, you should know, that women who befriend me and help me usually end up dead."

She heard the courtesan's gasp even over the noise of the dragon's flight. "What do you mean by that?" Callista asked.

"I just wanted you to be aware. Women I like tend to die, just like the men I like tend to be rogues, liars, and general bastards."

"Or bastard generals," Callista said, trying a light tone. "It's just your profession, and the circumstances. I'm sure if you were a seamstress in a quiet little village, your friends would live to a ripe old age. And your man would still be a rogue. I'll take my chances."

Linsha felt a warm rush of relief and gratitude. She hadn't planned to ask the courtesan for any more assistance, for she had already done far more for Linsha than expected or hoped for. But since Callista offered—and was still willing to risk her life—she wouldn't say no. "If you're serious, the first thing I want to do is find Varia."

"Oh, she's probably in the Tarmak headquarters. When Lanther gave me his instructions to take care of you. I also heard him tell an officer to take the owl and keep it alive until he came back or the man would die a slow and brutal death."

"That sounds like Lanther. Good! Varia first, then Crucible. We'll have to ride up to Duntollik to find the remnants of Wanderer's tribe and a shaman named Danian."

She thought she heard the faintest sigh behind her, but Callista agreed willingly enough. For someone who liked to loll in bed past dawn, the courtesan was as game as any newly knighted Solamnic.

"You really fell for him, didn't you?" Callista asked after a moment of silence. "A dragon and a man. That will not be easy."

Linsha twisted around to face the courtesan, but her eyes gazed far away to a dark horizon. "I met an elf once. Gilthanas. He was a friend of my grandparents who fell in love with a Kagonesti elf. When he found out she was really a silver dragon, he was furious and hurt, and he drove her away. He told me years later that his pride pushed Silvara away because he had been too proud to admit how deeply he loved her and how deeply her lie had wounded him. He was wandering through the world on the edge of insanity trying to find her. I don't want to end like that. I don't want to spend the rest of my life regretting that single moment of pride and anger on the battlefield." Her eyes focused again on Callista. "Do you believe it's possible to have a relationship with a dragon?"

The girl patted Sirenfal's scaly back. "Why not? Most dragonriders are connected to their dragons in ways far deeper and more subtle than most humans are with each other. You have the advantage of being a woman drawn to a dragon who spends much of his time as a man. There could be . . . advantages."

Linsha hardly knew what to say. She realized she was deeply attached to Crucible and for years she had been attracted to Lord Bight. But the revelation that they were one and the same had stunned her beyond rational thought. All she could accept now was that she missed Crucible fiercely and she was furious at Lord Bight for lying to her. How could she reconcile the two? And would it matter if she did? She didn't know with any certainty how he felt about her. Perhaps it didn't matter one whit to him what she felt for him. After all she was only human. Perhaps this was just another instance of her wretched luck with men.

"Of course it won't be easy for him either," Callista pointed out. "If he loves you, he will have to watch you grow old and die much sooner than he will."

"Or he could die the day after you return," Sirenfal interjected, entering the conversation for the first time. She tipped her head around so they could see the glow of her eyes. "Take what you are given and let the future work itself out. You worry that he is a dragon? Perhaps that is an insurmountable problem. For most people it would be. But the Tarmaks did not call you the Drathkin'kela for your skill with a sword or your green eyes. We have joined our thoughts, and I have felt a power in you, a sympathy for dragons many humans do not have. If Crucible is willing, a relationship between the two of you could be very beneficial."

Behind the dragon's words, Linsha heard the echo of another dragon's voice. *The bond formed between a dragon and a human is worth the effort to forge it.* Iyesta had told her that in a vision, but she hadn't explained any further or tried to discuss the difficulties of a human-dragon bonding.

More than anyone else, Linsha wished she could talk to

her brother, Ulin, at that moment. He was the only one in the family who would understand. He had been a dragon mage and had formed a deep friendship with a gold dragon named Sunrise. If there was anyone who could help her sort this out, it would be him. But he was gods knew where, and all she could do was find Crucible—if he was still alive—and try to work this out for herself. If he was dead . . . there would be nothing to do but grieve.

"I need to rest again," Sirenfal told her two riders. "I'm sorry."

"Don't be," Linsha said. "You are the one doing all the work."

She and Callista held fast as the dragon banked down and landed in the sea again. Sirenfal spread her wings, tucked in her head, and was immediately asleep. The women shared a little water and ate some dried bread, then Linsha kept watch while Callista slept. The courtesan had finally relaxed a little on dragonback and was able to sleep for a time.

When the crescent moon rose late in the night, Linsha woke Callista for her turn at watch, then she leaned against Sirenfal's warm neck and tried to sleep. The waves were a little rougher that night and the air was a little colder, a sign that they were moving closer to the southern seas and the approach of winter. But how much closer? How far had they come already? They were certainly flying faster than the Tarmak ship had sailed, and even with Sirenfal's numerous rests, they would arrive at the Plains faster than two weeks. But how much faster? Could they get to land before the food and water ran out? And what about food for Sirenfal? She was already skin and bones, and she did not have any strength in reserve. Maybe she could eat fish. As for that, she was a dragon with a powerful breath weapon. Maybe she would be willing to use her hot breath to cook a few fish for her riders.

On that hopeful thought, Linsha fell quietly asleep.

Sirenfal was not enthusiastic about eating fish. Fish were, she said, not one of her favorite meals. But she was hungry and knew she needed all the strength she could muster. She flew as low over the water as she dared until they found a school of some sort of silver fish swimming in a shimmering cloud just below the surface of the water. Sirenfal shot a short, boiling hot jet of air into the middle of the school and waited for the dead fish to float to the surface before she landed and began to feed on the precooked catch. Linsha pulled two fish out of the water that looked particularly well done and, using Callista's dagger, gutted their breakfast and cut it into serving pieces.

Even Sirenfal admitted the idea had been a good one.

They were still eating their breakfast when Callista grabbed Linsha's arm so hard that she dropped her fish.

"Look! What is that?"

The courtesan cried in such alarm that Linsha did not complain about the dropped food or the bruises that would likely appear on her arm. She looked to see what had disturbed her friend so badly and saw a gray fin slice through the water about a dragon's length away from Sirenfal. For one joyful heartbeat she thought the fin belonged to a dolphin, one of Crucible's favorite water companions, then she looked at it more carefully and saw the straighter line of the dorsal fin and the menacing movement of the creature in the water, and she recognized it as something very different.

"It's a shark," she said in disgust. "It was probably drawn here by the dead fish."

Callista actually squealed with dismay. "I hate those things."

Sirenfal cast a baleful eye on the shark. She nudged a few fish in the direction of the predator, luring it closer. The shark took the bait. The dragon's head flashed down. There was a big splash, a swirl of blood, and the dragon's head came up with an eight foot shark dangling from her mouth. She spat it aside.

"That'll teach it to steal our breakfast," Linsha said dryly

The food helped the dragon and enabled her to fly most of the morning. She rested again around noon for several hours and flew on until sunset when the wind shifted and stiffened to a strong headwind. Clouds drifted overhead, obscuring the setting sun and bringing on an early dusk. Although the clouds did not bring rain, the wind brought a choppy sea and waves higher than Sirenfal liked. Like a half submerged wreck, she wallowed and rolled on the waves and spent most of the night trying to keep her body facing the fast moving waves so they did not roll over her. Neither she nor the women got much sleep.

When daylight came Sirenfal forced herself into the air and continued the journey. But Linsha could see her flying was a real struggle. Her wings did not beat as well and the wheeze in her breathing was worse. Most frightening of all, the wound caused by the Abyssal Lance was red and swelling. Linsha knew she had not been the cause of the redness and irritation, because she had made a determined effort to avoid sitting on the spot or bumping it. Something underneath the skin was festering.

"Sirenfal!" she called. "We need to turn further west to find the Blood Sea islands. Surely we are close to Karthay."

"I don't know," came back the dragon's exhausted reply. "I don't know where we are. The wind comes from the west. I don't know if I can fly against it, but I will try."

She veered more westerly and flew doggedly on against the wind. The sky was overcast and the air cool. The sea below had turned to shades of gray and green, streaked with foamy white from the tops of the waves.

Linsha wished she had more than a thin tunic between herself and the wind, but all she could do was huddle down with Callista as close to the warm dragon as they could. While they flew, Linsha scanned the sea from horizon to horizon in search of land or even a ship, but all she saw were endless leagues of empty rolling sea.

Hours later, it was Callista, looking far to the right, who spotted the small island. Urgently she tugged Linsha's arm and pointed to the dark smudge barely seen against the clouds and water. Linsha breathed a silent prayer of thanks and told Sirenfal.

The dragon needed no urging. Wingsore and breathing in jagged gasps, she dropped down toward the island that from above looked like a mere scrap of land. She didn't care how small it was. It was land that didn't rock or roll or try to swamp her. Weary beyond measure, she came down heavily on a strip of beach and waited just long enough for her riders to slide off.

Linsha and Callista ducked out of her way and stood aside to watch as she found a patch of sand to the leeward of a large dune and began to dig. Sand flew in all directions. With the last of her strength, Sirenfal dug a crater in the sand just large enough to hold her curled body. Tucking in her wings, she crawled into her nest, curled tightly around herself, and dropped into an exhausted sleep.

The two women looked at each other. It took them only a short walk to reach the other side of the island and a slightly longer walk to come to the end of the island. It was little more than a scrap of land with a cove, a slight beach, some dunes, and some rocks. That was all. No habitation or shelter. No food and no water.

A fter some diligent searching, Linsha and Callista found a few pieces of driftwood and some dried seaweed, enough fuel to start a small fire. Linsha used an old method her father showed her once that involved rubbing sticks together very quickly over a tiny heap of tinder to start a fire. It took a while to catch, but eventually they had a small fire burning in the shelter of the dunes. They roasted a fish Linsha had saved from the morning, ate some bread from their tiny store, and drank a mouthful of water. They took turns keeping a watch that night, mostly to prevent the fire from going out.

Morning came and the wind died. The clouds drifted to the east. The sun shone benevolently on the island, and the seas moderated. But Sirenfal did not wake up.

"Is she all right?" Callista asked worriedly.

"She's alive," Linsha reported. She checked the dragon's breathing and heartbeat, and ran her hand gently over the livid wound on Sirenfal's shoulder. "Is she all right? I don't know. This wound really bothers me. It's become much worse. We'll let her sleep. All we can do is wait."

They spent the rest of the day scrounging for more fuel

183

for the fire and food to eat. Callista finally washed the soot and blood from her body, and Linsha cut strips from her pants to make coverings for her bare feet. Sunburn and thirst plagued them all day, and tiny sandfleas bit their skin unmercifully. The women slept fitfully in the dunes again that night, hoping fervently Sirenfal would soon wake. The water was almost gone.

When morning came and Sirenfal still slept unmoving, Linsha decided to try to reach the dragon with magic. Her mystic powers of the heart were not particularly strong and magic was still unpredictable, but if she could do something to help the dragon even for a moment, it would be worth the attempt. She knelt beside Sirenfal, took the two dragon scales in her hand, and leaned against the brass's warm shoulder. While Callista watched, Linsha turned her concentration inward and focused within her own heart and mind. She felt the power surge through her blood and to her skin and muscles. The answering power of a much older force rose from the scales in her hand to join hers, and as one the magic flowed out of her hands and into the ailing dragon. Linsha's thoughts went with it. She spread the power outward into the dragon's body to heal and strengthen, but to her surprise she met resistance. A clump of darkness, an evil malignancy, lay close to Sirenfal's heart. It clung tenaciously to her like a deadly tumor growing steadily toward her blood vessels and her pumping heart. Linsha recognized the taint of the evil. It was the same foulness she had felt in the bolt cut from the Abyssal Lance that she had pulled from Crucible's back.

Oh, Sirenfal . . .

I cannot fight it, the brass spoke in Linsha's thoughts. *I have tried.*

What can I do to help?

You have already helped me. You freed me. Now I will do what I can for you while I still have life within me.

Linsha felt the dragon stir under her hands. Sirenfal was

coming out of her deep sleep. "No!" Linsha cried, deeply worried. "Stay asleep. Give yourself time to heal and recover."

There will be no healing. I will not leave you and your friend alone on this island to die.

The spell broke, and Linsha's link to the dragon faded away. She was left standing beside the brass, feeling helpless, inadequate, and close to tears. Sand sprayed around her, forcing her to step back, as the dragon rose from her nest and spread her wings.

"It's time to go," she told her companions.

"Sirenfal, you don't have to do this," Linsha insisted. "If you fly now, the damage will spread faster. The splinters are close to your heart. The physical effort of flying could move them to your heart that much quicker."

"We'll find another island. One with food and water. I won't leave you here." She curved her neck down and noticed several of her scales had fallen off into the sand nest. With surprising delicacy, she picked up a brass scale with her talons and dropped it at Linsha's feet.

Linsha stared at the pale metallic scale for a long moment before she picked it up. "Iyesta would have been proud of you, you know," she said, looking up at the young brass through a blur of tears.

"Um, Linsha, what is going on?" Callista asked. "Is she feeling better?"

Linsha decided not to go into detail and worry Callista that much more. Sirenfal was right. If they stayed on the island without water and adequate food, they were dead. They would just have to take the risk of flying and hope the dragon could reach more land before the lance splinters killed her.

"She wants to go now," Linsha said. "Get the dagger and the waterskin."

Together they buried the tiny fire, gathered their meager belongings, and climbed up the leg of the waiting dragon. As

185

soon as the two women were settled on her back, the brass took a running leap into the wind and beat hard to gain height above the ocean waves. The island disappeared behind them and the sea lay wide and vast below, sparkling in the morning sunlight.

For a long while Sirenfal flew silently, concentrating on forcing her wings to beat. She did not fly high but stayed low near the waves. This way, if something happened to her she would not fall to the sea from a great height.

Unfortunately the lower altitude did not give Linsha and Callista the best view of the sea, and Linsha was terribly afraid they would miss something. Her best guess was that they were near the chain of islands that separated the Blood Sea of Istar from the Courrain Ocean and that the tiny island they had landed on had been a harbinger of those islands. But if that was the case, where were the larger islands? They had been flying for several hours, and Karthay, Mithas, Kothas, or even Saifhum should have been in sight by now. But she could see nothing. There was only water and a large, empty horizon.

All at once Sirenfal lurched lower. Her head began to weave as if she could not see where she was going. Her wing beats faltered. She gave a low, keening cry of pain.

"Oh, gods," Linsha muttered. "Hang on!" she shouted to Callista.

The two women clung desperately as the dragon shuddered beneath them.

Although the dragon struggled to stay aloft, she could not fight her dying body. She dropped lower and lower toward the water until at last she stretched out her legs like a rudder, spread her wings as far as they would go, and coasted the last few lengths into the sea. Water washed up around the women in two large waves, drenching them both. When it subsided Linsha and Callista found themselves gasping and sitting on a motionless dragon half-submerged in the surging waves.

"Sirenfal!" Linsha cried. She dove off the brass's shoulder and swam to the head that floated in the water. She prodded and patted the dragon's nose and rubbed her forehead, but there was no response. The dragon's light eyes were half-open; they appeared dim and cloudy. There were no bubbles coming from her nostrils.

I'm sorry, came the softest whisper in Linsha's mind— followed only by silence and an emptiness that tore at Linsha's heart. The world rocked.

"*No!*" Linsha screamed. She beat at the dragon's head with her fist, flailed at the water, and bellowed her rage at the absent gods. "No! Not again! I've had it! I can't lose any more! Do you hear me? Stop it! Stop it! I can't take any more of this!"

The grief she had kept inside for so many friends suddenly came boiling out in a raging, uncontrolled paroxysm of emotion she vented to the cruelty of the gods in a screaming fit that lasted until she was hoarse. Finally her screams dissolved into deep, wracking sobs. She cried for what seemed uncounted hours, purging the grief she had locked away for Sir Morrec, Sir Remmik, the Knights of the Citadel, the Legionnaires who had been her friends, Captain Mariana, General Dockett and the militia, the centaurs, the people of Scorpion Wadi, Afec, and especially Iyesta and Sirenfal. She thought she had handled the deaths so well, keeping them closed in a dark chest in her mind, staying cold and professional while she needed to be. But this loss of another friend, another dragon, was more than her will power could control. She held onto the dead dragon's neck and poured her tears into the uncaring sea until she was drained and exhausted.

Callista sat on the dead dragon's back and stared open-mouthed at her. After a while, when Linsha's sobs had eased to exhausted, hiccupping spasms, the courtesan gritted her teeth and eased into the water. Holding on to the dragon's neck ridges, she pulled herself along the neck until she reached Linsha's side and gently took her arm. She pulled Linsha back to the dragon's body and helped her climb up out of the water. Both women were chilled and soaked, and they huddled together to stay warm until the wind dried their clothes. Callista gave Linsha the last sips of water from the water bag.

Linsha felt drained and weaker than a kitten. With Callista's help, she lay down on Sirenfal's upper wing vane and fell fast into a deep slumber. She slept through the rest of the afternoon, the evening, and well into the night.

She was still deep in sleep when a familiar voice drew her out into a dream.

Linsha, my beautiful one. Come talk to me.

She twisted her head around and saw him standing on the water near the dragon's wing. Starlight filled his form with pale light and glittered in his blue eyes. He saw her eyes open and gave her his roguish grin.

That's good. Come out of your sleep. You have cried your tears for all of us, but now you must look to yourself.

"I didn't cry for you," she said. "Good gods, Ian! Why do you keep coming to pester me?"

He tried to look affronted but it didn't work on his spectral face. *Pester you? I believe I warned you the last time and helped save your life.*

She snorted at him, not willing to admit he was right. "So how do you manage to visit me? I thought Takhisis had all the souls of the dead under her control or something like that."

Something like that, he agreed.

"Does she know you come to visit a Solamnic Knight?"

Her mind is busy elsewhere.

Linsha slowly pushed herself upright and looked at Ian Durne's ghost hovering close to Sirenfal's shoulder. "What do you want this time? I know about Lanther now—and surely there are no draconians out here."

Green Eyes, don't you ever appreciate me? He grinned, charming and handsome even beyond the grave.

Her eyes suddenly narrowed as a thought occurred to her. "Tell me, sir knight, did you know Lord Bight was a dragon?"

He laughed. *Not until he bit my head off. If I had known that, I would not have gone after him with just a sword.*

"Do you know where he is now?"

Do you mean is he dead? No. Do I know exactly where he is at this moment? No.

Linsha put her head back down and closed her eyes to hide the sudden surge of relief. "Fine. If you're not going to be any help, you may leave."

Something cold like mist trailed over her face, and she opened her eyes again to see Ian hovering very close to her. His features were clear and sharp as crystal in the starlight and the look on his face was sad.

I did love you in my own way, he told her softly. *But there is another who is far more worthy of you. Stay alive for him. Watch out for the sharks.*

Sharks? The word jabbed through Linsha on a shaft of fear. She bolted upright just as Ian's spirit faded into the night breeze. "Ian, wait!" she called, too late.

Beside her, on Sirenfal's other wing, Callista jerked awake. "Linsha? Who are you shouting at?"

Dazed, Linsha stared around her and realized that Ian was gone—if he had even been there. She was awake now, trembling in the chilly night, and wishing she were still asleep. Even talking to Ian in a dream was better than sitting on a sinking corpse in a vast sea while her body ached from hunger and her throat burned with thirst. She studied the sea around her hoping to see a dark mass of land, the white phosphorescence in breaking waves on a beach, or even the lights from a ship. All she saw was a tint of light on the eastern horizon foretelling the rising of the sun.

"Ian said to watch out for sharks," she said.

"Who is Ian and how could he be talking to you now?" the courtesan asked.

Linsha shook her head to clear the cobwebs in her thoughts. "Ian is a better friend as a ghost than he was as a man. I don't know. Maybe he's just a phantom of my dreams. But he has a point. Sirenfal's body will draw predators. We need to be higher."

"She's also sinking," Callista said, a note of fear in her voice. "I don't know how she stayed afloat this long, but I can see her body is deeper in the water."

They crept off the wing vanes and sat together on the highest point of Sirenfal's back, waiting for dawn. They were lucky in one thing—the sea was calm and the sky was clear.

When the sun rose, Linsha saw indeed that the dragon's body was slowly sinking. Her head and neck were under water and the waves lapped up her sides almost to Linsha's feet. Dismayed, Linsha racked her brains for a plan, for a course of action, for something that would help. What would she do with Callista when the dragon finally sank? The courtesan said she couldn't swim, and Linsha knew she could not hold up the younger woman for long.

A shark fin sliced through the water near Sirenfal's head and vanished underwater before Linsha could cry out.

She heard a sharp intake of breath and Callista's hand grabbed her arm. "Did you see that?" the courtesan hissed.

They both felt a sharp tug on the corpse. A dark shape flashed by followed by a second and third. Something swirled the water near the dragon's submerged tail, and Linsha turned to see two more triangular fins cut through the waves close behind.

"They're all around us!" Callista cried, close to panic.

The corpse twitched and rocked a little as the sharks tugged on the scale-covered flesh. Blood swirled in the water.

And blood, Linsha knew, would attract more sharks. Anger roiled in her mind. She had to sit helplessly by while these beasts of the sea tore the dragon apart. In time they would probably kill her and Callista as well. This was not the way she wanted to die. She had survived wars and battles and duels, plagues and invasions, wounds and spells. Was she to die now in the teeth of some mindless creature that felt nothing but hunger? She would never know what happened to Crucible or Varia, never see her parents again, never fulfill her vow to save the brass eggs. This was not right! There had to be something she could do to get herself and Callista out of this mess.

"Give me the dagger," she said between clenched teeth.

Callista promptly handed it over. "What are you going to do?" she asked fearfully.

"I don't know yet. Something."

But there was nothing she could do. She had no boat, no tools, no real weapon against sharks, no help, and no escape. She sat and watched the sharks swarming around the body of her friend and tearing it to pieces underneath her.

One shark squirmed over the tatters of a wing and wriggled too close to Linsha's feet. She looked down into its bleak, fathomless eye and stabbed it in the head. Bleeding heavily, it slipped back into the water and was immediately set upon by other sharks.

Callista began to cry behind Linsha's back. "You can swim. Get off when you can and make a break for it."

"For what?" Linsha said as calmly as she could. "I wouldn't make it ten strokes." She kicked at another shark that came too close and noticed the water was now halfway up Sirenfal's sides. She pulled up her feet.

Sharks splashed and squirmed on both sides, tearing pieces off the dead dragon. In a few places Linsha could see the bones showing through the ragged flesh. Her anger grew sharper with fear.

All at once the body belched forth a huge bubble of trapped air and dropped deeper in the water. Callista screamed. Both women crawled to their knees and balanced precariously on the back of the sinking corpse. Linsha shouted furiously and fought off any shark that came close.

She was so preoccupied with the gray fins and the slashing teeth around her that she did not see the other gray fins that flashed by and disappeared in the swells. Nor did she pay attention to the faint voice that called in her mind.

Linsha.

Callista lost her balance and slipped into the water. Screaming, she grabbed for any hold on the polished scales. Linsha snatched her arm and managed to haul her back on the dragon's spine. Both women clung to each other, panting and shaking as the sharks milled around in the water just an arm's length away.

Linsha!

Linsha heard the call this time as clear and welcome as a morning bell. Her head snapped up. Her eyes lifted to the sky. "Varia?" she cried in disbelief. She turned her emotions inward and converted them to a mental cry for help, a cry she prayed her friend would hear. *Varia! I am here! Hurry!*

"What is it?" Callista demanded.

"Help," was Linsha's answer. "I hope."

Then the sea was filled with more gray fins, but these fins were shorter, rounder, and curved. The animals that swam beneath them were fast and sleek and utterly fearless. They charged into the midst of the feeding sharks and slashed and rammed them time and again with their powerful noses. Linsha and Callista stared down in disbelief as dolphins killed several sharks and harried the determined survivors that refused to leave their meal.

The significance of the presence of dolphins dawned on Linsha like the hope of a new day. Rising unsteadily to her feet, she looked to sky and saw a small shape come diving down. It was too small to be a dragon, but it was the right size to be an owl with brown and cream feathers.

"Varia!" Linsha shouted in delight.

The owl looped around her, singing an aria of warbles and trills and screeches of pleasure. She soared up and dove again to come spiraling downward in a flight of joy.

Suddenly there was a great roar and a huge splash behind Linsha. Startled she turned around and saw all the sharks were gone. The only creatures left in the water were the dolphins and—she slowly lifted her eyes—one large bronze dragon. He floated in front of Sirenfal's corpse, his wings half furled like sails and his bronze scales shining with water and sunlight. He lowered his head to look at her, and in that moment she stared into the depths of his amber eyes.

Her heart skipped a few beats; her head grew dizzy. Without thinking about sharks or Callista or Varia or Lord Bight, she jumped in the water and swam to his side. Without a word, he lifted a front leg so she could climb up his shoulder and wrap her arms around his neck. She pressed her face against his wet scales and felt her gratitude, hot and intoxicating, surge through her soul. He was alive and he had come for her.

"Crucible, I can hardly believe it," Linsha said, stunned by the effort he had made. "How did you find us?"

"Varia said you had been taken to the Tarmak's homeland," he explained. "She told me where to go. Fortunately my dolphins found you first."

"Thank Kiri-Jolith they did. We weren't going to last much longer."

"Who is this?" Crucible asked, nodding to Sirenfal's corpse.

Linsha realized he was veering away from any discussion of their parting or of his human identity or anything that might mar the moment of their reunion. She did not care.

She was so happy to see him and be back in his company that she did not want to talk about any of that either. In time they would have to, but not now, not while the joy of the rescue was so strong in her heart.

"Her name was Sirenfal. Lanther had her trapped on Ithin'carthia. He killed her eggs and experimented on her."

Crucible swam slowly around the remains of the brass while the dolphins frolicked and leaped around him. "Did she get you off the island? How did she die?"

"Ah," a small voice called from the back of the floating corpse. "That's a really long story. Do you think you could get me off before Linsha starts it?"

"Who are you?" the dragon asked.

Varia swooped low and hooted with pleasure. "Callista! You're here!"

"And I would not be here without her," Linsha said with a grin. "Please get her off. She can't swim."

"With pleasure," replied Crucible. He swam close to the dead dragon and extended his powerful front leg for the courtesan to climb over. Callista tossed the leather bag holding the stolen text to Linsha and stepped gingerly onto Crucible's leg. As soon as she was sitting safely on his shoulders behind Linsha, he veered away.

"Crucible, please do something for her," said Linsha, indicating the dead brass. "She doesn't deserve to be left to the sharks."

He made a sharp squealing noise that made the dolphins back away then took a deep breath and closed his eyes to concentrate. A brilliant bolt of fiery white light exploded from his mouth and played over the dead dragon.

The light was so intense that it forced Linsha to shield her eyes. She did not see the eruption of steam and bubbles as the bronze's breath hit the cool water and the corpse. She heard an odd noise as the body disintegrated in the beam of sizzling light. When she opened her eyes and looked at the place where Sirenfal had been, there was nothing but clouds of steam.

"Thank you," she said. She and Callista exchanged glances of mingled relief and wearied sadness.

Then Linsha raised her arm in an invitation to her long-lost friend, and Varia came swooping down to accept. She landed on the Rose Knight's wrist and sidestepped carefully up her arm to sit happily on her shoulder. Linsha buried her face in Varia's warm feathers and inhaled the owl's familiar scent.

"Thank you to you, too. I was not ignoring you."

"I know," the owl replied. "I can bide my time." She gently nibbled Linsha's ear. "It's just so good to see you alive."

"I think we all have stories to tell."

"And lots of time to tell them," said Varia dryly.

Followed by his pods of delighted dolphins, the bronze dragon turned in the water. Using his powerful tail, he began the long swim for the Plains and the Missing City.

At Linsha's plea, Crucible swam directly to the nearest island, a large mountainous chunk of land called Karthay, the northernmost island of the Blood Sea chain. Linsha was dismayed to learn it was only half a day's swim from where they had landed in the ocean. If Sirenfal had lasted a mere half-day longer, they would have made landfall. Not that it would have helped prolong the dragon's life, but at least she would not have died thinking she had failed Linsha and Callista.

They found a small cove where a stream poured down from the mountains into the sea, and they made camp that night in the shelter of a rock outcropping.

The women bathed in the fresh water, drank their fill, and filled the water bag while Varia went hunting. For dinner that night they ate roast duck and wild berries and finished the last of the Tarmak bread. It was, Linsha decided, one of the best meals she had ever had.

Late into the night they sat by a large fire and talked, telling their stories of escape and rescue and friends. In a small place behind her pleasure in the evening, Linsha wished Crucible would change into his human form so she could see Lord Bight. But he did not. He crouched by the fire beside her, his large body acting as a windbreak for the wind that swept in from the sea. Perhaps he did not want to chance her ire this night, or perhaps he did not have the strength.

"I still do not fly well," he told her. "Danian healed my wounds and repaired my wings, but he said it would be months before I could fly long distances, and even then there has been too much damage to expect a complete return to my normal flights."

"Then how did you come so far?" Callista asked, marveling at his journey.

"I swam most of it. I can fly short distances, then I have to swim."

"Have you had any ill effects from the barb?" Linsha asked. The death of Sirenfal rode heavily in her mind that night, and the thought that there might be splinters left in Crucible made her queasy with dread.

He shook his head. "None that I know of, besides an ache between my shoulders once in a while. Danian said you must have removed the entire thing. How did you know how to do it?"

Linsha's eyes fell to her hands in her lap and the scars that still discolored her palms and fingers. "Iyesta came to me in a vision at the Grandfather Tree. She gave me two leaves from the tree and told me I could help you."

The dragon dipped his head in thanks and gently nudged her. "But tell me what happened to you? I thought you were with the other centaur and he would bring you."

Once again Linsha told her tale from the battle on the Red Rose to the death of Sirenfal. She told him and Varia about the Tarmaks, Malawaitha, the Akeelawasee, and Afec. She thought for a moment about skimming over Lanther and their marriage, but she knew Crucible had to know that it happened and why, so she told about that too, as well as the death of the dragon embryo and the experiments done on Sirenfal. Crucible sat quietly through the entire telling without interrupting, and when she was finished he continued to sit and contemplate the fire.

Varia, on the other hand, could not contain her anger at Lanther or her joy that Linsha was free of him.

Linsha cast a worried glance at the enigmatic dragon and gently ruffled Varia's feathers. "What happened to you?" she asked. "How did you get away from the Tarmaks?"

"That was easy," the owl said disdainfully. "They kept me in a cage in the headquarters and put a warrior in charge of me who was being punished for something."

"One of the dog warriors?" Linsha asked curiously.

"Yes. I just waited until late one night when he was not paying strict attention as he fed me and I removed part of his finger. When he pulled his hand out, he didn't close the cage door fast enough and I flew out. Once I made it out of the city, I went to find Crucible."

"How did you know where to find me?"

"I listened to the Tarmaks. They talked about the Drathkin'kela going to Ithin'carthia to marry the Akkad-Dar and I knew it had to be you. Then, one afternoon, I heard your voice call me."

Linsha sat up a little straighter in surprise. "What? When?"

They counted the days and the hours, and Linsha remembered the night she had fought Malawaitha and sent a mental cry into the night. She and the owl looked at one another and smiled in wonderment.

"Would you have gone all the way to Ithin'carthia, if we hadn't escaped?" Linsha asked Crucible. She tilted her head to look at his horned face in the firelight.

"That was our intention," Crucible said, his deep voice a muted rumble in his chest. "You saved my life. I could not leave you there to suffer slavery or worse."

"But all the way across the Courrain Ocean?" said Callista. "That's incredible. You must really—"

Linsha abruptly reached across the courtesan for the leaf bowl holding the last of the berries and bumped her hard with her elbow, cutting off the words Callista was about to say next. "Not now," she muttered sharply. It seemed obvious to her that Crucible did not want to talk about anything more than simple subjects. If that was the case, then the last thing she wanted to discuss in front of Varia and Callista at this time was his feelings and motives for helping her. She wondered now if he had come to her rescue out of a lingering affection and respect for Iyesta and an ordinary obligation to the person who pulled the bolt from his back. After all, hadn't he just said so?

Callista stared at her curiously, but she finished the sentence with, "You must be really tired."

The dragon remained silent, his deep amber eyes glowing with firelight.

"Since you have seen Danian," Linsha went on, a little too brightly, "I am guessing Wanderer's tribe still survives?"

Varia bobbed her head, her "ear" feathers stiff with the importance of her news. "Oh, yes! That man is cleverer than a desert fox. He has a hidden fortress deep in the desert that the Tarmaks haven't found yet, and he's been gathering all the remaining warriors from tribe and clan to wage a clandestine war against the Tarmaks. Falaius is with him and the remaining militia."

"What about Sir Hugh and Leonidas?"

"Leonidas is fine. He took Crucible out of the battle to find Danian then stayed with Wanderer's group. There are some fine looking fillies there that I think have caught his eye."

"And Sir Hugh?" Linsha prompted.

Varia blinked and reluctantly answered, "I don't know where Sir Hugh is. He did not return after the battle and he has not shown up anywhere."

"He's dead?" Callista gasped.

Varia blinked again. "I don't know. I heard in the Tarmak headquarters that a large group of prisoners and slaves had been brought back for the Akkad-Dar. Maybe he is there."

"We will have to look for him when we go back for the eggs," Linsha announced.

Owl, woman, and dragon looked at her in surprise, but no one said anything about her plan, not yet anyway. They were all too tired and the night was growing late. While Callista curled close to the warmth of the fire and Varia found a perch on Crucible's back, Linsha crawled up to the dragon's warm side and lay down beside him as close as she could get. He peered down at her for a little while until she was asleep, then he curved his neck and tail around her and enclosed her in the protection of his body. He slept, too—deep and well for the first time since the day she had disappeared.

The next day they left Karthay on wing and flew south as far as the island of Mithas before Crucible had to rest his wings and swim. The bronze dragon was an excellent swimmer and had the streamlined body, the powerful tail with the webbed ridges, and the webbed feet that enabled him to move quickly through the water. He usually swam underwater, but with the two women and the owl on his back, he stayed on the surface and cruised south like a dragon-prowed warship, dolphins racing playfully beside him. Even on the surface he could still move faster than any man-made ship, and he had the great southern current to help speed him along.

By flying and swimming, they covered the distance to the island of Elian that sat poised at the northeastern edge of Malystryx's domain, the Desolation. Since they had no idea where Malys was, they decided to spend the night on the island, to rest, and gather stores, and leave before dawn the next day. The only way to avoid Malys's domain—and hopefully Malys's attention—was to swing wide to the east around the Desolation, then move southwest over the vast open expanse of the southern Courrain Ocean where the great southern current met the colder northern current flowing up from the Ice Wall to the distant south. The weather tended to be rough in that area, and the seas were often turbulent and dangerous. Crucible wanted to fly over as much of the region as he could bear so he did not have to inflict any rough weather on the thinly clad women. If all went well, they would be able to reach the eastern shores of Silvanesti in two days.

Luck for once was with them the next day. The weather remained balmy, and a steady wind from the north helped carry Crucible south across the expanse of water. They saw no sign of Malys, and the only ships they spotted were several large Minotaur warships that hovered on the horizon and quickly vanished to the west. Crucible made no attempt to chase them. Twice he had to land to rest his wings, but the waves remained moderate, and he was able to cover many leagues by using his tail for propulsion and his wing vanes as sails. They reached the elf realm of Silvanesti after nightfall of the second day, coming to shore on the long, narrow peninsula that was the easternmost tip of the elves' realm.

Varia told Callista and Crucible about the fall of the shield that had once surrounded the elven realm and the invasion of the Knights of Neraka, and Linsha told them about the destruction of Qualinesti by the great green dragon, Beryl, and the exodus of the elves across the Plains of Dust to their kinsmen in Silvanesti. They had fled the devastation of their homeland, not knowing the disaster that had befallen the forest.

Callista's eyes were huge as she listened. "What has happened since? Where are the elves now?"

"We heard that many are scattered, refugees with nowhere

to go," Crucible replied. "Some have gathered and are marching north toward Sanction."

Linsha winced when she heard the note of yearning in his voice. He desperately wanted to go back to his city, to learn its fate, to stand in the way of its oppressors. Yet he hadn't. She wondered why.

"We have heard rumors, too," said Crucible, "mere whispers on the wind, that Khellendros is dead, killed by Malys."

Linsha and Callista were stunned by the news. "Can it be?" Linsha whispered. The great dragon overlords were falling one by one. If only Malys would be next.

On the fourth day of their journey, Linsha insisted they stay on the beach where they had landed to give Crucible a day of rest. He had pushed himself very hard, and she could see he was exhausted. The bronze must have been in worse shape than she thought, for he did not argue but curled into a sandy nest and slept most of the day.

Meanwhile, Varia went on a reconnaissance flight and Linsha and Callista spent the warm autumn day napping and gathering crabs for supper. They saw no elves or Dark Knights on the isolated beach, and for that they were grateful. Linsha just wanted solitude and peace for one more day.

The weather changed the next day, taking a turn for the worse. Clouds gathered to the south, the heralds of an autumn storm, and the wind changed direction from the north to the southwest. Crucible had originally planned to fly over water so he could swim if he needed to, to reach the Plains, but when he smelled the ice on the wind and felt the changing pressures in the air, he decided to fly directly over a part of Silvanesti, past the city of Phalinost and the Towers of Eli, and hug the coast the rest of the way to the Plains of Dust. It meant more flying and the risk of being spotted, but it would be faster.

"And where do you plan to land?" Linsha asked, when he told her his plans that morning.

"Somewhere on the Plains where we can find shelter."

"What about Mem-Thon? It's close to Missing City and the villagers might be willing to help us."

"It was *too* close to Missing City," Crucible said in a loud grumble. "The Tarmaks wiped it out. They also set up a garrison at Sinking Wells and destroyed the entrance into the Scorpion Wadi. There is nowhere safe to go around Missing City. I am taking you to Falaius."

"Falaius!" Linsha felt a surge of temper. "I won't hide in some fortress buried in the middle of the desert!"

Crucible rose from his nest and stretched his wings before he said in a tone of real reluctance, "He's not in the fortress. He and Wanderer are bringing an army south through Thunder's old realm. The Tarmaks are spread thin through there and do not expect an invasion."

"What?" Linsha snapped. "Where are they going? Why didn't you mention this sooner?"

Callista and Varia watched the exchange for a moment and both quietly left for a more peaceful stretch of beach, leaving Linsha and the dragon to their argument.

"They are going to attack the Tarmak army before Lanther returns. They're hoping I will return with you before they meet the Tarmaks in battle."

Linsha felt a flush of heat in her face and a fiery hot ball of anger in her gut. "And you didn't see fit to tell me until now? Is this a habit with you? What other things are you not telling me? What is the matter with me that you cannot trust me? Is it because I am a mere human that can't be trusted or respected enough to be included in your important plans?" She marched up to his chest and yelled up at him, her anger radiating from every word. "Well, I don't care who is planning to attack the Tarmaks or who expects us to be there! Nor do I care where you go! I'm going to Missing City to get those eggs out!"

"Of course I trust you," he tried to say, "I just—"

"The blazes you do!" she yelled at him. "Turn back to Lord Bight and tell me that to my face!"

A sudden light flared across the dragon's scales, and Linsha jumped back in surprise. She hadn't really expected him to shapeshift to his human form, yet as she watched a brilliant, coruscating cloud of light enveloped him and transformed him from a large, four-legged dragon to a tall, two-legged man. When the magic had run its course and the light faded, Linsha saw standing before her the man she had once thought was firmly ensconced in Sanction. An odd feeling rocked her senses, and her rebellious heart began a slow pound. Gods, he was just a handsome as she remembered—tall and well muscled, his hair and beard a deep shade of gold, and his face elegantly chiseled. But it was the eyes that captured her and held her still. They gleamed like sunlight through amber, and in their depths she saw the same wisdom and character she had seen in Crucible's eyes.

He held up a hand as if to stop any accusation she might make. "I am sorry that I did not tell you the truth about my work as Lord Governor of Sanction. I kept my identity a secret for so many years by not trusting anyone, and since I did not know you well at first, I did not tell you."

Linsha barely nodded. That much she could understand. Her anger slowly abated. Looking at the man face to face, looking into Crucible's eyes, she could not sustain her hurt and rage at him. The man and dragon were one and the same. If she could forgive one, she had to be able to forgive the other. She would not be Gilthanas, doomed by his own pride. She held still and did not trust herself to speak.

"Later," he went on with a sigh, "I suppose I did not handle that as well as I should have. I have been posing as a man for many years, but I still do not fully understand human emotions where women are concerned. I became so close to you as Crucible, I did not want to jeopardize that by telling you I was also Bight. I see now that was a mistake. I should have trusted you to accept me in all my forms."

"Yes, you should have," Linsha said. "It would have made your lordship's appearance in the middle of a battle a little easier to accept. I would have known what to expect instead of learning for the first time that the man I respect and admire is also the dragon I love."

He inhaled sharply, unsure if he understood what she meant. "What about Lanther?"

Her expression turned severe at the mention of his name. "What about Lanther?" she shot back.

"You married him."

Linsha threw up her hands. He certainly had some things in common with human men. "Were you listening when I told you about Lanther? I hid nothing from you. I had the choice of marrying him or being left for his officers and men. Which would you prefer? The marriage has not been consummated and never will be. I think widowhood would suit me better!"

"I will see what I can do," he said softly. On its own accord, his hand lifted to her face and cupped her cheek in his palm. "I have learned much about you these past few months, and you are not a 'mere human.' You have more skill and talent and honor than many dragons I know."

He moved a little closer until the warmth of his body touched her skin. Linsha felt herself trembling as her muscles slowly melted in the heat of his nearness. She leaned her cheek into his palm and did not take her eyes off him.

"I promise there is nothing more I haven't told you. I didn't tell you about Wanderer's army from the first because, to be honest, I don't want to take you there or to the Missing City. I would rather take you far out of harm's way, because I really don't know if I can bear to—"

His words were cut off by a shout.

"Dark Knights!" Varia screeched. She came winging

205

back followed by Callista, running as fast she could in the sand. Close behind her raced five Knights of Neraka, intent on catching such a fine prize. They saw the second woman and an unarmed man and whooped with the thrill of an imminent capture.

Lord Bight snarled. He broke away from Linsha and spun around to face the charging knights. "Get behind me!" he ordered.

Linsha felt a powerful wrench at their separation, and the anger Lord Bight had fueled in her resurfaced and found another target. She laughed. "I've been fighting jealous Tarmak women in the Akeelawasee. These are boys in comparison."

Just as Callista reached them, Linsha dashed forward toward the nearest knight. The look of triumph on his face turned to surprise as she ran at him without a sword or a shield or a spear. Jamming to a halt, she dropped to her side in the sand and kicked his feet out from under him. The knight fell heavily. He tried to roll out of the way, but a second knight tripped over him, fell, and dropped his sword. Lord Bight snatched up the weapon and decapitated the man with a powerful swing of his right arm.

The remaining four men shouted with anger. The first knight on the ground tried to get up. He made it to his knees before Linsha clambered onto his back, wrenched the dagger out of his sheath, and stabbed it deep into the base of his neck just above the collar of his breastplate. She didn't wait for him to die before she jumped to her feet and went after a third knight. By that time it was too late. Lord Bight might have been in human shape, but he still possessed a more powerful strength and speed than any normal man. He killed two knights before they had a chance to defend themselves, and he turned with a roar on the last knight. The knight, terrified out of his wits, took to his heels and ran for the woods where more knights surely waited. Linsha flipped her dagger around, grasped the blade carefully, and threw it at the knight. It was a good throw, but it bounced off his armor.

Grinning, Lord Bight said, "This is better," and threw his sword. It caught the running knight between the shoulder blades, pierced his body to the hilt, and threw him several feet before he hit the ground, quite dead.

Linsha looked around at the dead knights in satisfaction. That would teach them to interrupt an important conversation. Unfortunately, it was a conversation that could not be continued now. These knights had probably been part of a talon on patrol. There would be more knights on the beach very soon. It was time to go. She saw the glow of light on the sand and stared up as Lord Bight shapeshifted back to Crucible. The transformation still amazed her.

Varia fluttered down and came to land on her shoulder. She peered around Linsha's tousled hair to see her face. "Are you all right?" the owl asked hesitantly.

"I am not angry with him—or you—if that's what you mean. I just wish one of you had seen fit to tell me, or warn me." She pushed a strand of hair out of her eyes and touched her cheek to Varia's warm feathers. "I don't think I will ever forget that shock of seeing Crucible turn into Lord Bight and knowing I could lose both of them."

"He would not let me tell you," Varia explained. "Iyesta did not tell you either, because she felt Crucible should be the one. She never laughed at you, Linsha. She always approved. I think that's why she asked you to defend the eggs. She knew Crucible would be there to help you."

Linsha gave a scant nod and bent to examine the dead knights. "I am still going to Missing City, with or without him, to get those eggs."

"I know," Varia said, "And so does he."

Linsha gestured to Callista to help her, and together they took two cloaks, a clean wool tunic, a pair of boots, a small pack full of trail food and utensils, a long knife, a sword, and a scabbard off the dead knights. Everything else they left because it was either too dirty or the wrong size. Body robbing was not something Linsha often indulged in, but this time she felt it necessary for their survival. She gave the dagger to Callista along with a cloak and the bag of food. She discarded her own filthy silk tunic, put on the warmer one, and secured it with the knotted belt Afec had given her.

Varia almost fell off her shoulder trying to see the knotted belt. "Where did you get that?"

"The Damjatt, Afec, made it. He gave it to help protect me from spells of the Keena priests. I don't know how well it works."

Varia chuckled in her throat. "Knot magic is *very* old. It is not strong, but I think it can ward off minor spells and abate more powerful ones. This Afec was a clever man."

"Yes, he was," Linsha said with fondness. She considered showing Varia the tome Afec had given to her then decided to wait. There wasn't time to explain the whole of her misgivings. She pulled a boot over her bare foot. "Now what can you tell me about this army that is marching toward the Missing City?"

"They've already defeated one army of Tarmaks in a battle. They're well organized, well led, and determined. They're trying to break the grip of the Tarmaks on the Plains. They don't really want the city, because their army is not big enough to take it. But if they can lure the main Tarmak army out and defeat it before the reinforcements arrive, they hope to free Duntollik at least."

"Then they'll be happy to know the reinforcements will not be here for a long time." Linsha grunted as she pulled on the other boot. She jumped to her feet. "Time to go."

The two women and the owl hurried to the dragon and climbed onto his back. Wasting no time, the bronze dragon crouched on the sand then sprang upward with a mighty leap that flattened his riders to his back. His wings swept down, and he was airborne, beating westward toward Missing City.

"Are you sure that is where you want to go?" he asked Linsha after a long silence. "I could take you anywhere. Even Solace."

"The eggs are in the city," Linsha said from the depths of her warm cloak. "I have seen them. I have also seen what the Tarmaks do to them."

"So have I," Crucible growled, resigned to her decision. "We'll go get them."

Into the City

17

Slipping into the Missing City was easier than Linsha expected. Although the Tarmaks patrolled the streets regularly and imposed a curfew on the inhabitants, there were not enough warriors to observe every back alley and hidden entrance into the city, and none of the Tarmaks knew the city as well as Callista and Linsha. Under cover of a steady cold rain, they came in through the ruins on the north side where the old city wall still lay incomplete. They found shelter in an abandoned house not far from the more populated Port District. They were lucky to find a house with a cellar, and while the food and stores had been cleaned out long ago and the roof of the house leaked, the cellar was dry and out of prying eyes.

Linsha wanted to start out right away to find the building where she remembered the eggs were housed, but Lord Bight said no. It was night outside and the Tarmaks would be patrolling for curfew breakers. What the four of them needed and needed badly was rest. They were all exhausted from the long journey. Everyone would think better if they had some sleep. Linsha was too tired to argue. They found a few old sacks and some moth-eaten blankets and bedded down on the cold earth floor.

Lord Bight eyed the floor and the thin burlap bags, then he winked at Linsha and stepped back to shapeshift. When the light died away, an orange tomcat stood before them. Purring happily, he snuggled in between Linsha and Callista and settled down like a furry bed warmer.

Linsha chuckled sleepily, "Dragons."

Linsha woke the next morning to a weight bouncing on her chest and a soft hooting noise coming from somewhere close to her face. Her eyes opened and she saw what she had longed to see every day she woke alone in the Akeelawasee—two large dark eyes surrounded by creamy feathers and a ring of darker feathers that looked like spectacles. Varia saw her eyes open and bounced again on her chest. Against her side and arm she felt the warmth of the sleeping cat.

She smiled sleepily at the owl. "Do you know how much I missed that?"

"A great deal, I hope, but I wanted to tell you Callista's gone."

Linsha sat up. "What?" She looked all around the cellar and did not see the courtesan anywhere. A dim daylight filtered down through the floorboards and from the open cellar door, but there was no sign of the young woman. Her cloak and sandals were gone. "Did you see where she went?"

"No, I was still asleep. I admit I did not hear anything."

"Where could she have gone?" Linsha scrambled to her feet and snatched a cloak, preparing to go out and find the courtesan.

All the rustling movement and voices woke the cat. He sat up with a big yawn and surveyed Linsha with golden eyes. *What are you doing?* he asked in her head.

"Callista is gone. I'm going to find her."

Give her time. She'll be back. Yawning again, he curled up to continue his nap. *She knows the streets well, and she is not as obvious as you are to the Tarmaks.*

There was some sense to what he said, so Linsha sat down beside him to wait. She would give Callista about an hour, then she would go out to find her.

Linsha promptly fell asleep again with Varia perched on her knee keeping watch.

The woman and the cat slept for nearly two more hours before Callista returned. Walking softly down the stairs, she gestured to someone behind her to follow her down. She slipped quietly into the cellar.

Linsha woke instantly and prodded Crucible the cat awake.

"Linsha, I brought a friend I thought could help," Callista said, waving at her cloaked companion to come closer. The person under a long, heavy cloak nodded to Linsha and pushed the hood back from her face.

Linsha smiled and jumped to her feet. The woman before her was in her late forties, as far as Linsha knew, of medium height, and wore her long red hair tied in a tight bun behind her head. Although she worked as a baker and was well dusted with flour from the baking that morning, for fifteen years she had been a member of Falaius's circle of Legionnaires working undercover in the city as a spy and a gatherer of information. The woman recognized Linsha as well and greeted her with pleasure.

The three women sat down together on the bags. Varia took a perch on a nearby empty cask, while the cat crawled into Linsha's lap and lay there quietly purring.

"I'm sorry if I gave you a start this morning," Callista said, "but I wanted to catch Mae before she left the bakery this morning. I thought she could tell us what is going on in the city right now."

The Legionnaire shook some rain off her cloak and

nodded. "I'm so pleased to see you alive, Lady Linsha. The last we heard, you were being carried away on their ships." She stopped, poised in mid-thought. "Does this mean the Tarmaks have returned? There were no ships in the harbor, but—"

Linsha hastened to reassure her. "Callista and I escaped. We came back a different way."

"Thank the gods for that. We know the return of the Akkad-Dar is imminent, but we are hoping for more time." Mae hesitated, looking from one woman to the other. "What? What you grinning about?"

"The Tarmaks' reinforcement fleet was destroyed," Callista told her, and she went on to explain about Sirenfal and the dragon's revenge on the Tarmaks.

Mae's face glowed with relief and pleasure. "The Tarmaks here don't know that yet. They're still making preparations for the Akkad-Dar's return. They're waiting for him to come back before they go out to face the rebel army."

"They'll have a long wait," Linsha said, "But I know Lanther will be back as soon as he can. All we have done is buy Falaius and Wanderer a little more time."

"We should let them know," Mae said thoughtfully. "It might change their strategy. I'll have to send a messenger."

Linsha shot a questioning look at Varia, who fluffed her feathers and nodded. "I'll send the owl. She would be faster, and she knows Falaius. All you have to do is tell me where the army is."

Mae described an old trail that bordered the easternmost branch of the Toranth River. "They are either near the river or headed toward the city."

"Good. As soon as I can write a message, I'll send her along," Linsha said, knowing full well Varia would be able to tell Falaius everything.

They talked more about the Tarmaks and the state of the people in the city. "The Tarmaks are doing a lot of rebuilding, particularly on the wall and in the harbor. They

213

use townspeople, prisoners, elves they've captured—anyone they can get their hands on. There have been no caravans in months, and only a few, selected merchant ships are allowed to land. Most of the food has been taken and hoarded by the Tarmaks, and many of the cattle have been stolen from their rightful owners. In fact," Mae said pointing a finger at Crucible, "be careful of your cat. Cats and dogs have become more popular on the dinner table these days."

Linsha chuckled and poked the tomcat in the ribs. "You hear that? Watch your scruffy hide or you'll end up in a stew pot."

Scruffy? Crucible grumbled. *Who are you calling scruffy? Have you looked in a mirror lately?*

"So—" Linsha turned serious again— "what can you tell me about the Treasurers' Guild building? I need to steal something in their vaults."

Mae looked surprised. "You came back here to steal money from the Treasurers' Guild? Why? There's hardly anything left. The Tarmaks kicked the guild out as soon as the Akkad-Dar returned from the Plains campaign."

"Not coins. Eggs. A clutch of brass dragon eggs. Lanther has them in the vaults under the watch of the Keena."

A light of understanding crossed Mae's face. "Ah, that explains the heavy guard on the building. We thought the priests were just using it as a temple or something."

"You keep saying 'we,' " Linsha said. "Are there more of you in the city?"

Mae's expression turned grim. "Only a few of us who were deep undercover. Most of our circle is dead. A few were captured in the field and are held in the slave pens, but there are not enough of us to free them."

"There are not enough of us," Linsha said, waving a hand at her small group, "to steal a dozen dragon eggs. We need a diversion, horses, a large net—"

"A net?" Mae interrupted. "What are you going to do with a net?"

Linsha shrugged, scratching the cat gently behind his ears. "Carry the eggs out of here. As you can see, we need a little help. Are there any slave pens near the Guild building?"

Mae still looked confused, but she didn't pursue it for now. The entire idea of stealing dragon eggs from the Tarmak intrigued her. "Yes, there's one nearby. They use the people in there for slave labor repairing the buildings and the harbor facilities. There are some militia soldiers, a few centaurs, a group of elves, and . . . oh, yes . . . one Knight of Solamnia."

"Hugh?" Callista and Linsha said at the same time. It had to be. As far as Linsha knew, he and she were the only two surviving Solamic Knights left on the eastern Plains.

Mae nodded, pleased she had been able to drop her own surprise into the conversation. "Tell me what you have in mind and I'll see if we can arrange it. It may take a few days."

"Of course," Linsha said. "I want to do this right the first time and get out." She was thrilled Sir Hugh was close by. With some good luck and good planning, they would be able to rescue him and the eggs in one night.

***

They found out that evening that there were three Legionnaires left in the Missing City who had not been caught or killed by the Tarmaks. They gathered one by one in the cellar of the abandoned house, bringing clothes and food and water, and staying to listen to Linsha and Callista tell them about the Tarmak island, Lanther, and the destruction of the Tarmak fleet. Varia, meanwhile, left shortly after nightfall to find the rebel army, and Crucible slipped out to do a little reconnaissance on his own.

When he came back late at night, he found Linsha on watch and Callista asleep on their blankets. Wearily he stretched out between them as before.

"What did you see?" Linsha asked. She stroked a hand down the soft fur on his side.

Mae is right. The building is heavily guarded, and those black-robed priests are everywhere. But I think with some archers and a good distraction, we can get inside. The problem will be timing. We need enough time to secure the eggs, carry them outside, and get them loaded in the net.

"Hmm. It's too bad Falaius and Wanderer are too far away. Have the Tarmaks dealt with a good fire lately?"

I don't know. I shall try to arrange one.

Linsha's mouth turned up in a small smile and her cheeks flushed a charming pink. "As much I like cats, do you think you could be Lord Bight for just a little while?"

The cat moved away from the two women and was quickly engulfed in the shimmering bright light of his magic. He changed back to the man who had been the Lord Governor of Sanction for almost thirty years and stood before Linsha with his hand held out to her like a supplicant.

Linsha unfolded her long legs and rose to take his hand. They moved away from the sleeping courtesan and sat down together side by side against a far wall. In soft voices they talked long into the night of inconsequential things, of her family and Sanction, of things they remembered from the summer of the plague when Linsha served in the governor's personal bodyguard.

"If I ever get back to Sanction," Lord Bight said. "I will need a new Captain of the Guard. Should you decide the Knights of Solamnia are no longer enough for you . . ."

Linsha was startled by his words. No longer enough? She hadn't thought of that. In fact she had concentrated so much on escaping Ithin'carthia and reclaiming the eggs that she had not thought about anything that might happen after this war. As far she knew, she would be on the Plains until the Grand Master relieved her or she died, whichever came first. And what about Crucible? Would he really leave her to return to Sanction? And what would she do with the eggs? The questions and the possibilities swarmed over her, until she wanted to scream. Not now! She could not think that far ahead. First they had to rescue the eggs and get them safely away. Then they had to deal with the Tarmaks. Then maybe, if they both survived, they could think about what next.

"Not now," she murmured. "Not now."

He opened his mouth, and she silenced him the only way she could think of. She leaned over and kissed him.

Egg Hunt

18

The next day the Legionnaires moved them to another place in a different part of the city to avoid drawing attention to movement around the abandoned house. They were led through backstreets and dark alleys to a door leading down into a deeper cellar where ale barrels stood empty and a few wine casks still sat on their racks. Several cheeses and an old ham hung from the ceiling beams and a bin of dried apples sat close to a wooden stairs that led up to a public house.

"It's the Orchard House," Linsha exclaimed. "I remember the proprietors. Delightful people, and the wife made the best apple pies."

"Why thank ye, Lady Knight. I remember you, too. Always paid your bill." A gray-haired woman leaned down from the upstairs door and squinted at her secret guests in the dim light of a single lantern. "There's not much left down there. The Tarmaks killed my man and ate me out of house and cellar. But you're welcome to anything you find. Just keep it quiet while there's customers in the bar."

Linsha and Mae waved their agreement and thanks, and the old woman stepped back and closed the door behind her.

"She said you can stay down here for a few days while we gather the weapons and work out the details," Mae said. "We have some men in hiding from the Tarmaks we will send to you to help. Do you know what you want to do for a diversion?"

"How are the Tarmaks organized to handle fires?" asked Linsha.

"They have our old fire fighting equipment—the ladders, the buckets, and the one hand pump. But we always counted on Iyesta to help us put out any fires in the city, so there is very little available to them. It's rained so much lately, I don't think they've given it much thought."

"Good. Is there a warehouse where they are storing anything worth burning?"

Mae's eyes twinkled and the laugh lines appeared around her nose and mouth. "They have a lot of their stores in a warehouse near the waterfront, but it's really too close to the guild building to be a good distraction. There is another one over in Mirage where they have stored much of the wine and spirits they stole from the farmers and merchants."

Linsha looked at Callista who grinned. Mirage was the name of the newer section of the city where many of the offices, warehouses, and shops connected to the harbor were located. The older guild buildings were mostly in the older city in the Port District.

"Wine and spirits," the courtesan said. "That should burn well."

Linsha looked down at the cat in her arms and winked.

<hr />

Three days later a cloudbank rolled up out of the south and settled over the Missing City in a dank, gray gloom. Darkness came early that night, and the citizens of the city hurried back to their homes and their meager meals, leaving the streets to the Tarmak patrols. By midnight, the streets were almost deserted.

Few people saw the large shape in the sky and no one saw where it came from. It swooped down from the clouds and hovered silently over Mirage for a moment. There was a brilliant streak of light like lightning, a thin clap of thunder, and the shape was gone as suddenly as it appeared. None of the Tarmaks who saw it could identify it because of the clouds and fog, but a few guessed it was a blue dragon from the burst of lightning. Others doubted they had seen it at all. It was probably just an errant storm cloud. What they couldn't doubt was the sound of warning bells. Smoke was rising from a warehouse in Mirage. Within moments the smoke became billows and the flames licked high through the roof. A massive explosion rocked the building and sent flaming debris flying in all directions. Smaller fires ignited on the roofs of nearby buildings and on a storage shed filled with fodder. Alarms bells rang throughout the city.

The Tarmak *dekegul* in charge of the city's forces collected his men and marched out of the old city to the harbor district to fight the fires. He took several dozen slaves with him to help, but he left the slaves in the large pen by the guild houses under guard, deciding they would be more trouble than it would be worth to take them along. They had a bad habit of trying to escape.

The prisoners were sheltered in a series of pens and stables that had once been a livestock market. Seeing the glow on the rooftops, they came out of their stalls to observe what was happening and were startled to see two women brazenly approach the pair of guards at the main gate. Both women were cloaked, and one carried a pie. One of the prisoners, a thin, haggard young man dressed in rags, nearly choked himself on a cry of recognition.

The taller woman said something in Tarmakian that caused the guards to laugh. She walked forward, arguing in a loud voice and gesturing with the pie as if she wanted to give it to someone. Just as the guards reached for the pie, she heaved it into the face of the nearest guard. The two women acted at the same time. The smaller one pulled out a crossbow from under her cloak and shot the second guard while the tall one pulled two throwing knives out of her belt and killed the guard with pie in his face and a third guard that came running.

Suddenly there was a swarm of movement all around the slave pen. Dark clad men slipped in to kill the remaining Tarmak guards quietly and quickly, and before the slaves really knew what was happening their rescuers threw open the gates and urged them to come out.

Linsha dashed into the pens. "Sir Hugh!" she called softly. "Are you here?"

Laughing and crying at once, the thin man in the rags came forward to hug her. "Gods, Linsha, I thought you were dead!" he cried. "And Callista! You are a sight for tired eyes. And . . . who are you?" he asked when a tall, blond man came to stand by Linsha.

"Lord Hogan Bight, this is Sir Hugh Bronan, Knight of Solamnia. Sir Hugh, this is the Lord Governor of Sanction. But you might know him better as Crucible."

The knight blinked. He knew he was tired and sick and not at his best and brightest, but surely she didn't mean what she said.

"It's a long story," she said dryly. "But now we need your help—all of you. We are stealing some brass dragon eggs that the Tarmaks took from Iyesta. If you help us, we will do our best to help you get out of town and join Falaius's army that is headed this way."

The slaves, made up mostly of prisoners of war, cheered raggedly. A few melted silently away into the darkness to make their own way out of the city, but the majority—nearly twenty men and centaurs—stayed. They quickly stripped the dead guards of all their weapons and dragged the bodies into the stalls. They also liberated a few horses housed in the stable. With a little luck the Tarmaks would be too busy to notice the pens were empty of slaves until it was too late.

Four male elves approached Linsha and Lord Bight and bowed low. "We will go with you," the eldest said, "for no dragon eggs should be held by these Brutes. But once we are out of the city, we would like to go on to Silvanesti."

Recognizing them as Qualinesti elves, Linsha returned their bow. "You may stay with us as long you wish. But you should know that the Knights of Neraka hold your kinsmen's Forest."

"Yes." The speaker sighed. "We learned that the hard way. We were trying to escape from the Dark Knights when the Brutes caught us just outside Mem-Ban."

Mem-Ban was another village located on the border between Iyesta's realm and the Silvanesti Forest, not far from the King's Road.

The elves, Linsha noted, were all young and had the look of warriors about them. She guessed they were stragglers from the main body of elves that had crossed the desert some time ago. Perhaps they had stayed behind in Qualinesti as part of a rear guard and only recently reached the Forest. What a welcome they had received, she thought.

Gathering together the freed slaves and the Legion men, Linsha led her small band toward the stone building that once housed the Treasurer's Guild. The building was constructed from the image of the original two-story edifice that had stood in the old elven city of Gal Tra'Kalas. It was an elegant design with large windows, columns on the front portico, and spacious rooms for the guild members to meet and socialize. Beneath the guildhouse was a large vault, waterproof and strong, built specifically to hold the steel and coins of the city treasury and the personal funds of the members of the guild. The treasury had been stripped,

Linsha knew, and much of the steel, gold, and silver had been sent to Ithin'carthia or spent by the Tarmaks on weapons, ships, and mercenaries. The only things of value in the vault now were the eggs. Or so Linsha hoped. She had not seen the eggs since the very brief viewing Lanther had allowed her before they sailed. But their placement looked permanent, and Mae had said the Keena were still using the place. Surely the eggs were still there.

In the deep shadows of an adjacent workshop across the street, Linsha and her company found Mae and the other two Legionnaires waiting for her. Looking pleased with themselves, they opened the wide doors of the shop and revealed a wagon hitched to two horses. Mae pulled back the canvas and revealed bows, which the elves and the centaurs happily took, and some swords and axes for the others. They also had a large bundle wrapped with canvas resting in the back of the wagon.

Linsha outlined their plan to the released slaves and watched in satisfaction as they spread out to obey her orders. Mae and Callista climbed into the wagon and took the reins to wait for the signal. For a few minutes, Linsha, Sir Hugh, and Lord Bight waited in the darkness for the attackers to take their position.

In that quiet moment before the attack, Linsha listened to every sound and she heard something she had not noticed before. Sir Hugh was having difficulty breathing. His lungs wheezed with every breath, and he was trying very hard to stifle a cough.

She moved close and said softly, "You are not well. Stay in the wagon with Callista. I will not lose you now."

His teeth shone pale against his bearded face as he smiled. "I have a cold. That is all. You will not deprive me of a little revenge for these past wretched days. Besides, seeing you has given me strength. You must tell me what has happened, and why you say that man is Crucible."

223

"Fair enough," she agreed. She pulled up her hood. "Ready? Stay behind me, both of you."

Tilting her chin up to its most arrogant angle, she stifled the nervousness in her stomach and marched out of the shop and into the street. The fire had been a distraction for the warriors in the city, but Linsha and the two men were to be the distraction for the priests and guards at the guildhouse. She walked boldly up the middle of the street where the Tarmaks could plainly see her. She behaved as if she had every right to be there and knew exactly what she wanted. It had worked before.

"Orgwegul!" she shouted in Tarmakian before the guards could challenge her. "Where is the Orgwegul?"

The guards by the front door hurriedly conversed, then shouted something inside. A heavily-armed officer came out. "I am the orgwegul," he said. "Do not come any closer, woman."

Linsha threw back her hood and revealed her face and hair. "You will use a more respectful tone to the Chosen of the Akkad-Dar," she snapped. "I am the Drathkin'kela and I have come to see the eggs."

The guards straightened and lost the sneering expressions on their faces. "The Akkad-Dar has returned?" the officer demanded.

"Of course," Linsha replied as if it were perfectly obvious. "He came ahead on a faster ship. We landed just a little while ago. But he is busy at the fires, and he gave me permission to see the eggs. I have the key." She pulled the key out on its chain and held it up for him to see.

"And who are those two?" he sneered, eyeing the disreputable looking men behind her.

"My slaves and bodyguards, of course. They were all that was left. Everyone else is fighting the fire."

The Tarmak officer stared thoughtfully at the distant glow on the roofs of the buildings in the distance. He could not see the harbor from where he was standing, so he could not confirm that a new ship had arrived. But he recognized the auburn-haired woman and the key to the egg vault. "Very well," he grunted. "You may approach."

Just then a black-garbed Keena stepped out onto the portico. "What is going on here?" he demanded.

Linsha and her bodyguards moved closer while the officer explained her errand. She held up the key for the priest to see.

But he didn't look at her. He shot a look in the direction of the harbor. "But that can't be," he said, confused. "The Akkad-Dar's ship was spotted just a little while ago. He couldn't have landed yet."

Linsha felt as if someone had just kicked her in the stomach. Lanther was coming! By all the absent gods, how did he get here this fast? Her anger blew high. He was not going to deprive her of those eggs. Not when she was this close.

"Now!" she bellowed. She, Hugh, and Lord Bight threw themselves to the ground as a flight of arrows flew past them. The three Tarmak guards and the priest were killed instantly. Linsha rolled over and unstrapped the two swords she had carried behind her back. She tossed one to Hugh. Behind her she heard shouts and the clash of weapons. Bows twanged and someone screamed. There was a rumble of wooden wheels on stone paving, and she knew the wagon was on its way. Half a dozen freed Legionnaires and the elves ran out of the darkness and joined them.

"Come on!" she yelled to Hugh and clambered to her feet.

"What about him?" Hugh shouted, pointing to Lord Bight, who stood quietly on the street.

Linsha grinned. "He's busy."

Linsha and Hugh dashed into the building, followed by the men and elves. They met immediate resistance in the long central hallway where the guards and priests were charging out of various rooms and side halls. The small company fought well, but there were more Tarmaks than Linsha expected and this was taking too long. She ducked into a side room and signaled to her forces to fall back.

"Down!" she yelled. "Take cover!" Then she shouted out the door, "Now, Crucible! *Now!*"

The fighting abruptly stopped as a large draconic head appeared in the door. The Tarmaks and humans alike gaped in surprise. The dragon inhaled, and the humans and elves dropped to the floor. A brilliant white light shot down the hall and exploded on the Tarmaks. Once, twice, and again Crucible fired his breath weapon over the heads of the attackers, wiping out clusters of Tarmak warriors and priests. Smoke curled from the walls and the hall filled with the stench of burning wood, scorched stone, and cooked flesh. The hallway became silent.

More of Linsha's men ran in the door. "The guards are dead outside," a Legionnaire reported.

"Let's get the eggs," she said tersely. "Lanther is coming." She caught Hugh staring at Crucible's form just outside the portico.

"Where did he come from?" the knight asked in astonishment.

She just laughed, a sharp, edgy sound of tense humor. "I'll tell you later."

The company of egg hunters continued through the building to the stairs that led down to the vault. More Tarmaks attacked them, but there were very few warriors left, and those were disorganized and scattered. The Legionnaires and the few militiamen spread out to find the remaining guards while Linsha and her group hurried downstairs. They entered a stone hallway and found the way barred by half a dozen Keena priests. The black-robed Keenas held round bucklers and short swords.

This would be good time for some of Afec's sleeping powder, Linsha thought. Without that, they would just have to do it the hard way.

"Back away!" she yelled down the stairs. "All we want are the eggs!"

A priest yelled something back that Linsha did not have to translate to the others.

The elves fired a barrage of arrows down the steps that wounded a priest, killed another, and scattered the rest. Under cover of the arrows, Linsha and her men charged down the stairs. The remaining priests fought zealously, but they were outnumbered by the ferocious rebels. The fighting was hard and bitter in such close quarters, and when it was over the priests and four of Linsha's company were dead.

Cursing, she plunged her sword into the throat of the last priest and stepped over his body. She drew out of the key and thrust it into the lock, praying it would work. It did. The key turned, the lock opened, and the door swung open. A wave of heat washed over her. She caught a glimpse of firelight and glowing braziers when a hand reached through the door and grabbed her sword arm. A second hand clamped to her face and wrenched her inside. The door slammed shut behind her.

Pain exploded in her head.

L insha gasped, her head reeling. The pain seared through her, shaking her resolve and stoking her fear. She tried to see who was speaking to her, but her vision was blurred and unsteady. All she could see was yellow light and a dark arm extending away from her. Sweat poured down her face and into her eyes, making her vision worse.

"I am Shurnasir, Priest of the White Flame and guardian of the dragon eggs," a voice snarled at her. "Who are you that you dare disturb the peace of this sacred place?"

She gritted her teeth and fought back her fear. This was not Lanther. This was a mere priest, a second rate Tarmak, and like the Keena at the imperial palace, this priest did not have the same skill or strength that either Akkad had shown. The pain ebbed a little. Perhaps Afec's belt was interfering with the magic that pounded at her head. Linsha did not know why the pain would be abating, and at that moment she did not care. She forced her hand upward to the three dragon scales that hung around her neck. They were heavy and sometimes irritating to her skin, but never had she been more grateful for them. She focused on the inherent power within each one and drew it forth, leeching out the magic of three different dragons.

"I am the Drathkin'kela and those eggs are mine!" she croaked.

Her other hand dropped the sword and clamped around the priest's wrist. His eyes opened wide with surprise. His spell snapped and he fell back, crying with pain. She held onto him, bending his hand back in an unnatural angle, forcing him to his knees. Her green eyes turned to flint.

"How many eggs are here?" she snapped.

His face screwed up in agony and his reddish skin turned pale. "Nine," he croaked. "The Akkad-Dar took two with him."

"That bastard," she swore, unconsciously putting more pressure on the priest. Something snapped. He moaned and flopped to his side. Linsha let him go, for at that moment she noticed the eggs. "They're different! These are darker and duller," she said. "Where are the brass eggs?"

She hauled the priest to his feet again and shoved him close to a hot brazier that glowed under a metal tray containing a layer of sand and one egg.

"We've been treating them," the priest admitted. His eyes rolled back to see the brazier and his hands plucked nervously at her wrists.

"Treating them? Treating them with what?"

There was a tremendous shout in the corridor and the door slammed open. Sir Hugh and the rebels charged in prepared to rescue Linsha. When they saw her, her expression fearsome and her prisoner well in hand, they skidded to a halt in relief and surprise.

"What have you been treating them with?" Linsha repeated. She glanced at the soldiers around her and nodded. Several hurried away.

"I don't know," the priest gabbled. "A mixture the Akkad-Dar gave us."

Linsha threw up her hands, shoving him aside. "Kill him," she said to Sir Hugh. "He won't cooperate."

The knight drew back his sword to strike the priest, but Shurnasir cowered down. "All right! We're treating the eggs with a special potion to make them hatch faster."

Linsha couldn't believe her ears. "Is that possible?" she asked the elves.

The four Qualinesti studied the eggs for a moment, looked at each other, and shrugged. "We have never heard of such a thing," one said.

"But they do look as if they are ready to hatch," commented the elder. "I have seen a clutch of brass eggs at this stage and they hatched within days."

"Why would you do this?" Linsha demanded. "Those eggs aren't supposed to hatch for years. You could be destroying the embryos."

"Not so far," the priest said, a touch of smugness creeping into his voice. "We have examined several the past few months, and their progress has been excellent."

Linsha's anger flared again. "Examined them!" she exclaimed. "I've seen your examinations. It's a wonder there are any left at all! Why would you do this?"

He quailed back from her anger and the power he felt in her. "The Akkad-Dar wants them to hatch early so he can use them."

"Use them for what?"

Sir Hugh glanced uneasily out the door and said, "Linsha, I think we need to take those eggs and go. If Lanther is really on his way, we don't have much time."

The reminder was like a bucket of cold water dashed on her head. Her temper cooled and reason returned. Her head still throbbed from the priest's spell and her own surge of magic, but she knew Hugh was right. There was still much work to do. "Tie him up. We'll let Lanther deal with him."

The priest's eyes grew huge, and he groaned. He scrambled to his feet and bolted for the door. Two arrows struck him at the same time and sent him spinning to the floor.

Linsha nodded to the elves. "That was probably far kinder than anything Lanther would have done to him," she said.

The company quickly got to work. Linsha found a pair of heavy gloves, and using those to lift the eggs from their hot nests, she placed them carefully on heavy wool blankets. The eggs were wrapped, put in thick feed sacks, and carried gently outside. When the last egg was removed, Linsha took a final look around the stone vault. Sir Hugh stood beside her, his face flushed as if with a fever.

"You know, you were rather scary," he said. "I've never seen you that angry."

"Dratted eggs," she said, rubbing her aching temples. "They're worse than children."

He laughed. "You'll be a good mother."

"The gods forbid," she said, turning on her heel. "Those eggs aren't supposed to hatch for years."

She pulled the door behind her and just before it swung completely closed, she tossed the key inside.

———————

"Those eggs will hatch in a matter of days," Crucible snarled when Linsha stepped out the front door. "What happened to them?"

Linsha told him what the priest had said while she walked around the bundle of eggs. The three undercover Legionnaires had done a fine job, she noted. They had brought a large fishing net, as well as the blankets and bags, and while the eggs were being brought up they had spread the net out on the ground and piled on more blankets. Now the eggs were securely tied in a tight, warm bundle in the middle of the net, ready to be carried out.

Crucible grumbled at the Keenas' unprecedented experiment, but there wasn't much to be done about it except get the eggs away.

"Can you manage it?" Linsha asked, worried for his wings.

"Of course. They are not that heavy."

They heard the clatter of hoofbeats and saw some of their centaurs come along the street with a string of horses. The elves and the men quickly mounted. Those too wounded to ride were loaded in the wagon with Callista. Mae stood beside the wagon, holding the horses' reins.

She handed the reins to Sir Hugh and joined her two companions. "Good-bye!" she called. "Good luck."

Linsha was startled. "Aren't you coming?"

"No. We agreed. We're staying here. We can help more in the city and gather better information this way. Tell Falaius we're here, if he needs us."

Linsha and Callista waved farewell just before the three Legionnaires disappeared into the mist and darkness.

"Let's go!" Linsha called. She climbed onto the wagon seat beside Sir Hugh. The mounted men and elves, the centaurs, and the wagon headed north on a road that led into the Artisan's District and eventually out of town.

Crucible waited until the horses were out of sight before he sprang aloft. Carefully he grabbed the net with his feet, lifted it above the roof line, and winged into the foggy night.

Run for the Hills

20

The Akkad-Dar stood at the threshold of the Treasurer's Guild and frowned. Dead guards and priests lay slumped on the floor, on the front portico, and in the halls. Blood was everywhere. The front hall was a scorched mess, littered with burned debris and scattered bodies. Some of the bodies had been stripped of their cloaks, weapons, boots, or clothes, and several piles of tattered rags lay on the floor.

Lanther kicked one ragged tunic with his toe, knowing full well what it meant. Beside him, the city *dekegul* stood silently, making no excuses.

"So," the Akkad-Dar said in a voice edged with steel, "the bronze dragon is still alive. Good. I can kill him myself." He strode into the hall and worked his way through the mess to the stairs leading down to the vault. He knew what to expect, but he wanted to see for himself. The *dekegul* went with him. They walked down the stairs without saying a word and studied the devastation below.

"These priests were brave, I'll give them that," Lanther muttered. He stepped over the bodies and pushed open the door. The emptiness mocked him. The eggs were gone, every one of them. There were only empty trays and the body of his chief priest lying on the floor.

A small shape caught his eye and he leaned over to pick it up. It was the key he had given his wife on the day of their joining. A cold smile flicked across his face, and he pocketed the key for safekeeping. He would give her that key back soon, he vowed.

He turned around and nearly bumped into his silent officer. He cursed, about to raise his sword and behead the fool for falling for such a trick, but he paused and gave it some thought. "Be at ease," he said at last. "Better men than you have been outwitted by that woman. Be responsible for her capture or the capture of the bronze dragon, and I will let you live with your honor. Fail and you may kill yourself."

The *dekegul* nodded his appreciation for the second chance. They were very rare from the Akkad-Dar.

Lanther stalked back upstairs and went outside, away from the smells and the scenes of loss. By the graciousness of the Dark Queen, he prayed for vengeance on his stubborn, treacherous, perfidious wife and that vile dragon that held her affections in a way he had never been able to do. They couldn't go far, he knew that. The eggs were heavy and had to be kept warm. They would have to find a place to keep the eggs safe until the hatching. And of course, there was the rebel army that was obligingly marching toward the Missing City. With the help of the Dark Queen, his beloved goddess, he would be able to rid the Plains of their army and rid himself of Crucible at the same time.

"Bring me the Abyssal Lance."

───────────────

"This isn't good," Linsha muttered beside Sir Hugh. She scanned the blackness on both sides and saw nothing. "This reminds me too much of the ambush when Sir Morrec was killed. All we need is the rain." A cold, queasy feeling settled into her stomach at the memory of that night. She never wanted to repeat it in any manner.

"Are you thinking they will ambush us?" Hugh asked in a voice just above a whisper, while keeping his eyes on the draft horses pulling the wagon.

Although the fog, the late hour, and the fire in the warehouse district had served to cloak their escape, the Tarmaks were not completely lax. Several patrols had already attacked, and they had been forced to slow down and fight their way through the dark streets. They had finally entered the ruins of the North District where many of the streets and buildings had never been rebuilt and the old city wall still lay in ruinous disrepair. There were no lights in this part of the city, no torches or lamps or fires, only eerie shadows and the fogbound darkness of night. The wagon and its escort had to slow down even more to avoid injury to the horses. There was only one road that had been repaved and repaired to serve as a highway out of the city, but it was difficult to follow in the mist, and to either side lay treacherous sunken holes, half-buried foundations, and heaps of rubble.

"It's possible," Linsha replied. "There are surely warriors by the wall, even if the wall isn't complete. The Tarmaks are fanatical about setting guards and keeping watch. They would have heard the warning horns, and they know this is one of the few roads out of the city."

"They can see the glow from the fire, too. Maybe they'll think that's the problem?"

Linsha continued to peer into the darkness. "It's too bad Varia went to find Falaius."

Sir Hugh looked up. "Is Crucible still flying up there?"

"I don't know where he is."

They rode on in tense silence, listening to the moans of the wounded in the wagon behind them and the clatter of hooves on the old road around them. The thick mist began to settle in a light drizzle that quickly soaked clothes and chilled the skin.

Linsha, Crucible's warning spoke in her mind. *There are Tarmaks ahead. Stop where you are.*

"Stop the wagon," Linsha ordered. "Everyone stop. Now!"

The wagon and the riders drew to a nervous halt. "What is the problem?" asked the eldest elf from the back of his small horse.

A gust of wind blew over them and they caught a glimpse of a large, winged shape flying in the mist overhead.

"Crucible sees something in front of us," Linsha replied in a hushed voice. "Since they're not too close, he can deal with them."

They waited, not daring to move or even breathe too loudly in the dense blackness.

A horn blew one single note before it was cut short by an intensely white beam of light that shot through the clouds and mist somewhere on the road ahead. There were muffled shouts and sounds of confusion. A second beam seared from the sky to the ground, creating more chaos.

Crucible called to Linsha again. *Go, now, while the Tarmaks are disorganized. There is only so much I can do while I'm carrying the eggs.*

Linsha gave the order, and the troop started out once more. They urged the horses into a canter in spite of the road and hurried as fast as they could through the ruins. They reached a curve, followed it around, and there in front of them was the smoking ruins of a Tarmak patrol. A few bodies lay sprawled on the ground, and the two large wagons that had been used to block the road burned furiously. The troop pushed on without a second glance. A stray arrow flew at them from the scattered Tarmaks in the ruins, but that was all. There was no sound of pursuit from behind.

The foundations of the old wall appeared before them, and they saw a crude stone gate, a watchtower, and a small group of sentries who raised their bows and drew the strings to their cheeks. Then the tower, the sentries, and a section of the wall vanished in a bright explosion of fiery light and thunder. Smoke billowed up into the mist.

Linsha blinked in the sudden light, and when she could see again, the portion of the wall was a smoking ruin.

"He is very useful to have around," Sir Hugh said, "Now that he can fly again. I take this to mean you got that bolt out of his back."

"Yes," Linsha said, as they drove past the wall. "With a little help from the Grandfather Tree."

"When will he leave for Sanction?"

Although his comments sounded terse to her, from what she could see of his face in the dark, he looked cold and fatigued. She reflected for a moment about his words and what he was not saying. "Are you angry about the Scorpion Wadi? You were there, weren't you? We thought for a while you had been killed."

"Fellion, I, and a little girl were the only ones who survived the massacre and the capture." He hunched forward over the reins and glared at the night. "He should never have left, Linsha. No city is worth that many deaths."

"No, it's not. But he's not clairvoyant, Hugh. He never thought the Tarmaks would do that. None of us did. His first loyalty was to another city that needed him, a city he called his home. So he left, thinking we would be all right for a while."

"And what about now? Is he going to dump those eggs somewhere and leave again?" He stopped and listened to his own question. Eventually he wiped his damp face with his sleeve, and sighed. "Could I sound any more petulant?"

She smiled at him in the dark, relieved by his change of mood. He really was exhausted. "You could add a little more whine."

He coughed hard but managed a smile. "You will have to

tell me what has happened to you—and to him." His voice dropped into sadness. "And what happened to Mariana."

"I will tell you everything when we have a few hours of peace. For now, we need to put as much distance between us and that city as possible. If Lanther really is here now, he will be after us with all the warriors at his command."

"Lanther," he said. "The traitor. I can still hardly believe it."

Linsha did not reply. Her shock at Lanther's betrayal had worn off the past months, mostly because of her constant proximity to him and the Tarmak people. But what had not worn off was the hurt and the outrage that he had so thoroughly deceived her to the detriment of everything she held dear in the Missing City. Crucible had deceived her about his identity, too, but whereas he had hidden his human shape out of the mistaken concern that she would hate him for his lie, Lanther had hidden his monstrous self in the desire to harm. She could forgive Crucible. She would never forgive Lanther.

She glanced back into the wagon bed and saw Callista wrapping a crude bandage around a man's slashed leg. The other wounded men were either unconscious or groaning on their rough pallets. The wagon jostled them over the rough road, but no one complained.

They continued their journey through the night, taking a northerly course along the old rutted road that wound its way through the Rough, the rocky, scrubby grasslands on the outskirts of the city. A few miles beyond the end of the Rough, the road broke into a path that forked east and west. The company came to a halt, and some distance away Crucible flapped down to lay the net of eggs on the ground. He landed heavily beside them and tucked his wings against his sides. The weary riders dismounted to give their horses a rest.

Callista earned the gratitude of one and all by revealing a supply of water, trail food, and a bottle of homemade blackberry brandy that Mae had left for them in the wagon.

They passed the bottle around to salute their escape and the liberation of the eggs.

The four elves drank their share and came to make their farewells to Linsha and Sir Hugh.

"We must part ways here, Lady Knight," the oldest said. "We shall go find our families."

"Although your undertaking is so intriguing, it is hard to leave," quipped a younger one.

The eldest elf nodded, his fair hair wet against his head. "Do you know yet where you will take the eggs?"

"Away from the Tarmaks," she said.

"If I may make a suggestion, there is an old volcano called Flashfire to the west. It is only about two days' ride from the source of the river. Perhaps the dragon could make a nest there that would be defensible and dry? Those eggs need to be settled as soon as possible."

Linsha bowed low in gratitude. It sounded like an excellent suggestion.

The elves said good-bye to their fellow prisoners, bowed to Crucible, and trotted their horses onto the eastern path where the sun would soon rise. The heavy mist quickly swallowed them.

"Did you hear that?" she said to Crucible.

The dragon rumbled an assent. "I don't know the volcano, but I will look for it. It might suit the eggs well. Will you come?"

Looking at the men around her, at Callista and Sir Hugh, Linsha felt torn. She desperately wanted to stay with the eggs, but she had been responsible for freeing these men and centaurs. She had promised them she would help them escape if they came to help her get the eggs. She did not feel it would be right to leave them now, with days of travel still ahead and the Tarmaks in pursuit. She would at least see them to the safety of the rebel army. "I have to stay with them," she said, hoping Crucible would understand.

Her decision did not please him, but he did understand. She was a Knight of the Rose. She could not do otherwise. "I will be back," he said. Rising on his wings, he lifted the net of eggs and flew west toward the headwaters of the Toranth River and a suggestion of a volcano.

The rest of the company shared a quick meal and did what they could for the four wounded men in the wagon. One had died of his wounds during the flight from the city, so they piled rocks in a cairn over his body and left him behind. At dawn they hurried across the open grasslands while the sun lightened the sky to the east.

Varia found them the afternoon of the second day of their journey. She came wheeling from the sky with a hoot of welcome and swooped in to land on Linsha's outstretched wrist. Hopping off, she perched on Linsha's knee and blinked up at the Lady Knight with wide, dark eyes.

A few of the men stared in astonishment at the raptor on the woman's lap, but most of them were familiar with Linsha and her talented "pet" and continued to ride without comment.

"I have seen Falaius," Varia said softly, so only Hugh and Linsha could hear her over the rattle and creak of the wagon. "He was so pleased to see me, he gave me a whole rat. He wants to know what you are planning."

"Where are they?" Linsha asked, scratching the back of the owl's neck.

Varia clicked her beak with pleasure and bent her head so Linsha could reach every part of her neck. "Coming south down the eastern Toranth River. They're planning to ford the river in the next day or two, as soon as the water becomes shallow enough for the baggage wagons, and then strike eastward. They want to lure the Tarmaks out of the city. But how do you get those Brutes to come to a place of your choosing?"

"Tell them where the eggs are," Sir Hugh said.

A glint of deviltry gleamed in Linsha's eyes. "That would do it."

"Where are the eggs?" the owl asked. "And where is Crucible?"

Linsha pursed her lips as she thought about Varia's news, the eggs, and the probability of Lanther's fury. She twisted around and studied the faint tracks unwinding behind their wagon as they moved over the wet ground. It had rained in fits and starts for two days, making the earth soft beneath the hooves of the horses. They had tried to hide their tracks and finally decided it was a waste of time. The ground was just too barren and too muddy. The only thing that would help would be cold weather to freeze the ground, but the late autumn had been surprisingly mild so far. The centaurs, natives to the plains, told her when the warm weather ended, it would probably end with a snowstorm.

"What are you looking at?" Varia hooted, peering around Linsha's cloak.

"A way to lure Lanther to the eggs," she replied. "Are you too tired to fly again?"

"I just need a short rest," the owl replied, fluffing her feathers.

"Good. There here's what I want you to tell Falaius." She explained carefully, while Sir Hugh and Varia listened, and when she was finished both man and owl approved.

While Varia fluttered down into the bed of the wagon to sit with Callista out of the wind and take her nap, Linsha turned the reins over to Hugh and hopped out of the wagon. She jogged over to a centaur she knew only as Mennaferen. He was a grayish roan stallion of middle years, with reddish hair, deep brown eyes, and the long, powerful legs of a runner. He had seemed very steady to her, and he looked to be in the best condition of the escaped slaves. He glanced down at her jogging beside him and slowed to a walk so she could keep pace with him.

"Would you be willing to take a message to Crucible?" she asked.

"Of course, Lady," he said in a deep, smooth voice. "Where has he gone?"

She told him of the elves' mention of a volcano somewhere near the source of the river. His grave expression never altered.

"My clan is from the north, but I think I have heard of such a place."

"If you can find it, tell Crucible to go seek Falaius, and tell him we are going to turn northwest."

"Are you going to lure the Tarmaks away from the new nest?" Mennaferen asked.

"Yes—and into a battle, I hope." Linsha said, "so take an indirect route."

"Then I will go." He bent low and winked at her. "But don't have the battle without me." He said his farewells to his companions and galloped away.

The other riders and centaurs, about fifteen in all, gathered around Linsha to learn what was happening. She told them her plan.

"Make no effort to hide your tracks," she said. "We want Lanther to follow us."

"And what if he catches us?" one man said.

She lifted her hand to her sword hilt. "Then we'd better make sure we are close to the rebel army."

"How do we know the Tarmaks will leave the city and come after us?" asked another.

Linsha's mouth tightened into a thin line and her expression turned bleak. "I know the Akkad-Dar. He's probably already left."

"Perhaps, Lady," said a light bay centaur with a sword

cut on his flank, "it would be wise to leave a scout behind who could watch the rear and warn you if the Tarmaks are coming."

"That's an excellent idea," she said, glad he had mentioned it. "Do you feel well enough to volunteer?" She hated losing another good archer, but the centaurs were the best choice for scouts.

"Of course." He stamped a hoof, ready to go.

Pleased, Linsha returned to the wagon and climbed back onto the driver's bench beside Hugh. The party moved on, and a short while later the bay centaur fell back into a cluster of treeless hills and vanished into the eroded valleys between. The wagon and its escort began a gradual drift to the north. By evening they were traveling northwest toward the river but away from the eggs. If all went well, the Tarmaks would follow them to a place that Wanderer and Falaius chose, a place where a battle could be fought and won.

A second wounded man died that night in spite of Callista and Linsha's best efforts. His wounds had not been bad, but the constant travel in a rough wagon and the cool, wet weather had taken too much from him. They concealed his body in the deep crevice of a large rock outcropping and piled more stones on top. Instead of lightening the load of the wagon, they added rocks to the wagon bed to maintain the weight and the illusion of a load. They pressed hard the next day, knowing there were still many miles to go. Neither Varia nor the centaur scouts returned, and all Linsha could do was worry.

Sir Hugh distracted her for a while by asking for her tale of Lanther and Ithin'carthia, and he told her about his capture, the terrible long march back to the Missing City, imprisonment, and slavery. He had changed, Linsha realized, in the time since he had tried to intervene for her during her trial those long months ago. Was it only months? It felt like years. All sense of boyishness in Hugh had disappeared. He was harder, withdrawn, and more angry. His once muscular body was tempered to lean muscle and bone, and sometimes when he moved, she caught glimpses of scars and whip marks on his legs, arms, and neck. What would he do, she wondered, if he survived this war? Would he stay in the Solamnic Knights? Was it all worth the pain and suffering? She didn't ask him, but the thoughts stayed in her mind like an insidious weed, and she heard Crucible's words again in her memory—*Should you decide the Knights of Solamnia are no longer enough for you* . . .

By the gods, what was enough?

On the fourth day, Crucible came, winging from the clouded sky to the west. He came without net or eggs, only an expression of satisfaction. His scarred wings backflapped carefully and lowered his bulk to the crown of windy hilltop some distance from the nervous horses.

To prevent the wagon team from bolting in fear, Linsha climbed down from the wagon and ran to join the bronze on the hill. Hurrying to him, she could not help the smile that lit her face.

He lowered his head to greet her and inhaled her scent with pleasure. "I found the volcano," he said as they walked side-by-side paralleling the moving wagon. "It is an old one, but the cone is still there and I found some lava tubes and an ancient chamber that I rearranged to make a spacious nest. They will be warm in there for a while."

Linsha was pleased. She knew building a nest for brass eggs would not be a problem for him. He had tamed the ferocious forces of the three volcanoes around Sanction, allowing the city to grow and thrive, so he certainly had the skill and power to manipulate one old, extinct shell. She had just worried that he would not be able to find anything suitable. The volcano had been a gift.

"Do they still look close to hatching?" she asked.

"Too close. I don't know what those priests used on the eggs, but it has sped up the development by forty years or more. I don't want to leave them for too long. But Falaius has a message for you, and I could get here faster than anyone else."

A shiver of alarm chilled her. "Is Varia all right?"

"She's just worn out by all the flying back and forth. She came to find me, so I left her sitting with the eggs and brought you the message myself."

An image formed in Linsha's mind of the small brown, spotted owl trying to sit on nine dragon eggs at the same time. She started to giggle and a breath later she laughed uproariously for the first time in a long dry stretch. "Can't you just imagine?" she gasped between fits of hilarity.

Crucible laughed with her, but he really didn't see what was so funny. He hadn't meant that the bird was literally sitting on the eggs. They were too hot for any avian. Nevertheless, he liked to hear her laughter and see her smile.

She sobered down after a while and tried to breathe normally. "Sorry. I am so tired, some things just seem silly." She rubbed her face, took a deep breath, and said, "Now, what was your message?"

"Falaius and Wanderer will meet you here." He scratched a rough map in the earth with his claw. "Here is the river. Here is the volcano, and here about twenty miles north is a low butte in a broad, fairly flat valley. The butte is a remnant of this ridge that stretches toward the river. There are low hills here and here. We will set up a trap in this valley, using the butte as our 'dragon nest.' "

"How do we find this place from here?"

He dragged his claw through the dirt toward the east. "You are already due east of there. Turn west. If you stay on a straight track, you will soon see a string of buttes to your right hand. Stay to the south of those and you'll find a runoff riverbed. It's usually dry, but it's sandy and has some water in it now, so you shouldn't miss it. I think you'll be able to get there in two days."

"Is Falaius there now?"

"His vanguard is. He and his scouts just found the place last night. He is very pleased to hear you are back."

"Tell him I will see him soon," Linsha said. "Does anyone know where the Tarmaks are?"

"Not yet. The scouts haven't come back yet, Varia is too tired from carrying messages, and I have been too busy. We need to find them. Perhaps a quick, high flight overhead? Lanther would expect that."

She put a hand on his leg and felt the warmth of his sleek, gleaming scales. "He still has the Abyssal Lance, Crucible. Be very careful."

"My back aches, my wings will never be right, and I still shudder at the memory of that lance. Trust me. I will be careful."

They said good-bye, and Linsha watched as the dragon took a running leap off the hilltop and glided into the air. She wanted so much to go with him, but she couldn't. Not yet. She still had her duty.

She jogged back down the hill to catch up with the wagon and told Sir Hugh what was being planned.

They turned the company west and raced for the river and the comparative safety of the Plains army.

Later that evening Crucible came back briefly to report he had found the Tarmak army. As Linsha had suspected, Lanther had gathered every warrior he dared spare from Missing City and sent them into the field. The army was stretched out in a long line and was a scant two days behind Linsha and the wagon.

"Two days!" she exclaimed. The Tarmaks must have run all the way.

"There is a unit of cavalry in the vanguard, and they are closest. They have almost reached the place where you turned north. We will soon see if they believe you have the eggs."

"What if they don't follow us?"

"I don't know. I will talk to Falaius and Wanderer before I return to the peak to check on the eggs. We'll let you know."

And he was gone again, flying away into the dusky blue skirts of evening.

The Akkad-Dar did not bother to have his large tent erected that night. He ordered only a small camp tent and sat inside in the glow of a single lamp studying maps while his army gathered around him. He had sent orders down the line that the scattered units were to be moved up without rest until the entire army was together. The enemy, he knew, was coming to meet him, and he reveled in the thought of the coming battle. But he wanted all his forces at his disposal, not stretched across the plains. True, he had pulled this march together very quickly, thanks to the foresight of the officer in charge of the city's garrison, but many of the *ekwullik* had needed weapons, arrows, food, and supplies for a long march. They had needed some time to ready themselves. Other units were ready to go. So the Akkad-Dar's army had left the city in pieces. Now it was time to bring them together.

He pored over his maps of the Plains, a legacy from the Akkad-Ur, and wondered for the thousandth time where Linsha and Crucible would take the eggs. He knew the eggs were close to hatching and would need to be nested very quickly. He also knew the dragon could not fly long distances.

After the damage done to his wings, it was a wonder he could fly at all. So, where would they go? Did Crucible have the eggs? Or did Linsha? Was Linsha in this wagon his trackers were following? Were the eggs? And where was the text Afec had stolen?

He pounded a fist on his table. He did not know the answers. He needed more information!

He heard a loud commotion outside his tent and rose to his feet to quell the noise. Before he could leave the tent, his second *dekegul* threw back the tent flap and saluted. "Akkad-Dar, the trackers have brought in a centaur."

Perhaps the answer to a prayer, Lanther thought. He breathed a silent word of gratitude to his goddess and strode out of the tent. He found three of his scouts surrounding a bound and angry centaur. Two more stood back with crossbows aimed at the stallion's back. The horseman was a light bay who had the looks of an escaped slave. He was thin, haggard, dirty, and had a wound on his flank that had been broken open again in the scuffle with the guards. It bled heavily down his leg. He glared ferociously at the Akkad-Dar, but Lanther was pleased to see a tremble in the centaur's hands and a nervous step in his hooves.

"Akkad-Dar, we found this one watching the camp," one of the scouts reported. "He will not speak to us."

Lanther crossed his arms and studied the centaur. His arms had been tied and his legs hobbled, but he was not gagged. "Were you with the traitor, Linsha Majere?" he asked. "Where are they taking the eggs?"

The centaur did not answer.

"We have been following a trail out of the Missing City that includes a wagon and a number of horses and centaurs. This group split off near the city, and the larger group went west." Lanther's voice turned sharper and came out hard and demanding. "Now they have turned northwest and are going . . . where?"

The centaur panted in fear. His eyes shifted left and right, and still he said nothing.

"All right," Lanther said. He flexed his fingers and nodded to the guards. They swarmed over the helpless centaur and slammed him to the ground. Stunned and gasping, the centaur stared up at the Akkad-Dar in growing terror. Lanther stepped to the centaur's front and clamped his hand over the horseman's face.

All was quiet for a short time until the silence was shattered by the centaur's agonized scream. The centaur twitched and writhed under Lanther's hand. His legs jerked in violent spasms. Patches of sweat darkened his bay hide. He screamed again, then abruptly he fell silent. His body trembled then subsided to stillness. His breathing stopped.

Lanther stepped back, satisfied. He glared distastefully at the corpse and indicated that the guards should haul it away.

The *dekegul* beside him bowed expectantly. "My lord?"

Lanther stared into the darkness of the Plains night. "The eggs are not in the wagon. The dragon took them. The wagon is a lure." He thought for a few more minutes while his officer and the remaining guards waited in silence. "We will go after the eggs and make the rabble come to us." He turned on his heel and returned to his tent.

Flashfire. The name played in his mind. He had seen that somewhere on one of his maps. His hands flew over the stiff parchments and old hides. It was there, somewhere. And then he had it—an old peak, a dormant volcano. Of course! He would take his army there and make the Plains rabble come to him. The dragon would be a fearsome defender, of course, but Lanther had several weapons to deal with him. Linsha would come, too, and when the battle was over and the eggs were in his possession again, he would have his wedding night and his revenge. She would live just long enough to bear his son, the child of prophecy, the Amarrel.

And . . . perhaps he would let her see him take possession of the hatchlings so she would know that she had failed completely. Yes, that would be the best.

* * *

One more day to go. In one more day of hard travel, if the wagon did not break a wheel, or a horse did not go lame, or the food held out. If everyone could keep going for just one more day . . .

Linsha looked at her companions and knew they could not go much farther. They had endured weeks of forced labor, starvation, and miserable conditions only to be freed unexpectedly and encouraged to trek across the open plains in wet, cold weather with inadequate food and not even a fire at night to dry their clothes. The two wounded men were holding on, but just barely, and the rest of the troop was exhausted and worn and hungry. The only thing that kept them going was the hope that tomorrow would bring them to the butte and the camp of Falaius's army. Then, hopefully, they would have a day or two to rest before the Tarmaks arrived.

Linsha glanced back at Callista, who gave her a wan smile. The courtesan was as exhausted as everyone else, for she spent most of her time caring for the wounded men—and lately, for Sir Hugh. The young knight's cold had turned nasty and left him with a racking cough and a fever. He sat with Linsha sometimes while she drove the wagon, but much of the time he sat in the back with Callista and coughed. Linsha hoped Danian had traveled with Wanderer's tribe and would be with the army. The healer would certainly have some medicines for such a bad cough.

A shout drew her attention to a faint sound coming behind them. She twisted in the seat and realized the sound was hoofbeats. Someone was coming up fast on the trail behind. The men and centaurs wheeled around and drew weapons while Linsha reined her team to a halt. Sir Hugh climbed up beside her, and they waited in tense expectation.

A form appeared on the far hill and came galloping toward them, waving and shouting. The centaurs relaxed.

"It is Menneferen!" one of the horsemen called to Linsha.

The roan centaur skidded to a halt by the wagon. His coat was muddy and damp, and his sides were heaving for air. "The Tarmaks," he gasped between breaths. "Didn't take the bait. They're not . . . following the wagon."

Linsha spat a curse and slammed her fist on the wagon seat. "Where are they?" she cried.

Menneferen took several more deep breaths and replied, "Crucible sent me to tell you. The Tarmaks are marching toward the river in the direction of the volcano."

Linsha threw up her hands, feeling angry and frustrated. "How did they find out?"

"Crucible thinks they may have captured someone and learned the truth that way."

The other centaurs exchanged glances. There was only one other scout away from the troop that knew where they were going, and they had not seen him in two and a half days.

"So Crucible knows," Sir Hugh said. "Where is he?"

"He is going to Falaius to warn him. They must move the army south."

A wordless groan drifted around the listeners. Their hope of finding rest and food the next day dwindled to nothing.

"And what are we to do?" Linsha demanded. She knew what she wanted to do, but she had volunteered to stay with this band, and she would not abandon them now.

"Crucible said, if you can make it, go to the volcano and wait for him. It is about thirty-five miles from here."

Thirty-five miles. At the rate they were going, it would take two days—maybe a day and a half if they really pushed.

"Is this volcano warm and dry?" Sir Hugh asked, with the barest twinkle in his eyes.

"Crucible made the nest inside," Linsha replied for everyone to hear. "It is warm as baked bread and as dry as the desert."

There was a subtle shift in posture and expression among the whole group. The members of the little company looked at one another and shrugged. Thirty-five miles was nothing when they had already come so far. They could make that final push, especially if there was a warm, dry cave at the other end.

Since there was no longer a need for subterfuge, they shoved the rocks out of the wagon and turned southwest. Menneferen took the lead to find the best path for the wagon. Fortunately, the ground in this area was mostly grassland on gently rolling hills. The way was not difficult, just long and tedious.

Yet they had to hurry. They had to find the volcano before the Tarmaks reached it. If need be, Linsha decided, she and Crucible would move the eggs again to keep them out of Lanther's grasp. They just had to get there first.

Crucible stayed with Falaius, Wanderer, and the rebel army long enough to see them packed and on their way. They had twenty miles to travel over the wetter, more overgrown terrain of the river valley. It was anyone's guess who would get to the volcano first, but Crucible decided he would be there to welcome whoever it was. He rose over the river on the evening breeze and flew south toward the conical peak he could see jutting up against the darkening sky. He flew swiftly, hoping the small owl he had left to watch the eggs was still watching unharmed. He hadn't told her that if the dragons hatched they would be looking for food—any food. Perhaps he should have warned her of that.

At first he was so preoccupied with his worries for the coming day that he did not realize that something had changed, something drastic in his own city so far away. Crucible did not know exactly what was happening, but he understood it was vitally important and it was happening in his city. His entire being yearned to return in a desire so strong it made him hurt.

But he couldn't go. His heart knew that. Even if his wings

had been strong enough to fly him to Sanction in one night, he could not leave Linsha and the eggs in the path of Lanther and the Tarmak army. Sanction would have to wait. With a low moan, he turned and flew south again, turning his back on the city he loved.

When he reached the volcano, he found Varia perched on a rock outside the cave entrance. She looked strangely agitated. Her "ear" feathers stood straight up, her feathers were puffed, and she paced side to side, bobbing her head. When she saw him land, she flew to him and landed on his horn.

Do you feel it? she asked before he could say anything. *What is happening?*

The owl had odd abilities and was very sensitive to the world around her. She, too, must have felt the strange currents in the winds of the world. *I don't know*, he told her. *But it is happening in Sanction.*

We are not the only ones facing battle then, she said.

━━━━━━━━━━━━━━━

They were nearly there. Everyone could see the peak standing stark and alone above the plains. Dark patches of pines grew around its base, in sharp contrast to the reddish dun colors of the dried grass and the barren rock. A pale afternoon sun washed the peak in light and set it aglow against the first blue sky the small company had seen in days.

Linsha squinted hard to see a cave entrance or some sign of Crucible, but the volcano looked empty. Of course, they were still about five miles away, and she could be missing something. But it didn't matter. It was only late afternoon, and it was possible her little group would be the first to reach the peak.

They had certainly tried. Everyone worked hard, taking only two rest stops during the night and pushing themselves to the limits of their endurance. They deserved a good rest, a hot meal, and a dry place to sleep. Linsha just hoped they would get it.

They traveled closer to the peak. The land, shaped by the ancient throes of the volcano thousands of years before, became more rugged around the base of the cone. It rose and fell more sharply into eroded gullies and steep valleys. Weathered outcroppings of rock protruded from the ground like old bones. Without Menneferen to help them find a path, they would have had a difficult time making their way to Crucible's new cave.

They were only about two miles from the peak when a steep, narrow valley cut cross their path. They took their time angling down the slope and gratefully reached the bottom with the wagon still intact. To their right a grove of pines grew on the valley's floor and hid the ground in shadow; to their left, a huge outcropping of rock blocked part of their view and hemmed them close to the trees.

Linsha looked up from watching the team of horses as they reached the bottom of the slope and noticed the trees only ten paces away. She glanced to her left and saw the hump of rock. Something small flashed in the sunlight on the stones in that outcropping. She stiffened, every alarm in her head going off. She slammed off the brake that had held them on the hill and reached for the whip.

But she was already too late. Large forms with skins painted blue erupted out of the trees and from around the outcropping and swiftly surrounded the small party. The Tarmaks formed a tight circle around the wagon and its escort and stopped with bows drawn and spears ready to throw.

"Surrender!" a voice called out of the trees.

Linsha threw the reins down and held her hands up where the Tarmaks could see them. Sir Hugh and the others reluctantly did likewise.

A group of five Tarmak warriors came out of the trees and

surveyed the prisoners with contempt. "Take the women and kill the others," an officer snapped in Tarmakian.

"No!" Linsha stood up in the wagon and drew herself up with all the arrogance she could muster. She switched to Tarmakian to make her case stronger. "You will not kill these men. They are my escort."

The officer looked amused. "Why wouldn't we? Who are you, woman, to argue?"

"You know well who I am, because the Akkad-Dar sent you to capture me." It was just a guess, but Linsha figured it was a good one. "I am the Drathkin'kela, the Friend of Dragons, and I am the Chosen of the Akkad. If you kill my escort, I will have no reason not to fight you, and when you have killed me, you will have to report to the Akkad-Dar that you were responsible for my death."

The officer did not move or speak but observed his prisoners as if contemplating her words. He glanced at the weary riders, centaurs, the wounded, the woman in the back of the wagon, and the fierce Drathkin'kela that defended them all. He nodded once.

"Bring them all," he ordered.

"Do not fight back," Linsha said to her troop. "Cooperate for now."

The men and centaurs tossed down their weapons and fell in behind their captors. A Tarmak climbed up on the wagon and pushed Linsha to the back so he could drive.

They turned down the valley past the bulge of rock and headed toward a much larger hill surrounded by trees and cut by eroded gullies. Linsha was not surprised when they turned into the trees and found the Tarmak army camouflaged in the shelter of the woods.

Fear bubbled in her stomach. Lanther was waiting for her. Lanther and his anger at her betrayal. She began to wonder if fighting the Tarmak to the death might not be a better choice than putting herself in Lanther's hands again. She saw him in a clearing in the midst of his commanders, his body painted blue and his face covered by the mask of the Akkad. In spite of his shorter stature and smaller build, he radiated an arrogant confidence and a sense of justified superiority that made him obvious even in a crowd of taller warriors. She felt her stomach twist into knots.

The *dekegul* stopped his warriors near the Akkad-Dar's position and ordered two of them to get Linsha.

She decided not to make matters worse for the others by fighting. She squeezed Callista's hand, gripped Sir Hugh's shoulder, and climbed out of the wagon without urging from the Tarmaks. Before the warriors could prompt her, she strode directly to the Akkad-Dar and accosted him, her arms crossed and her expression radiating anger. She noticed he was wearing the dragon scale cuirass and a sword big enough to remove a minotaur's head.

"How did you get here so fast?" she asked in a voice of total outrage.

"It's good to see you, too." He crossed his arms and mimicked her posture. "Did you think I would let my wife go to war without me? The dragon did not burn every ship." He took a step closer and gripped her jaw with his fingers. "Why did you leave?" he hissed in her ear.

His fingers were like steel and buried themselves into her skin so hard that she could not move her jaw. Her eyes met his through the mask. Terror seared through her that he was going to use the spell that seemed to rip her mind apart. She wrenched herself away from him so hard she tripped over a rock on the ground and fell hard on her back. Her head slammed into the earth. Through the ringing pain she heard laughter and the sharp snap of orders.

Someone lifted her to her feet and bound her arms. Lanther watched as the warriors restrained her, and when they were finished, he searched the wagon and found the leather bag. Holding it close to her face, he said, "When this is done, we will consummate our marriage, and when I am finished with you, no man will ever touch you again."

"What is so important about that book?" she croaked. "What do I care about Lord Ariakan and his Amarrel?"

He gave a self-satisfied chuckle. "Afec's greatest prophecy, given five years before I came to the Plains. The Emperor, the Empress, and I were the only ones who heard it." He leaned in close, and she felt the cold metal of his mask against her ear as he whispered, "The Amarrel has not been born yet. Ariakan deceived Khanwhelak's father. The Warrior Cleric will be *Drathkin'kelkhan*, the son of the Chosen of the Dragon. And *I* will be his father, my dear Drathkin'kela."

Linsha was too stunned to comprehend. All she could do was stare at him through a fog of pain and disbelief.

He turned to the others of her company. "That one!" he pointed to Menneferen. The centaur eyed the Brutes around him and walked to the Akkad-Dar.

Linsha looked at him, but her vision was blurry and all she could see was his reddish hide. "Please don't kill him," she whispered.

"I have no intention of that," Lanther said. "He is going to do something for me. Now, listen carefully, centaur. You will go to that peak, around to the west side. You will see the entrance the bronze dragon made in the side of the volcano. Go to that entrance. The dragon is there."

He was speaking to the centaur like an adult sometimes speaks to a dull-witted child, and Linsha found it very annoying. She squirmed in her tight bindings, but the warriors who gripped her arms ignored her.

"You will tell the dragon." Lanther went on, "that the Tarmaks have attacked your party near the river. Lady Knight Linsha Majere desperately needs his help. You will do what you must to get the dragon to leave the cave, or I will kill these fine folk. If you try to tip him off, I will kill all of them. Do you understand?"

The centaur nodded, his face expressionless.

"Good." Lanther lifted a finger.

Linsha heard the snap of a bowstring, the whirring flight of an arrow, and Menneferen jolted back and groaned. Frantic for him, she struggled to clear her vision and finally saw a Tarmak arrow penetrating his rump. It was not a fatal wound, but it was painful and it bled enough to make a dark red patch on his hide.

"You may go now," Lanther said with a wave of his hand.

Limping, the centaur jogged out of the clearing and took the most direct route toward the peak.

Linsha felt herself picked up and slung over the shoulder of a burly warrior. She lifted her head enough to see the others rounded together and led off into the trees. There was nothing more she could do for them but hope she would see them again. Callista waved once to her, and they were gone out of sight in the heavy woods.

Then there was no more time to wonder. She was carried through the trees and brought out into another valley where a string of large horses stood in the shadows of the pines. Linsha recognized them as Damjatt horses from Ithin'carthia. Lanther and his guards mounted and readied themselves to ride while Linsha was placed behind Lanther on his horse. He took an extra length of rope, wrapped it around her wrists, and tied it to the horn of his saddle.

The riders urged their horses into a trot and rode in single file through the woods around the base of the hill. Linsha's head cleared enough so she could see where they were going, but she wasn't strong enough to do anything about it. She had enough sense left to know that Lanther held the rope tied to her wrists, and if she jumped or fell she would only break something. She sat behind him and nursed her strength for a better opportunity.

In the shelter of the pines, the riders stopped and waited.

Linsha looked around. She still felt dizzy and her back ached from her fall, but her vision was clear and her strength was returning. She saw the peak ahead of them, looming against the blue sky. The Tarmak riders were on the west side now, for the sun was behind them, and they were very close.

"There he goes!" a warrior said in Tarmakian, and they watched the bronze dragon charge out of the cave and take wing. As soon as he was out of sight, the riders kicked their horses into a gallop.

The Damjatt horses burst out of the trees into the sunlight. They may not have been fast, but they were very sure-footed. They galloped across a wide, open field and up the steep, rocky foot of the volcano without missing a step.

Linsha held on to Lanther as the horses plunged up the slope and came to a sliding stop on a wide ledge in front of a hole in the side of the peak. The hole was rounded, large enough for an averaged-sized dragon to slip through, and it penetrated deep into the flanks of the volcano. The Damjatt horses caught the scent of dragon and balked at the entrance.

The Akkad-Dar and his warriors slid off their horses. Several Tarmaks took the reins and led the horses away from the cave's mouth, while the others loosened their swords and lit torches. Lanther yanked Linsha off his horse and wrapped the end of her binding rope around his hand to keep her close.

"Inside." With a jerk of his head, he indicated the cave entrance. "We will drink the *Awlgu'arud Drathkin* this night!"

The warriors cheered.

"No!" Linsha screamed.

He was turning to answer when a warrior yelled, "Akkad-Dar! He comes!"

All heads snapped around; all eyes stared toward the woods in the valley where the Tarmak army lay hidden.

A winged shape soared over the trees as fast as his wings

could bear him. Sunlight shone on his bronze scales. He bellowed his fury and loosed a powerful beam of fiery light into the trees where the thickest numbers of warriors waited. The trees exploded into flame. Wreathed in smoke and swirling ash, the dragon banked toward the peak and charged at the group on the volcano's ledge.

Shouting a curse, Lanther dropped the rope and lunged for the horses. It was only then in the sunlight by the side of the cone that Linsha noticed another thing Lanther had brought with him. It was tied to the back of one of the horses, and as a warrior unwrapped it and brought it to the Akkad-Dar, Linsha recognized its rusty-red barb and the long black shaft —the Abyssal Lance. Her fear for Crucible grew tenfold. The Akkad-Dar hefted its weight to his shoulder and gave Linsha a vile look. He mounted a horse and leveled the barb on the bronze dragon.

"Crucible! Crucible, no!" Linsha screamed. She ran in front of Lanther's horse, but a Tarmak snatched her arms and heaved her up over the saddle in front of Lanther. She landed hard on her belly and lay gasping, her chest aching and her head ringing with pain.

The dragon's roar thundered off the peak, and dragonfear radiated from him like waves of heat. He shot one short burst of flame at the warriors, killing several, and flew by, his head craned around to look for Linsha.

Linsha felt the *whump* of wind from his wings as he passed overhead. A storm of dust and grit blew up from the ground. In almost the same moment the horse carrying her and Lanther reared in terror, and the surviving Tarmak warriors fell on their faces, groveling in fear.

Linsha struggled to stay on the terrified horse, for she knew as well as Lanther that Crucible would not attack him as long as she was in the way. If only she could get Lanther to drop the lance. She twisted her head up and saw Crucible curve around.

"Tarmaks!" bellowed Lanther. "On your feet! Use the steel arrows! The poison will bring him down!"

Linsha went cold. What poison?

Obedient to the Akkad's will, the warriors struggled to their feet. They drew out arrows tipped with barbs forged and tempered in the smithies of Ithin'carthia. Lifting their bows high, they stood firm and sighted on the approaching dragon.

Lanther's horse squealed in terror. In spite of the horse's panicked attempts to bolt and Linsha's added struggles, the Akkad-Dar stayed on his mount and kept his grip on the lance. With a ferocious jerk of the bit, he forced the horse's head around and settled it briefly on its feet.

Linsha heard the flap of Crucible's wings and the snap of bowstrings. The dragon fired another bolt of searing fire at the warriors, then he lurched sideways and snarled in pain.

"Did you hit it?" Lanther yelled.

Those few still standing gave a ragged cheer. At least one of the specially made arrows had penetrated the dragon's tough scales.

Frantic, Linsha caught a glimpse of Crucible in the sky. He winged upward then angled around to make a third pass.

All at once the dragon' head lolled and his wingbeats slowed into a ragged flap. As he lost control of his flight, his heavy body fell. Writhing and twisting in the air, he dropped out of the sky and crashed on the slope of the volcano a few hundred feet downhill from the ledge. His body lay motionless; only his wing vanes twitched in the wind.

Linsha could not make a sound, so stunned was she by his sudden fall.

Filled with triumph, the Akkad-Dar shouted a warcry, raised the lance, and kicked the big Damjatt down the hill toward the fallen dragon.

The saddle banged painfully into Linsha's ribs and stomach; her arms throbbed from the strain of holding on. She fought to stay on the horse, not just to help Crucible this time but to prevent herself from falling on the rocks or under the horse's heavy hooves. Her hands clutched at Lanther's legs and his waist, and her bouncing weight dragged at his unsteady balance. He cursed her, but he could not drop the reins or the lance to push her off.

Grimly they hung on while the horse charged down the slope toward the stricken dragon. In a flash of panic and fear for the bronze, Linsha summoned her strength into one desperate effort. She hauled her upper body off the saddle and made a grab for the red shaft of the lance.

Her sudden movement threw the horse off-stride. He staggered sideways, and the black barb that was aimed for the dragon's rib cage jerked sideways, slammed off a boulder, and stabbed deep into Crucible's haunch, penetrating his poison-induced stupor. The bronze roared, his agony drowning out all other sound in the world.

The sudden impact knocked Linsha and Lanther from the horse and sent them tumbling to the ground near Crucible. The horse, relieved of the thrashing weight on his back and the vicious pain in his mouth, bolted down the hillside.

Linsha lay sprawled on her back while the world whirled around her and tears trickled down her face. Crucible had stopped screaming. She hurt in every bone, muscle, and fiber of her being. She didn't want to move, but she could hear movement from Lanther in the rocks and Crucible's labored breathing. At least the dragon was still alive.

She rolled over to her side and pushed herself to her knees. Dizziness and pain shook her, but nothing seemed to be broken—just bruised, battered, lacerated, and pounded. She felt like a side of meat prepared for the fire.

"Curse you!" Lanther shouted at her. He staggered to his feet and drew his sword. His mask had been torn off in his fall, and blood streamed down the blue paint on his face from a wicked gash above his eyebrow. He limped forward and lifted his sword, ready to drive the point through Crucible's eye into his brain. Linsha reached for the closest weapon at hand—a fist-sized chunk of rock—and heaved it at the Akkad-Dar's back. Years of juggling had given her excellent eye to hand coordination, so the rock flew unerringly and struck him on the back of his neck.

He pitched forward, his arms flailing to keep his balance, and the sword dropped from his hand to fall close to Crucible's head. He reached for the sword as Linsha grabbed for another rock. She drew back to throw again when Crucible stirred. One eye crept open; his head moved.

Lanther barely snatched his hand away from the sword before the dragon's teeth clashed together just above the blade. Thwarted from the sword, Lanther lunged after the Abyssal Lance that hung at an angle from Crucible's back leg.

"No, you don't!" hissed Linsha, and she pelted him with more rocks.

Frustrated and enraged, the Akkad-Dar backed away from the dragon. Emotions crawled over his blood-stained face—hate, anger, jealousy, and pain, then his blue eyes flared like lightning and he turned on his boot heel and ran up the hill toward the cave.

Linsha knew where he was going, but she could not leave. Not yet. She clambered around to Crucible's head, her eyes shimmering with tears.

"You're still alive," she marveled and touched his cheek, his eye ridges, his neck as if she could not quite believe the evidence of her eyes. "Stay with me! Fight the poison. *Fight it!*"

I will try. His message came to her mind in barely a whisper.

Her hand wrapped around the scales on her chain and she reached deep into herself to summon the healing power of the heart. She had to heal him, for the thought of his death tore at her like a nightmare. Try as she did, she could not complete the spell. Her magic bubbled in her blood and immediately drained away, sucked out by the souls of the dead around her.

"I'm sorry," she whispered.

Don't be. Go. His eyelid slid closed. *Save the eggs.*

Her tears fell on the shining scales of the dragon's nose, and it took all of her will to leave him lying on the side of the volcano and pursue the Akkad-Dar. She left Lanther's fallen sword where it lay, for it was too heavy for her to handle. There would be others on the ledge. She hurried up the rocky slope.

When she reached the ledge, she discovered all but two of the Tarmak warriors who had accompanied them were dead. The two survivors stared at her as she scrambled over the edge onto the level ground in front of the cave. Their swords drawn, they moved toward her.

Horns blared in the trees to the north and were echoed on the skirt of the peak to the south. The two Tarmaks stopped and stared out at the meadow below. The ranks of warriors that had survived the dragon's fire were pouring into the meadow below to escape the smoke and flames. Their horn-blowers answered the challenge with a pealing call of their own. All at once a dark flight of arrows soared out of the trees and dropped with deadly accuracy into the milling crowds of warriors. The Tarmak horns sounded another warning as a long line of mounted Plainsmen and centaurs came out of the trees. There was another flight of arrows, and the horsemen charged underneath them into the line of waiting Tarmaks. A thunderous clash of bodies and weapons, the shouts of fighting men, the screams of horses, and the pounding beat of drums filled the valley.

On the ledge of the peak the three antagonists stared at the attacking army of Plainsmen. The two Tarmaks glanced uneasily back at the cave and scowled down at the battle, now joined in ferocious intensity. Linsha took advantage of their distraction. She darted past them for the cave, snatched up a sword from a dead Tarmak, and loped to the cave's entrance. The two Tarmaks did not follow.

She hurried inside, and the sunlight faded quickly behind her.

Maternal Instinct

23

The tunnel lay straight and true, its sides smooth and its floor level. Dense darkness surrounded Linsha, forcing her to move to the wall and follow the tunnel by touch. She noticed immediately that the air was warm and dry and smelled faintly of molten rock. She jogged blindly down the passage and feared with a sick certainty what she would find when the tunnel ended—the eggs in a nest, waiting to hatch. Lanther would smash them, and she would fail. She wondered briefly where Varia and Menneferen were and hoped they had left when Crucible flew away.

Shortly she saw pale light ahead and realized the tunnel was about to come to an end. She didn't bother to slow down but hurried toward the chamber and the light. The Akkad-Dar, she knew, would be waiting for her. Her sword gripped in her hand, she stepped out of the tunnel. Her eyes widened with surprise and she looked up with wonder at a mound in front of her.

Crucible had found a chamber fashioned long ago by the internal workings of the volcano's fiery core. He had leveled the floor, enlarged the chamber, and bored two small ventilation shafts through the side of the cone that allowed both air and light into the cave. He had also built a nest in the center using sand and earth to create a mound for the eggs. It sloped up nearly eight feet and was about twenty feet in circumference. A thin shaft of light from the western ventilation shaft penetrated the gloom and shone on the side of the mound like a beam from a thief's lantern. The air was very warm in the cave, prompting Linsha to wonder if Crucible had heated rocks or something to add extra warmth for the nest.

"Come up here."

She looked up the mound and saw Lanther standing on the top holding an egg. It occurred to Linsha that he was not using gloves to carry the round orb. Had the eggs cooled that much?

"What are you going to do?" she asked.

"Come up here, or I will smash every one. Leave your sword."

Linsha knew she had little choice. There was no sign of either Varia or Menneferen, and no one else knew she was there. Her heart in her throat, she jabbed the sword into the dirt at the base of the mound and climbed warily up the steep slope.

At the top the mound fell away into a bowl-shaped depression lined with sand. Nestled in the warm sand lay eight of the nine eggs. They were darker than she remembered. They appeared softer, too, for she could see indentations and creases in the shells she hadn't remembered before. One of them rocked slightly.

Linsha blinked. She looked again, but the eggs stayed motionless. Surely not, she thought. It was too soon.

"You never had any intention of giving me those eggs. You would have said anything to persuade me to come to Ithin'carthia. What made you think I would be the mother of a Tarmak demi-god?" she asked, her soft voice full of derision. "Or that you would be the father?"

Lanther was gazing into the distance, his attention drawn to something only he could see. At her words, he jerked slightly and focused his eyes on her face. "Afec foretold it," he replied. "And I saw it in my vision from Takhisis when I took the Test in Neraka. From my goddess I saw it all—the fall of the Missing City, the conquest of the Plains, my union with the Drathkin'kela. Our son *will* be Amarrel, the Warrior Cleric who brings peace and prosperity to my people for a thousand years."

Linsha leaned forward and said, "Takhisis is gone. She abandoned this world. You have been deceived. And I will die before I ever bear any get of yours!"

A smile as cold as the winds from the Ice Wall lifted his lips and frosted his eyes. "You are wrong, my lady wife. Takhisis is here, in the world. She has come to claim this world for her own."

The Akkad-Dar's face was masked in blood and dirt, and his skin was disguised by blue paint. But there was no mistaking the gloating arrogance of victory that exuded from his body in an almost palpable aura. With cold deliberation he slammed the dragon egg to the dirt and smashed it with his foot.

It did not shatter as Linsha would have expected, but split with a sickening crunch and tore open under the impact of his boot. A small dragonlet flopped on its back in the ruins of its shell. It cried piteously, waving its legs. Lanther's laughter filled the cave.

Horrified, Linsha snatched at it, but Lanther's arm rose and he slammed the point of a dagger into the small body. He held it up by the limp neck for her to see. She screamed in rage and threw herself at him and brought them both crashing to the dirt. Her hands groped for the dagger as they rolled and strained on soft earth.

It wasn't the smartest way to attack a man taller, heavier, and better trained, but Linsha's only thought was to protect the young lives contained in the eggs. The body of the dead dragonlet mocked her. The pain of its murder galvanized her into a fury. She fought hard with fists and feet, elbows and knees, to reach the dagger and get Lanther away from the eggs.

The Akkad-Dar struck back, equally determined to punish her. He punched her hard in the cheek with a sharp jab and wrenched away from her. His dagger flashed out with deadly speed in the soft light and ripped through her sleeve, slashing the skin of her forearm.

Linsha caught his arm and forced it aside. Her face throbbed and her arm burned, but she hardly noticed. She slammed the palm of her hand into his nose and noted with brief satisfaction that the cartilage crunched under her blow and blood poured down his mouth. She hit his broken nose again, then again, blood spraying them both. His eyes rolled, and she lunged again, struggling to take possession of the knife, but he stumbled backward and the blade remained just beyond her reach.

As they grappled on the soft rim of the mound, Linsha felt something shift. The earth, gravel, and sand that comprised the nest had been piled quickly and had not been packed into place. Abruptly the dirt gave way underneath them, and Linsha tumbled down the slope in a small avalanche of dirt and gravel. Lanther fell beside her, dropping the dagger in his fall. A cloud of dust rose and danced in the band of sunlight that shone on the eggs.

Choked on dust, Linsha coughed and tried pick herself up. Too late. Lanther slammed her down against the slope of the mound and pinned her with his knee. His hand clamped down on her throat. His mouth twisted into a sneer, he reached over and picked up the dirty, damp corpse of the baby dragon.

"My goddess *has* returned," he hissed, spitting blood out of his mouth. "Through her and through the magic of the

271

dragons comes my power." He laughed then, and his blue
face became hideous with hate and spite. "I loved you once
and hoped to enjoy your body and your mind. But since you
have chosen to fight me, I will settle for your body. You do
not need a mind to be a womb for my son."

His words brought terror to Linsha's thoughts. He would
destroy her soul, leave her with nothing but an empty head
and a dead heart. She tried to push herself deeper into the
mound to loosen his grip on her throat; she tried to squirm
free of his weight on her chest. Nothing she tried freed her
of his hold. Her eyes stretched wide with fear. Her heart
pounded furiously in her chest.

His eyes closed, he muttered a string of incomprehensible
words and spun a spell to leech the latent magic from the
body of the dead dragonlet and the dragon scales of the cuirass he wore. Dark magic filled him and flared around him
like sheet lightning. He lifted his hand from her throat and
gripped her forehead.

The pain lashed into her soul.

<hr />

Far to the north in the city of Sanction, another battle
raged. Gold and silver dragons, Knights of Solamnia, elves,
and men fought the forces of the Dark Queen Takhisis for
the city Crucible had rebuilt. While men and elves died in the
skies and at the walls of the city, the goddess herself arrived
in a storm of black clouds to descend in a chariot drawn by
five dragons. She stepped from her chariot into the sands
of a killing arena and surveyed the captive audience that
awaited her pleasure. They would witness her entrance into
the mortal world, and they would grovel before her.

One woman waited for her on the dismal sand. A young
woman—a girl really—with short red hair, amber eyes, and
the power to lead an army. This girl had given everything

to her Queen and now she waited, her head bowed, her soul willing to make the sacrifice of life itself for her One God.

Takhisis stretched out her hand to take the girl's offering.

She met resistance. Before her eyes her power failed, and her forces retreated in dismay.

She, who had dared to steal a world and hold in it thrall, realized her plans were collapsing around her.

The other immortals had found her at last, had found the world she had hidden from them.

The gods had returned.

Clear and bright as sunlight on morning dew, a warbling song pierced through the darkness of the tunnel. It sprang into the cavern and echoed off the walls like the first bird songs of spring. There were words in the joyful melody that stripped away the black fog of Linsha's mind and spread through her thoughts with dawning comprehension.

Varia burst into the cave crying at the top of her impressive voice. "The gods! They have returned!" She swirled and dipped overhead, singing in delight.

Linsha felt Lanther falter. His magic, once so powerful and overwhelming, seemed to drain from her mind. The pain faded to a throbbing ache.

Lanther shook his head. "No! Takhisis, hear me!"

He got no answer. Linsha had spoken many times of the gods. She had used their names, listened to her parents' stories, and talked to Solamnic clerics who refused to give up their belief in the deities. But not once had she ever truly beseeched a god for help . . . until she felt the magic of the Akkad-Dar fail and sensed with unutterable certainty that the gods of her people had finally returned to their world.

Kiri-Jolith! she implored to the god most beloved of the Solamnic Knights. *Help me!*

For the first time in her life, her prayer was answered. Love, hot and sweet, filled her muscles and bones; reassurance surged through her mind. She rose out of the soft earth, knocking Lanther off her chest. He reached for her throat, but she slammed his hands aside and grabbed a fistful of his dragonscale cuirass.

He had sought to use the magic power of the dragon scales for his own evil, but the scales were brass. Brass dragons were metallic—dragons of good, dragons of the light. Their power could not be corrupted for long.

This time a Majere sought the magic of the scales, and there was nothing to stop her. Her own inherent talent and empathy for dragons drew the magic into her mind, increased it five times over, and bent it to her will. She sent it lashing back into the Akkad-Dar, reinforced by all the pent-up grief and anger he had caused.

The magic exploded within him. His hands clamped on his head, and his face contorted with his inner agony. He screamed until his voice broke. He toppled backwards, pulling the cuirass out of Linsha's hand. His body convulsed a few times and then he lay softly moaning, his eyes staring vacantly at the stone ceiling.

The power faded from Linsha's control, leaving her both weak and exhilarated. Shaking, she stepped around the mound to fetch the sword she had left. Lanther appeared to be in a stupor, but unconscious or not, she was going to finish what she should have done in the garden house at the imperial palace. Lanther would not live to see another day.

"Linsha!" Varia called. "Come up here! Something is not right!" The owl fluttered above the mound, looking down at the eggs.

All thoughts of Lanther and the sword vanished. Linsha climbed up the soft side of the mound and saw with alarm that the eggs were rocking back and forth.

"Oh, no," she breathed. "I don't know anything about hatching dragons!"

"Don't they just do it themselves?" Varia asked, dropping down to her shoulder.

Linsha swallowed hard. The depth of her lack of knowledge about baby dragons hit her like a punch to the abdomen. She didn't know what to do to help them.

"Most of the time," she said. "I . . . I think. But these have been . . . altered. They are hatching too soon, and these eggs are different! Those shells are soft, but they're tough. They won't crack. Maybe the membranes are too thick. If the dragonlets can't get out of their shells . . ."

She couldn't finish the words. She climbed down into the nest with the eggs and gently put a hand over one. A silent, frantic plea for help radiated from the egg into her head. She stretched out her hands over all the eggs and felt the same desperation from each one.

"They're in trouble!" she cried. "What do I do?"

"Stay with them. I think they will sense your presence. I will go find Danian."

Varia hooted and swooped out of the cavern.

The assurance that the tribal shaman was close by and could come to help steadied Linsha's panicky thoughts. Danian had nursed Crucible back to health. He could find a way to help these babies. She thought of Kiri-Jolith again, and after saying a heartfelt prayer of thanks, she added one more plea for the health of the babies and the life of the bronze dragon who had given so much for her.

"Hold on, Crucible," she whispered.

"Linsha!"

She was startled to hear a familiar voice call down the tunnel. Hooves pounded on the stone floor, and to her great relief and delight, Varia flew into the cave followed by a centaur she knew very well. Leonidas. The young buckskin trotted into the cavern carrying two men on his back—one an older tribesman with milky blind eyes and the other a young fair-skinned Outlander with red hair. They both slid off the centaur and hurried up the mound.

"Leonidas, remind me to tell you later how glad I am to see you," Linsha called down before she greeted the two newcomers. Swiftly she told them about the eggs and the Tarmaks' insidious experiments.

Danian knelt in the sand beside Linsha and laid his hands on an egg. His sightless eyes stared thoughtfully into the distance. "These babies are in distress," he said. "They must be released from their eggs."

"I know," Linsha replied impatiently. "What can we do?"

"First, you must comfort them."

Linsha looked at all eight eggs and said, "What?"

He took her hand and laid it on the leathery shell of a twitching egg. "You must be mother to them. Comfort them. Tell them you will help them, but they must *not* fight the shell. When they are relaxed, we can try to slice the eggs open without hurting them." He seemed to sense her confusion and dismay, for he turned his blind eyes to her and nodded. "You can do this. I have seen a great power in you. I did not understand it at first, until I spent some time with Crucible."

She tried to force out a deprecating chuckle, but it just sounded like a gagging noise. "I may be a Majere, but the talent for magic went to my brother. Not to me."

Danian shook his head. "You are wrong. Your magic is simply different. You have an empathy for dragons, and they sense it and respond. Use that for these babies."

An empathy for dragons? She had suspected it. Afec told her as much. Was such a thing possible? She knew she liked and respected the native metallic dragons. Could it be that her appreciation for them was based on something innate within her mind and blood?

Her eyes sought Varia, one of the wisest creatures she knew, and looked questioningly into the owl's steady gaze. Varia tilted her head slightly. One brown eye slowly winked.

"Leonidas," Linsha said slowly. "Will you please go to Crucible? Tell him the eggs are hatching. Stay with him. I will be there as soon as I can."

The centaur agreed and trotted through the exit.

Linsha drew in a deep breath. In spite of the return of her magic, she felt exhausted. "I don't know if I can sustain this long enough to reach all eight eggs."

"I don't think you will have as much trouble," Danian said. "The souls of the dead have been freed. They are no longer under Takhisis's control."

Linsha paused. She hadn't thought of that. For a surprised moment, a stream of familiar faces passed through her memory—Sir Morrec, the knights, Sir Remmik, Mariana, Iyesta, Ian, and a host of others who died and whose souls had been trapped in the living world. She hoped Danian was right and they were free to go—not only for their sakes but for the state of magic. How wonderful it would be to create a spell and have it complete its task without being ripped apart by the souls of the dead.

Kneeling among the eggs, Linsha spread her arms to include them all. She closed her eyes to concentrate better and began the withdrawal into her self to find the power she needed. When all was quiet in her mind, she focused on the beat of her own heart wherein lay the power of her birthright.

Be a mother, Danian had said. But she had been a knight all of her adult life. She didn't know how to be a mother.

Yes, you do, whispered a part of her instincts, the instincts she had hitherto ignored. Think of your own mother.

Remember compassion. Strength. Love. Sacrifice. The willingness to do anything to protect your child.

She felt the magic energy burst like a spark from a flint. She nursed it carefully on the tinder of her will and felt it flare like never before. She had used the power of the dragon scales to stun Lanther, but this was different. This was her own magic, drawn from her love, from her blood, and it ignited in her heart, burned in her spirit, and set her mind on fire.

Children. She transferred her thoughts to the small lives within the eggs. *Do not fear. I am with you.*

Eight living minds responded to her touch with such a clamor of fear and confusion that she gasped and clutched her head in her hands. They were so desperate! She felt their need tear at her. It was easy to talk to one dragon like this, but eight was more than she could bear. The connection with their minds began to slip away.

"Hold on to them!" Danian reassured her. "They will listen to you."

From the oldest memories Linsha had of her mother, she summoned feelings of comfort, caring, and assurance. Warmth suffused her from the ends of her hair to her toes, giving her strength and confidence. She stretched out her arms again and gathered the eight frantic streams of emotion to her.

"It's all right," she whispered, and she sensed her magic spread out from her heart to her hands. It enveloped the eggs and settled like a gentle touch over each one. *Lie still, little ones*, she crooned in their minds. *Lie still and we will help you.*

The frightened struggles slowly eased within the eggs. An aura of nervousness and tension still surrounded them, but Linsha eased their fears with soothing thoughts. They reached out to her and felt her confidence in them and her love.

Danian pulled a small knife from his healer's kit and

handed it to Tancred. "Carefully, lad, make a small slit in one of the eggs and see what is there."

His redheaded apprentice obeyed, gently making a cut through the tough, leathery egg shell. "The membrane is really thick," he murmured as he made another slice with the knife.

"You may have to pull them apart," Danian suggested.

Ever so carefully, Tancred grasped the edges of the slice he had made in the egg and pulled it apart, dumping the wet, struggling dragonlet into Linsha's lap. She did not move as the creature keened and tried to flap its crinkled wings.

"Do the rest," she hissed. "Hurry!"

Firmly gripped in the center of her magic, Linsha did not hear Varia's furious shriek or see her dive at something behind her. Her attention remained fixed until Tancred looked up and yelled, "Lady! Behind you!"

She dragged her thoughts away from the eggs and turned her head just as Danian's body slammed into her back and shoulders. She heard the crunch of steel against bone.

Tancred screamed in grief and rage. Varia shrieked like a striking eagle.

Out of the corner of her eye, Linsha caught a glimpse of Lanther, blood streaming down his face, his expression twisted into a feral grimace of hate. Behind her, Danian lay limp against her body, his weight pressing into her back. The dragonlet in her lap hissed and struggled in her arms as Tancred scrambled over the sand after the Akkad-Dar.

In the sudden crush of distractions happening around her, Linsha felt her link with the baby dragons begin to fade. Frantically she shut her mind to everything but the eggs for fear that if she lost the connection now, the dragonlets would panic and die in their shells before someone could help them. She heard, as if from a distant place, the struggle happening behind her between Tancred and Lanther and Varia, but she could not help them yet. She had to get the babies out of

279

their eggs. She gathered the magic from her heart in one last desperate surge and poured it into the minds of the remaining seven.

Be strong, children. It is time!

She moved quickly. Using the utmost care she broke open the eggs and helped the awkward creatures out. In a matter of moments, Linsha found herself surrounded by keening, wet baby brasses, each about three feet long from head to tail. Her magic spell ended, leaving her drained, but the dragonlets's joy filled her mind until she flung out her hands and burst into laughter. Their little lungs filled with their first breaths, and the warm air of the cave and the residue of Linsha's magic lent them a sudden, fierce strength.

"Linsha!" Varia screeched.

Her head whipped around and she saw Lanther had pinned Tancred to the sand. The Akkad-Dar's eyes were wild with madness, and in his hand was the dagger he had used to kill Danian. Hatred, thick and dark as tar, filled her mind, and she struggled to climb out of the pile of dragonlets.

But the baby dragons lifted their heads and hissed. Their small eyes gleamed with sudden fire, and their untried muscles bunched under their scales. In one unified movement, they leaped out of the remains of their eggs and pounced on Lanther.

Lanther screamed a Tarmak warcry. He stood, the newborn dragons swarming him, twisting their tails round his limbs, clawing, biting, rending, tearing . . .

Screaming in rage, Lanther tumbled backward over the side of the mound. Once more he shouted in fury, but it broke in his throat, and his cries turned to panic and agony. Linsha could not see him, but she heard his shrieks, each more desperate and frantic than the last, and in between she heard tiny claws shredding skin and flesh, small jaws biting.

Linsha closed her eyes. She made no move to stop the little dragons. Surely they were hungry, and after all that

Lanther had done to their siblings, they deserved their revenge. She paid no attention to the scream cut short or the sounds of eight tiny mouths feeding that came from the base of the nest.

She stared down at the body of Danian, lying in a muddy puddle formed by his own blood. His chest did not move, and all light had gone from his eyes. She prayed to the gods to watch over the old man's soul.

Tancred crawled over and cradled the healer's head in his hands. Tears streamed down his face. He stared at Linsha with frightened eyes. His hands were stained with blood from a slash on his arm and the mortal wound on Danian's back.

"I don't know what to do without him," he said hoarsely.

"Yes, you do. In here—" Linsha tapped his forehead— "and here—" she tapped his heart. "The magic has returned, Tancred. Use it."

They heard a soft flap of wings and Danian's kestrel sailed into the cave, circled once, and dropped gently to the sand beside the dead man. The bird cried a question.

Varia crooned softly, her voice aching with sadness.

The small raptor tilted his head, his bright eyes as sharp as obsidian chips, then he stepped gently up Danian's arm and perched on the man's shoulder. He chirped a brief message to Varia.

The owl's head swiveled toward the entrance. "The kestrel says Crucible needs you now."

Linsha grabbed Tancred's hand and hauled him to his feet. "Come on, healer. I need your help." She pulled him down the mound, and without looking back at the corpse of her enemy, her husband, her nemesis, she strode out of the cave.

Down the slope in the valley at the foot of the volcano the battle thundered beneath a calm sky. Smoke towered above the burning woods and flames had begun to lick out across the grass of the meadow.

Linsha ignored it all. The whole of her attention focused on the form of the bronze dragon. She could see the black lance, in obedience to its evil spells, had penetrated deeper into the dragon's haunch. While it would not kill him immediately, if they didn't remove it soon, the barb would eventually work its way through into his lower body and kill him. She ran down the hill to his head and caught his nose in both hands.

"Crucible, I'm sorry. Lie still now, and we'll get the barb out."

"You're back," he moaned, barely able to speak.

"Of course," she reassured him.

"Lanther?"

"Dead."

"The eggs?"

"Eight hatched. The gods have returned, Crucible. They have restored their magic to our world. Takhisis is defeated."

"Good." There was no mistaking the sound of triumph in that one word. He twisted his head around and looked at her with one golden eye. "We have come so far."

"We will go the rest of the way," she replied. "Together."

Strengthened by her resolve, Linsha nodded to Tancred and indicated the lance that dangled from the dragon's leg. "Take the dagger and cut out the barb. I will keep him still." His eyes grew huge and she added, "Danian taught you well, Tancred. Remember his faith in you."

Linsha watched the young man study the length of the big bronze and the leg that trembled under the weight and agony of the Abyssal Lance, and she knew she need say no more.

Still holding Crucible's head, she knelt in the rocks and pushed his head down. She knew Tancred had begun work removing the barb when Crucible's body stiffened and the breath rushed through the dragon's throat. He held still, motionless as a statue beneath her touch. While she waited, she gathered the reserves of her magic—the magic to heal, the magic to unite her feelings, thoughts, and empathies with a dragon—and as soon as she heard Tancred yell, "Lady Linsha, it's out!" she released the power through her fingers into Crucible's mind and body and filled him with the strength to heal. She sensed lingering shreds of dark magic in his leg and realized this second wound from the Abyssal Lance would not be so easy to heal.

She felt Crucible stir under her hands. His horned head lifted, his body rolled around to his belly. He leaped to his feet, and his scarred wings spread overhead to cast the two humans in shadow.

Linsha saw the wound on his leg was only partially closed and the scales around it were blackened. But the lance was out and there were no splinters. For that she gave thanks.

Crucible dipped his head to Tancred and nudged the young man. "Thank you," he said. But to Linsha he send a silent message that held no words, only the glorious intensity of his feelings for her.

Then he sprang into the sky and spread his wings on the wind.

The Tarmaks had mounted a fearsome defense and almost overwhelmed the slightly larger Duntollik army when Crucible joined the fray. Healed by Danian and Linsha together, the bronze still ached from the half-healed wound caused by the lance, but his wings could carry him and his fury bore him swiftly over the field of battle. He smashed into the Tarmak lines, seared the mounted warriors on their horses, and sent the Tarmaks fleeing across the Plains. The few that were left were harried unmercifully by the Plainsmen and centaurs. Only a few determined Tarmaks returned to the Missing City to report their defeat and the death of the Akkad-Dar.

The field was left a smoking ruin. The Plainsmen helped their wounded, stripped the Tarmak dead of the weapons that had not melted under the dragon's breath, rounded up the surviving horses, and lit a bonfire to celebrate a victory that had been long in coming.

Linsha returned to the satiated dragonlets in the cave and waited while they settled down. After a quick glance, she avoided looking at the mangled mess of shredded clothes, armor, and gore that had been the Akkad-Dar. When the last dragonlet had found a place in the sand and fallen asleep, she left them under Varia's watchful eye and went to find Callista and Sir Hugh.

The members of her party had been freed by some of Falaius's men, so she and Callista went to help Tancred. The young healer needed all the willing hands he could get to help. Linsha worked late into the night before she said goodnight to Tancred and trekked up the hill to the cave entrance. She found the brasses still asleep, but this time they were crowded around the recumbent form of Crucible. Varia perched on one of his horns, her eyes closed, her brown body almost invisible in the dark cave. The remains of Lanther's corpse were gone.

The big bronze didn't so much as twitch an eyelid when the Lady Knight came in. Grinning to herself, Linsha crawled over a baby dragon and found a comfortable spot by Crucible's front leg. Happier than she had been in many years, Linsha joined the dragons in sleep.

Thank you.

A voice spoke quietly in the darkness, a soft but powerful voice that woke Linsha with a start. She blinked, still groggy with sleep, and saw a large form in the darkness. A pale light like silver moonlight emanated from its shape, outlining its edges just enough to reveal a dragon.

"Iyesta?" Linsha said sleepily.

Yes. The voice filled her mind. *I had to come to say thank you.*

Linsha sat up against Crucible's leg and looked down at the sleeping dragonlets. "I didn't do very well. The Tarmaks killed many of them."

There are eight who will be grateful you honored your vow.

"Thank you for trusting us."

Iyesta lowered her head. *The young ones are in good hands. I must go now. The dark goddess no longer holds us.*

"Iyesta," Linsha said. It was important to her to let Iyesta know. "I know who Crucible is now."

The dragon's pale eyes glimmered. *It will not be easy.*

"What won't?" Linsha asked.

The bonds between a human and dragons are worth the effort to forge them.

Dragons, Linsha noted.

Iyesta began to fade, her outline blurring into darkness.

"Good-bye," Linsha called. "And if you see a good-looking man named Ian Durne? Tell him I said good-bye." And thank you, she added quietly to herself.

Silence returned to the cave.

farewells

24

By the next day, the baby brasses could fly well enough to make circles around the volcano while Crucible watched. He reported to Linsha that the dragonlets were healthy, considering everything they had gone through during their interrupted incubation and early hatching but that they would need a little time to grow and gain strength before they could move anywhere. He could only wait to see if the magic used by the Tarmaks to speed up their embryonic development would have any affect on their growth.

That same day Wanderer and Falaius gathered in the wounded and the scattered units and began making plans to return to Duntollik before winter set in. They knew there was little they could do to take the Missing City back. They had broken the back of the Tarmak army, with Crucible's help, but the Brutes still held the city, and the winter was too miserable to allow for fighting. They had to regroup and plan a campaign for spring before the Tarmaks rebuilt their ships and came back in increasing numbers.

Linsha spent her day caring for the wounded, playing with the dragonlets, and trying not to think about the future. The truth of the matter was she was exhausted in mind and body. She couldn't think clearly, and she didn't know what to do. Falaius, once he finished his effusive welcome to her, encouraged her to return to Duntollik with them. However, she and Sir Hugh were the only Knights of Solamnia in the area. By their orders, they should be in the Missing City, perhaps working undercover against the Tarmaks. Linsha personally felt that if she never saw another Brute again, it would be too soon.

Then there were the dragons to consider. Linsha knew she should talk to Crucible about his plans, but she dreaded what she thought he would say. She put off talking to him for several days until at last the Plains army was ready to march back to Duntollik. Falaius asked her again to join them, and Linsha knew she had to make a decision.

She waited until the brasses were asleep in their cave before she asked Crucible to join her outside. For a long while she leaned back against him and stared silently at the two moons that hung like pearls in the sky, one silver and one red. Their new presence in the night sky still amazed her. For all of her thirty-four years there had only been one pallid moon, but now that the gods were back, the moons of Lunitari and Solinari had returned to grace the darkness. And, she knew from a dozen childhood tales, somewhere in the darkness between the stars, black Nuitari looked down on Ansalon.

Finally, she told Crucible of the Legionnaire commander's offer.

"I don't know what to do," she confessed.

The dragon did not hesitate. "Whatever you decide, I will come with you. I cannot bear to lose you again."

"I will die long before you do," Linsha said. "And what about Sanction?"

"I could die tomorrow," he said, curling his neck around her. "I would be dead, if it weren't for you. I will not hide that I want to go back to Sanction. It is my city and I want it

287

back. I don't know what is waiting for me there, but I want you to come. You and the brasses."

She threw up her hands, so tired she was close to tears. "I don't know what I must do. I am still a Knight of Solamnia. I am bound to the Grand Master in Sancrist."

"Is it what you want?" he asked. "Is it enough?"

"It was always what I wanted," she replied. But she thought of Lord Bight/Crucible and the brasses who had bonded with her as surely as her own children, and her heart filled with doubt. "I don't know," she whispered.

She agonized over her decision through the night, and discovered the next morning that the weather had given her a reprieve of sorts. A snowstorm moved in during the night and prevented anyone from leaving the area. The snow lasted for several days, then in the vagaries of autumn weather, promptly melted in a brief warm snap. By then Wanderer and Falaius knew it was time to go before the cold and the snow settled in for months.

Linsha finally declined the offer to go to Duntollik, at least for now. She released Sir Hugh from any decision of hers and suggested he go. But Sir Hugh refused. He wanted to stay with his superior officer. As long as they were together, he argued, they were a circle, of sorts. His choice did not ease Linsha's mind at all.

Callista, however, did decide to go to Duntollik. "There is nothing left for me in the Missing City," she told Linsha. "I've never been to Duntollik. Perhaps there I will find another profession." And she smiled at Tancred.

The next day, Linsha had to say good-bye to many friends. Some of the partings were pleasant; some were very difficult. Leonidas gave her a fierce hug and a dagger of centaur design he had carried from Duntollik. Callista wept and promised to come see her when she settled somewhere. Falaius made her an honorary Legionnaire and told her to join him any time. Tancred, his arm already healed, bowed low to her. She gave him her heartfelt gratitude for helping her heal Crucible.

"It was an honor, my lady," the young healer said. "I think we will both find our way."

Then the horns sounded, the horses stamped in anticipation, and the Duntollik army marched west for home.

Two days later the decision was taken out of Linsha's hands. On a cold, cloudy morning a silver dragon appeared above Flashfire and bugled a greeting to Crucible. The two Solamnic Knights and the eight brasses watched in amazement as the silver dipped and soared over the volcano and winged in to land in the level ground in front of the cave. The small brasses crowded around him. Varia hooted a welcome.

"Chayne?" Linsha cried. "Is that you?"

The young silver male dipped his head in a bow. He had once been one of Iyesta's close comrades and had flown with her on the journey to see Thunder in his lair. He had disappeared the night of the storm and no one on the Plains of Dust had seen him since.

"My apologies, Lady Linsha, for leaving at such a time. I was drawn away from Krynn with all the other silvers and golds and held prisoner until just recently. When we were released, we flew to Sanction and fought against the Dark Queen's forces. I am only now returning to the Plains to learn what has happened. I also have a message for you."

Linsha, Hugh, and Crucible glanced at one another. "Do you know what has happened here?" Linsha asked.

The silver ground his teeth. "I know some. I found Falaius and the Duntollik army just yesterday. They told me about Iyesta and the Brutes. They said you were here and could tell me much more. But first I want to tell you that when the Solamnic commanders heard I was going back to the Missing

City, they asked me to tell Sir Morrec to return to Sancrist to report on events in the city. They are trying to contact all the Solamnic circles."

"Sir Morrec is dead," Sir Hugh said without emotion. "Sir Remmik is dead. The entire circle is dead. Except for Lady Linsha and me."

Chayne nodded his shining head. "Yes, that is what Falaius said. So I guess I'd better take you both back."

"I don't think—" Linsha started to say.

The silver, eager to please, cut her off. "Oh, it is no problem. Someone should tell the Solamnics what is happening down here, and since I cannot return to the city right now, I will take you. We can fly there in a few days. Otherwise, it would take you months."

Linsha swallowed hard against the lump that suddenly blocked her throat. "Of course," she said.

"Perhaps we had better go now," said the bronze dragon. "There is still plenty of daylight, and the dragonlets and I can get a good start."

Linsha and Hugh gathered what food they had and wrapped themselves in all the warm clothes and blankets they had been able to collect. Hugh climbed onto Chayne's broad back while Linsha rode on Crucible with the owl nestled comfortably in front of her. Bouncing with excitement, the dragonlets gathered between the two adult dragons and bugled their readiness to begin.

A Sort of Homecoming

25

The High Justice, the head of the Order of the Rose, leaned back in his chair and steepled his fingers. "I want to be sure about this point, Lady Knight. You said the Akkad-Dar was a Dark Knight accepted by the Tarmaks. Would you say he acted in accordance with the orders of Takhisis or his own ambitions?"

Linsha sighed and shared a glance with Varia, who sat silently on her shoulder. They had been over this before. Several times.

The High Council, after hearing of her arrival at the great Castle uth Wistan, had convened to hear her testimony on the destruction of the circle in the Missing City. They had only given her a day to rest and eat a hot meal before they summoned her to the presence of the Grand Master, Sir Liam Ehrling, the three High Knights of the Orders, and a small troop of scribes. The last time she had been summoned to a council at the castle, it taken weeks for anyone to get around to it.

For two hours she had talked, telling them the events of murder, trials, death, invasion, war, massacres, capture, battles, slavery, and escape. The only thing she left out was any mention of the text of the Amarrel and Afec's prophecy. It was probably just the ravings of an old man, but he had given the book to her, and she wanted to translate it before she turned it over to anyone. She told the council about the ambush, her trial and sentencing, and Sir Remmik's obsession with her guilt. She told them, too, about Crucible, Iyesta, and the brass dragon eggs. When she was finished and thought back over her choices and decisions, she decided there was little she would change.

Then the questions began.

"How was the ambush arranged?"

"Who sat on the council at your trial in the Citadel?"

"How was Lanther able to fool the Legion and the circle for so long?"

"Why did you chose to accept Iyesta's request to guard the eggs?"

"Tell us about the leadership of the Plains tribes."

"What is your assessment of the Tarmak ability to rebuild their fleet?"

And on and on for several more hours.

She responded to the best of her ability and answered each question without overt emotion, as befitted a Rose Knight. The council seemed to react well to her honesty and treated her with respect and only mild suspicion.

When at last they finished, the room fell quiet. The only sounds Linsha could hear were the crackle of the embers in the fireplace and the scratch of the scribes' quills as they finished the last few words.

Sir Liam finally stirred as if returning from a deep meditation and bent toward the other knights. They deliberated quietly among themselves.

The room grew warmer. Linsha leaned her head back in her chair and felt her eyelids grow heavier and heavier. If the knights didn't hurry and release her soon, she feared she would fall asleep. To keep awake, she looked around the elegant, wood-paneled council room and felt decidedly shabby. Her armor was gone, her hair was long and unkempt, her clothes were a mismatched collection of things donated from other people, and the only weapon she had left was a centaur dagger. She did, however, have three dragon scales and her honor.

The High Knights sat up in their chairs and looked down at her from the dais.

Sir Liam spoke for them all. "Your report is excellent, Lady Linsha. We had no idea of the full extent of the disaster in the Missing City or of the growing threat of the Tarmak empire. Sir Hugh's testimony has corroborated most of your report concerning the circle and certain events of the war. However, there are parts of your tale that are . . . disturbing— your escape from the Citadel after the trial, your collusion with the Akkad-Dar, and most especially the killing of this . . . Malawaitha. These actions of yours are transgressions against the Measure, yet you have given extenuating circumstances that have painted these events in a different light. Unfortunately, there are no witnesses present to confirm or deny these exact circumstances—"

"Of course there are!" Varia said, cutting him off. She fluttered down to Linsha's knee and stared at the four astounded knights. She had been quiet as an owl until that point, and now her avian temper was aroused. "You have not asked me or Crucible! Nor have you summoned Callista, Falaius Taneek, or the shaman Tancred. What Lady Linsha has told you is the truth. There should be no question of her honor."

"What magic is this?" demanded the High Clerist.

"None of her doing," hooted Varia. "I am my own being. I stay with the Rose Knight because of her courage, her willingness to sacrifice, and her sense of honor."

Linsha hid a small smile. She was surprised Varia had chosen to speak in front of the knights. Surprised and very touched.

"If I may, my lords," said Varia, "I would like to bring in a witness for her defense."

Without giving the council a chance to respond, Varia loosed a piercing whistle.

Someone knocked on the council doors. Bemused, the Grand Master nodded to the guards who opened the door to admit a guest.

A tall, golden-haired man with a trim beard and eyes the color of dark amber limped into the room and bowed to the knights. He was dressed in the most splendid finery befitting the Lord Governor of Sanction, and he outshone everyone in the room. Standing straight before the High Knights he radiated power and assurance like a lion among kittens.

Linsha felt her heart race and her face flush with pleasure. A grin spread over her face to see him. Gods, she thought to herself, all he had to do was walk into the room and she turned to mush.

"Lord Bight," welcomed Sir Liam. "It is a pleasure to see you. We thought you were dead."

"Or fled," remarked the High Justice to the Grand Master's right.

"I was detained," Lord Bight said.

"How is your leg?" Sir Liam inquired.

"It heals slowly."

"Do you wish to address the council?"

Lord Bight tilted his head in a slight nod. "Perhaps later. At this time I have brought the results of Linsha's oath for your consideration." He turned, motioned to the doors, and spoke a word in the ancient tongue of the dragons. The doors opened wide, pushing the guards aside. There was a sudden outburst of bumps, bangs, scratches, squeaks, and rustlings as all eight dragonlets tried to get through the wide doors at once.

Linsha smiled in delight and held out her arms. Snorting and growling at each other, the eight sorted themselves out and rushed to greet her. Varia fled to a ceiling beam.

It was impossible to embrace them all at once, but Linsha touched, patted, or scratched them all as they crowded around her, all of them trying to talk and be near her at once.

The High Knights watched the scene with amusement. Finally Sir Liam signaled to Lord Bight, who shouted an order for silence. The young brasses obeyed, and a welcome silence settled over the council room, though one of them hissed at the Grand Master.

"Lord Bight, your point has been duly noted."

The knights leaned together to talk quietly among themselves again.

While they talked, Lord Bight walked to Linsha's chair, took her hand in his, and waited quietly with her. The dragons gathered protectively around her, and Varia flew back to her shoulder.

Linsha settled back in her chair and closed her eyes.

"Are you frightened?" Lord Bight whispered.

"No." And it was true. She felt as comfortable and content as she had the night in the cave. It didn't matter to her anymore what the council decided. One way or another she would find a way to stay with Crucible and the dragonlets. The gods had brought them all home. Surely they would not separate them now. "Are you?"

"No. I am with you."

She felt hot blood rise up her neck and into her cheeks. "They could send me on a mission to the Abyss as penance, you know."

"Then I'll help you dig." He smiled down at her.

Sir Liam spoke out, "Lord Bight, you know Sanction has had a very difficult time. Are you planning to return?"

"It is my desire. I would have given my life to the city, but the Tarmaks decided otherwise."

The knights considered his words in the light of his newly revealed identity.

"You are one of the few dragonlords left to our world," the Grand Master pointed out. "Your services would be invaluable."

Lord Bight lifted a single eyebrow. "Indeed."

The council studied the group around Linsha and weighed her testimony. Then they looked at one another and nodded.

Linsha waited. Her fingers tightened around Lord Bight's hand.

Sir Liam put his elbows on the table in front of him and looked down at Linsha. "Lady Knight, it is written, 'Courage is the will to strike a blow for the cause of good, no matter what sacrifice the effort demands.' You have certainly shown the courage to be true to your sacred oath to Iyesta. Your escape from Solamnic justice, under the circumstances, was warranted. Sir Remmik's zeal, sincere as it seems to have been, left him . . . misguided. Your collusion with this Akkad-Dar seems to have been a genuine effort to protect others he would have most certainly harmed. However, there is still the matter of the murder of Malawaitha. Torn by two oaths you might have been, but in no way can the Oath and the Measure sanction one of our own turning assassin. Pure as your *motives* might have been, this council must judge your *actions*. You have sinned, Lady Majere."

Varia ruffled her feathers, and Lord Bight opened his mouth to speak.

"Please, Lord Bight," said the Grand Master, cutting him off. "Let me finish. Lady Majere, you have violated the Oath and the Measure. This Malawaitha might well have deserved punishment, but your challenge to her—forced as it might have been—can in no way be excused." He looked to the men sitting to each side of him. Each of them nodded. "Penance must be dealt. You are hereby removed from the active lists. You will be a Knight-in-Exile until such time that you have redeemed yourself. For your penance, we assign you the task of continuing the task Iyesta swore you to do. Your oaths, both to the Knighthood and to the dragon Iyesta, bind you still. Guard these dragonlets, guard your honor, and guard those in need—with your life if need be. In regard to the young dragons, we believe Lord Bight can be of assistance. When they are grown and have gone their own ways, you may return to this castle and petition to be reinstated. This council is dismissed."

With that, the three High Knights stood and left the room, their scribes gathering their parchment and following them out.

A glow of delight spread over Linsha's face. She was being punished by swearing to do the one thing her heart told her to do? Thank you, Kiri-Jolith! She leaped to her feet and threw her arms around Lord Bight.

"Do you feel like another flight?" she whispered in his ear.

He nodded, holding her close the entire length of their bodies. The dragonlets squirmed with suppressed excitement.

"Then let's go to Sanction," she said. "I just want to stop in Solace on the way. My family should be present when we are married."

Varia and the dragonlets crooned together in delight.

The End

IMPORTANT CHARACTERS AND TERMS

Solamnic Knights

Castle uth Wistan — The center of the Solamnic Knighthood in Ansalon. Located on the isle of Sancrist.

Grand Master — The highest-ranking Knight of Solamnia.

High Council — The Grand Master and the three High Knights form the High Council, which conducts the Solamnic Orders' affairs.

High Clerist — The head of the Order of the Sword.

High Justice — The head of the Order of the Rose.

High Warrior — The head of the Order of the Crown.

COMMANDERS
Grand Master Sir Liam Ehrling — The head of the Knights of Solamnia.

Sir Barron uth Morrec — Former Lord Commander of the Solamnic Circle in Missing City. Killed in an ambush on the night of the Great Storm. See *City of the Lost*, Chapters 7-8.

Sir Jamis uth Remmik — A high-ranking Knight of the Crown, killed by the Tarmaks. See *Flight of the Fallen*, Chapters 23-24.

Lady Linsha Majere — Daughter of Palin and Usha Majere. A Knight of the Rose whose last assignment was to serve as the Third Commander in the Circle of Knights at the Solamnic outpost in Missing City.

KNIGHTS
Sir Fellion — A Knight of the Sword. Friend of Sir Hugh Bronan.

Sir Hugh Bronan — A Knight of the Sword. Close friend of Linsha Majere.

Sir Johand — A Knight of the Sword.

Sir Korbell — A Knight of the Sword.

Sir Pieter — A Knight of the Sword. Sir Pieter was the youngest knight serving in the Circle in Missing City.

The Legion of Steel

Falaius Taneek — Commander of the Legion of Steel in Missing City.

Lanther Darthassian — Son of Bendic Darthassian and member of the Legion of Steel in Missing City.

Mae — An undercover operative in the Missing City.

Tomarick — A member of the Legion of Steel in Missing City.

Tarmak Characters, Sites and Terms

Afec — A Damjatt apothecary and one of the chief slaves of the Akeelawasee.

Akeelawasee — "The Place of the Chosen Ones." A part of the imperial palace set aside for the women of the imperial family.

Akkad (pl. Akkadik) — Tarmak term for general. Literally translates as "chief" or "topmost." The Akkad answers solely to the Emperor.

Akkad-Dar — The Tarmak title given to Lanther Darthassian

Akkad-Ur — The official title of Urudwek.

Amarrel — The Warrior Cleric, a prophesied holy leader among the Brutes. It is commonly believed that Lord Ariakan managed to convince the Tarmak Emperor Kankaweah that he was the Amarrel, thus solidifying his leadership over the Brutes.

Awlgu'arud Drathkin — Literally "the egg-drink of the dragon." A potion made from the embryo and amniotic fluid of dragon egg. It is believed to substantially increase vitality and aid one's ability to wield magic.

Berkrath — A Tarmak goddess.

Brutes — A colloquial term used by the people of Ansalon to describe the Tarmak.

Damjatt — An indigenous culture on the island of the Brutes that was subjugated by the Tarmaks. They have largely assimilated into Tarmak culture. They are renowned on their island for the breeding and training of extremely large warhorses.

dekegul (pl. dekegullik) — Officer in charge of one dekul. The dekegullik answer to the Akkad.

dekul (pl. dekullik) — A unit of the Tarmak army consisting of 1,000 warriors.

dodgagd — A bitter tasting berry of Ithin'carthia. From it, the Tarmak make a juice, which they believe promotes good blood-flow.

Dog warriors — When a Tarmak soldier is punished, he is relegated to being a "dog soldier," the lowest ranking worker delegated to the most menial and degrading tasks.

Drathkin'kela — A title meaning "Chosen of the Dragon" or "dragon friend."

Drathkin'kelkhan — A title meaning "child of the chosen of the dragon."

ekwegul (pl. ekwegullik) — Officer in charge of one ekwul. The ekwegullik answer to a dekul.

ekwul (pl. ekwullik) — A unit of the Tarmak army consisting of one hundred warriors.

Imshallik — A Keena high priest.

Ithin'carthia — A large island and homeland of the Tarmak, Damjatt, and Keena peoples.

Kadulawa'ah — The Tarmak name of Takhisis, Queen of Darkness and Mother of Dragons.

Keena — An indigenous culture of Ithin'carthia that was subjugated by the Tarmaks. They have largely assimilated into Tarmak culture. They are the most philosophically and religiously inclined culture of their homeland, and many Keena find roles as priests, scribes, and scholars.

ketkegul (pl. ketkegullik) — Officer in charge of one ketkul. The ketkegullik answer to a ekwul.

ketkul (pl. ketkullik) — A unit of the Tarmak army consisting of ten warriors. Ten ketkullik comprise one ekwul.

ket-rhild — Tarmak term for a formal challenge, a battle to the death.

Khanwhelak — The current Emperor of the Tarmak.

Loruth — One of the women of the Akeelawasee.

Malawaitha — A minor daughter of Emperor Khanwhelak. Her mother was a slave.

marthtok — In the Tarmak tongue, it means literally "ill-shaped," but the term is most often used to describe deformity, especially in infants.

Mathurra — A Tarmak soldier.

Orchemenarc — A fortified tower and lighthouse that stands on a promontory outside the harbor at Sarczatha.

orgwegul (pl. orgwegullik) — Officer in charge of guards and sentries.

quartal — Among Tarmak aristocracy, the family or clan symbol. Usually a bird of some sort.

Ruthig — A guard in the third *ketkul* currently assigned to guard the Akeelawasee.

Sarczatha — Capitol city of the Tarmaks and seat of the Emperor.

Shurnasir — Keena priest among the Tarmak forces in Missing City.

Tarmak — The dominant culture on Ithin'carthia. They subjugated the Damjatt people of the island many years ago and finished their conquest of the Keena people just a few years prior to the Summer of Chaos.

tazeer — A powerful drink made from leaves, bark, and other ingredients. Supposedly, it increases mental vitality and fertility.

Tzithcana — First wife of Emperor Khanwhelak and current Empress of the Tarmak.

Urudwek — Akkad of the Tarmak forces sent to subdue the Plains of Dust. Official title: Akkad-Ur. Killed by Sir Remmik. See *Flight of the Fallen*, Chapter 23.

Miscellaneous Characters, Sites and Terms

Abyssal Lance — A weapon of great evil created during the Chaos War. The lance has an ensorcelled barb that works its way deeper into the victim until it kills.

Amania — A young girl living among the refugees of Missing City.

Ansalon — The southernmost continent of Krynn.

Ariakan — Son of Ariakas and the goddess Zeboim. Founder of the Knights of Takhisis. Prior to the Summer of Chaos, he established the Dark Knights' alliance with the Tarmaks and brought many of them to Ansalon to serve in his armies.

Azurale — Centaur member of the Missing City militia.

Bendic Darthassian — Father of Lanther Darthassian.

Beryllinthranox — Green dragon overlord. Commonly known as "Beryl."

Blood Sea of Istar — The large sea to the northeast of Ansalon.

Callista — A beautiful courtesan.

Caphiathas — Centaur officer of the Missing City militia and the uncle of Leonidas.

Carrebdos — Centaur. Chief of the Windwalker Clan.

Chaos War — The war fought during the Summer of Chaos.

See *Dragons of Summer Flame,* by Margaret Weis and Tracy Hickman.

Chayne — A silver dragon.

Cobalt — The blue dragon companion of Sara Dunstan.

Courrain Ocean — The great ocean east of Ansalon.

Crucible — Bronze dragon and erstwhile guardian of the city of Sanction.

Cyan Bloodbane — A green dragon most noted for aiding in turning the realm of the Silvanesti into a cursed forest of nightmare. He was later enslaved by Raistlin Majere, but when Raistlin entered the Abyss, Cyan returned to Silvanesti to exact his revenge upon the elves.

Danian — A blind healer dwelling among the Plainsmen.

Desolation, the — An area of east-central Ansalon devastated by the great dragon overlord Malystryx.

Dockett — General of the militia of Missing City and unofficial commander of the refugee forces after the fall of the city.

draconian — "Dragonmen" created from the corrupted eggs of good dragons during the Age of Despair.

Duntollik — A region of the northwestern Plains of Dust.

Elian — A large island off the eastern coast of Ansalon.

Ereshu — A centaur clan of the Plains of Dust.

Flashfire — A dormant volcano in the Plains of Dust.

Gal Tra'Kalas — A city founded by the Silvanesti on the eastern coast of the Plains of Dust. It was destroyed during the Cataclysm.

Gilthanas — A prince of the Qualinesti.

Goldmoon — One of the famed Heroes of the Lance. Widow of Riverwind. Now head of the Citadel of Light on Schallsea Island.

Grandfather Tree — A gigantic vallenwood tree growing in the Plains of Dust. It is revered by the local inhabitants. Some even believe it is a manifestation of the god Zivilyn.

Hogan Bight — Lord Governor of the city of Sanction.

Horemheb — Centaur of the Willik clan of Duntollik.

Ian Durne — Commander of Sanction's city guard, who later turned out to be an assassin of the Dark Knights. See *The Clandestine Circle*, by Mary H. Herbert.

Iyesta — Brass dragon overlord of the eastern Plains of Dust. Commonly known as "Splendor."

Karthay — A large island to the northeast of Ansalon. It is due north of the Minotaur Empire.

kefre — A hot drink found in Khur that is gaining popularity throughout Ansalon.

Kern — A region of northeastern Ansalon that borders the realm of the dragon overlord Malystryx and the Blood Sea of Istar.

Khalkist Mountains — A range of mountains that run along eastern Ansalon.

Kharolis Mountains — A range of mountains south of Qualinesti and west of the Plains of Dust.

Khellendros — A blue dragon overlord. Sometimes known as "Skie."

King's Road — One of the only major roads through the northern Plains of Dust. It once served to link Silvanost with Tarsis, but it has fallen into disrepair.

kirath — The elite warrior scouts of the Silvanesti.

Kiri-Jolith — The god beloved by the Knights of Solamnia

Knights of Neraka — The so-called "Dark Knights," originally formed to serve the dark goddess Takhisis.

Kordath — A nomadic tribe of the southern Plains of Dust.

Kothas — The southernmost of the two islands of northeast Ansalon that, along with Mithas, forms the Minotaur Empire.

Krynn — The world.

Leonidas — Centaur member of the Missing City militia and close friend of Linsha Majere.

Lunitari — Goddess of Neutral magic, incarnate as the red moon.

Malys — see Malystryx.

Malystryx — A red dragon overlord with a vast realm in eastern Ansalon. Malystryx is the most powerful dragon in Ansalon.

Mariana Calanbriar — Half-elf captain of the Missing City militia.

Mem-Ban — A town in the northern Plains of Dust.

Mem-Thon — A coastal town to the northeast of the Missing City.

Mennaferen — A centaur.

Methanfire — The blue dragon of Bendic Darthassian.

Mina — A young Dark Knight who has led the armies of Neraka in several successful battles in Ansalon. See *Dragons of a Fallen Sun, Dragons of a Lost Star,* and *Dragons of a Vanished Moon* by Margaret Weis and Tracy Hickman.

Missing City — A city on the eastern coast of the Plains of Dust. This city was rebuilt by the Legion of Steel and served as the center of Iyesta's realm. It was captured by the Tarmak shortly after the great storm in the summer of 38 SC.

Mithas — The northernmost of the two islands of northeast Ansalon that, along with Kothas, forms the Minotaur Empire.

New Sea — The great inland sea of central Ansalon, so named because it was formed during the Cataclysm.

Nordmaar — One of the northernmost realms of Ansalon.

Nuitari — God of Evil magic, incarnate as the black moon.

Onysablet — Black dragon overlord. Commonly known as "Sable."

Orchard House — A public house in Missing City.

Phalinost — A city on the southeastern border of the Silvanesti Forest.

Plains of Dust — A vast arid region of southern Ansalon.

Qualinesti — The forest realm of the elves in southwestern Ansalon.

Red Rose — A river in the Plains of Dust.

Riverwind — One of the famed Heroes of the Lance and husband of Goldmoon. He died fighting the dragon overlord Malystryx. See *Spirit of the Wind*, by Chris Pierson.

Rough, the — The rocky, scrubby grasslands on the outskirts of the Missing City.

Sable — see Onysablet.

Saifhum — A large island that lies between Karthay and Kern in the Blood Sea of Istar.

Sancrist — A large island west of mainland Ansalon. It serves as the home for the Knights of Solamnia.

Sara Dunstan — Founder of the Legion of Steel.

Scorpion Wadi — A large canyon northwest of the Missing City.

Silvanesti — The forest realm of the elves in southeastern Ansalon.

Silvanost — The capital city of Silvanesti.

Silvara — A female silver dragon who fell in love with Gilthanas.

Sinking Wells — A favorite campsite of the Legion of Steel in the Plains of Dust.

Sirenfal — A brass dragon.

Solinari — God of Good magic, incarnate as the white moon.

Sunrise — A gold dragon and companion of Ulin Majere.

Splendor — see Iyesta.

Stenndunuus — Blue dragon overlord of the central Plains of Dust. Commonly known as "Thunder."

Takhisis — Evil goddess, also known as the Queen of Darkness.

talon — A unit of the Knights of Neraka consisting of nine knights and a commanding officer.

Tanefer — Centaur member of the Missing City militia who goes with Linsha and Lanther to find the dragon eggs in *City of the Lost* by Mary H. Herbert.

Tancred — The apprentice of Danian. See *Bertrem's Guide to the War of Souls*, Volume Two.

Tarsis — A city in the western regions of the Plains of Dust.

Thon-Thalas River — The river that runs from the Khalkist Mountains, through the Silvanesti Forest, and into the Courrain Ocean.

Thunder — see Stenndunuus.

Toranth River — A river in the Plains of Dust.

Towers of E'li — The towers that guard the entrance to the Thon-Thalas River from the Courrain Ocean into Silvanesti.

Ulin Majere — Son of Palin and Usha Majere. Linsha's brother.

Varia — A sentient owl and friend of Linsha Majere. Varia possesses the ability to speak with a wide vocal range and has a talent for telepathy and reading auras.

Wanderer — Son and eldest child of Riverwind and Goldmoon.

Windwalker — A clan on the Plains of Dust.

World Tree — see "Grandfather Tree."

The Minotaur Wars

Richard A. Knaak

A new trilogy featuring the minotaur race that
continues the story from the *New York Times*
best-selling War of Souls trilogy!

Now available in paperback!
NIGHT OF BLOOD
Volume One

As the War of Souls spreads, a terrible, bloody
coup led by the ambitious General Hotak and
his wife, the High Priestess Nephera, over-
takes the minotaur empire. With legions of
soldiers and the unearthly magic of the Fore-
runners at his command, the new emperor
turns his sights towards Ansalon. But not all
his enemies lie dead...

New in hardcover!
TIDES OF BLOOD
Volume Two

Making a bold pact with the ogres, and with
the assurances of the mysterious warrior-
woman Mina sweetly ringing in his ears, the
minotaur emperor Hotak decides to invade
Ansalon. But betrayal comes from the least
expected quarters, and an escaped slave
called Faros, the last of the blood of the lawful
emperor, stirs up a fresh, vengeance-driven
rebellion.

The War of Souls is at an end, but the tales of Krynn continue...

THE SEARCH FOR POWER:
DRAGONS FROM THE WAR OF SOULS
Edited by Margaret Weis

After the War of Souls, dragons are much harder to find, but they should still be avoided. They come in all hues and sizes and can be just as charming and mischievous as they are evil and deadly. The best-known DRAGONLANCE® authors spin tales of these greatest of beasts, in all their variety and splendor.

PRISONER OF HAVEN
The Age of Mortals
Nancy Varian Berberick

Usha and Dezra Majere find that a visit to the city of Haven might make them permanent residents. The two must fight both the forces of the evil dragon overlord and one another in their attempts to free the city—and themselves.

WIZARDS' CONCLAVE
The Age of Mortals
Douglas Niles

The gods have returned to Krynn, but their power is far from secure. Dalamar the Dark, together with the Red Mistress, Jenna of Palanthas, must gather the forces of traditional magic for a momentous battle that will determine the future of sorcery in the world.

THE LAKE OF DEATH
The Age of Mortals
Jean Rabe

Dhamon, a former Dark Knight cursed to roam in dragon form, prays that something left behind in the submerged city of Qualinost has the magical power to make him human again. But gaining such a relic could come at a terrible price: his honor, or the lives of his companions.

October 2004